The Admiral's Choice

The Terra Prime Series

Book Three

Terry A. Hurlbut

ISBN: 978-1-958700-01-3 (paperback)
ISBN: 978-1-958700-00-6 (ebook)

Published by Conservative News and Views.
https://www.conservativenewsandviews.com/.
Cover by Andrew Dobell - Creative Edge Studios.
www.creativeedgestudios.co.uk.
Printed in the United States of America.

To Andrea

Contents

Chapter 1 1

Chapter 2 19

Chapter 3 39

Chapter 4 53

Chapter 5 67

Chapter 6 85

Chapter 7 103

Chapter 8 121

Chapter 9 125

Chapter 10 141

Chapter 11 161

Chapter 12 173

Chapter 13 187

Chapter 14 205

Chapter 15 223

Chapter 16 239

Chapter 17 251

Book Four Preview 271

    Chapter 1 1

    Chapter 2 19

    Chapter 3 25

What Did You Think? I

Acknowledgments III

About the Author V

Chapter 1

Jacques-Yves de Grasse turned away from the sun, now setting over *le bassin d'Arcachon* far away to the west. He faced his visitor squarely. "Would you care to say that again?" he asked. He had unconsciously slipped into a voice he had not used for fifteen years. The last time he'd spoken this way had marked the beginning of his retirement.

No, not retirement. *Exile,* said a voice in his mind. He ignored it.

Vice-Admiral Ramón Ordoñez-Pizarro USN frostily replied, "I believe you heard me the first time, Rear-Admiral de Grasse. A dangerous revolutionary movement has sprung up, right here on Sol d. And one of *your* former officers is at the heart of it."

"I won't bother asking you why don't you just say 'Earth,' if you still say 'Sol.' Instead, I will proceed to the next question: why come to me?"

"For the obvious reason that, if anyone can reach Lieutenant Commander Morrow and persuade him to stand down, you can."

Sacré salaud, he didn't say. "You fellows—or at least the Admiralty as then constituted—didn't seem to want my help fifteen years ago, when it might have mattered," he said. "They as much as told me, 'Go back to your family vineyard and be happy. This matter is in the hands of top men.' Well, obviously, your 'top men' have failed you. So now you come to me and say, *'Amiral-arrière,* we need your help!'

"*Connerie!*" he shouted. He was a vintner, not a rancher, but still a man of the country, and swore like one. "I ought to tell you and your superiors what to do with yourselves," he went on. "And before you upbraid me for a lack of manners, let me remind you: I am retired. For fifteen years have I been retired, and not by my choice, either. And as it happens, you are standing on the land of my ancestors, which belongs to me by the direct guarantee of *les cinq dames* themselves. So I don't have to accord anyone an ounce of respect who has not earned it. And you, *mon vice-amiral,* have not."

The Vice-Admiral made a big show of clearing his throat. Then he said, "I read the brief. So I understand how sensitive a subject this is to broach with you. But a moment's sober reflection—perhaps over a few glasses of the excellent wine for which your vineyard and winery are famous throughout the Galaxy—will, I am sure, convince you of both the urgency of the situation and your value to us in resolving it."

That part about the fame of his wine struck home. His father had often regaled him with the diary entries of his *multi-arrière-grand-père* Alain. In them, he described how he obtained the guarantee of which the Vice-Admiral had just spoken, from Mdlles. Francisca Ordoñez-Pizarro, Kanesha Preston, Ruqayya Tamraz, Jawahir Otayf, and, of course, Mdlle. Secrétaire-générale Gunilla Thorsell, their leader. And very lucky had his multiple-great-grandfather been to obtain it nearly four centuries ago. Everyone else forfeited his land, which then underwent *le rendu à rétro-sauvage*. Now, to look beyond the borders of the De Grasse 400-hectare holding, none could tell that the surrounding lands had ever been anything but wilderness.

Of course, his guest knew all these facts. Best, therefore, not to antagonize him *too* much.

"*Touché, mon vice-amiral,*" he said. "By all means, let us continue this dialogue at my house."

The two walked to where the Vice-Admiral's magnetically levitating vehicle, his flag lieutenant, and his Marine chauffeur waited.

* * *

Jacques-Yves didn't have to ride with the Vice-Admiral. After all, he had his own maglev car. But that car, like every car on Earth (very few of which existed), was fully autonomous. So all he had to do was dispatch the car to the garage, where it would find its own stall, at least as well as a horse would. Then he mounted the Vice-Admiral's vehicle.

Once aboard, he closed the passenger door. Then he took off his hat, revealing his perfectly bald and shiny head. He needed a hat, and a light coat, against the slightly nippy air.

The trip back to the main house took about fifteen minutes. Jacques-Yves spent the time enjoying the scenery. Though actually, the view was less enjoyable now. How forlorn the vineyard looked at this time of year! The wine was long since laid down, and wine that had finished aging had gone out to the nearby town of Cadillac. There, stevedores loaded it onto barges for the trip down the Garonne to Bordeaux, as had happened for centuries. All this had happened two months ago, in the month *Vendémiaire*, the month of wine-pressing. At least now, he could better appreciate the view than he could have a month earlier. *Brumaire*, the month of fog, always shrouded his vines.

At last, they arrived at his house. Upon arrival, Jacques-Yves alighted first and acknowledged his butler, Michel. He then snapped rapid-fire orders to draw wine and serve it to him and his guest in the library.

The guest, upon entering the library, immediately fell to scanning the shelves that lined the walls. "Impressive," he said. "You're one of the few people in all the United Systems who keeps cloth-bound books. Vice-Admiral Brandon Nelson did the same following his second retirement, from command of *Bonaventure III*. Why do you do it? Surely you can access even texts like these on the Network."

"Not all of them. Besides, like wine, a true book is best appreciated when one can hold it in one's hand and turn its pages."

"Is that a Christian Bible I see on your shelf?" the Vice-Admiral asked with a faint note of disapproval.

Jacques-Yves ignored it. "Yes," he said. "A *Louis Second* edition, translated from the original Authorized Version of the British Royal Commission on Bible Translation, which they issued in … Wait, wait, wait … Em-zhee-day-enn minus nine zero six double zero, give or take a couple hundred."

"Did you just calculate that?" asked Ordoñez-Pizarro, now sounding impressed.

"Actually, no," said Jacques-Yves. "I memorized it long since. I'm far more accustomed to converting between MJDN and French Republican. For instance, today is MJDN 204195, is it not?"

"Of course."

"Well, to my way of thinking, it is Primeday, first day of the Third Decad in the month *Frimaire* in Year 626 of the French Republic."

"Why use such a calendar?" his guest asked. "The Gregorian calendar, that I might understand."

"Not when you reflect on the memories of war that attach to that calendar."

"But they attach to the Republican Calendar, too, no?"

"Yes, but the French Revolution is more remote. Besides, the month names are ideal for a farmer—or a vine-dresser and winemaker. They tell the seasons of weather or agricultural or horticultural or viticultural activity. And quite accurately, too—as these last fifteen years have confirmed. But all that suffices—and forgive my manners. Please seat yourself."

The Vice-Admiral sat in one of the two cushioned armchairs in the library. Jacques-Yves took the other. Just then, an underbutler arrived, bearing a wine carafe and two glasses on a silver tray. He set this on the small table between the two armchairs, then left. Jacques-Yves opened the carafe and poured for himself and his guest.

Taking one of the wine glasses, Ordoñez-Pizarro said, "Rear-Admiral, I offer a toast. We can drink to the resumption of your sadly interrupted career."

Jacques-Yves took his own glass and touched his to his guest's, but with considerable deliberation. "That's almost as provocative a statement," he said, "as your broaching to me that you need my help in quelling revolution." He paused to sip his wine, then said, "You do realize, I trust, that, thanks to the Admiralty, I have received no briefings since they relieved me of my command, arrested my second officer, scattered my last command from one end of the Quadrant to the other, and even decommissioned my ship. Almost as if they wanted to bury not only Lieutenant Commander Morrow but myself and my command as well. Are you now prepared to tell me why?"

"Why your relief and retirement and the decommissioning and the rest of it, no," said his guest. "Mainly because I know not these things myself. And by the way, we're going to be working very closely with one another. Can we not call one another by our first names?"

"Very well … Ramón. And I am called Jacques-Yves."

"Thank you a thousand times … Jacques-Yves." Well! Now Jacques-Yves could be impressed. Though they were speaking Standard, Ramón had just used a French idiom. Most Standard speakers would have thanked him a *million* times, through a misreading of the French phrase.

Taking another sip, he said, "It's not important. What is important is this 'revolution' my former second officer Matthew Morrow is supposed to be making. As I said, I have received no briefing."

"True," said Ramón, sipping from his own glass. "That is why I, not some more junior officer, am here. I must emphasize the extreme sensitivity of what I am about to impart to you. I am the eyes, ears—and voice—of the Admiralty and even of the security council and first secretary."

"More provocative still," said Jacques-Yves. "Just what has Matthew Morrow done?"

"He has conquered completely the prison and reservation complex of Botany Bay," said the Vice-Admiral. "In the process, he has gathered to himself not only the prison population but also the entire population of the American Reservation on the western third of that continent."

"*Cinq dames!*" Jacques-Yves cried. "The American Reservation—and how quickly *that* demonym rolled off your tongue. Surely you don't think I have forgotten that the name *America* is a name with which to frighten small children. And the American Reservation … the prison of the descendants of the last Americans who refused rehabilitation. You are telling me that Matthew Morrow has recruited *them* to aid him in his … quest, whatever that might be. Now, just *when* were you going to brief me about this!?"

"I am doing so now, Rear-Admiral, and that is the important thing."

"How did he accomplish this feat?"

"He escaped from the Botany Bay Psychiatric Institute in the New South Wales District."

"And why was he confined there?"

"That's not important. What *is* important is that, in the process of that escape, he hijacked an LCG prison transport. Using that, he traversed the Southern Ocean, then attacked the force-field generator at Sharp Point and introduced himself to an American cavalry force—horse cavalry, if you can believe it! —that was reconnoitering that generator at the time. After that, it was a simple matter to recruit the Americans. The Special Security Forces had restricted their technology to pre-electric inventions. How, is unimportant."

"You seem to regard a great many things as *unimportant* to which I would assign a great deal of import," said Jacques-Yves with a tone he almost regretted using.

Ramón seemed to take no notice. "The point is that the Americans had cavalry and mobile artillery. I must observe that the SSF were fearfully lax in this regard. They ought never to have permitted the Americans to reorganize their society as they did. But, *tacaños* that they always have been, they didn't want to expend effort building barracks, reformatories, or mess halls, and did not want to mix the Americans in with the regular populations of adult and juvenile inmates in the Victoria and South Australian districts. They insisted on leaving the Americans to their own devices, to fend for themselves. Oh, what can they do? We'll just raid them once in a while if they ever try to develop electric … ah, sorry. Forget I said that."

Jacques-Yves smiled thinly. *"D'accord,"* he said.

"And now see what! The Americans had built an army, and your former second officer recruited them. With them, he swept Botany Bay from Perth to Sidney and every installation in between."

"A moment, Ramón. How could he do that, given the force fields that, I'm sure, demarcate the various districts of Botany Bay?"

"By creating, almost as if he had done so immediately, a virus program that took down every force-field generator at once."

Jacques-Yves sighed. "Pray, continue," he said.

"Worse than that, in the administrative centers in Adelaide, Melbourne, Townsville, and Sydney, he has captured all the ancient aircraft that once belonged to the Royal Australian Air Force, plus a B-52 Stratofortress that once belonged to the United States Air Force. The SSF were conducting research on them, trying to design a gravity generator that would enable one of our pilots to fly them without risking vertigo or blackout from the accelerations attendant on air-to-air combat. But your second officer recruited, if you can believe it, *adolescent boys* to fly them as they were!

"And fly them they did, to embarrassingly good effect. Those SSF who did not die in action, now languish in the prisons they once guarded. And Matthew Morrow has made sure to confine them the old-fashioned way, with physical bars and fences, not force fields. All the produce from the penal farms and ranches of Queensland is now lost to us. He has set up a 'capital city' in the Canberra Administrative Center, and makes regular propaganda broadcasts from, as nearly as we can tell, the ancient Sydney Opera House. Thanks to him, riots have broken out in Mumbai, Rangoon, Phnom Penh, Hanoi, Ho Chi Minh City, and lately in Beijing, Shanghai, Nanjing, Chunjing, Auckland, Wellington, Christchurch, Seoul, Pyongyang, and Tokyo."

"Have any riots broken out in France?"

"Not yet, Admiral," said Ramón. "But the Latin Quarter in Paris is getting restive. I stopped in Bordeaux on my way up the Garonne to see you. No riots yet, but a whispering campaign. My sources also report more whispering at Alise-Ste-Reine. My staff suggested to me that the Five Ladies perhaps ought to have removed the statue of Vercingetorix," Ramón paused. "Ah, well," he said, "that is of the past. The present is our most pressing problem."

"Which could be worse," said Jacques-Yves. "I take it that's why you haven't moved against Matthew in force."

"You are pleased to joke, Jacques-Yves. We can't possibly land any troops on Botany Bay. First, that B-52 carried air-launched flying bombs with which he destroyed the spaceports of New Zealand. Matthew Morrow's rioting gangs have taken over every other spaceport from which you could cross to Botany Bay over water alone. We tried once to drop troops into the American Reservation—and the American militia killed or captured them all. Trying that again would give his revolution more publicity—and more fire-power and transport capability—than the Admiralty would care to risk. And there are other reasons, which I am not authorized to disclose, why the Marines *and* the Navy are stretched thinly at the moment."

"Do you mean to say," said Jacques-Yves, "that we are under attack from The Hive, or the Far-elves, or some such enemy?"

"No," said Ramón. "At least we have no attacks from *those* quarters. More than that, I cannot—must not—say."

"But what you *are* saying," said Jacques-Yves, "is that you don't want to assault Matthew Morrow's position with main force. I suppose you also hope you don't have to destroy him. You do know that I know exactly what he is and how formidable he can be. The Five Ladies know how he saved a key mission for me. Two, in fact. Except the second one happened shortly before his arrest."

"All perfectly true, Jacques-Yves. Believe me; we don't want to destroy him if we can help it. That's why we need you. But you need to know more about the arsenal he now appears to have at his command."

"Meaning *more* than aircraft of the twenty-first century? Do tell."

"We know that he has acquired at least five LCG prisoner transports, in addition to that twenty-first-century 'air force' he now has. And we suspect—and this is the most sensitive intelligence I have to share—that he now possesses a wet navy."

"A wet navy?" asked Jacques-Yves. "Ramón, just how long has he been operating?"

"Since MJDN 204154."

"And within forty-one days, he has constructed a number of ships of war that can float on the water? Impossible."

"I never said he built a wet navy," said Ramón. "Only that he possesses one."

"How? And where did he get it? The United Nations decommissioned every ship of war it possessed more than two centuries ago. You know that. No vessel that could possibly serve as a warship is even permitted on the oceans of Earth today."

"These photographs show us what he has," Ramón said. He then snapped his fingers. His flag lieutenant, a slight-looking gentleman wearing two silver lieutenant's bars and the shoulder lanyard of an aide-de-camp, walked to the table where his superior—and his host—sat. He carried something Jacques-Yves thought he'd never see again. It was a genuine *porte-documents* or "briefcase" in Standard. Holding this out in front of him, the flag lieutenant opened two snaps and flung open the lid. Ramón reached into it and drew out another incredible set of objects—hard-copy photographs.

"You said this was a sensitive matter," said Jacques-Yves, soberly. "For any other matter, you would hand photographs like these to me on a microdrive."

"You never saw these photographs," said Ramón with emphasis.

Jacques-Yves nodded and took them. And goggled at the first one. *"Incroyable!* This is the United States Ship *Constitution*—or as perfect a replica of that vessel as ever I could imagine."

He stopped abruptly as he noticed Ramón turning pale. "How would you know what that vessel looked like?" he asked, voice dropping to a near-whisper.

"Now *you* are pleased to joke, Ramón," said Jacques-Yves. "I built a model of this vessel as a boy. She's a legend in Earth naval history. Surely I needn't tell you of the most famous sea battle of the Anglo-American War!"

"We had wondered whether that was the original," said Ramón, still whispering. "And I assure you, this is no joke. Look at the rest of those photographs, if you please."

Jacques-Yves did. And goggled again. "Why, these are priceless!" he said. "They are perfect replicas of four of the first colony ships to carry settlers from Great Britain to what became the United States of America. I recognize them. *Mayflower. Susan Constant. Godspeed. Discovery.* Do you realize the value of these vessels? All five! No civilized human being has set eyes upon any of them since…"

He broke off. Then he asked, "Ramón, how closely in your confidence do you keep your flag lieutenant?"

"As closely as my own person," the other said. "If a flag officer cannot trust his flag lieutenant, whom can he trust?"

"Just as well," said Jacques-Yves. "I was about to say that none have laid eyes upon these vessels since the Aztlán Climate War. *Constitution* remained active, as a museum ship, ever since that other war in which she figured. As the Climate War broke out, she vanished. Along with all these other vessels—replicas all, belonging to two different historical societies. Now, how in the Five Ladies' names did Matthew Morrow acquire them? And if he did, then he commands a crew for each! Where did he recruit them? I tell you frankly, Ramón, that you have a very serious problem on your hands, to be sure."

"But that's only the half of it, Jacques-Yves," said the Vice-Admiral. "Look at the last photograph."

Jacques-Yves didn't know quite what further shock to expect. But in that last photograph, he got the worst shock of all. It depicted two block-like ships with the oddest shape he'd ever seen. Hull and deckhouse sides alike sloped inward. A word came to him, a Standard word: *tumblehome*. Even L'Académie Française still had trouble with that one. Tumblehome referred to the inward slope of the upper part of the hull—if a ship had such a slope. But these two vessels had tumblehome extending to the very waterline, even below it! Even the ships' bows had inward sloping edges! Then he noticed catalog numbers on their bows: 1000 and 1001.

Unbidden, the phrase came to him: the *Zumwalt* class. Then he looked again at the vessel numbered 1000 and could plainly see signs of some kind of repair—repair of battle damage that might have occurred centuries ago—to a vessel without access to a proper drydock.

"Ramón," he said, "your problem is more severe even than I first imagined," he said.

"Why? As if the Admiralty knew not."

"Because these are the very vessels—USS *Zumwalt* DDG-1000 and USS *Michael Monsoor* DDG-1001—that sank the third member of their class, NAS *Lyndon Baines Johnson* DDG-1002, and then vanished, like the other five. *Zumwalt* must have taken the brunt of the battle damage; she's had repairs that still show. The only reason such modern vessels as these could survive, other than their power plants running on natural gas instead of uranium, is that they must have made port—somewhere." He broke off. "Where have they been hiding all this time? And how could Matthew Morrow have found them?"

"I have one idea," said Ramón.

Jacques-Yves looked up in surprise, for his guest was almost *snarling*. "Would you care to share?" he asked.

"As you might guess from my last name," Ramón began, "I have a famous ancestor."

"Francisca Ordoñez-Pizarro?" Come to think, the Vice-Admiral certainly looked it, with his jet-black hair, round face, and slightly darker-than-suntanned skin. All attributes *la directrice générale du Nouvel-Aztlán* had possessed. Not to mention fiery black eyes, like those that allowed Francisca to rise so high. Those eyes were flashing just now.

"Well, of course, she, too. I can understand that you would think first of the first Director-General of New Aztlán. But I have a more recent ancestor, her lineal descendant, Bernardo Ordoñez-Pizarro. The last commandant of the United Nations Climate Force. He begged the Security Council to let him keep searching for any more of *los estados-unidenses* who might have escaped the grasp of Lord Steele, the first commandant of that Force. The Security Council waved him off, called him paranoid, and disbanded his force anyway. Well, *now*, at last, they can apologize to my family!"

"Ramón, surely you don't think the original United States of America still exists?"

"It's not what I think, Jacques-Yves. It's what I know. What I feel in my bones."

"Ramón," said Jacques-Yves, doing his best to sound patient, "the entire region between the two coastal strips that make up *le Nouvel Aztlán* underwent the Retro-Wild Rendering … excuse me, Re-Wilding, after the Climate War."

"Then how do you explain these ships, eh?"

How *did* one explain how seven vanished ships could suddenly turn up? "Well," said Jacques-Yves, "I could speculate endlessly about how the original crew of each became a 'generation' crew, literally training generation after generation of their descendants to take over vital crew functions. Including some of the best shipfitters in the history of naval architecture. Keeping those wooden vessels afloat for nearly four hundred years was certainly an achievement. Those two *Zumwalt* class destroyers are even more remarkable—for *Zumwalt* herself obviously underwent considerable repair.

"I'll admit that I cannot explain their reappearance. And I have already observed that the Admiralty has a problem. There shouldn't be any wet-navy warships afloat in the oceans of Earth.

"But something's missing here, Ramón. What does Matthew Morrow say? I admit it might seem an idle boast, but a rebel's boast is another officer's lead, is it not?"

"We *hope* that's their entire Navy," said Ramón. "But there's more with which to scare the Admiralty—*if* they can wrap their minds around it."

"And what is that? After all, what you've shared with me already suffices to shock."

"That last photograph? Look at it again. Look closely."

Jacques-Yves reached for his antique magnifier. A crude substitute for the "zoom" function on an *écran moniteur*, but effective. "What am I looking at?" he asked. Then he said, "Wait! Each of those vessels is firing its big shore gun! But those guns were supposed to be useless! The last government of the United States never appropriated the funds for the special ammunition those guns were to carry."

"And how did you know *that?*"

"Ramón," said Jacques-Yves, "look behind you. That shelf," said Jacques-Yves, pointing.

The Vice-Admiral turned to look. "What about it?" he asked.

"What series of bound volumes do you see?"

Ramón leaned over to look more closely. Then he said, "Is that *Jane's Fighting Ships?*"

"Yes, in the editions of the twenty-first century. Elsewhere I have a copy of every other edition I could get my hands on. From the last editions, I know all about that fiasco with the Advanced Gun System and the too-costly ammunition they never made. Except that someone *has* made it, or at least a serviceable substitute. Clearly, Matthew is engaged in serious business."

"Exactly. But there is more. Our satellites were lucky to snap that photograph. For in the next instant, there was … nothing to see. Only the wooden flotilla remained. Of those two ships, the satellite could detect no sign!"

"That's impossible!"

"Nevertheless."

"Then do you mean to imply that those vessels are cloaked?"

"Again, you score."

"Well," said Jacques-Yves, "if anyone would ever cloak a wet-navy vessel, these two ships would be the perfect candidates."

"Does *Jane's Fighting Ships* give you that historical insight?"

"It does. Even in their heyday, vessels of the *Zumwalt* class would typically appear as fishing vessels on the sensor systems of that day. Add to it that those shore guns, originally useless, now have ammunition they can use. And now, total cloaking. I can see why you regarded Matthew Morrow's movement as dangerous. But what can possibly have driven him to do all this?"

"That," said Ramón, "remains classified."

"*Pardon?*" Jacques-Yves said, lapsing into a string of French. Then he took a deep breath and went on in Standard, "Excuse me, Ramón, but I must insist that you and the Admiralty be totally candid with me. How can I get through to Matthew if I know not all that he is saying?"

"Trust me on this," said Ramón. "He is making a lot of incredible accusations, most of which are false. As such, their substance need not concern you."

"*Need not concern me?* Ramón, that *substance* has convulsed more than a dozen cities on the oceans immediately surrounding Botany Bay and a few thousand miles inland. It has reached the city of Paris and likely reawakened the memories of the original national hero of France—going back to before France existed. As you, yourself, now admit. And you come to *me* for help in persuading him to stand down. How can anything he says *not* concern me?"

"All you need to know is that he has gone, quite simply, insane. And he might very well have allied himself with a nation-state we all thought destroyed."

"Which, need I remind you, Ramón, is your unsupported hypothesis, nothing more."

"I know I can't expect you to believe that. Nevertheless."

Jacques-Yves sat where he was for ten seconds. During that time, he tried to process all the information he had received and identify the information he had *not* received.

"Will you stay for dinner?" he asked. That might be one way to find the missing pieces.

"Thank you, no," said Ramón. "I have other matters that require my attention. For one thing, we are still trying to establish a two-way channel of communication. Matthew Morrow has cut off all communication with Botany Bay except the broadcast stations, which he is now operating to make pirate broadcasts. But as soon as we can be sure he'll listen, we will call upon you. Never fear."

"I promise you," said Jacques-Yves, "that *fear* is not the word—not in this context. I will eagerly await your further communications."

* * *

"The *vice-amiral* has taken his departure," the butler said about half an hour later. "At what hour does *mon amiral* wish to dine?"

Jacques-Yves looked up from his copy of *Jane's Fighting Ships,* edition 2016. "I will dine at seven hours, Michel," he said. "My habitual meal will do."

"Thank you, sir."

Michel turned to go. Jacques-Yves got up from his armchair, tucked *Jane's Fighting Ships* edition 2016 under his arm, and started for his study. After two steps, he stopped and raised a hand. "Wait."

"Sir?"

"I'll need some references in my study—*Jane's Fighting Ships,* editions 2013 through 2021. You will note I have the 2016 edition already in my hand. Have someone pull the rest from their shelf and bring them to me directly."

"Yes, sir. Will that be all, sir?"

"Yes, thank you."

Michel walked to the shelf, obviously to pre-select the volumes in question by pulling them partway out. Jacques-Yves left him to it and walked briskly to his study. Here he kept the records attendant on running the vineyard and winery. Here also, he kept the records of his naval career and the research projects he had begun upon his retirement. Those things, quite simply, kept him sane. The project that excited his interest now was his history of naval architecture. He hoped to publish it someday. In this New Economy, he couldn't hope to recoup any remuneration. The Five Ladies had abolished copyright and patent, along with much else. But there was always satisfaction. Satisfaction that someone would always know the truth about some things, as only a naval officer could see them.

Two ships interested him most of all now. Thankfully he didn't have to wait long before a valet brought in the books he had asked for—nine weighty landscape-style books.

"Set them on that table, if you please," he ordered, pointing to a simple four-legged table. The valet knew his job well. He set the books down and waited. At a nod from Jacques-Yves, he left.

Jacques-Yves continued to read the 2016 edition. Here was the treasure trove. For in that year, in the Gregorian Calendar, the United States Navy commissioned *Zumwalt* and launched her sister ship *Michael Monsoor.*

He knew instantly where to find the information he now wished to review. Outboard profile, top and bottom plan, bow and stern elevations, inboard profile, and deck plans. He had studied these only briefly before, though slightly more carefully than usual. The curious histories of those two vessels had prompted the extra study. But now—now he must study those vessels far more closely. For here was his best clue to Matthew's intentions, until Ramón Ordoñez-Pizarro cared to reveal more.

What was the Admiralty hiding? Surely Matthew had published some sort of manifesto. Why not share that with him?

Jacques-Yves thought about Ramón's fantastic theory about the original Americans. *Could* they have survived—and in sufficient numbers to service these two vessels? These vessels were the key. They were, without a doubt, the most powerful ships afloat today.

And how could Matthew have fashioned ammunition for those shore guns? Even the Americans didn't do that before the Climate War. *Zumwalt* fought her battle with *LBJ* alone, using the low-altitude, terrain-following guided missiles the Americans had developed long before. That much, a court of inquiry later established. *Mansoor* left her station, and everyone assumed she went to *Zumwalt's* aid. Of the three vessels, the hastily assembled United Nations Navy recovered the wreckage of one: LBJ. The other two apparently vanished off the face of the oceans.

And now they were back. Only Matthew—or someone else—had made them capable of shore bombardment and taken over all of Botany Bay, which once had been the continent, and Commonwealth, of Australia.

But why, why, *why!?* What did Matthew hope to gain? Botany Bay was as isolated as was Cruria Australis, the cold, snow-blown continent that lay beneath the Southern Cross. Jacques-Yves still had the old world portrait globes that identified that continent as Antarctica, the continent opposite the Bears' Ocean—the Arctic Ocean. The Five Ladies had changed the name, saying no geographical feature should ever have to self-identify relative to another. They had also renamed North and South America, assigning the names *Aztlán* and *Amazonía*.

The United Systems had changed Australia to Botany Bay and evacuated the entire civilized population from the Commonwealth that once held sway there. They had done it by the oldest expedient of all: loading them aboard a colony ship to settle another world. That suggestion had come, actually, from the Elves. Only the Aborigines remained in their Northern Territory. Tasmania had undergone *le rendu*. And each of the remaining "states" of the old Commonwealth had gotten a particular set of United Systems rejects. Western Australia had become the American Reservation. South Australia had received the juvenile offenders; Victoria and Queensland the adult offenders, with Queensland given over to penal farming. And in New South

Wales, once the nucleus of Botany Bay? There, the United Systems dumped the dangerously insane among their people.

But now … now that entire continent was hostile. Matthew Morrow had done this. But what did he plan next? What could he do, staging out of an isolated continent, with seven wet-navy ships? Five wooden, and two metal—and heavily armed, and cloaked. Plus a B-52 Stratofortress, with fighter escort, and all those other aircraft! Did he have Chinook helicopters? He seemed to remember that the Royal Australian Air Force did once have them. Those banana-shaped troop carriers with the dual counter-rotating main rotors could easily jump from Queensland to New Guinea and hop their way across Indonesia to Vietnam. Any ground forces using them would thus have access to three continents. To say nothing of *Constitution*, which could carry a platoon at least and escort the other four wooden vessels, each of which could act as a transport.

What are you after, Matthew? he could only wonder.

A sudden commotion in the *foyer* broke through his reverie. *Now, what was going on that Michel couldn't handle better than this?* He heard Michel's voice … and a woman's voice. From the cadence, slightly artificial. And yet, somehow familiar. But at five hours of the afternoon?

He rose from his desk and strode to the *foyer.* Unconsciously he affected the stride he once used in the passageways of his last ship, *Bonaventure VII.* He didn't often affect that manner, except when something annoyed him— as it did now.

"What passes?" he barked in French as he burst into the *foyer.* "What is this noise? Forget you that I am at home to no one at this hour…"

He froze. Michel turned from the argument he'd been having with the female visitor—or intruder. "My excuses, my Rear-Admiral," the butler said. "I tried to tell the *mademoiselle* that you are not receiving, but…"

Jacques-Yves silenced him with a quick hand gesture. For he had eyes only for the woman.

"*Bonjour, mon capitaine,*" she said. And, of course, she called him *"captain."* For that's what he had been to her when last he saw her. She stood one hundred eighty meters tall and had the same bright red hair and hazel eyes.

She wore what looked like Marine camouflage fatigues, and the silver bar on each shoulder marked her rank. But they also bore an insignia he did not recognize: a stylized symbol of Earth, depicting the Eastern Hemisphere, but sporting dove's wings. In her hand, she carried the single-visor canvas hat, also in fatigue colors. And that voice identified her convincingly.

But it did not change the fact that she was supposed to be dead these twenty-five years. Yet, here she stood … No, wait. Her skin was gold—like the skin of an officer they both knew.

Barely able to speak, he answered, "Hello … Lieutenant."

Chapter 2

The gold-skinned woman held out her hand—not continental socialite style, but Marine style. *"Comment allez-vous, mon capitaine?"* she continued in flawless French. "Or … pardon me. It's Rear-Admiral now, is it not?"

"That's exact," he said, taking her hand. Hard, artificial, likely strong enough to crush his fingers. At least she knew that incredible strength she now possessed; she squeezed just enough. Matthew would have done the same.

Turning to the butler, he said, "Quite all right, Michel. Allow me to present Lieutenant Natalya Fyodorovna Bronskaya, late of the Corps of Marines of the United Systems—and formerly a ranking officer in my last command." He couldn't help noticing that Natalya seemed faintly awkward to hear him mention her old service. Did that winged-globe insignia have any bearing on that?

"Lieutenant Bronskaya is my guest this evening," he continued. "Carry on with your duties."

"Yes, sir," said Michel. "Shall I set another place at the table?"

Jacques-Yves turned to Natalya, who nodded. "Yes, definitely," he said. "The same meal. I will notify you of any change. Carry on." At least, he *hoped* that would be satisfactory—to her.

Michel left down one hallway. Jacques-Yves turned to his latest guest. "Pray, come with me," he said. "We will continue in my study."

"Thank you, Admiral," she said, turning to follow him. As soon as they arrived in his study, he brusquely said, "Pray, seat yourself," gesturing to an armchair. "And by the way: *can* you dine, in human fashion?"

"Yes, thank you, Admiral," said Natalya, taking the offered seat. "Since Matthew could, I can."

"Of course," said Jacques-Yves ruefully as he sat behind his desk. *Jane's Fighting Ships* still lay where he'd been reading it. He closed it and shoved it to his left side. "No, there's no 'of course' about it," he said. "Lieutenant, what *bizarrerie!* First of all, that's not a standard Marine uniform. What's that insignia that you wear? What does it represent?"

"The Revolutionary Forces of Free Earth."

"*Les forces révolutionnaires!?* And what can that want to say? Do I infer that *you* have turned revolutionary?"

"Yes, Admiral."

"*Quel bizarrerie,*" he said again. And then, "*Quel! Biz! Zarre! Rie!!*"

"Admiral," said this … this metal-and-plastic body that looked so like Natalya Bronskaya and spoke with her voice, "when I tell you *why* I have turned revolutionary, you will not find it so bizarre. And more than that, you will join me."

Jacques-Yves de Grasse stared at his erstwhile security officer and strike-force commander for a very long time. Then her voice—or rather that chillingly accurate facsimile of it—broke upon his reverie. "A sou for your thoughts, Admiral," she said softly.

"Eh? Ah, yes—back to the days when we had something called 'money' to spend. I was just thinking of when we first met. I was a junior pilot officer, on my first deep-space posting."

"USS *Napoléon Bonaparte* CC-65," said Natalya. "How could I forget? I suppose you would think back to that first time, after all," she sighed, and her eyes—at least they looked real—took on a faraway look. "Novy Mir," she said. "And a polity calling itself *Soyuz Sovyetskikh Sotsialistichyeskikh Respublik.*"

"Or in my language, *l'union des républiques socialistes soviétiques.* Yes, I remember. What foolish rosy-eyed idealists those were, who petitioned *le conseil des colonies* for permission to settle a new colony world, and reproduce—and without benefit of printers—the economic model of the polity with that very name, that once stood for Russia and several other countries in eastern Europe and central Asia. And it took that polity about as long to fail as the old one did."

"Seventy years," said Natalya. "And I was there for the last sixteen years of it. Sixteen years, during which I learned how to survive. As I had to."

"It's not as if they didn't pick a good spot," Jacques-Yves went on. "Kepler-438 b. Twenty percent heavier than *la Terre* and eighty-eight percent similar. If that experiment could have worked on any world, it would have worked there. But of course, the Navy lost contact with it and sent our ship to investigate and, if necessary, evacuate. I still remember the officers who served with me—including First Lieutenant Warren Maczak of the Marines, our strike-force commander. He was aboard my LCG, leading the First Platoon and also commanding the whole company. You know, of course, that they rewrote the doctrine on urban warfare while pacifying Novy Moskva. What an appalling disaster that was—half the buildings burned, and gangs occupying the other half."

"One of which," said Natalya grimly, "was holding *me* captive at the time. My father was lying dead in the streets, his body only then turning cold. I trust we don't need to go into the ways that gang used me."

"No," said the Admiral hastily. "Lieutenant Maczak briefed all the officers. After which, Captain de Gaulle charged us all never to disclose anything we saw or heard in that action."

"Funny that you should think back all that time."

"I am trying very hard," said Jacques-Yves, "to understand what has driven you to such an extremity."

"Admiral," she said with a smile, "aren't you the least bit curious to find me alive … and changed?"

That brought him up short. "Yes," he said after three seconds, "indeed I am. I rendered your remains, as I thought, to a funereal transport after that dreadful business on Rigel g. No one ever told me what was so urgent about shipping you off to Sol d. And in cryonic stowage, at that! What can Doctor Girard have overlooked? And what is this change in you?"

She merely smiled.

Jacques-Yves sighed. "I mean, more than the obvious physical change, Lieutenant," he said. "That gold skin—your incredible strength—and for what it's worth, they reproduced your voice exactly. That's a Frankel total-body prosthesis you are wearing, is it not?"

"Yes, Admiral," Natalya said. "Containing not only my brain but my entire central nervous system, plus my eyes, inner ears, and all twelve cranial nerves on each side."

"Actually, I start to wonder why no one saw fit to tell me at the time."

"Don't ask me, Admiral," she answered. "The Botany Bay Psychiatric Institute did this."

"*That* name again!" he cried.

"You've heard of that institution before?"

Jacques-Yves took a deep breath, then said, "Yes. This very day, in fact."

That caused her to sit bolt upright. "What!" she cried. "From whom?"

"From Vice-Admiral Ramón Ordoñez-Pizarro, Director of Naval Intelligence."

"*Der'mo,*" Natalya growled.

"*Pardon?*"

"Oh, excuse me. *Merde.*"

"I know what the word signifies," said Jacques-Yves, drily. "Lieutenant Maczak said that was your every other word on Novy Mir. I gather the Vice-Admiral's visit presents a problem?"

"And how! It means I have less time than I thought I had."

"Time to do what?"

"To recruit you, of course."

"You are pleased to joke," he said with deadly calm.

"I assure you, Admiral, I do not joke."

"Tell me this," said the Admiral. "Do I infer correctly that you are here as Matthew Morrow's ambassador?"

"Well, it's none too soon for you to grasp that! Of course I am. And I tell you frankly: he would be absolutely furious to see you in this mausoleum in which you have installed yourself."

"Mausoleum?" Jacques-Yves caught himself. He mustn't shout; that would bring Michel asking how he could be of assistance, which was the last thing he needed now. More quietly, he said, "Lieutenant, this happens to be my home and the land of my ancestors."

"Ancestral land or no," Natalya said, "a mausoleum it still is. One would think you came here to die—except that you didn't. I know you didn't. Which means you don't belong here. You were never meant to be a vine dresser and winemaker. I don't care if your wine is the best-tasting Bordeaux in the Galaxy. Nor even that you inherited some land patent with tenuous tenure at best. This is not the life you were meant to lead. You belong in your conning chair on *Bonaventure*, whether it's the sixth or the seventh, makes no difference. You commanded a capital ship; that's your life. Or at least, you belong on the deck of a capital ship, in command of a task force. They took that from you, just as surely as they took Matthew's liberty from him."

She now leaned forward and actually held out her hands toward him. "Admiral," she said, "please join me. Join *us*. Take your life back."

"I cannot promise any such thing," said the Admiral. "Not until I hear much more. All right, then. So Matthew Morrow sent you, and you have confirmed it."

"What finally gave you the key?"

"The Botany Bay Psychiatric Institute. Matthew Morrow was confined there."

"Did Vice-Admiral Ordoñez-Pizarro tell you that?"

"He did indeed. But never mind that. How do you propose to recruit me—and what has gotten into you and Matthew both, that you contemplate such a drastic step as revolution?"

"Well, tell me this, Admiral. You have acknowledged the change in me. Why do you think it came about? And why should the Botany Bay Psychiatric Institute be in charge of a program to develop the Erich Frankel prosthesis for widespread use?"

"All right," said Jacques-Yves. "I confess, I had wondered about that. That Institute is a place of confinement and treatment of the criminally insane. I can barely understand Matthew winding up there, but not you. Never you."

"But why Matthew?"

"*Zût alors!* How should I know? These black-clad security personnel board my ship one day, take him off, and then announce that I am to retire and my ship is to go for scrap."

"And you never thought to ask why?"

"Lieutenant, one does not question the orders or the motives of officers of the Navy."

"And that's the problem, isn't it?"

"And what do you want to say, *'that' is the problem? What* problem?"

"The problem of a society that is inherently unjust and is about to collapse."

"You stack enigma upon enigma. Pray, come to the point."

"Well, I scarcely know where to begin. But I'll begin with the printers."

"What about them? Other than, they can't make good wine? My ancestor got a land patent from the Five Ladies on the strength of that, by the way."

"I mean, Admiral, that whatever the printers were supposed to be able to make, they are making less well every year. And in the last fifteen years, the problem has become noticeable—and worse."

Jacques-Yves paused to reflect. He steepled together the fingers of both hands and rested his chin upon them, then reflected on several interesting expansions he'd made over the years. Like expanding into textiles …

"You might have right—that is, be right—at that," he said. "I must ask Michel to review for me all the substitutions he has made these fifteen years. Now and again, he'd mention to me something about 'real things' being of significantly better quality." He broke off as he noticed Natalya taking a certain alarm. "Lieutenant … No, may I call you Natalya?"

"I wish you would, Admiral," the rebel officer said. "I did, after all, come here to renew an old friendship."

"Then tell me right now, if you please, Natalya: what do you have? You look alarmed."

"Admiral," she said, "does any of your food come out of a printer?"

"Odd that you should ask," he said. "Michel has lately sought my authorization to hunt wild game to put food on our tables. Or at least to take some of the excellent two-meter-long Atlantic sea sturgeon that breed in our river, the Garonne. Naturally, I can't countenance such a thing. But more to the point, long ago, we started to grow flax and establish a textile mill. Now he wants to grow wheat, rye, corn, and such things and rehabilitate an ancient water-driven mill."

"Admiral," said Natalya, "I don't know what your Michel … your butler?"

"Yes. What about him?"

"I don't know what he knows or suspects. But if you value your life and your sanity, you will at least start planting food-staple crops, even if you can't bring yourself to hunt."

"And why should I have to do that?"

"Because … Oh, pardon me. I had forgotten. Admiral, I'll pose you another question. Might you have noticed, perhaps forty-five or so days ago, your thoughts becoming clearer?"

That struck home. "Yes," he said. "Natalya, again, you score. You were right—perhaps I *am* in a mausoleum of my own making. At about the time you name, I began to resent my present situation. And I know not—knew not—why. After all, this is my home, as I told you. Yet every day, I hear a voice in my head telling me I am in exile. Again, I know not why, or from where, that voice comes. But how would you know that it happened forty-five days ago?"

"Because that's when Matthew released a virus to all the printers of the world, to cause them to leave out a certain ingredient in any food or beverage."

"And that ingredient would be?"

"A derivative of a major tranquilizer called promazine."

Jacques-Yves was suddenly very glad he had been seated before he heard that. He actually felt his heart race. "Do you mean to tell me," he said, "that the people of this planet, and possibly every member of every ship's crew, has been taking … a *toxin*, and not by their choice?"

"On the button, Admiral."

"I … I am without voice. I literally cannot believe what I'm hearing. I distinctly remember Matthew bringing a serious programming error to my attention—along that very line. I told him to correct it. Now you tell me it was no error, but the *intent* of the authorities…" Then something else occurred to him. What was that time span? "Wait, wait, wait. Forty-five days?"

"That's what I said, Admiral. Is that important?"

"Yes," he said grimly. "Ramón told me," said Jacques-Yves, very deliberately, "that Matthew Morrow had regained consciousness, at the Botany Bay Psychiatric Institute, on MJDN 204154. Except that was forty-one days ago, not forty-five. So how could Matthew have acted earlier?"

"Simple. Your Admiral Ordoñez-Pizarro lied to you. Matthew Morrow first regained consciousness on MJDN 204109. And not on Botany Bay at all, but at Bethesda Naval Hospital."

"Bethesda … Maryland? In New Aztlán?"

"That's the only Bethesda I know that has a naval hospital."

"Now *that*," said Jacques-Yves, who now stood up from his desk and began to pace, "is an entirely new pair of arms. If Matthew Morrow has, in fact, been conscious for nearly ninety days, why should Naval Intelligence keep *that* from me?"

"I can explain that, Admiral," said Natalya, "when you agree to join me."

"And that, Natalya," he said, "is blackmail. And you have yet to answer my question: how came *you* to get mixed up in revolution?"

"It's very simple," said Natalya softly. "I owe Matthew Morrow my life."

Jacques-Yves froze in place and stood that way for a quarter of a minute. "All right," he finally said, "at least tell me this much. How comes it that you owe him your life?"

"Gladly," said Natalya. "But first: did Vice-Admiral Ordoñez-Pizarro mention me?"

"No."

"Well, we already know he's a liar," said Natalya. "He surely knew that my, for lack of a better term, *resurrection* would be difficult to explain."

"Why don't *you* explain it, then?"

"Certainly. I need not go over that last rescue mission. By the way, how did that mission go?"

"If you mean, after the hospitalmen evacuated you to the ship and your second-in-command took over, then it went well. No further casualties among the officers—though a few more Marines won their listings in Memorial Hall." He named them. "So, what do you remember next?"

"Waking up in a body that was not mine, holding up hands that were not mine, and speaking with a voice that was not mine, though, at least it sounded right," she said angrily.

"And next?"

"What do you think? I was so shocked; I simply shut out the world and everything and every*one* in it. Matthew tells me that lasted for twenty-five years."

"*Dégueuelasse,*" he said. "And how did you get out of that state?"

"Matthew brought me out of it."

"How?"

Natalya's eyes actually seemed to sparkle at that. "Admiral," she said, smiling, "all I can say is that the fairy-tale collectors and composers were right. When a woman loves a man, as I loved Matthew and now love him all over again, his voice can reach her in the deepest depression. All he had to do was talk to me."

"So you're telling me that you loved Matthew?"

"You can put that in the present tense, Admiral," she said. "Though, I suppose, I must apologize. I never told you when it happened."

"I think I know. On shore leave, was it not? And a month into our first cruise," said Jacques-Yves. "Your manner underwent a definite change at the next wardroom meeting—and I remember Matthew's almost studied ignorance at that same meeting. So now you admit that you broke discipline, to say nothing of taking advantage of…" He couldn't speak.

Natalya smiled again. "Admiral," she said, "I've already made my apologies to Matthew."

"I should certainly hope so," he replied frostily. Then he took a deep breath and sat down again. "On second thought," he said more calmly, "if Matthew accepted your apology, that ends the matter. And would, even if I were still in command and you two were still in my wardroom. But that is of the past. So, he said some things to you that recalled whatever had passed between you twenty-five years ago."

"And that was all I needed to hear. Of course, he let me cry for what I'd lost, and then assured me that I hadn't lost the most important thing, as far as he was concerned." She smiled again, "Admiral, you cannot know what that meant to me."

"I'll take your word for it. And what did he tell you next?"

"At first, only that he must have seen something he shouldn't have," said Natalya. "Something the Admiralty didn't want known. That, and how Doctor Folsom had informed him of your retirement."

"Doctor Folsom? Who's he?"

"*She.* Director of Psychiatry at the Botany Bay Psychiatric Institute."

"I see. And what is her role in this affair, other than her position?"

"Her predecessor had sought to duplicate Doctor Erich Frankel's work. It was he who placed my central nervous system in this body. She was his second-in-command and eventual successor."

"You spoke correctly about Vice-Admiral Ordoñez-Pizarro," said Jacques-Yves, grimly. "He would not have dared speak to me about what happened to you. I might have strangled him if he had. I swear to you, Natalya, that I knew nothing of this. Certainly not what happened to you."

"But why did you leave Matthew where he was?"

"I told you before: one does not question the orders…"

"Or the motives of one's superiors. Matthew told me … and forgive me for saying this … that this was your worst failing. Only that's not quite true, is it? Do you think I don't know the direction your career took after I had to leave your command? Matthew shared all with me. Including the other missions you ran between my apparent death in combat and his arrest. For instance, he told me about your fielding an improvised task force to establish a blockade during the First Morgenetic Civil War. Matthew was not likely to forget that incident. You actually let him command one of those ships. And a good thing, too, as it turned out. Do you remember what you told him after he delivered his after-action report? And submitted himself for discipline?"

"Yes," said Jacques-Yves. "I told him no commanding officer should ever apologize, even to his officer-in-tactical-command, for acting on a piece of intelligence that he could not report up the chain by … How does one say it in regulation-ese? Ah, yes…'because of the delay involved or for other clearly obvious cause.' And that went double when his quick action saved the operation—and that is no exaggeration.

"But how does that apply to my case? I wasn't in the field then. We were in orbit around this very world!"

"Oh, Admiral," she said, almost wistfully, "does your duty really require you to be so trusting? Don't you want to know what Matthew saw that was so sensitive?"

Jacques-Yves took a deep breath and let it out. "All right," he said. "What was it?"

"First, I'll tell you what he reported: an anomaly in Protected Wild Space, west of the Bethesda complex. In NRD-01-VA-Lucketts. That report led to his arrest."

"Was *that* all? No, Natalya, there was something else."

"Indeed, there was, Admiral," she said, with that grim tone returning. "It was a game preserve."

"A game preserve? In *Protected Wild Space!?*"

"But not only that, Admiral," she said. "The game was not wild animals. It was children."

"Impossible!"

"Quite possible," said Natalya. "And with evidence to prove it." She reached into a pocket of her fatigues and pulled out a microdrive. "A complete copy, Admiral," she said, tossing it onto the desk. "Only, I wouldn't play that before bedtime if I were you."

He picked up the microdrive and stared at it for a good long time. Then he pressed a button in the kneehole of his desk. The one bare surface he maintained turned into a computer workstation, which, of course, had a jack for inserting a microdrive. He inserted this one, navigated the file-management display that came up, and selected a video file at random.

Afterward, he didn't know what shocked him more: that such an installation would exist or that the Elfin Ambassador would be involved. For among the scenes that played out was the killing of that ambassador by his intended victim—a twelve-year-old girl.

"Nauséabond, en effet," he said, feeling nauseous. "But you said he did not tell you all this at first. Why not?"

"Because he didn't remember it just then."

"What does that want to say, 'he didn't remember it just then'?"

"He escaped from Bethesda Naval Hospital," Natalya said. "Three people escaped with him, including a chief information technician. That person helped him slip through the Barrier into Protected Wild Space. There he reconnoitered that installation."

"I sense that this recording is redacted," said Jacques-Yves.

"I regret very much that I must 'compartment' certain information. Let it suffice that he found some valuable allies. They helped him capture that installation and rescue the children in it, and took charge of those children afterward. But they also enhanced him. Greatly. And equipped him with a program by which he could erase his secondary memories and lockout his primary memories in case of capture."

"That explains the discrepancy between the two dates," said Jacques-Yves. "So he escaped from Bethesda Hospital on MJDN 204109, and then encountered you on Botany Bay on MJDN 204154."

"Correct."

"Then what if I were to tell you," he said slowly, "that Vice-Admiral Ordoñez-Pizarro has formed the theory that the original Americans, who once occupied the middle part of the continent called Aztlán today, still exist, and have maintained their society even in the face of the Re-Wilding?"

Natalya almost—but did not quite—take that without flinching. After three seconds, she said, "I will neither confirm nor deny an account of events I did not witness. I prefer to let Matthew Morrow tell you about that himself—again, if I can persuade you to join us."

Then it was true. But that did not begin to tell him exactly where his duty lay. Aloud, he said, "I will consider it. By the way, does he still call himself a lieutenant-commander these days?"

"No, Admiral. He holds the rank of Field Marshal."

"How appropriate," said the old Admiral. "I knew he was ambitious, but I knew not how much."

"Would that *ambition*," said Natalya. "explain why a rocket force, unknown to me previously, tried to destroy us with a thermonuclear missile?"

"*WHAT!?*" He stared back at her in literal open-mouthed astonishment.

She started to repeat that last. Jacques-Yves, cutting her off, said, "I heard you, I heard you, I heard you, I heard you!" Now he buried his head in his hands.

For five seconds, he held that pose. Then he raised his head, took a deep breath, and let it out. "All right," he said. "Come over here." He got up again and crossed to the corner of his study where he kept his world portrait globe.

"What is this artifact?" Natalya asked. "It's very attractive."

"It is a three-dimensional map of this Earth."

"Really?" Natalya gasped, and her eyes widened in wonder. "But why not simply call up a holographic display?"

"I happen to like solid objects," said Jacques-Yves. "I think I'll show you my library. Now let us see." He spun the globe until he could see the continent marked *Australie*. Then he spun the frame on which the globe was mounted so that he was looking directly at the landmass.

"Now then," he said, "from where did that missile launch?"

She pointed to a spot in the Manchuria region of China.

"And how do you know that?"

"Matthew has acquired an air force of sorts," she answered. "Including LCG prisoner transports, easily capable of seeing such a launch."

That confirmed what Ramón had told him. "And the target?"

She pointed to the old capital city of Canberra.

"*La vache*. What kind of other secrets is the Admiralty keeping? Come to think, Ramón was very evasive with me. Imagine keeping a brace of missiles within striking distance of Botany Bay and not telling anyone! But why Canberra?"

"Because that's where Matthew and I happened to be standing at the time," said Natalya. "It will be a very long brief. For now, let it suffice that there were three of us cyborgs on Botany Bay at the time. The third ... well, of him, the less said, the better. Like Matthew, he came from Berks' World."

"The failed colony on Proxima b?"

"The same. And we can now solve an important mystery about that colony."

"Are you telling me this other person was the one who opened all the airlocks and killed everyone?"

Natalya nodded. "Everyone but himself and Matthew," she said. "The fact of the matter is that they knew one another as boys. Stefan Weiss—that's the name of this other cyborg—was the bully and Matthew was his target. The two of them died in an accident involving a school bus. Doctor Frankel made cyborgs out of both of them, not Matthew only."

"Let me guess," said Jacques-Yves, "Stefan Weiss went insane."

"Or simply drunk on the power Doctor Frankel gave him. He couldn't tolerate Matthew surviving with him. So he destroyed the colony."

"And lately," said the Admiral, "*both* of them were on Botany Bay. *La vache*, what was Doctor Frankel, and what were those officers on Botany Bay, trying to do? Create some new kind of ultimate warrior?"

"That's what Matthew and I believe. But I've been digressing. Matthew started with the American Reservation, in a campaign to sweep across Botany Bay. As he was closing in on the New South Wales District, he used the official announcement station to call out Stefan Weiss. The two fought their last battle outside Canberra."

"And Matthew won."

"Yes."

"And then," said Jacques-Yves, now feeling angry again, "the enemy— that is, the Special Security Forces—passed an alert that Matthew had won the fight. And the Admiralty—or someone in high authority—decided to destroy Matthew by any means necessary. How in the name of every officer under whom I ever served did you survive? Are you that robust?"

"Happily, we never had to test that," said Natalya. "A truly wonderful woman … a heroine of our revolution … flew an LCG directly at the missile and rammed it. We believe the missile had at least one warhead with a contact fuse."

"Which blew the others up. And at what altitude?"

"Four hundred kilometers."

"*Zût*. No wonder all those Chinese cities are running riot. Electromagnetic pulse effects, a flash bright enough to blind, plus radiation effects … and all of them happening over Manchuria. I tell you, someone is going to pay for this."

"Not so, Admiral," said Natalya, more soberly still. "We've already figured out that the Admiralty, or the SSF, or whoever gave that order, has already found a scapegoat. The pedophile game preserve alone would justify revolution. The missile makes all other courses impossible."

"Are you sure about that?" asked Jacques-Yves. "Are you truly sure? You're telling me that absolutely no one in the Admiralty or the Security Council is trustworthy."

"Admiral," said Natalya with a sigh, "think. Who would appoint a monster like Holger Tildblad to direct the Botany Bay Psychiatric Institute?"

"He's the one who gave you this … er … body."

"Yes. And how could he get away with a thing like that? Why didn't Brianna Belle Folsom, his successor, intervene and lay information about the project? How could she get away with the atrocities Matthew and I have documented, and in some cases, suffered? Who put a promazine derivative into everyone's food and drink if anyone was trustworthy? Surely you know that things like these must have had approval at the very highest level."

"Heads-of-state have had ranking subordinates run their own projects before, without the knowledge or authorization of those same heads-of-state."

"All right, then! What about Doctor Frankel on Berks World? Who covered up the full extent of that project? They even tried to erase Matthew's earliest childhood memories. But by the time he revived me, he had recovered them. Admiral—face it! He has information sufficient to embarrass the entire government! You already know the Admiralty is lying to you. Why shouldn't the corruption go as high as the Secretariat? As old as this secret is, do you really think anyone could become first secretary who had not even knowledge of these things? No—a first secretary must support them with all his heart!"

Jacques-Yves turned away. Burying his head in his hands, he walked across the room to the far corner. For several seconds he held that pose. Mercifully, Natalya kept silent until, at last, he could lower his hands, turn, and face her.

"Natalya," he said, "I apologize. You must think I regret to see you again, after these many years. I assure you, I am very glad to see you. You were an officer under my command. I thought you killed in action. To see you alive once more … Why, it's as if I had lost a daughter and gotten her back. But what you have brought me, I find extremely difficult to believe."

"I comprehend, Admiral," she said soberly. "But ask yourself: what have I to gain by lying? And have I ever lied to you?"

"Nothing, and no," the old Admiral said. "But a lie is not the same as a misinterpretation. A logical explanation, far less dire than you have brought me, might still exist."

"It might, Admiral," said Natalya, shaking her head sorrowfully. "But it does not."

At that moment, Jacques-Yves heard Michel's discreet knock. "Yes?" he asked.

"Dinner is served, *mon amiral.*"

"Thank you, Michel," Jacques-Yves said. "Natalya, let us leave this for later. After dinner." And he crooked his right arm toward her.

"Delighted, Admiral," she said with a smile as she took the offered arm.

* * *

"So that's what you meant by not being able to countenance hunting or fishing," said Natalya. "You turned vegetarian, even vegan, did you not?"

"Yes, I did," said Jacques-Yves. "I will not even *pretend* to eat meat."

"But this food is still printed, is it not?"

"Yes. But didn't you say that shouldn't present a problem?"

"Admiral, if you please, let me act as your taster."

"Are you sure?"

Natalya smiled. "Remember, Admiral—this is a prosthetic body. Promazine and its derivatives can't harm me." She picked up her soup spoon and scooped up a sample of the *vichyssoise* before her. She carried it to her mouth and swallowed as Jacques-Yves waited. Finally, she smiled. "It's safe, Admiral," she said.

"*Bon.* Then I shall play the host from now on. Michel, the wine."

Michel produced a bottle of white wine—the de Grasse vineyards grew grapes for white wine as well as red. He uncorked it and poured some into the glass that Jacques-Yves held out for him. The old Admiral sniffed it, then nodded to Michel, who then poured full servings for Jacques-Yves and Natalya.

"Will that be all, *mon amiral?*" the butler asked.

"Yes, thank you," said Jacques-Yves. "Pray, leave us now."

The butler withdrew, leaving the two old friends alone.

"May I offer a toast?" said Natalya. At her host's nod, she raised her wine glass. "Let us drink, then, to old friendship—and comradeship-in-arms."

"*Oyez, oyez,*" said Jacques-Yves, who touched his glass to hers. As she sipped her wine, he watched her closely. He was used to the wines from his winery, but …

"Truly, your wine is excellent, Admiral," she said. "I can readily see how your ancestor managed to get a land patent for this vineyard."

"As my ancestor wrote in his diary," said Jacques-Yves, "only a few glasses of wine sufficed to convince the Five Ladies that even the new printers from the Elves could *never* produce wine as good as any that came out of the soil. The *terroir* of good Bordeaux wine is simply non-duplicable."

"But if I may so observe, Admiral, that applies also to the fruits of the land," said Natalya. "Michel is correct. This soup tastes as if made from mutant ingredients. Believe me—I can tell."

"I can just imagine," said the Admiral. "And to what do you attribute that 'mutant' taste?"

"Simple errors of copying built up over time," said Natalya. "Like actual mutants one occasionally encounters in the wild."

"See here," said Jacques-Yves, "if the food is not to your liking, then…"

"I don't mind," she said. "I apologize for seeming to find fault with everything. It's just that Matthew has taught me to question *everything* I encounter. Without exception."

Jacques-Yves took a deep breath and slowly let it out. Then he said, "Natalya, obviously, you could not leave the discussion until after dinner. I ought to have expected that. But if I may ask, are you sure you're accounting fully for all your emotional reactions?"

"I'm not sure I understand."

"Simply this," said the Admiral. "I accept that your waking up 'wearing' a total body prosthesis came as a profound shock. But perhaps you've let your shock cloud your judgment of other matters. Like these apparent printer errors. And while I cannot condone the introduction of an anti-psychotic drug into everyone's food, I remain hopeful that the right person will, if we inform him, correct the problem."

"Is Matthew letting his own emotions cloud *his* judgment, then?" asked Natalya.

"Yes, he is. And I lay the blame squarely with the Naval Criminal Investigative Service. How they, and those Special Security Forces, could have treated him as they have, is beyond my comprehension. Had they not, we would be having a far different conversation."

"Or maybe we wouldn't be having any kind of conversation," she answered. "Because I would still be catatonic. I am quite desolated, Admiral. I must reject your notion that Matthew and I are not behaving logically. But I recognize that you could not see the justice of our cause as clearly as do we."

"I have fear that I cannot see at all the justice of your cause."

"Admiral, I'm going to tell you a story. It's a story from Novy Mir, before the *Napoléon* came to rescue the survivors of our 'great experiment.' Pardon me for describing this, but … well, since we didn't print anything, we ate as humans everywhere ate before the Elves came. We took lots of flora and fauna with us—or at least the founders did. Frogs among them. And sometimes, I would stew them."

Jacques-Yves made a slight moue of disgust at that thought.

"Yes, I know how you feel about that. But I needed to set some background. Sometimes when I was foraging for food, I would capture a frog to eat. But I didn't throw it into boiling water. I did at first, and found that was the fastest way to lose one's meal. So I started lowering the frog into a pot full of lukewarm water, and *then* lighting the fire underneath it. It was very effective. I could easily cook a frog before it even knew it was cooking. Heating the water slowly and gradually made things much easier than heating the water to a boil before throwing the frog in."

"You are telling me," said Jacques-Yves, "that the authorities are stewing me slowly and gradually, like your frogs."

"That's exact, my Admiral," said Natalya softly. "And not you alone. Everyone."

"And to what end?"

"To an end as old as civilization itself, Admiral—to maintain control. As I told you: the grand experiment is failing. They ought never to have authorized the Novy Mir colony. That exposed the central weakness. The printers compensated for that weakness—until now. Matthew, of course, captured hundreds of them as he conquered Botany Bay. From the errors they are already making, he calculates that the system will fail catastrophically in five years' time—six at the outside. And already the air is polluted again."

"Is that another subtle change I'm not supposed to notice?"

"Yes, indeed. Matthew noticed it immediately upon his awakening in Bethesda. At Botany Bay, it's worse. And he's traced it down."

"To where?"

"To China. Which is now the seat of industry."

"There is no industry on *La Terre!*"

"Oh, but there is, Admiral," said Natalya. "A *munitions* industry."

Sighing, Jacques-Yves said, "Well, Ramón did tell me about a 'classified' reason that the Navy and Marines were stretched thin. I don't suppose you or Matthew have the key to *that* mystery."

"Indeed we have, Admiral," said Natalya, who suddenly sounded grim. "Revolution has broken out in the Nine-o'clock Quadrant."

Chapter 3

"You don't want to say that the Metamorphs have regained their strength?"

"No, Admiral. The Metamorphs didn't start that war, or so our informant tells us."

"Who could possibly inform you of doings in the Nine-o'clock Quadrant?"

"Doctor Udayan Thakur," said Natalya. "Former Base Surgeon aboard Station Midgard, and now—well, his story is almost as interesting as Matthew's or mine. He's a 'renegade augment,' through an 'arrangement' his parents made. It made him capable of realizing any career goal he chose, or even more than one. So when revolution broke out, he decided he wanted to act the part of a 'secret agent.' He literally parachuted from orbit into Sidney after Matthew and I, and our allies, secured it."

"And how exactly did your Doctor Thakur parachute down to Earth from orbit?"

"In a personal re-entry capsule."

"I did not know the Marines were deploying that at scale!" said Jacques-Yves.

"They aren't. It's still experimental," said Natalya. "Then-Captain Medea Mercouri of USS *Argo* developed it during her passage across the Twelve-o'clock Quadrant."

"Are we talking about USS *Argo* CLG-711? The light cruiser that can land on a planet's surface? The ship that vanished into an uncontrolled wormhole shortly before the Metamorphic War broke out? And then returned from the Twelve-o'clock Quadrant seven years later?"

"The same."

"Do I take it the *Argo* is in our Solar system as we speak?"

"Yes, Admiral. Holding station near Ultima Thule, so Dan tells us."

"I remember him," said Jacques-Yves, drily. "He put us all to shame when we visited Station Midgard, and he examined Matthew. He treated

Matthew as just another officer, not … well. That's of the past, of course. So Dan Thakur is now involved in another revolution—about which the good Admiral Ordoñez-Pizarro refused to brief me. I gather you can?"

"Yes, Admiral," said Natalya. "Relax. This will be a long brief. First: did you know that several humans and Midgardians established settlements in the Nine-o'clock Quadrant, after the Metamorphic War ended?"

"Only what I read on the popular news networks."

"Then this you might not have heard. Two years ago, that quadrant fell out-of-contact."

"*La vache.* That *would* have been less than comfortable to explain. So that's how long this other revolution has been proceeding in the Nine-o'clock Quadrant?"

"Yes. I'll tell you what Dan Thakur told Matthew and me. Four years ago, the United Systems started to levy taxes on these new settlements. You have to remember: the United Systems was and is debt-ridden. Printer stocks are not infinite, and at the end of the Metamorphic War, they were scarce. While the settlements—which now call themselves the Free Systems—are free and clear."

"So the United Systems tried to tax them."

"That's exact."

"And how did Medea Mercouri get mixed up with the Nine-o'clock Quadrant?"

"Well, when she brought her ship, the *Argo*, back to Six-o'clock, the High Command debriefed her on a rather striking set of adventures deep in Hive territory. How she managed to get through that space without the Hive totally assimilating her crew, even Dan found it too difficult to explain. But for her reward, they assigned her as CinC9, in charge of all Navy and Marine assets in the Nine-o'clock Quadrant. She always considered that an insult and a waste of her talents and intelligence—both the gathered kind and the in-born kind.

"Well, when the Security Council passed those new taxes, she rebelled. She absolutely refused to enforce them. Even when a cadre of Beringians from the new world of Oklahoma—under the leadership of her old ex-oh, by the way—destroyed a shipment of tea from Earth, she refused to take any enforcement action. So then the Navy recalled her to Earth. Not only would she not go, but she declared the Six-o'clock government illegitimate and threw in with some civilians on the colony world of Terra Nova who were already urging independence. Dan estimates that one-third of her forces, including the crew who inherited the *Argo*, went with her. The rest remained loyal and now answer to a new CinC9, an Admiral William Howe.

"Two years ago, things came to a head. Admiral Howe sent down an LCG to a city on Terra Nova called, believe it or not, Lexington, and…"

"A 'shot heard round the Galaxy' rang out. Exact?"

"Exact. The Nine-o'clock Quadrant has been at war ever since."

"And do you believe this account from Doctor Thakur?"

"Implicitly."

"It would explain," said Jacques-Yves, "why the Navy and Marine Corps are 'stretched thin.' And it might explain why the Admiralty are afraid to take any further overt action. May I assume that Matthew has been 'sharing' this account in his 'propaganda broadcasts'?"

"That he has."

"And Ramón told me that Matthew had gone insane. *Quel bizarrerie, en effet.* Then again, your very appearance is bizarre in itself. If I can accept that, I have to accept much else. The question is how much I *can* accept."

"Admiral, I say again: think. What was so special about Matthew, the late Stefan Weiss, or me, that anyone should go to the trouble to outfit any of us with total-body prostheses? Didn't you ever wonder about Matthew himself? Let me tell you, Admiral: I did."

"Why should you? Beyond being, and forgive me for saying it, pruriently curious about him?"

Natalya chuckled. "I deserve that," she said with a smile. Then, turning serious again, she said, "But remember, Admiral: as commander of your Marine strike force, I also was in charge of security. And it always struck me funny that anyone would invest such resources in a project of that kind. I tried investigating the project but kept running into dead ends. Privacy locks I could understand—but these locks had 'top secret' or worse labels."

Natalya paused for a second or two.

"What have you?" asked Jacques-Yves.

"I never told you this, Admiral," she said. "But I went on that particular shore leave boiling with frustration because I couldn't figure out where Matthew came from. I let you believe I just plied him with drink to test how he would respond. And got drunk myself on the strength of it. But what I didn't tell you was that I was interrogating him. I was never drunk, either— I took a prophylactic alcohol antitoxin before I even went down on that shore leave. That's how it started; what you called a 'prurient curiosity' developed in the course of the evening."

"If you're trying to shock me, Natalya," said Jacques-Yves, "you've failed. What's that, next to having you show up on my doorstep when I thought you dead? So tell me: did your 'interrogation' succeed?"

"No, Admiral," said Natalya. "Because he knew even less than I'd been able to find out. It left me burning with shame, though, for more than one reason."

"We discussed that quite sufficiently long ago," said the Admiral, who suddenly paused again.

"Now, what have *you*, Admiral?"

"Nothing. Just..." He trailed off.

"Admiral," she said, voice hardening, "with all due respect to your rank, talk to me. Please."

Very deliberately, Jacques-Yves said, "The after-action report from your second-in-command contained a few hints that I dismissed at the time. Lieutenant Kress was even more obsessed with security than were you— which made him a most worthy successor to you. I suppose it comes with the territory, he being a Morgen himself." Leaning forward, Jacques-Yves went on, "He told me that the enemy dispositions on Rigel g always struck him as indicating advance knowledge, not only of our presence but who would be commanding the Marine detachment. He swore that the enemy commander must have received detailed intelligence about you personally.

We could never prove that, of course, and obviously, he won the battle anyway. But he mentioned other things. Like how those evacuees got themselves into such a strife that they would need rescue."

"What was so strange about that?"

"They violated several security protocols to get into that situation. Or so Lieutenant Kress wrote in his report. I still have it. Would you like to read it?"

Natalya surprised him. She made a very angry face. "Yes, Admiral, I would like that very much," she growled. "It rather sounds as though someone set me up. And why not? Someone who had survived a failed colony, then became a Marine, and qualified for OCS faster than ... well, than most." Abruptly she stopped growling. In a softer tone, she continued, "In fact, my background is very close to a few things about Matthew's background that he only recently remembered. That's how he could sympathize with me when I finally put my shame aside and told him everything about me." Now she bowed her head. "Excuse me, Admiral, I ... I..."

Then she did something he would never have expected, something that changed his entire outlook on this affair. She reached up with her left arm and wiped her eyes. Her breath came out ragged, and that's the *last* thing he would expect from a cyborg ...!

"Pardon ... pardon me, Admiral," she finally said, her breathing settling down. "I should have expected to find out something like this eventually. But that doesn't make it any easier."

"I should think not," said Jacques-Yves, grimly. *"C'est absoluement dégueuelasse.* I owe Kress an apology; I knew your death upset him, but now I know why, and I blame myself for that. I never followed up on his report. My fault entirely. And I owe *you* an apology. And Matthew."

"Why Matthew?"

"For more than the reasons you think, Natalya. You see ... I never briefed him on Lieutenant Kress' suspicions. Lieutenant Kress briefed me directly, as was his right as a Marine, not a Navy, officer." Again he clawed at the air. *"Zût encore!* Perhaps if I *had* briefed Matthew, we could have stopped all this!" Then another thing occurred to him. He went on, more softly, "Of course that might have meant…"

"It might have meant that my death would have been permanent," Natalya said when Jacques-Yves didn't finish his sentence. "Have no fear, Admiral. I've struggled with that thought myself. Matthew told me from the first that he was heartily glad to find me alive. And since then, he's made me feel just as glad."

"Which does not alter the fact," said the Admiral, "that I failed both of you."

"Does that mean you'll join us?"

"Not yet," said Jacques-Yves sharply. "I could never make such a decision merely to expiate my self-disgust for a bad decision. I need to meditate on everything else you've told me."

He hung his head. What else could he say, knowing how he had really put his finger in his eye? Words were totally inadequate. He was still searching his mind for *anything* to say when he heard something that made him look up. She was whistling a tune. He had heard that tune before … but not from any celebrated composer.

He looked straight into her eyes. "Did Matthew share that with you?" he asked.

"Yes," she said, smiling. "I never knew he could compose…"

"He couldn't," said Jacques-Yves. "Not, at least, until *Débora* operated on him to take out the chip that had been blocking his emotions. He well and truly loved you, as I'm sure he's told you. The first thing he did, when your loss crashed into his mind, was to go to the ship's music room and play the most heart-rending interpretation of Tchaikovsky's *Pathétique* Symphony—specifically, its Fourth Movement—that I or anyone else on board had ever heard. And then … then he wrote that music. He called it your theme."

"You should hear it with a full orchestra playing it," Natalya said.

"I have," said the Admiral. "We had enough instrumentalists on board to make at least a small orchestra. Matthew arranged it."

"Ah, but you likely never heard it played on wind instruments with real reeds or stringed instruments made of wood, drums made with real membranes, and so on."

"And you have?"

"The New American Symphony played it for me in the Sydney Opera House," said Natalya, her voice now seeming to swell with pride. "I recorded it. I can record anything now and upload it, too."

"You almost persuade me to join your revolution, just for that," said Jacques-Yves. "Even that will not suffice, however—but do upload it. I should like to hear what a real orchestra sounds like."

"Only too pleased."

They finished their meal in silence, after which Jacques-Yves had Marcel conduct Natalya to the guest bedroom. He himself retired to his own bedroom. Only instead of taking *Jane's Fighting Ships*, edition 2016, with him, he took some far more pertinent reading matter. To wit: the after-action report by Lieutenant Kress, USMC, concerning an action on Rigel g.

Neither he nor Kress could have known where events would take both men. Kress had changed the gold bar on his shoulder to a silver one, thus becoming *First* Lieutenant Kress, after taking over permanently as company commander. Then had come that dreadful mission that had ended in the wreck of *Bonaventure VI*. Lieutenant Kress had jumped two grades and become *Major* Kress, commanding a full battalion of Marines on Station Midgard during the Metamorphic War. Jacques-Yves understood that Major Kress had found his own love interest, an affair that ended tragically when the other officer was killed in action.

Then, incredibly, he had figured in the second of two civil wars that convulsed the Morgenetic Empire. Jacques-Yves had run a little side action in the first—and during that time, Kress had laid down his Marine commission and taken part in the fighting within the Empire. After all was over, Kress had taken up his commission again. But after the Emperor had made some thoroughly bad decisions that almost lost the war for the United Systems/Morgenetic Alliance, Wolfgang Kress had done something Jacques-Yves still couldn't get over. He actually *challenged the Emperor to a duel*—and won. With the eventual result that Jacques-Yves' old officer was now Emperor.

What would his old friend think, knowing that Natalya had lived? The more Jacques-Yves thought about this after-action report, the more sense it made. Why had he not seen Kress' logic before? Because it led too close to home, perhaps?

Jesu-Christ once said that a prophet was not without honor, save in his own hometown. Did an enemy risk detection, save only when said enemy was always in charge?

Jacques-Yves was still pacing his room, the after-action report in his hand, when again, he heard a commotion from another part of his house. He donned a robe, belted it, and reached for the intercom. But before he could touch it, a hall boy knocked at his door.

"*Entrez,* he ordered.

The hall boy entered.

"What passes out there?" the Admiral asked.

"*Mon amiral,* Marcel gives his respects and rather urgently requests your presence in the *foyer.*"

"For what cause?"

"*Monsieur,* we have an intruder."

"Lead the way," said Jacques-Yves, and followed the hall boy down the corridor.

The noise got louder with every step they took. At last, they emerged into the *foyer,* where Jacques-Yves beheld a scene he scarcely expected. He saw Natalya, still in uniform, holding a man about thirty centimeters off the floor with her right hand locked around his throat! The prisoner wore an outfit that looked a little like combat fatigues, except for being black as jet. At Natalya's feet rested a black balaclava-style headdress and a pair of black gloves. Taking in the outfit, Jacques-Yves saw a jacket with many pockets in it. Natalya held him up effortlessly and snarled, "Are you going to talk, or shall I end your miserable existence right here and now?"

"Cela suffrira!" Jacques-Yves bellowed. Everyone, except the hapless prisoner, turned to look.

"Put that man down," he ordered. "But hold him securely. *I* will question him."

Natalya let the prisoner's shoes touch the floor but still held him in that same neck grip.

"Marcel," said the Admiral, "report. How came you and Natalya to take this prisoner?"

"*Mon amiral,* he entered the house surreptitiously," said Marcel. "We found on his person the most sophisticated burglars' tools anyone ever carried. I suspected at once that he was no ordinary burglar. So on my own cognizance, I had Lieutenant Bronskaya awakened so that she could at least give her opinion. What she found … well, if you will permit, perhaps she can explain."

"Well, Natalya?"

"Admiral," she said in her no-nonsense Marine voice, "this man is a spy. The equipment he was carrying would be available to no one other than Naval Intelligence or, as I strongly suspect, the Special Security Forces. I was just about to ask this *crotte* about that when you appeared."

"And now, whoever you are," said Jacques-Yves, now thoroughly angry. "What are you called? To what service do you belong? And how came you to enter my house without an invitation?"

The man glowered and said nothing.

Then Jacques-Yves remembered that he had spoken in French. So he tried again in Standard, "What is your name, rank, and service? Why did you break into this house? This is private property, and you are trespassing."

"*Nothing* is private in our modern society!" the prisoner spat. "Maybe you don't understand that anymore, *Admiral* De Grasse. In any event, if you let me go, it *might* go better for you in court."

"Court? You wouldn't mean a court-martial because you know I'm retired."

"I mean the special tribunal set up for hard cases like yours. And I'm not going to tell you another thing."

Jacques-Yves considered that for a few seconds. Then, switching back to French, he ordered, "Search him."

With an efficiency Jacques-Yves would not have expected from his staff, four servants bore the prisoner down and held him fast. Natalya let go of the man's throat, took hold of his jacket in two handfuls at the neck, and pulled. She continued to tear his jacket down the middle. Within five minutes, she had laid out a rather impressive kit—a Personal Digital Device, another crude-looking device that looked like nothing so much as a hand-held antenna array—and several black canisters.

Jacques-Yves bent down and picked up one of the canisters. He hefted it, looking carefully at the prisoner as he did. The prisoner's eyes bulged.

"*Tiens, tiens!*" he said. "This frightens him. I wonder why?"

"*Mon amiral!*" cried Natalya. "Pray, handle that canister carefully! It is an aerosol."

"How dangerous can that be?"

"Very. Considering the other equipment this man had on his person, I think you would find that it contained an aerosol solution of cyanide of potassium. Except that I would not test that if I were you!"

Jacques-Yves' blood ran cold. He handed the canister to Marcel, who set it down as delicately as if it were a grenade. Then the Admiral picked up the hand-held "antenna array" and looked it over more carefully. And his blood ran colder still.

"Natalya," he said, handing her the device, "what do you make of this?"

She took it from him and seemed to examine it more closely still. Then she looked up with a very grim expression. "This," she said, "is an electromagnetic pulse projector. Why Doctor Folsom at the Botany Bay Psychiatric Institute didn't try to use that on us, I'm not sure. But someone obviously thought they could paralyze me with this."

"Could they?"

"I think I have a defense against this sort of thing about which its inventors knew not," she said, still speaking French. "Perhaps I'll keep this, to analyze it and make sure I could defend against it. But everything should be obvious now. The Special Security Forces traced me here—and intended to kill you all and capture me."

"Is that correct?" the Admiral asked the prisoner in Standard.

Again the prisoner stood mute.

"Marcel," he ordered next, this time giving the order in Standard, "if you had to defend against a gas attack, could you?"

"Oh, yes, my Admiral. It just so happens…"

"Never mind what 'just so happens.' You will break out some of your defenses, enough to protect yourself and as many men as you need. Then you will take the prisoner outside, to the rear garden, and test that canister on him."

"NO! I'll talk! I'll talk!"

Jacques-Yves looked the prisoner in the eye. He stared into the other's eyes for a long time.

"Never mind," he finally said. "You have already told us everything we need to know from you, from your reaction alone." Then to Marcel, speaking in French, he said, "Take him outside and dispatch him. Don't bother with the canisters; I want you to take care of the matter quickly. And then … then I have much fear that we shall have to abandon this house."

Marcel, in the same language, said, "*Mon amiral,* if I may?"

Jacques-Yves looked his butler in the eye and caught an expression he'd never seen before. This man obviously knew something and had not shared it with him. Something sensitive. Aloud, Jacques-Yves said, "Continue."

Marcel, as Jacques-Yves half expected, countermanded his order—to a degree. First, he ordered the hall boy, who hadn't said a word since rousing Jacques-Yves, to summon three other members of the staff. When they arrived, Jacques-Yves noticed that these were three of his burliest hired hands. "This man is a prisoner of war," Marcel told them. "Take him into the rear garden, at least one hundred meters distant from the house. Be sure to take with you something you can use to signal me at need. Wait there with him for further orders—but keep him alive. *No molestation.* Do you comprehend?"

"Yes, sir," said their obvious leader. And with an efficiency Jacques-Yves had thought to see only in Marines, the three took the prisoner away.

"And now, Marcel," said Jacques-Yves, "exactly what was that in aid of?"

"You were correct, *mon amiral.* This house and these lands could never withstand siege, and we shall have to evacuate. But I have a plan, for I have been preparing for such a moment for some time. Long ago, I came into contact with a revolutionary group who call themselves the 'Zealots.'"

Natalya gasped. "What did you just call them?" she asked.

"The Zealots, *ma lieutenante.* Their leader is one we know only as the 'Lady of the Lamps.' She has taken an interest in the Admiral and wants to make sure that, if ever he comes under such an attack as this, he can evacuate. And that his property, or as much of it as we can preserve, we will preserve."

"And she will want to interrogate the prisoner, is that not so?"

"Yes, *ma lieutenante.*"

"Admiral, I recommend you trust these people implicitly," said Natalya. "I think I know who this 'Lady of the Lamps' must be. Though I have not heard that name, I have heard of the Zealots. We can safely assume that this is the same group."

"And what is your plan, Marcel?" Jacques-Yves asked.

"That we pack as many of the historical artifacts as we can safely move. Every member of your staff knows the plan; have no fear. But the plan also calls for your own evacuation."

Now Natalya spoke again. "You may tell your Lady of the Lamps that Lieutenant Natalya Fyodorovna Bronskaya thanks her a thousand times—but that Rear-Admiral de Grasse has an important mission to perform that necessitates his evacuation to a place of my choosing, not hers."

Marcel bowed. "At your pleasure, Lieutenant," he said.

"And what," said Jacques-Yves. "is *that* in aid of?"

"Admiral," said Natalya with a tight-lipped grin, "it is time for you to join the revolution. And to meet at least some of my other allies."

Chapter 4

"I still can't believe it," said General Kevin Carlson. "All the old references said that all these islands housed a thriving nation-state having almost as many people in it as the original United States. And here we are, building a new settlement on one of these islands, after it became totally wild."

Field Marshal Matthew Morrow lowered his binoculars and turned to smile at his newfound friend. "Surely, Kevin," he said, "you remember the prevailing ideology of those who sent you to the American Reservation? According to it, Earth—or Sol d as my former service calls it—was overcrowded and needed immediate relief. But more to the point, the authorities had special plans for the continent of Australia. A prison requires isolation, and what better isolation than to have thousands of nautical miles of ocean and uninhabited islands separating it from the nearest cities?"

"So they evacuated Indonesia? Seventeen thousand islands, and they evacuated them all?"

"Yes. Actually, they felt the need rather acutely. Indonesia's total fertility rate hadn't yet dipped below replacement level. That gave the United Nations an excuse to say these islands were becoming seriously overcrowded."

"Well, I won't swear that we'll wind up crowding those islands to that extent. But it's certainly nice to have some breathing room. Both here and in the former Penal Farm district—Queensland, wasn't it?"

"That's what they called it before the Great Evacuation," said Matthew, raising his binoculars again. He was looking out to sea toward a spot about two hundred yards from the beach on the island of Timor. "Did you know," he said idly, "that a famous Royal Naval officer lost his first command to a mutiny in these waters? And barely made it to this very island in an open launch?"

"I seem to recall that particular legend, yes," said Carson. "That would be Captain Bligh?"

"The same. Lieutenant William Bligh, Royal Navy, assigned to and commanding His Majesty's Armed Vessel *Bounty*. If he hadn't trained under an even more famous officer, Captain James Cook, he might never have made it. Imagine navigating an overcrowded launch three thousand miles! Why, that boat wasn't even as large as most of those boats you see out there."

He meant, of course, the incredible flotilla of pleasure boats beyond Timor, to the south and east. Some rode at anchor, with much smaller craft bringing people and equipment onto the beach. Others were just coming in or heading back out to sea toward the continent.

"I'm not sure I'd want to try navigating that distance even with one of those," said Carson. "Though, of course, these have come a long way. Then again, we both have."

"Yes, we have, you and I—but especially you. How does it feel to be truly free?"

"Words can't describe it, Matthew. To have actual possession of the continent is a great gift in itself. To have the opportunity to settle other lands is a greater gift. Only, how difficult was it to persuade the New Zealanders to make all these boats available?"

"It wasn't that difficult at all, really," said Matthew. "The only reason the UN didn't evacuate New Zealand is that the Special Security Forces wanted a place to enjoy leave. As I understand it," he said, his voice darkening slightly, "the SSF took more than the usual liberties we in the United Systems Navy used to take. Now the tables are turned, as I believe you say it. New Zealand is home to a tribe, the Maori, with an excellent reputation for producing warriors. I've appointed them as guards over most of the SSF prisoners. The rest of the population, as I understand it, have made their own arrangements with your people."

"Yes, they have. But now I suppose you'll be leaving us."

"Yes. I leave for Vietnam in the morning."

"Vietnam," said Carson. "Another legendary place—though not so pleasant a legend."

"Because a force calling itself 'American' failed to achieve its objective there. Yes, I know. And the Naval and Marine personnel I will be leading know it, too."

"But it's not the same, is it?"

"Not at all. But it's still a vital objective. If what Doctor Folsom blurted out to me is accurate—and I have no reason to think she would lie about a thing like that—then the Vietnamese cities of Hanoi and Saigon—or Ho Chi Minh City as the official maps call it—are in the hands of rioters, with help from some United States Marines."

"Those would be from the original America, right?"

"Right."

"Another thing I can't fathom. An underground society!"

"Oh, they send hunters and foragers to the surface, from time to time. But more to the point, they are experts at tunneling. That's how they captured the Great Circle Tube Line that runs all the way from Saigon to Rio de Janeiro in South America. The problem is, they can't hold out forever. They face considerable opposition in Beijing and even in Hanoi and Saigon. I need to get to Saigon and tip the scales for them."

"Yes, but with only two companies of Marines?"

"That's as much as my ships can carry."

"And wooden ships, at that."

"Yes—all replicas of the original colony ships that settled the original America. Except for *Constitution*, of course—she has always been a warship. And then don't forget the other ship you can't see—because she's designed to make herself invisible."

"Just one more thing, Field Marshal," Carson asked. "Why aren't you using those aircraft we discovered in Adelaide?"

"They haven't the range," said Matthew. "Any flight from Australia will be a one-way flight. My new Air Marshal won't send any aircraft until he knows they have a place to land."

"I'll take your word that that's necessary, Field Marshal. Do you suppose I'll have an opportunity to see this "original America"? To see all these wonderful things you describe?"

Matthew considered that. *Someday, perhaps. But a lot of things have to happen first.* Aloud, he said, "Tell you what, Kevin. You do your part in the revolution for Earth, and you will."

"Thank you, sir."

"You're welcome. And I'm not just talking about military operations, as important as they are. I also mean this expansion project. And recreating a shipbuilding industry and electricity. And all other kinds of industry."

"Your friend Captain Jones—or Admiral Jones—already gave us the plans for our first power plant. It seems he needed a facility to split water into the two gases that make it up, so he could re-fuel. Since we already had steam, we could adapt that technology easily. Still, what you're talking about will take generations to accomplish."

"Some of it will. But I'd like to see your people building ships as rapidly as possible. Those larger vessels out there—and the one vessel you can't see—are all that's left of the United States Navy. That can't last. The Navy must be made larger—much larger. That's why I made sure your people had the full plans of the USS *Constitution*—and a design for an even larger class of vessel. And remember, the other side, as far as I know, does not have a Navy on the water. Not yet, anyway. That's your advantage. Press it."

"That we will, sir."

"I know you will." Matthew held out his hand. "Goodbye, General," he said. "It was a long campaign, and I might even call it glorious."

"Thank you again, sir," said Carson, taking the offered hand. "For everything." He then saluted.

Matthew returned the salute and turned to head down the beach. He went through the steady stream of construction workers making their way inland to the site the Americans had picked out for their first village on Timor. Their equipment would no doubt strike some of his other American friends—the Navy and Marine personnel who had come from North America, as they called it (the United Nations called it Aztlán)—as appallingly primitive. Still, it had one virtue: with it, a settlement could rise quickly from materials available here on the island. A phrase came to him, from the plans for settlements on the Moon and Mars: *in situ resource utilization*. But of course, such plans had never come to fruition. Thank the Elves for that. With their intervention, human beings had surrendered their destiny, though the Elves pretended to take a secondary role in the formation of the United Systems.

The Elves, Matthew knew, must soon strike back in some way to prevent losing all they had spent the last four centuries (or nearly that) building. Matthew was determined to be ready for that.

As he walked, Matthew came upon another team of specialists standing around a heap of slag. He singled out the obvious team leader. "How's it going?" he asked.

The leader looked up from his study of the slag heap and smiled, "I was just about to ask you something about this, sir," he said.

Matthew smiled, "You're not in the Army, so you don't have to say 'sir.'"

"Well," said the leader, "everybody does, after what you did for us. Anyway, we were wondering whether the Army could spare us any of those new—what do you call 'em—'dew' weapons."

Matthew looked more closely at the slag heap. "Yes," he said, "I can see how one of those advanced weapons could make this job go much faster. Do you have paper and stylus for me to write on?"

"Stylus—oh! A pencil. Yes, of course." He provided the articles, and Matthew wrote a quick order on a single sheet. "Pass that on to the next boat back to the continent," he said. "Say that the Field Marshal himself made it a top priority to send three of these to you as soon as they can find them. You'll probably have to sail all the way to Perth; that's where we found the armory."

"Thank you. Ah, what was this, anyway?"

"That," said Matthew, smiling, "was a force-field generator. It was intended to keep anyone off this island who managed to reach it. Except that I passed a virus program to every generator like it, telling them to overheat and melt down. I wasn't sure the program would jump to any of these islands, but obviously, it did."

"A virus program—is that what I think it is?"

"That depends on what you might think, but yes, very likely. The kind of virus you're used to, spreads from person to person and gives you a nasty cold. A virus program does much the same. It copies itself from machine to machine and makes the machines 'ill,' or, in this case, dead."

"Would that affect any of our equipment?"

"Happily, no," said Matthew. "The kind of machines that sort of program 'infects,' require electricity to run—and electricity is something the United Nations didn't allow you, which means you need not worry. By the time you do start using electricity, that virus program will be long gone."

"Good to know," said the leader with feeling. "Thank you again."

"You're welcome," said Matthew and walked on.

Finally, Matthew came to the training camp that Lieutenant Walston—now *Captain* Walston—had set up. Walston had been very self-conscious about this—for, after all, he'd barely finished Officer Candidate School two months ago. That is, until Matthew reminded him that his was a brevet rank, reflecting his position as the senior U.S. Marine officer present. He had literally recruited other officers—and as many as 150 men—from the United States Cavalry and Militia from the American Reservation.

Matthew could only approve of this camp. He watched the recruits, who were obviously running a war game: one company attacking and the other defending. The contest looked to be inconclusive—but that was because each side was trying its hardest, and the two sides were evenly matched.

Captain—and Brevet Rear Admiral—Ronald Jones, United States Navy, stepped up and exchanged salutes with him. "I'd say they're ready for anything, Field Marshal," he said.

"I agree," said Matthew. "Brevet Captain Walston knows his business, and he's obviously serious about turning these nineteenth-century-style cavalry troops into Marines. By the way, are your ships ready?"

"They just finished revictualling, and *Monsoor* is fully fueled. Hydrogen, of course—we helped them adapt some of their steam engines to build their first power plant in return for their supplying power for electrolysis. But there's one thing that worries me."

"And that would be?"

"The weather. The prevailing winds are all right—in fact, they couldn't be more favorable. From here, they blow straight toward Vietnam, all the way. That is, if this weather holds."

"Why wouldn't it?"

"Tropical cyclones, sir. The season for them, in these waters, began last month. You'll recall that I steered my fleet past one in the North Atlantic on my way here. It kept us out of sight from space, I'm sure, but I didn't find it pleasant."

"How hard do they blow in these waters?" asked Matthew.

"I had a chance to talk to Kevin Carson about that," Jones said. "The hardest blow they ever had, was two zero eight statute miles per hour. That works out to one eight zero knots. The locals actually named that one 'Camille,' after the third named North Atlantic tropical cyclone of 1969. That was about two hundred years ago. They haven't had one since. Now ordinarily, I'd say that meant we'd be one in a million getting a storm like that. But, you see, I happen to think things like that happen in cycles. Which means ..." he stopped talking.

"Which means we're overdue, is that it?"

"Yes, Field Marshal, I'm afraid it does."

"As I recall, the original *Mayflower* passed through a series of storms on her way to what became Massachusetts."

"True, but nothing as bad as that. Even at that, *Mayflower* barely made it. She broke a beam during that passage. If some passenger hadn't invested in a jackscrew, which he then lent to the task of reinforcing that beam, they never would have made it. And you know we have two other vessels that are smaller."

"Then we'll just have to trust to your seamanship and that of our officers," said Matthew. "And, of course, make sure that your present *Mayflower*, and the other ships, carry a jackscrew for just such an eventuality."

Jones smiled, "You're right, sir," he said. "We weathered that hurricane, and we'll handle any typhoon—or whatever they call it down here. And I've thought about that contingency already. We have one break: compared to the society that designed the originals of these replicas, this society was advanced by two hundred fifty years. Our ships are not only revictualed, but refitted. I would have liked to have them build more vessels like *Constitution*, but..."

"But there's no time for that," said Matthew. "I've delayed as long as I dare to get to Vietnam and relieve that siege. And by the way: 'typhoon' is as good a name as any, considering where we'll be heading."

"When do we weigh anchor?"

"Promptly at zero six hundred tomorrow. That gives you…" Matthew glanced at the sky, marking the rough position of the sun, now hanging to the northeast, "twenty hours," he said.

"Will these other islands be as easy to go ashore as this one?"

"If the virus reached them all, yes," said Matthew. "But in case we run into any intact force field—say on Borneo or Sumatra—make sure your guns and missiles are ready."

"Aye-aye, sir. Anything else?"

"Not so far. Use your PDD if you have to reach me."

"Aye-aye, sir." Jones saluted. Matthew returned the salute and continued up the beach.

* * *

Matthew decided he could use some company, even briefly. Natalya was not here, of course. He did not know precisely where she was, only that she was likely somewhere in the North Atlantic and, hopefully, about to land in France, if she hadn't already. But he still had one old friend whom he could visit right now.

He walked the rest of the way up the beach, then inland. Eventually, he came to his objective: an LCG, a gravity-driven craft capable of single-stage-to-orbit flight even when taking off from a planet like Earth. He walked to the stern of the saucer-shaped craft, to the stern landing leg. There he showed an identity card to the Marine PFC standing guard. The guard nodded, and Matthew climbed the boarding ladder set into the leg. At the top of the ladder he showed his identity card to another Marine—a sergeant. He smiled. "Hello, Color Sergeant," he said. "Make that *Gunnery* Sergeant."

Gunnery Sergeant Sean O'Shea saluted him. "Good morning, Field Marshal, *sir!*" he said with a wide grin.

Matthew returned the salute. "At ease, Gunnery Sergeant," he said. "How is the prisoner?"

"She's her usual arrogant self," O'Shea said.

"And how are you keeping yourself?"

"Ready in all respects for the next operation, sir."

Matthew looked around—and affected his most baleful frown. "No, you're not, Gunnery Sergeant. Is this your idea of shipshape? For your information, this ship will depart at zero six hundred hours tomorrow. If I didn't know any better, I'd think this ship would never be ready by then. Now I have to see someone aboard, and when next I cross this country, I want no hint of the sloppiness I see around me. Understand?"

"Yes, *sir!*" O'Shea saluted again—nice and crisp.

Matthew returned the salute and started for the distinguished passenger stateroom.

But another voice stopped him—female, Caucasian by its timbre, and middle-aged. A voice he knew well. The voice of his former warden: Captain Brianna Belle Folsom, United Systems Navy.

"Commander Morrow?" she asked.

Matthew sighed. "On second thought," he said, "I might as well talk to the prisoner. Carry on." And he turned reluctantly and walked down the short, circular passageway that held the cells until he came to hers.

"*Field Marshal* Morrow to you," he said. "As I know you remember."

"I refuse to address you as an officer holding a rank the Admiralty did not assign you."

"That does not matter. I make the rules now. A thing Doctor Frankel should have thought of when he gave me this body."

"Without it, you would be just another autistic kid who attracted the attention of a bully you could never handle in your natural body. Don't try to impress me."

"I don't know who's worse—you or Stefan Weiss," said Matthew, thoroughly unruffled. Whatever this arrogant woman wanted to pretend, *he* was the master here, and they both knew it. "I pick you," he went on. "As a psychiatrist—a healer of souls—you're supposed to know better. Anyone would expect you to recognize Stefan Weiss for what he was, what he became, and how he became that. But you and Doctor Tildblad—and Doctor Frankel before either of you ever saw either one of us—chose to exploit him. Now he's dead—and I had to execute him, because I'm the only one who could. You will stand trial for your crimes—and your failures as a professional and human being.

"I can't imagine what you even want to say to me just now. But all right, if you have something to say, say it. But make it fast—I have a lot of demands on my time, and I do not like to waste it."

"Still the same, aren't you?" she asked. "I don't care what you think of me. I only did my duty."

"An argument that didn't work for the defendants at a place called Nuremberg."

"You have it backward, Matthew Morrow," she said, almost spitting. "The Americans were civilization's worst enemies. A fine choice of friends you made."

"Nobody asked my opinion at the time I acquired this body," said Matthew. "And no American built those pedophile game preserves. And in Protected Wild Space, too. Tsk, tsk, tsk. If that's civilization for you, I'd take wildness, if I didn't know you and your superiors were lying."

"As I said before, you are not scientifically trained, so you cannot possibly know what you are talking about."

"I know enough never to trust you," he said. "And I have the assurance of someone who had some of the same training you have, that I am in the right. Now, if that's all you have to say, fine. I have better things to do with my time than to make 'small talk' with you. But I do have one order. Make this cell shipshape. We're leaving tomorrow."

"Oh?" Now she seemed to be taking an interest. "And where to?"

"To the United States Naval Prison, deep in the extension to the Cumberland Caverns."

"And just how do you propose to take me there?"

"You're so smart; you figure it out. Good morning to you, Doctor." And he left the prison ward section. He was sure she was staring at his back but didn't care.

Matthew crossed the guards' country he had inspected when he first came aboard. Gunnery Sergeant O'Shea must be just finishing up chewing out his soldiers and cleaning up the disarray that had greeted Matthew's eyes earlier. He spared the Sergeant one small nod of approval as he continued to his real objective.

Outside the stateroom, a private—another part of the force he had recruited in the Botany Bay Psychiatric Institute—snapped to attention and saluted.

"At ease, private," said Matthew, returning the salute. "Is Doctor Conroy in?"

"Yes, sir. Shall I announce you?"

"Please do."

The private touched an intercom switch as Matthew listened to the sounds of a ship whose crew were getting ready for action. He heard a woman's voice he knew well: "Yes?"

"The Field Marshal is here to see you, ma'am."

"Thank you, Private. Please send him in."

The private nodded to Matthew, who walked to the inner door and stepped through it.

Dr. Diane Conroy Kendrick stood up and flashed him her warmest smile. "Good morning, Field Marshal," she said, holding out her hand.

He shook it, saying, "First names always between us, Diane."

"Thank you, Matthew," she said. "Won't you have a seat?"

Matthew took the chair in front of the desk. "I trust you find your accommodations satisfactory?"

"Eminently so," said Diane. "And thank you for this assignment. Though taking charge of that female prisoner has been a bit unrewarding. I wish I could report progress, but I can't."

"I've just had another fruitless interview with her myself," said Matthew, resting his left ankle on his right knee. "I don't expect her to yield until the day comes when a judge pronounces her guilty. Anyway, I came to tell you to make at least preliminary preparations for getting under way."

"So we're leaving for Saigon, then?"

"Yes, at zero six hundred tomorrow," he said. "I've waited long enough." He explained the tactical situation as he had to Kevin Carson and Ronald Jones.

"That sounds serious," she said.

"We've both faced worse, as you know."

"Yes," she said soberly. "But that was under an officer we both respected."

"Jacques-Yves de Grasse," said Matthew.

"Do you think Natalya will have trouble recruiting him?"

"Actually, to use the usual military turn of phrase, my confidence is high. Confidence in Natalya's ability to explain the situation to him, and *his* ability to understand."

"Begging your pardon," said Diane, "but Natalya should be heading up the strike force to hit the beach at Saigon. She has the experience for that."

"That's true as far as it goes," said Matthew. "But she's also the only person qualified to reach Rear-Admiral de Grasse—unless you count myself. Besides, the Americans sent me a good officer to meet us outside of Canberra. Vietnam actually has a historical significance for him—I asked him. He'll also be connecting with forces he knows. But I need to know one thing more. How are those four other officers I assigned to you?"

"I think you'll find them eager to leave," said Diane. "You must have filled their heads with some mighty tall tales about America."

"I assure you, everything I shared with them is true. But I should speak to Andrew now."

"I'm sure he's in his quarters."

"Good. In the meantime, good day to you, and it was nice seeing you again."

"And likewise."

He left the stateroom and walked further down the passageway to a door labeled *Command Quarters*. This door also had a guard, who, like the other, came to attention and saluted.

Showing his identity card, he said, "Give Captain Blakely my compliments, and tell him I'd be pleased to see him."

The guard touched an intercom and exchanged a few greetings with the man inside. Then the door slid open, and Matthew entered.

Andrew Blakely stood at his desk, his hand already raised in salute.

"At ease, Captain," Matthew said as he returned the salute. "I'm here to give you your operational orders."

"Then we're shipping out?"

"That we are. The entire task force will be moving out at zero six hundred tomorrow. Gunnery Sergeant O'Shea is already making his men shipshape. From now on, you'll coordinate with Brevet Rear Admiral Jones aboard *Monsoor.*"

"Yes, sir. Will you be traveling with us?"

"No, instead, I'll travel aboard *Monsoor.* So you'll have no one aboard any more senior to you than Doctor Conroy. Well, technically, there's Doctor Folsom, but she is relieved of all duty and authority."

The younger man grinned, "I quite understand," he said. "Though it feels a little strange wearing a title like 'Captain' when, technically, I'm only a lieutenant."

"That doesn't matter. Aboard this ship, your word is law. To avoid confusion, you may address—and refer to—your distinguished prisoner simply as 'Doctor.' And I know that *really* seems strange to you: having authority over Brianna Belle Folsom. Understand this: whatever she might have been before the revolution, she is now a prisoner—*your* prisoner. Don't forget that, and don't let *her* forget it, either."

"I won't, sir," said Andrew.

"I know you won't. You understand exactly what I'm saying; I can tell by looking at you. Oh, and one more thing, Captain. I need to requisition a DEW weapon—the heaviest you have in your armory."

"That would be our Mark Eight. It's the same as the one Sergeant O'Shea carries. It sounds as though you plan to go ashore with the invasion force."

"I have to. There are things only I can accomplish, and only in Saigon."

Andrew took paper and stylus and scribbled out a brief order. He then handed it to Matthew. "Show that to Sergeant O'Shea," he said. "He can fix you up."

"Thank you, Captain. Carry on."

Andrew saluted with an even more confident smile.

Chapter 5

"**Y**ou presume a great deal, Lieutenant. You do know that?"

Natalya smiled. "Yes, Rear-Admiral."

"However," said Jacques-Yves, "your point is well-taken." He turned to Marcel. "You will activate your plan at once, subject to the modifications Lieutenant Bronskaya has just suggested. So let's set some assumptions, shall we? To begin with, the Lieutenant and I will need to head directly west, to Arcachon Bay, through the savage lands. Is that not so, Lieutenant?"

"That's exact," said Natalya, smiling.

"Very well. Marcel, have someone draw out my rough-country fatigues. And weapons for the Lieutenant and myself. One long gun and handgun for each of us—and spare charge packs."

"Yes, sir. Will you have need of anything in particular from your library?"

"My Louis Second Bible, and my copy of *Les Misérables*. Also, *Jane's Fighting Ships*, Edition 2016. In addition, pack my world portrait globe and see that the Lady of the Lamps gets it. She might find it useful. Along with all the rest of my library."

"*D'accord.* Will you have need of anything else?"

"Let's see … best speed through untamed savage lands is slightly faster than three kilometers per hour, so it should take us twelve hours to traverse that country. One day's rations of food and water, then."

"Admiral, if I may suggest," said Natalya, "I'd make that one day's ration of water for yourself. I'll provide for you." It was on the tip of his tongue to ask how, but he instantly dismissed that as a foolish question. She was still the fine ground-combat and security officer he once knew.

Aloud he said, "Do that. One day's ration, as she said. Then get yourselves out of this region, *toute de suite*. I have much fear that you will not have a great deal of time. Waste none of it."

"Yes, sir."

Jacques-Yves returned at once to his bedroom, where a valet was already laying out a full set of camouflage fatigues for him. He nodded to the lad, who left the room. Then he quickly stripped out of his nightclothes and put on the fatigues with a facility that surprised even him, when he stopped to think about it. Already he noticed a spring returning to his step, one he had not felt for fifteen years.

And so the exile returns, said that voice in his head. *Felicitations.*

He picked up a camouflage visor cap, then regarded himself in the mirror. *Well, apart from having no insignia, you might as well be in uniform.* But of course, he couldn't wear any insignia. He was literally a man without a country now. *Not true,* said the silent voice. *You are returning to the country you should never have left behind. The sea, whether of waves or stars, is your country.*

And it was true. Why had he lost sight of that? Natalya was right. Only a steady diet of a drug could have made him forget his true place in the universe. This vineyard and its associated winery were attractive enough but were not his true calling and never had been.

As he stepped out into the hallway, Natalya met him. She wore a haversack on her back, a long gun slung on her left shoulder, and a gunbelt with a handgun in its holster. Now she handed him his gunbelt, which he fastened on. Then the long gun—remarkable that he still remembered how to carry one, though he had rarely borne such weapons during his service.

Finally, his own haversack. "You'll find everything within it, as you ordered, and according to Marcel's plan," she said. "He is already an excellent soldier of the revolution. Your staff are waiting for you in the great room, by the way."

"To say goodbye, no doubt," said Jacques-Yves. "Well, they have been my crew, as it were, for fifteen years. I'll think of something to say to them. Shall we?"

They walked rapidly to the great room to find Marcel and as many of the household staff as could fit into the room. Jacques-Yves caught his breath. This would be a little more difficult than he anticipated. Then he noticed something he'd least expected. His staff were also under arms, some armed even better than he was.

He signaled to Marcel, who crossed the room to him. "Marcel," he asked, "do I assume correctly that you have lately built a secret addition to my armory?"

"Yes, sir," he said. "The Lady of the Lamps suggested it."

"Just so," said Jacques-Yves. He wouldn't even ask where the extra weapons had come from; obviously, this Lady of the Lamps was very resourceful. "Well done," he went on. "Now, I must address everyone." Squaring his shoulders, he turned to the crowd and said, "Ladies and gentlemen, we all are going on a great journey. I am near-desolate that I cannot share it with you. However, my path, and yours, must now diverge. I must say, in the fifteen years during which it has been my privilege to be the master of this house, this vineyard, the winery, and every other part of this establishment, not one of you have ever given me cause to complain. For that, I thank you all very much. And now we go our separate ways, for time is indeed short."

His staff all made a slight bow, which he returned. Then he found that if he stayed much longer, the scene would only turn maudlin. So he turned to leave.

Natalya fell in beside him as they went out the front door. As they did, Natalya handed him a set of goggles, which he put on. When he did, he found that he could see very clearly ahead of him, almost as if it were daylight. Then he noticed she wasn't wearing any.

"Is your night vision good enough without such enhancement?" he asked.

"Yes, sir," she said in a tone that clearly indicated she would rather discuss *nothing* until they were well away. He took the hint at once. Together they descended the steps, then turned to the right, which, of course, was west. As he moved through the vines, he watched the vine dressers doing … something.

"What do you suppose they're doing?" he whispered. "In the fifteen years I have managed these vineyards, I've never seen any such activity as this. It's almost as if they're planting something else among the vines."

"Admiral," Natalya said, "you do trust Marcel, don't you?"

"Implicitly."

"Then, if you'll let me advise you, you should trust that this is part of his plan. Perhaps it would be best not to interfere."

The two walked rapidly in silence for about twelve minutes, to a spot Jacques-Yves had rarely visited. In fact, it was the western gate of his landholding, about one kilometer from the main house at its center. Beyond lay totally savage land, with an electromagnetic force field to keep intruders out—or him in, he realized with an ironic smile. He was about to ask Natalya how she proposed to get through that never-used gate, when she took out a slender metal stylus-shaped object, about ten centimeters long, and pressed a small button on it. At once, the slight shimmer of the force field stopped, and the two passed through the gate, which then "resealed" itself behind them.

From now on, the going would be much slower since they had no trail—no, that was not quite accurate. For he *did* perceive a trail. But of course. "You blazed this trail, is it not so?" he asked.

"Yes, sir. And may I say that you have adapted well. But we probably will be able to make better time than you calculated."

"Of course; I was forgetting that to return is always faster than going forward—and for you, this is a return trip, is it not?"

"Indeed, yes. Just like old times, *mon amiral-arrière*. Or it is for me."

He had opened the conversation in French and decided to keep it that way, seeing that she was more than willing—and able. "Part of the burden of command, *ma lieutenante*," he went on. "The notorious Brandon Nelson could get away with personally leading landing parties. But by the time I started command school, standing doctrine called for dispatching my executive officer, my strike-force commander, perhaps both, but never going on landing party except under the most extraordinary circumstances."

"I assure you, sir, that was all for the best," said Natalya. "Only now, my mission is rescue and evacuation, and you are my protectee."

"And where are we going, other than to Arcachon Bay?"

"To make rendezvous with USS *Elmo Zumwalt*, of course. Your instincts served you well, to bring along the reference most likely to describe her."

"But surely she is much changed since she rated an entry in *Jane's Fighting Ships!*"

"Not as much as you might suppose, sir. True, she no longer has that natural-gas power plant. In fact, her power plant, if you call it that, consists of a large electric battery. But she still has all the armament she originally had."

"Including the shells for her big shore gun. Amazing!"

"Yes, isn't it? But, *mon amiral,* haven't you noticed something about yourself just now?"

"What do you want to say?"

"Well, as we say in Russian, you are definitely back in your own plate. You have been out of it for these fifteen years, and it showed. Perhaps you never noticed, but of course, *I* would, not having seen you for fifteen years, and remembering you still as the captain of a ship."

"If I comprehend you justly, *ma lieutenante*, you are saying that I am in my element once again." He smiled, "And I'll let you in on a little secret: I am, indeed. Rescue, you said? You've already afforded me rescue."

"I'll take that as a high compliment, sir."

"Which I intend it to be. You've earned it. Of course, you have me at a considerable disadvantage. You haven't aged a day since I saw you last, and you're so much stronger. You move through this forest far faster than your training would account for and smooth a trail as no one else can. What, do you have night vision built into you somehow?"

"Flattery, *mon amiral?*" asked Natalya, now sounding serious.

"I assure you I intended nothing as empty as *that!* But I sense much disquiet. Have I said something wrong?"

"Oh, no. It's just that…"

Jacques-Yves could kick himself. "Please accept my deepest apologies, Natalya," he said. "I keep forgetting that which you have lost."

She smiled a slightly twisted smile, "Oh, well," she said, "Matthew and I talked about this often enough. Nothing's the same for either of us, but especially for me, because I lived with a normal adult body, and he didn't."

"Yes, and he lived without emotions, too."

"I still wonder about that ... about his getting his emotions back, I want to say."

"Shall I tell you how that came to pass?"

"Pray, tell me, sir," she said. "I have only Matthew's perspective, and I suspect he's holding back on me."

"Yes, and I can't blame him, though I've decided this is something you've a right to know. Frankly ... well, you know how he was when our ship was preparing for commissioning. Awkward, and making everyone around him feel awkward. Well, he came to a perfectly logical conclusion that he would be a better officer if he could get in touch with his emotions. Commander Shaka, the engineer, took it upon himself to examine him in detail, something even *Débora*—that is, Doctor Girard—had never done. She admitted to me that she wouldn't know how. So, after Eric identified the chip, I called a wardroom meeting to consider the problem. We heard from Matthew, who did finally express a wish to have Doctor Girard remove the chip, though it was very hard for him to express that. So I dismissed him from the meeting, and we all came and went at the problem for five minutes. And finally, I said, 'It is his right.' That was all Doctor Girard needed to hear, so she scheduled surgery at the next opportunity."

"And how did it go?"

"Well, *Débora* told me the surgery itself went well. The adjustment afterward created the problem, as Diane—the psychiatric associate—warned us it would. For one full day, Matthew would laugh uncontrollably, usually at the same basic thing: some joke Commander Shaka, or Commander Kendrick, had told him, and he never got. Until after the surgery, that is. But as soon as he was off duty ... *Ma lieutenante*, I'll tell you what Diane told me. All the sadness, especially from losing you, crashed in on him at that moment. Naturally, I wouldn't have known anything about it because even a ranking officer won't always come to his captain about anything troubling him.

"I can remember it as though it happened yesterday. I got a call from Diane, asking me to meet her *toute de suite* in the ship's music room. I came as quickly as I could. And the sounds coming from that room … I … Forgive me, *ma lieutenante,* but this is more difficult than I supposed…"

And, of course, it did come back to him: music that was positively haunting in its tone, like a man crying out in despair and extreme sorrow. Tears came to his eyes, as they still did after so many years. Finally, he came to himself and could speak again: "Matthew Morrow had never made music properly before. Any time he performed anything, it was by brute memory, even by reproducing exactly someone else's interpretation of a work. But on that day … he chose, as I told you earlier, Tchaikovsky's *Pathétique* Symphony, the fourth movement. And at last, he was playing it with his own emotion. Diane cried at the strength of it. I muttered some bit of nonsense, something like having the fear that I would lose him to the concert circuit or some such thing. He apologized to us both for disturbing us … Well, evidently, he forgot that a ship's music room is soundproof anyway. We left him to himself, and two days later, he said he would like to give a concert. I permitted it, and he did. That's when he played for us his original compositions. *His original compositions.*"

"Including my personal 'theme,' as he called it."

"Yes. And it suits you, if you don't mind the opinion of a musical dilettante."

Natalya laughed—and how much more pleasant she sounded when she laughed. "You don't do yourself justice, *mon amiral,*" she said. "I never had the chance to tell you how much I respected you, and that's even allowing for your taking part in rescuing me from Novy Mir. Seeing you back in your own plate—back to your old self—is the most wonderful thing in my life so far, except for Matthew coming back into it."

"But I still have the same problem. *I'm getting old for this sort of thing.*"

"Nonsense. You're as old, or as young, as you feel." Then, in an even more serious tone, she said, "And at the present moment—all jokes aside— I need my old commander. This world needs you. The *Galaxy* needs you. Matthew would tell you the same if he were here."

Abruptly the night-vision goggles whited out. He stripped them off and noticed that the forest around them was much lighter. *How could that be?* They were deep into the forest, but now a distinct glow was coming from behind them, from the east.

He looked back to see a wavering, bright orange glow … realization set in.

Fire.

"*Mon amiral?*" said Natalya. "What passes … *Oh.*"

The two of them stared wordlessly. Then Jacques-Yves spoke the unspeakable. "It's my ancestral vineyards. Burning. Very soon, nothing but ashes will remain. Oh, how glad I am that my ancestor Alain is not here to witness this!"

"How awful! Is this Vice-Admiral Ordoñez-Pizarro's idea of revenge?"

"No," said Jacques-Yves. "Absolutely not. I don't know him, but I know the Admiralty and the authorities they serve. They would still want the wines from the De Grasse winery no matter what they thought of me, even if they had to put someone else in charge of them. Never would they destroy them. But Marcel would. I think he did. We saw him preparing to do precisely that."

"But why?"

"For three reasons. Partly for misdirection—the authorities will likely think I decided on suicide, or even that the fire started by accident, and I perished in it. Partly for diversion—the authorities will be too busy trying to fight the fire to bother with a few people making their way inland, or wherever Marcel will take them. Not too pleasant for us, of course, so we must keep moving, reach the shore, and make contact with your allies *tout de suite.*"

"Agreed. But what was the third reason?"

"That if a De Grasse is no longer there to run that vineyard and winery, no one will. Not exactly the demonstration I would have made, but Marcel was thinking of me. For that, at least, I thank him."

"I hope he thought to save the seeds."

"I'm sure he did," said Jacques-Yves. "You and I can perhaps work for a day when anyone, not merely a few elite government officials, can enjoy a good Bordeaux wine. When that day comes, we'll want to replant those vines. But that is for the future. For the present, we ought to keep moving."

The glow was already dying as he turned away. He put the night-vision goggles back on, and they showed as clear a way as ever. Natalya took the lead, and they resumed their westward run.

* * *

An hour. Two hours. Actually, Jacques-Yves lost all track of time. After watching his vineyards burn, even briefly, he and Natalya didn't talk. They just kept moving. She, of course, could move effortlessly. He kept going strictly on what *Débora* would call an adrenaline rush. Every time he thought he was flagging, he would remember where he was, where he had to go, and who very likely was sifting through the ashes of his former landholding, looking for clues and spewing out horribly obscene descriptions of the De Grasse family and Jacques-Yves' personal habits.

Yet even he had to admit that he was running out of energy. And before he could bring himself to mention it, Natalya did.

"Stop, *mon amiral*," she said. "You've had no rest since you got up yesterday morning—for it is after midnight—and you're getting dehydrated. I can tell."

He did stop, breathing heavily. "I told you … I was getting old … for this…"

Natalya smiled. "Not a problem, sir," she said. "At least not an insoluble one. I knew this was going to happen. I simply waited until you ran out of energy."

"Do your talents extend to medicine, then?"

"Not beyond wilderness first aid, but my enhancements might make me better able to tell when someone desperately needs it, as you do now," she said. "You should take water."

He slipped off his haversack, brought it around, and opened it. Easily he spotted the two canteens, one on each side. Almost greedily, he grabbed one, twisted it open, and started to gulp.

"Not too fast, sir," Natalya warned. "You'll only spit it up if you do. Nice and easy."

He took her advice and, with the first swallow, realized the soundness of it. "Thank you, *ma lieutenante*," he said. "Thank you for respecting my dignity."

"As I told you, I've always admired you, ever since Novy Mir," she said. "I put in for your command after that dust-up that almost ruined the peace talks with the Morgens. And I was glad to get that assignment, too. But even you have your limitations. You've hit your limit, and you have to rest."

"We cannot rest until we are at sea," he insisted. "To paraphrase Victor Hugo, I am Jean Valjean, and Javert is already after me—after us."

"And does that make me Cossette?" Natalya asked, grinning.

"You occupy her place, yes," he said. "But you are more capable than she."

"I like to think so," she said. "But still: you need rest, and yet, as you say, we must keep moving. Happily, I have an answer to that." As she spoke, she slipped off her own haversack and opened it. From it, she withdrew something he had not seen except in one setting: a long, ribbon-like elastic bandage. He had seen that sort of thing in the sick bays of the various ships he commanded over the years. But then Natalya did something with this one he definitely had not seen. She fashioned a carry harness out of it.

"If you would, sir," she said, "first put your haversack back on, then climb into this."

Carefully he re-closed the haversack and slipped it onto his back. Then he climbed into the harness, as she had asked. The next thing he knew, she had slipped her arms through it, back to him, and stood up. And he was riding, quite comfortably, on her back, as if he weighed no more than a feather! Actually, they had her haversack between them. Such a load would have staggered anyone else, but Natalya bore it as if it were nothing.

"Let your arms dangle in front of me—just so—and you won't fall," she said. "And try to get some sleep."

At first, he doubted that last. But as she moved off, he found he could not keep his eyes open. So he did sleep—not very comfortably, but more comfortably than he'd a right to expect.

* * *

He awoke, no longer slung on Natalya's back but lying down. What had passed? How much time had passed, anyway? He checked his wrist chronometer—such a crude device; why hadn't Marcel packed a PDD in his pack? But of course. Personal Digital Devices were traceable, something neither he nor Natalya could afford. This chronometer would not be. Marcel had chosen well, even allowing for Jacques-Yves' fondness for ancient devices of all kinds. This particular device was mechanical, with a "movement" that could even give the day of the week (in French abbreviations) and the date.

MAR 12. *Mardi*—the day of Mars. A Gregorian day name. But why? Then he remembered—this wrist chronometer dated back to pre-Great Climate War days. Back then, the Gregorian calendar was current even in France. And the month name would be *décembre,* which once had been the tenth month of the year, back in the day of the *calendrier julien.* Today it would be the twelfth month.

Five hours of the morning, the chronometer told him. But why had Natalya abandoned him like this? No, not abandoned. *Hidden.* For several fallen branches covered him. Could that mean that the enemy were already near?

Gently he pushed the branches aside. It was still dark—but of course, the moon would not rise before the sun, it being two days past the new. He waited for his eyes to adapt to the darkness, stood up, and looked around.

His haversack stood leaning against a tree trunk to his left, as did his long gun. His gunbelt rested next to these.

And then he heard the unmistakable noises of battle.

First, several high-pitched howls, followed by Directed Energy Weapons, discharged at killing strength. Then several men's voices, all crying out in pain and surprise and terror, then falling silent. After that came the thuds of blows—the crunches of bones breaking—and Natalya's voice, in rapid-fire grunts, each punctuated by a thud.

He looked about for his night-vision goggles—and found those near the top of the haversack. Quickly he put them on. When he did, the forest stood out in its usual stark relief.

This forest was a good deal denser than he remembered from starting out. So he must now be well into the old Gascony Heath Regional Natural Park that separated his landholding from Arcachon Bay. *Le rendu au rétro-sauvage* had effectively extended this "park," but evidently, that hadn't stopped Natalya. She must be able to run like the wind, even with such a load on her back.

Again he heard Natalya's voice, almost roaring. The voice came from the west, toward the Bay. Quickly he donned the gunbelt, slung the long gun, and picked up the haversack—he knew he'd have to drop it when he came close to the battle. Finally, he drew the handgun and set off west.

He heard a scream, then distinctly saw a man's body—black-clad, shoulders bare of rank insignia—flying through the air. His body struck a tree trunk and bent backward around it—and the scream rose to a high pitch and abruptly cut off. He then fell to the ground in a tangle of arms and legs. No living body ever fell like that.

And then something like St. Elmo's Fire lit up the pre-dawn sky.

Jacques-Yves stood almost transfixed as he beheld Natalya, long gun in both hands, standing rigid, bathed in a blue-white arc that looked exactly like a lightning strike. Then he glanced at the black-clad sergeant holding a weapon he recognized all too well: a long gun with three antenna-like arrays at one end. *So this is what an Electromagnetic Pulse weapon does to a Frankel total-body prosthesis,* he said grimly to himself.

The St. Elmo's fire died, and Natalya fell prone, as if pole-axed.

Jacques-Yves did not hesitate. He dropped his haversack, aimed his handgun, and fired.

The bright DEW beam burned through the sergeant's heart. He dropped his weapon and fell supine.

Now Jacques-Yves holstered the handgun and unslung his long gun. Holding it point down, he advanced to where Natalya lay. But before he could even roll her over, another onslaught of armed figures approached.

He shot the first black-clad attacker he saw, then took cover behind the nearest tree. That was almost unavailing because he felt, rather than saw, another DEW beam lance through the air, close enough to singe him. He fired a wild shot in that direction and must have missed because he heard someone scrabbling to a slightly different spot. So he fired again—and a most satisfactory yowl of pain rewarded him. Then two of the figures almost caught him in a cross-fire. By sheer instinct, he fired at the assailant to his left, then turned around to face the other one—two other ones.

The two moved as one to fire at him …

Suddenly, a series of rapid-fire explosions scared every small animal that was still around to witness the battle. The two assailants went down, bleeding not from thermal wounds, but from *puncture* wounds. He heard a man's voice—a baritone, with an accent he could not quite place—shouting at him, "Get down!" in Standard—or at least it sounded like Standard. Without thinking, he flattened himself on the ground as the battle continued. He heard more of the peppering explosions of the strange weapons the intruders carried, and the DEW fire of the original black-clad assailants.

Finally, silence fell. He heard several voices, all speaking Standard but with an accent he had never heard before. Then the voice that had shouted to him to "get down" spoke again. "Rear-Admiral Jacques-Yves de Grasse, if you can hear me, you can trust me. I am Sergeant Peter Jameson, United States Marine Corps. Please give me a signal!"

Did he dare trust this Sergeant Jameson? Of course. That unfamiliar accent told in his favor. Carefully he stood up, holding both hands waist-high. "I am Admiral de Grasse," he announced to the back of the first figure he saw. The person turned around.

Jacques-Yves beheld a Black man, standing roughly 175 centimeters tall, wearing a helmet and a dark green-and-khaki uniform that blended in beautifully with the night. His name JAMESON was stenciled above the pocket on his right chest, and over the left pocket, Jacques-Yves read another name: MARINES. Sergeant's stripes decorated his shoulders—along with a red, white, and blue flag sporting thirteen alternating red and white stripes and a blue field with stars on it. Jacques-Yves made a quick calculation: five rows of five stars, and four of four. Twenty-five plus sixteen. Forty-one. Odd.

"Are you all right, Admiral?" the Sergeant asked.

"If you mean, am I in order, yes," said Jacques-Yves. "Sergeant Jameson, I presume?"

"Yes, sir," said Jameson, who made a most impressive display of transferring his weapon to his left hand and raising the right in a smart salute. Jacques-Yves returned it.

"May I ask—"

"Sergeant!" another voice cried in that same accent. "This must be Lieutenant Bronskaya! She's hurt and unresponsive!"

Jameson brought his gun to a point-down carry posture and set off at once to where Natalya lay. Jacques-Yves retrieved his own long gun and followed.

Natalya. Instantly he was at her side, not caring who was watching. He reached to roll her over—and winced. He had forgotten how heavy she was. But before he could give any orders, Sergeant Jameson already had four of his men on one knee on Natalya's right side, hands underneath her.

"In three. Two. One. *Go!*" he ordered.

The four expertly rolled Natalya over onto her back. And then Sergeant Jameson knelt beside her, on her left side. Carefully he felt along her left flank. He must have found what he was looking for because he pressed what must be some kind of touch pad. Then he counted down from ten and withdrew his hand.

Natalya opened her eyes and looked around her. Her eyes lit on Jameson. She smiled, "I see you remembered your drill, Sergeant," she said.

"Yes, ma'am," he said, saluting again.

She returned the salute. Then, at a bound, she was standing on her feet. "Report," she said.

"The ship tracked an obvious maglev AFV coming out of Bordeaux," Jameson answered. "They signaled us, so I took my fire team into the forest. If I may say so, we got here just in time. Did they fry your innards with that EMP device?"

"Yes. Fortunately, my memories and routines are hardened—and your use of my reset button was excellent. They will not catch me that way again, I assure you."

"It is *I* whom you have to assure, Lieutenant," said Jacques-Yves briskly—in Standard, which was what everyone else was speaking. "Now tell me truly: are you fully recovered?"

"Yes, Admiral. I've run a full diagnostic, and everything checks out."

"Good. Now then, Sergeant Jameson. Did you take any casualties?"

"Your pardon, Admiral, while I take a muster?"

"Make it so."

Jameson raised his voice, "Fire Team! Call off! One!"

"Two!" cried the Marine who earlier had found Natalya.

Then silence.

"Nicholson! Call off!"

"Four!"

"Marines!" cried Jameson. "Shannon didn't answer. We search for him."

"Wait, Sergeant," said Natalya soberly. "I think I can sense him." And without a word, she led Jameson and Jacques-Yves to a spot about ten meters distant. There the missing Marine lay—dead.

The full Fire Team stood around their fallen comrade and doffed their helmets. Jacques-Yves and Natalya doffed their hats as well.

Jacques-Yves let ten seconds pass, then said, "Marines, cover."

All three Marines donned their helmets again.

"Now then," Jacques-Yves went on. "As senior officer present, I assume command of this expedition. May I assume that this maglev armored fighting vehicle rests nearby?"

"Yes, sir," said Jameson. "We were headed straight for its projected elzee when it landed, and those SSF goons got out of it. It carried a full squad. We're pretty sure that we got them all—or at least those whom you and the Lieutenant didn't get."

"So they didn't even leave any reserves on board," said Jacques-Yves. "Foolhardy of them, but good for us. You'll find that I am fully qualified to fly such a vehicle. May I assume that your ship carries an MH-60R utility helicopter?"

"Yes, sir. We've improved it some, but we saw no need to carry more than one."

"Then your ship's hangar will have room for the maglev as well. So here is the plan. We will all take off in the maglev with the body of your fallen comrade here. The SSF can rot where they lie for all I care; we haven't time to do the usual battlefield clean-up, and I am sure the SSF know exactly where their vessel landed. I have fear that we haven't much time—but I can assure you, a maglev can cross water. Does your helicopter have a separate crew?"

"Yes, sir. They'll be waiting for us."

"No good. If you can signal them, tell them to strike whatever camp you've pitched on shore, then take off and return to your vessel. If you cannot signal them, I will."

"I can handle that, sir," said the Sergeant.

"Make it so. Then let us gather our friend here, and as many of the small arms as we can carry, and set out for the maglev."

"Yes, sir!"

Jameson used an even cruder two-way radio to send his signal. *Crude, but effective,* Jacques-Yves told himself. *At this range, the SSF will never hear it.* Then Natalya slung Private Shannon's body over her shoulder, and they set out for the maglev.

They found it easily. Under Natalya's direction, they put Shannon aboard first and strapped him down as best they could. Then they fanned out to recover all the small arms. Jacques-Yves recovered his weapons and backpack, and when he rejoined the party, they had loaded an impressive arsenal of DEW weapons aboard the maglev.

Natalya greeted him at the boarding ladder. "You'll find everything in order," she said in French. "I also have found and disabled everything that could serve as a homing device."

"*Excellent,*" he said. "Now, let us prepare to take off. Carry on."

She saluted and went aft.

Jacques-Yves entered the small cockpit. He reached for the control screen and activated the public-address system. "Now, all hands, this is the Admiral," he said. "Secure for take-off."

"All secure, sir," said Natalya from behind him.

Now he brought up a control display and, using only his fingertips, lifted the tiny ship off the ground, turned to the west, and headed out, skimming over the treetops. Now, of course, he could fly much faster than a man could walk. There—sixty kilometers per hour. That should do it.

Chapter 6

Natalya came forward to join him. "Just like old times, isn't it, Admiral?" she asked in French.

"If you want to say that these controls differ little from those of that LCG I piloted during your rescue from Novy Mir, yes," he said. "But if you want to say that it reminds me of any mission I ever flew while in command of *Bonaventure* Sixth or Seventh, no. This is something entirely new."

"I comprehend," she said.

"And now, if you please," he went on, "let's have an after-action report. Why did you conceal me and leave me behind?"

"As a reserve, *mon amiral.*"

"You deliberately engaged an enemy of vastly superior strength, and alone?"

"Superior in numbers but not in total power, sir," she answered. "At least, that's how I calculated the risk. Obviously, I miscalculated."

Jacques-Yves considered that. Then he said, "Then you did well to leave me behind as a reserve. I see that my old strike-force commander hasn't lost any of her strategic or tactical skills."

"I'm grateful to you, sir, for intervening when you did."

"Of nothing, *ma lieutenante.* In truth, I wouldn't have cared to lose you twice."

Even as he caught the tenderness in his tone, he could see Natalya's expression softening. And to think this was a total-body prosthesis he was looking at! He decided to say more: "Cybernetic organism though you are, you are still the same dear friend who fell in action on Rigel g, and the often impetuous officer who graced my wardroom before then. Don't forget that."

"That means more to me than you know, *mon amiral,*" she said. "Thank you a thousand times."

"Of nothing … No, that is much more than a mere 'nothing.' It proves you're still alive."

"And I thank you for that, too."

"Now, if you don't mind talking about your 'enhancements,' as it were, did I witness a demonstration of some of them back there?"

"If you mean when those SSF fired their DEW guns at me, and I reflected their beams back at them, yes," said Natalya. "Matthew taught me that trick."

"But surely the Frankel prosthesis didn't include an electromagnetic body shield!"

"Not the original. But I understand that Matthew learned how to make one in his little brush with Hive raiders. He taught me."

"But how? An enhancement like that requires hardware as well as software!"

"Credit one of *his* enhancements. Before he found me again, Matthew received a kind of nanobot that, in great numbers, works even better than a printer and internally. When he had himself brought to the Psychiatric Institute, he managed to give me my own nanobot army. I'd prefer not to say how. But through that agency, I got many more enhancements, including the body shield. Except that I had not tuned it sufficiently to ward off an electromagnetic pulse attack. Now I have."

"Amazing. Now about that flag these men wear. Why forty-one stars? I understood that the original United States of America had fifty States, not forty-one."

"Forty-one is the number of States they now have," said Natalya. "Matthew briefed me, and Sergeant Jameson confirmed it. And I must say that you catch on fast."

"That signifies nothing. Of course, you could not tell me openly that the United States of America actually exists, even if Ramón Ordoñez-Pizarro already suspects it. But *where?* They can't be visible from space!"

"Underground, Admiral."

"*La vache!*"

"Surely you remember that the visionary inventor Leon Vincent invented a technique for tunneling, along with his automotive and aerospace ventures?"

"Yes, but I hardly dared believe that even *he* could have anticipated something like the Great Climate War!"

"He didn't. But others did. They rescued him from the prison to which the United Nations and their allies took him. Then when the fireballs started to strike—deliberately, too—the Americans retreated into various drift mines and started tunneling from there, using his techniques."

"Again, I am without voice. But of course, they've had literal *centuries* to recreate their entire civilization. But I hope they haven't grown complacent about living underground."

"Some of them had," said Natalya softly. "Matthew also briefed me on a battle he had to fight in those undergrounds against some very highly placed traitors. But he also briefed me on something else. The Americans aren't the only civilization that retreated underground from the United Nations-Elfin alliance. There also are the Israelis."

"I had heard that the State of Israel also fell in the Great Climate War. So they accepted American hospitality?"

"Not exactly. They built their own Caves, beneath what was once 'up-State New York.'"

"And may I assume I will meet them as well?"

"Actually, you have already made contact, however indirect, with a member of that civilization."

"And who might that be?"

"The 'Lady of the Lamps.' That is, if it's the one I'm thinking of."

"I comprehend not."

"Then, next time you consult that Louis Second Bible you brought with you, look up a book called *Juges*. Then look for the story of one called *Débora, femme de Lappidoth*."

"*Débora*. Now that's a name I will always speak with great emotion, as I'm sure you understand."

"I had wondered whether you and our ship's surgeon had a relationship."

"Actually, she is the widow of my last commanding officer, before I received my first independent command. Imagine my surprise when I found her part of PCU-81. But of course, we are not talking about the same person."

"Oh, no. But I don't suppose you ever wondered about that name *Lappidoth*."

"Should I have?"

"Well," said Natalya, "it's something of which no one would take notice, except a student of Hebrew. First of all, it's feminine—and a man's name would be masculine. Second, it's a plural. And if you change the ending to a singular ending, you come out with *lapidah*, which stands for *torch*. Or, more generally, *lamp*. A hand-held lamp, but still a lamp."

"The Lady of the Lamps," Jacques-Yves almost whispered. "Surely you don't want to say that *that person* has somehow returned to walk this Earth?"

Natalya laughed. "Oh, no," she said, "nothing as melodramatic as that. But someone whom Matthew and I knew well—the same woman who sacrificed her life to save ours, or so we at first believed—has decided to follow her example."

"And that's why you were so quick to trust Marcel when he uttered that phrase," said Jacques-Yves. "And to think I found Matthew's fascination with ancient languages quaint but unavailing. Again I owe him an apology. He just might have saved our lives."

A soft chime sounded from the board in front of him. "And here we are," he said. "That, of course, is Arcachon Bay, and ahead of us, on the shore, is an anomaly. I'll just magnify it." He quickly did so. "Yes, as I thought," he said. "The remains of Sergeant Jameson's camp, including landing-gear markings for an improved Seahawk helicopter. Remarkable that anyone will still be flying such an inherently unstable vehicle. And now, Natalya, I have need of your assistance. If I remember my *Jane's Fighting Ships* correctly, the ship for which we search will be difficult to find."

"Not entirely, Admiral," said Natalya. "I have her. A very small sensory signature, but recognizable, if one knows for what to look." She tapped her own screen several times. At once, a tactical overlay manifested on the realistic visual display before him. Targeting lines converged on an outline he recognized from the work he had cited. Surely that was USS *Elmo Zumwalt* DDG-1000, now moving away from shore at a respectable fifty kilometers per hour.

"My word," said Jacques-Yves, "she must be making flank speed, or nearly so. For such an exotic-looking vessel, she is very fleet. I am impressed."

"Range, six-point four-five kilometers," said Natalya. "But we'll have to move much faster than this to catch her."

Jacques-Yves again made several more rapid taps on his console. "There," he announced when he had finished. "One hundred kilometers per hour. At this speed, we should catch that ship in less than eight minutes. So perhaps I should address her."

"I thought you might, Admiral," said Natalya. "I have a channel open."

Of course, she knows the correct channel to address that vessel, since she sailed in aboard her. He began to speak in Standard: "USS *Elmo Zumwalt* DDG one triple-zero, this is SSF Fighting Vehicle Six One Six, Rear-Admiral Jacques-Yves de Grasse commanding. I have your Fire Team and one other officer aboard with me, together with, I regret to say, the body of a casualty. I request permission to land and come aboard."

He didn't have to wait long, for a man's voice answered him: "Fighting Vehicle Six One Six, this is USS *Elmo Zumwalt*, Commander Jack Arthur in temporary command. We have you on radar, but would ask that you let us talk to the other officer you mentioned."

Jacques-Yves turned to Natalya, "What can he want to say by that?"

She smiled, "Let me talk to him."

"The channel is yours."

Natalya spoke: "USS *Elmo Zumwalt*, this is First Lieutenant Natalya Fyodorovna Bronskaya, RFFE, assigned to Operation Naboth's Vineyard."

"Six One Six, voice and passphrase confirmed. All permissions granted. And on behalf of the United States Navy, welcome aboard."

"Thank you a thousand—no, a *million* times, *Zumwalt*," said the old Admiral. "I am somewhat familiar with your design, but no doubt you have an approach controller who will wish to talk to me."

"Six One Six, that's affirmative. Stand by one."

Jacques-Yves muted his microphone and turned to Natalya. "This American Navy impresses me the more," he said. "By the way, I wonder that I slept so long, back in that forest. Was I that fatigued?"

"You were, Admiral," said Natalya. "You were in as deep a sleep as anyone I've seen."

Another voice filled the cabin, "Sierra Sierra Foxtrot Six One Six, this is *Zumwalt* approach control. Do you copy? Over."

"*Zumwalt,* this is Six One Six," the Admiral said in reply. "I copy you, how do you say it, 'five by five.'"

"Yes, that's how we say it, Six One Six. You are now three nautical miles downrange of us, but we are about to turn to port. Turn left, to new heading two six five."

"Acknowledged. Turning left, to heading two six five. We still have you on our own tactical."

"All good, Six One Six. You're looking good here. By the way, you need not acknowledge further transmissions unless we so advise."

Jacques-Yves again muted his microphone. "Did you need to ask me something?" he asked.

Natalya said, "I was wondering whether that reference to 'nautical miles' would confuse you."

"*Jane's Fighting Ships* had more than ship-design descriptions. It also discussed United States Customary and Nautical measuring systems. One 'nautical mile' is one minute of latitude, is it not?"

"Or one minute of longitude, but only at the equator. But you have hit the mark. The Americans use their own system of measurement, which now has nothing to do with *Système Interstellaire*."

"Did Matthew brief you on that, also?"

"Oh, yes," said Natalya, smiling again. "In fact, he arranged for me to carry a set of EEPROMs re-defining all the Seven Constants of the Universe, and also defining nautical miles and 'knots.'"

"Yes, of course, the Americans would need their own definitions of the Seven Constants. They no longer had access to the Paris Center for Weights and Measures, for one thing."

"And for another, they thoroughly repudiated all things having to do with the United Nations."

Again the outside voice sounded: "Two nautical miles downrange. Course good. Reduce speed to four zero knots. You are cleared to land."

"That would be seventy-five kilometers per hour, sir," said Natalya.

"Very well," said Jacques-Yves, who reduced his speed accordingly.

"One nautical mile downrange. Advise when you can spot us."

Jacques-Yves used a forward-looking directional radar—risky, but he sensed that he ought not advertise his position to any installation in the Arcachon Commune if he could avoid it.

The radar image could have been that of a small fishing vessel. But Jacques-Yves knew better.

"*Zumwalt*, we have you on radar," he said.

"Roger, Six One Six. Make straight-in radar approach. Godspeed."

Not long afterward, he could barely make out the vessel, with its deckhouse and two forward weapons launchers. His target, he knew, was the flat deck aft of the deckhouse.

Then, with a skill he thankfully had not forgotten, he matched the speed of the larger vessel and brought his magnetic craft over the cross-haired circle on the flight deck. He was about to set his craft down when he noticed a man in overalls, a simple visor cap covering his head, holding two arms straight up. Behind him, a large door in the center of the aft bulkhead before him gaped open.

"I see he wants me docked more fully than a simple landing," he said softly. "Well, let's see how well I remember all of my docking procedures."

He edged his craft forward. Ahead, the man in overalls started to backpedal, still holding his arms straight up—and then he inclined his right arm slightly inward, palm inward and down. Jacques-Yves steered slightly to the right, until his signaler was holding both arms straight up again. From then on, he steered straight.

It didn't take long for him to enter the dark enclosure. With his night-vision goggles, he could still see the far inner bulkhead well enough to stop well clear of it—that is, when the man in overalls crossed his arms in front of him as an obvious signal to stop.

The signaler then extended both arms forward, palms down. Jacques-Yves responded by settling his craft down. And then he was surprised to find his craft moving to starboard.

"Did I land on some sort of deck sled?" he asked.

"Oh, yes, *mon amiral.* That's how they recover helicopters."

The sideways motion stopped. Jacques-Yves then noticed the space they were in growing darker. When it grew as black as jet, bright lights snapped on.

He was in a vast hangar behind a closed folding door. To port, the MH-60R helicopter, main rotor blades properly folded, rested on its own deck sled.

Now he re-activated the public-address system. "Now hear this," he said. "We have successfully returned to your vessel. Make all preparations for egress from this craft."

* * *

As Jacques-Yves stepped down the short boarding ladder, he watched as a man in a white uniform—combination cap, white tunic and trousers, a silver starburst on each arm, and shoulder boards with three stripes each—walked toward him. This man stood about 180 centimeters tall and probably weighed not much more than 75 kilograms. He stopped about two meters away and raised his arm in salute.

Jacques-Yves, more from force of habit than anything else, returned the salute, whereupon the man extended his right hand. "Welcome aboard, Admiral," he said.

"Commander Arthur, I presume?" said Jacques-Yves, taking the offered hand to shake it.

"You presume correctly, sir."

"Why 'temporary' command? Is your captain indisposed?"

"Negative. But in the absence of a flag officer, he assumed command of the Australia expedition, but sent me back to ferry some guests back to the States—with a slight detour here to pick you up. I am normally the executive officer of this vessel."

Jacques-Yves released his grip, then said, "I commend you for doing a fine job thus far. Though I regret to say that your Marine contingent suffered a casualty."

"Yes, I am aware of that. I believe they're taking him off now."

The commander gestured back to the AFV, where two hospitalmen were bearing the body of Marine Private Shannon off the vehicle on a litter. A third figure detached itself from that melancholy group and strode up to the two senior officers.

"Sergeant Peter Jameson reporting back aboard, sir," he said, raising his arm in salute.

The commander returned it, saying, "My highest commendations on a well-run extraction—and my condolences on the death of your fellow Marine."

"Thank you, sir."

"And now, if you will, Sergeant, get into your Class As. Pass my compliments on to the rest of your Fire Team, and tell them I would be pleased to have you all join the Admiral, Lieutenant, and me in my sea cabin for breakfast. Zero seven hundred."

"Aye-aye, sir!" said the Sergeant, grinning broadly.

* * *

Jacques-Yves looked at himself in the mirror. Before him stood the man he once had been, if only briefly, fifteen years ago. Two stars replaced the four bars he had worn on his collar for so many years before. Thank the stars Marcel had thought to pack his ribbons, and even his medals, with his uniform! Of course, that uniform likely wouldn't pass muster in the United States Navy. But he was here as a guest, not as a regular officer in line of command. That, he supposed, made a difference.

This was not an occasion for medals, so he wore only the ribbons. But those looked impressive enough. Oh, the stories each could tell if they could but speak—of his intervention in the Morgen civil war and even two actions against Hive raiders who had managed to strike in the very Solar System itself. And many others, too numerous to name.

He had little thought that now he would be fighting a war against his own authority.

Around him spread the moderately luxurious flag quarters of USS *Elmo Zumwalt*. For all the brutal efficiency that wet-navy ships obviously required, Jacques-Yves de Grasse would not trade a day in quarters like these for all his years in command quarters aboard *Bonaventure VI* and *VII*. He actually *felt* a part of this ship in a way he had never felt aboard any other ship he had served. And what marvelous furnishings! A bunk that folded up into the bulkhead, freeing up space for walking or reading. Or drafting a battle plan. A drafting table with compasses, dividers, graphite styluses, rubber erasers, and graduated straightedges! Primitive such equipment might be, but all he needed was a good-enough light source, and he could draft any battle plan he could imagine. And a library, all his own, with books by legendary names.

His thoughts strayed to the library he left behind on his landholding. He hoped the Lady of the Lamps, whoever she might be, would make good use of it.

Last of all, he picked up another instrument he thought he would never set eyes upon. A genuine sextant for determining latitude by the Pole Star! How thoughtful of the acting captain to leave this for him—and how revealing of these people's fondness for solutions that might not be technological but had served mariners for many centuries before the invention of the first *ordinateurs* during the Second World War.

He heard a knock on the wooden door. "Come," he said.

The door opened. A Marine, in utility uniform but wearing the distinctive broad "cover" of his service, entered and saluted. Jacques-Yves returned it.

"The acting captain's respects, Admiral," the Marine said. "Will you be joining him for breakfast?"

"*Tout de suite*—that is, straight away. Lead on, Marine."

The Marine turned about and walked out into the passageway. Jacques-Yves followed. The Marine led him a short distance aft, then knocked on another door. It opened from the inside, and the Marine led Jacques-Yves through.

Commander Arthur greeted him with another handshake. "Good morning, Admiral," he said. Then he took another look at Jacques-Yves' uniform and said, "My word, look at all that lettuce. And to think they mothballed you for fifteen years over some silly misunderstanding!"

"I gather," said the Admiral, "that it was rather more than that. Didn't the Lieutenant tell you?"

"She has—many times. And as often as I hear that story, I still can't believe it. But please, sit down. You must be famished." He led Jacques-Yves to a spot at one end of the long table. Natalya sat to his right; two seats to his left remained vacant for the moment. At the far end of the table, Commander Arthur sat, with Sergeant Jameson to his right. Two other Marines took the remaining chairs.

Another knock sounded at the door. The single Marine at the door opened it to admit two other officers.

Involuntarily, Jacques-Yves stood. "Doctor Thakur!" he almost shouted.

"Captain de Grasse! Oh, wait—it's Rear-Admiral, now, isn't it? Good to see you!"

The speaker—about ten years younger than Jacques-Yves, standing about 180 centimeters tall and, Jacques-Yves, knew, weighing 80 kilograms—entered the cabin and shook Jacques-Yves' hand. As he did, he said, "Oh, pardon me, Rear Admiral. May I introduce my new friend, Jake Boddicker? Lieutenant Jake Boddicker—direct commission, actually."

"What interesting company Field Marshal Morrow keeps these days, to be sure," said Jacques-Yves, his flesh crawling. "Let me guess: you're a Syndicate man."

Jake Boddicker smiled a toothy, ingratiating smile. "Touché, Admiral," he said. "I specialize in weapons. Matthew sent me to the States with special orders—but I'll let Dan here tell you about that."

"Gentlemen," said Captain Arthur, "if you two would take your seats, we can get on with the business of the morning."

The two newcomers took the vacant seats. Boddicker at least knew where he stood with Jacques-Yves; he didn't presume to shake the older man's hand.

"And now," said Commander Arthur, "the roster, as it were, is complete." Turning to the Marine at the door, he said, "Pass the word to the steward's mates that they may serve us breakfast." The Marine saluted and left.

"Gentlemen and lady," he went on, "I asked you all to join me so that everyone could be properly introduced. Rear-Admiral, you obviously know Lieutenant Bronskaya, Sergeant Jameson, and, I believe, Lieutenant Commander Thakur. And now you know Lieutenant Boddicker as well."

"Don't forget these other two Marines," said Jacques-Yves. "Without them, I'm not sure that either the Lieutenant or I would be here."

The two Marines who were the subject of that complement smiled sheepishly—only for a moment. Commander Arthur took up the conversation again: "What you do *not* know, or at least I don't *think* the Lieutenant has had time to explain, are our orders concerning you. And, what *I* would like to know are your wishes and desires. My orders are fairly simple: first, to assist the Lieutenant here in extracting you, and second, to ferry you, the Lieutenant, Sergeant Jameson, Commander Thakur, and

Lieutenant Boddicker to the States. I'm not sure I understand why, but there it is."

"Sending a battle destroyer, one of only two in your Navy, merely to ferry four passengers to your home port? That scarcely seems logical."

"But she's one of the two fastest ships afloat, and neither Captain Jones nor Field Marshal Morrow wanted to waste any time. You may consider yourself a very important person, Admiral."

"In that case, it's rather bold of you to sail directly into the Bay of Biscay and then into Arcachon Bay. Had you no fear of detection?"

"None, Admiral. You see, in addition to our very slight radar signature, Field Marshal Morrow taught us the secret of a technology he called 'cloaking.' This ship is, for all intents and purposes, invisible as well as undetectable on radar. We engaged the cloaking system immediately after securing that flying soup bowl of yours in our hangar and closing the hangar door."

"Then it is true—both that this ship and your sister ship are cloaked, as the Director of Naval Intelligence himself told me yesterday, and that the former Lieutenant Commander Matthew Morrow really is calling himself a Field Marshal these days. In my country, we say that such a man has long teeth. Too long, I would say—were it not for the positively atrocious discoveries Lieutenant Bronskaya shared with me."

"That would be funny were it not so sad," Arthur said. "I read the minutes of certain courts-martial and civil trials resulting from the Pedophile Camp Raids—the first of which Matthew Morrow himself led. We knew we faced an enemy with a thoroughly black heart. We did *not* know just how spiritually corrupt that enemy was."

"Lately," said Jacques-Yves, "that enemy tried to kill me. I have, believe me, no further loyalty to the society I once served. And to see Lieutenant Bronskaya alive again was an even greater shock. Has she explained to you who she is, what she is?"

"Yes," said Arthur—and Natalya seconded that with a firm nod.

Before Jacques-Yves could say anything else, the cabin door opened again. Eight steward's mates entered, each carrying a covered tray. They placed one in front of each of them, even before Natalya. Then, at a signal from Arthur, they uncovered all the trays at once.

Jacques-Yves noticed the flavors first. Then he looked at the breakfast before him: baked apples, hot coffee, and a stack of the thickest crêpes he had ever seen—three of them, flavored with butter and thick, sweet syrup.

Commander Arthur picked up his fork, a signal for everyone to begin eating. Jacques-Yves tried the crêpes first. They were delicious—and better tasting than anything he had ever eaten before.

"Natalya—that is, Lieutenant Bronskaya—briefed me on a rather astonishing point—for me, anyway," he said. "Do I take it these meals came from an actual functioning galley?"

"They did indeed," said Arthur. "Not exactly the printed food you're used to, is it?"

"It tastes far better. In fact, the only thing I've truly enjoyed for fifteen years has been the wine that came from my vineyard and winery. And that was the only…"

"The only what?"

"The only thing on my table that was real," the old man finished. "And does every member of your crew eat as well as this?"

"Indeed, yes. The same galley serves us all, from a distinguished passenger like you, down to the lowliest seaman apprentice. Though I could regale you with many thrilling stories of how this ship survived after the Battle of the Gulf and her crew had to hunt, fish, and forage to fill her galley … Oh, pardon me. I think I said something wrong."

"It's the hunting and fishing part," said Jacques-Yves. "I told myself I ought never pretend to eat meat if my society professed such a revulsion at animal husbandry that it substituted a genetically modified sheet mushroom for all meats, and then extended that to imitating all other foodstuffs. That is an argument I shall have to have with myself."

"Understandable—which is why I chose this particular meal."

"I thank you for that. If that's the worst misunderstanding I'll ever have in my new life, I shall count myself most fortunate."

Natalya smiled—a jaunty smile. To his left, Dan Thakur grinned. Jake Boddicker smiled sardonically—his kind could never be anything *but* sardonic.

"I'm curious," said Jacques-Yves. "This really is the same vessel that defeated one of her sister ships and then vanished, with the remaining one, centuries ago?"

"Yes, it is. She's had a few refits, but we like to keep her appearance as close as possible to the original, in memory of that battle."

"I'll take your word for it. But how many decades passed before she made port again?"

"About twenty."

"*Twenty!* You are saying this ship, and her sister, became generation ships. How could that be? Pardon me for stating the obvious, but I see no females in your crew."

"Well, for one thing, *Zumwalt* and *Monsoor* both had women in their crews—about twenty percent, in fact, and that even included officers. But even that isn't the real reason. The real reason is one of the most interesting traditions of this ship—and part of the reason why no one ever had the heart to scuttle her, preferring instead to do endless refits. You see, both ships had some members of their crews on family leave—another hangover from the 'gender equality obsession' days. In this ship's case, it included the first lieutenant and one of each first-class boatswain's and machinist's mate. *Monsoor* had some of its engineering ratings on leave at the time. How they managed to get all the spouses of both crews together, and *then* book passages for them on a Caribbean cruise—another kind of excursion unknown today—well, that would take too long to tell, and it amazes us even today. The hardest part was prevailing on the cruise ship's Captain to, in effect, come looking for *Zumwalt* and *Monsoor*. Some of the events were less than pleasant, right up until word reached the ship from the 'home office' ordering them back to port for decommissioning. Faced with that, the Captain agreed to lead the search. By the most incredible seaman's luck, he found us. So we all sailed away together."

"Incredible. Did that passenger ship survive?"

"Oh, yes—refitted largely as a hospital ship—maternity hospital, of course."

"Of course. Now, I also understood that this vessel was the most advanced of its day. So who installed an archaic drafting table and tools in the flag quarters?"

"That was Admiral Scott's idea," said Commander Arthur with a grin. "He said that, even if all the information systems went down, the senior officer on board should have something to work with that wouldn't break down. We even carry paper sea charts for that same reason."

"My compliments to your Admiral Scott. That is an eminently sensible policy—and one which makes me feel quite at home. But I would like to learn more about your information systems—and all this ship's systems."

"Your tour begins when our meal ends," Arthur said. "Commander Thakur and Lieutenants Bronskaya and Boddicker know every square inch—or make that square centimeter—of this ship. They can tour you."

"I look forward to that."

* * *

The tour began on the forward weather deck, with the two low-lying protuberances forward of the deckhouse.

"This one," said Jake Boddicker with a feral smile, "is the ship's main gun. It fires a most unusual shell—chemically propelled and even guided after firing."

"As I recall, the original United States Congress funded the three vessels in this class but not those projectiles. That rather made this gun useless."

"Not anymore. Those guns were decisive at the Battle of Sydney. It almost makes me jealous just to think of it," he finished with a chuckle.

"I can well imagine. And the other mount?"

"The missile launcher," Boddicker went on. "This ship carries a dizzying variety of surface-to-surface missiles—radar-guided, heat-seeking, you name it. When we go below, you will see where they store the missiles."

"I see that you are making good use of your old trade," said Jacques-Yves. "Did Captain Arthur make you his gunnery officer?"

"Unofficial assistant gunnery officer, yes. But now that you're on board, I'm attached to you."

"I look forward to hearing more—later. For now, let us continue the tour."

The four then entered the deckhouse, where the tour began in earnest. They began with the command bridge, and the combat information center looked almost like what he had on *Bonaventure VII*—but a good deal more compact and efficient, he saw at once. Natalya showed him the various sensory and weapons systems, including sophisticated radar and sonar.

"Reading about all this in a reference is one thing," he observed. "Seeing it first-hand is another. And I notice that this ship, for all her size, makes a very slight wake."

"The tumblehome design ensures that," said Dan Thakur. "While also reflecting radar and other active sensors to one side, not directly at most sources. If you're not approaching from the air at exactly the correct angle…"

"I know," said Jacques-Yves. "Don't forget that I piloted a maglev out here. Even with her cloaking system offline, I could barely see her."

The party continued down various ladders to see the other ship's systems, including quantum computer servers (each independently powered and shielded), the missile racks forward, the crew's quarters, sickbay, galley—and down below, the boathouse below the flight deck (housing two very large surface boats), and—furthest below—the fuel cell rooms (where the largest fuel cells he'd ever seen produced not only electricity but hot water), the battery room, and the engine room.

"And now," said Jacques-Yves when he had seen it all, "to business. Let us continue in my quarters."

Chapter 7

"**I** have waited patiently during the tour to ask you three some questions to which I will need answers," he said to his guests as they were all seated in the flag sea cabin. "Doctor Thakur, you first. Natalya said you were a 'renegade augment,' a concept she never explained. Perhaps now you can."

"Gladly. First, let me tell you that I've been fighting that canard all my life. I received no kind of genetic therapy—but I did receive the best early education for which any child could ask if he knew to ask. My father is a pediatric neurologist. He insists that our education systems do not begin to realize the full potential of the pupils and students in their charge. When I was born, he sensed that I was brighter than most and invented an educational program as challenging as it was enjoyable. So that, when I began schooling, I already knew how to read, write, and count.

"I don't know how the canard that I'd had some kind of extra therapy got started. I will tell you that I dealt with petty jealousies throughout my schooling. Then when the time came for me to choose an academic track, the Board of Admissions of the University of Earth had no idea where to send me. So I elected the Naval Medical Academy. Well, in the Navy, my situation got so sticky that no less an authority than the Judge Advocate General reviewed my case. There's no telling how that review would have ended in any other circumstances than those in which it took place."

"And those circumstances were?"

"The Metamorphic War, of course. The Navy couldn't afford to cavil at allowing an officer who could do anything when the situation required it, to retain his good standing, merely because such a course offended someone's notions of 'equality' and 'equity.' And I recognized that I was lucky to get what standing I got. But when Vice-Admiral Medea Mercouri joined the Free Systems in the Nine-o'clock Quadrant, I joined her cause in a trice. I make no bones about it, Admiral. She represents a cause that celebrates individual merit, and does not suppress it because failure to do so might make someone jealous."

"Why *did* she join that cause, I wonder?" asked Jacques-Yves.

"Are you kidding? No, of course not—you don't know. Well, when she returned from the Twelve-o'clock Quadrant, she had a wealth of insight on how to manage a crew and keep a ship together without regular visits to a base. So what did the Navy do? They sent her to the Nine-o'clock Quadrant as commander-in-theater. It was a bloody waste of her talents, and she resented it bitterly. Not that she would let it show; she was too much the consummate professional to let a thing like that slip. But I recognized the signs and looked for an opportunity to share my own frustrations with her.

"That's when the United Systems started demanding taxes of printer-stock materials."

"And that," said Jacques-Yves, "is what prompted the rebellion, is that not so?"

"It certainly is. She wasn't about to enforce anything as ridiculous as that. Can you imagine her doing that? She, who taught her crew how to keep a ship running and in repair *without* printers, enforcing the collection of a tax to keep printers going halfway across the Galaxy? That would be funny were it not so outrageous. So when the civilian populations on Terra Nova organized the beginnings of a federation, she defected to this federation. Took about a third of the Navy and Marine assets with her, including her old ship. And me. The insights I just shared with you came to me during our first interview."

"I see," said the old Admiral. "And it makes perfect sense. Now, how much do you know about the doings on this Earth—or Sol d, as is her official name?"

"I've had an earful—from Matthew Morrow. But also from the four that I had as my advisers during the Metamorphic War. Admiral, the powers-that-be have treated them abominably; I can describe it in no other way. I met them again after I landed in Canberra. They were all glad to see me again, of course … but the stories they told…!" Dan Thakur went on to narrate those stories in detail. Stories of psychological experimentation involving the worst sort of criminal acts.

"I hope," said Jacques-Yves when Dan Thakur caught his breath, "that the officer responsible for those atrocities will be suitably punished."

"Matthew Morrow is holding her pending trial before a public tribunal. Frankly, I think she deserves summary execution. But Matthew won't do that. His sense of justice won't allow it."

"That 'sense of justice' might be the only thing keeping him sane, don't forget."

Dan Thakur fell silent, obviously thinking about that. Then he said, "You're right, of course. He shared his own story with me—the one involving the childhood bully who wound up as the third Frankel prototype. The only reason Matthew dealt summarily with *him* is that literally, no one else could. So he handled that in vintage Matthew Morrow fashion."

"And what does that signify—that is, what does that mean?"

"It means," said Jake Boddicker, grinning as usual, "that Matthew couched his 'dealing' as trial by combat. I ought to know—I helped arrange it."

"Now *that* almost *is* amusing—and a very elegant solution to an ethical dilemma only he would think he faced. I must congratulate him if I ever have the chance to meet him.

"But now tell me this. What exactly are your positions on board this ship? Doctor Thakur?"

"Before you came aboard, I was a barely tolerated 'guest surgeon' in Sick Bay. Today I'm attached to you, sir, now that you're aboard. As is Natalya here."

"And you, Mr. Boddicker. What is your history—your story?"

"As you obviously figured out—I guess I'll always give off a Syndicate smell—I was serving time for weapons dealing when Matthew, as I learned later, took down all the force fields on Botany Bay. By the time Matthew showed up with the whole United States Cavalry, I had already taken over the Adult Detention District. As I told you during the tour, Captain Arthur put me to work in the gunnery department. But now, like Dan here, I belong to you."

"Now, suppose you tell me why Matthew is sending you to America?"

"I'll tell you part of the reason; I'll let Doctor Thakur here explain the rest. I understand that America—that is, the real America, not that admittedly good imitation called the American Reservation of Botany Bay—has one of the best weapons industries I am likely ever to have seen. Matthew seems to believe I can pass along a few secrets to improve American battlefield and other weapons even more."

"Of that, I have no doubt. Now you, Doctor. What exactly was *your* mission? And just how came you to have yourself fired out of a missile tube to re-enter Earth's atmosphere?"

Dan grinned. "Oh, you heard about that," he said. "Captain Park—that is, the Captain of *Argo*—wasn't at all sure it would work. But obviously, it did.

"But to answer your question, I am a spy. I suggested to Admiral Mercouri that our war for independence would have a better chance of success if revolution were to break out on Earth itself. So she sent *Argo* here, with me on board. And what did we see when we stood off in a far orbit? A missile—an intercontinental ballistic missile—taking off from Manchuria and then detonating prematurely—while it was on a trajectory leading to impact on Botany Bay. Naturally, I insisted that Botany Bay was where I needed to make contact. Captain Park fired me out the launch tube, as you guessed—and against his better judgment, or so he'll probably tell you if you ever see him. I parachuted into Canberra and made contact with Matthew Morrow—and with Jake Boddicker here. So now, here I am."

"I still am almost without voice to think that Matthew Morrow still thought of me."

"Command instinct, sir, if I may make so bold," said Dan. "He knew you'd come as soon as Natalya could brief you."

"And I," said Natalya, "knew I could convince you if I could just present myself to you."

"Which you did, as one coming back from the dead," said Jacques-Yves, drily. "Doctor, you will readily appreciate that it took more than her talking to me to convince me. It took the actions of certain government agents—to say nothing of the removal of a certain psychoactive drug from the food-and-beverage programming of all the printers."

"Yes, I heard about that too. Neo-chlorpromazine. Yet another outrage."

"But that is of the past. Let us come to the present. Doctor, I need your honest opinion. Yours too, Mr. Boddicker—for against my better judgment, I have decided to trust you, little though I like you. Is this ship truly invisible? Isn't its wake detectable if one is close enough aboard?"

"Yes, sir," said both men in chorus.

"Would you care to explain?"

"I can," said Boddicker. "Matthew Morrow adapted a cloaking system suitable for a ship in outer space, to a wet-navy ship. The only reasons you *wouldn't* detect this ship while under cloak, would be either that she was lying to, or you wouldn't know where to look for her, or you literally were nowhere near her."

"And that's the problem, is it not?"

"Oh, yes, Admiral," said Dan Thakur. "There is something you need to know, something the three of us didn't want to mention in front of the Captain. During the entire cruise from her hidden harbor in the Gulf of Mexico to her entering the Southern Ocean off Australia, this ship and her sister ship—that would be USS *Michael Monsoor* DDG-1001—encountered several sonar traces—sonar ghosts, the bridge watch called them. *Undersea* sonar ghosts. You understand the problem?"

"Perhaps," said Jacques-Yves. "What exactly did these 'ghosts' sound like?"

"That's the nagging problem, Admiral. Sometimes the sonar operators thought they were hearing whales copulating—all very well, except it was out-of-season. Then someone else decided they were hearing seaquakes."

"So? What's the problem?"

"The problem, Admiral, is not only that these sounds never went away, but also that they were happening at regular intervals. Entirely *too* regular to be either thing they sounded like."

And then, realization struck Jacques-Yves like a blow to the temple. He almost whispered, "In other words, a magneto-hydro-dynamic drive."

"What's that? I never heard of it."

"Me neither," said Boddicker. "And I thought I'd heard of every kind of drive."

"But I would scarcely expect even you to know anything of wet-navy ships," said Jacques-Yves. "I, on the other hand, have the benefit of *Jane's Fighting Ships,* which I studied extensively. A magneto-hydro-dynamic drive is literally a water jet, but one that uses powerful magnetic fields in place of propellers or impellers. It consists of two tubular conduits running lengthwise fore-to-aft, with magnetic field generators at regular intervals. Such a drive, having no moving parts, would be exquisitely quiet. The Japanese Naval Self-defense Forces once built two prototypes—small, but no less successful. And they would indeed sound exactly like a school of whales, or a seaquake—and from which a regular water hammer would build up in the tubes."

"Which is exactly what we heard! I knew it!" cried the doctor. *"Something* shadowed this ship and her task group on her way to Botany Bay. That I will swear on a stack of hardcover print editions of *Schwartz' Principles of Surgery* as high as the combined height and draft of this ship. The sonar recordings clearly show it, and Captain Jones knew what he had seen. But he couldn't prove it, and Captain Arthur doesn't understand—not fully anyway."

"And why would you take an interest in the ship's sonar system, anyway?"

"In addition to medicine," said Dan, "I also know information science. I've already made a few enhancements to this ship's information-handling systems."

"Good to hear. But there is but one puzzle. If the shadow were an enemy, why did she never engage? Why did she let a fleet cross two oceans without challenge and strike a decisive blow in Matthew's cause?"

"Even Captain Jones doesn't know that, Admiral. I think that's part of the reason he sent *this* ship to make a 'ferry run.'"

"And assigned you both on board," said Jacques-Yves. "Well, from now on, you both are attached to my staff, as you said. And don't you *ever* hold back on me. Questions?"

"None, Admiral. I understand—I *comprehend*—perfectly."

"So do I," said Boddicker. "You can count on me, Admiral."

"And that," Jacques-Yves said to Natalya, "goes for you, too."

"Yes, sir," she said with a jaunty smile.

"Now then. For the moment, I'll have to speak to our Acting Captain about our place here. What did he mean about ferrying so many of us to America? Mr. Boddicker has already explained his reasons. What about yours? And everyone else?"

"I can tell you about Sergeant Jameson," said Natalya. "He's an officer candidate. Lieutenant Walston—his Marine officer-in-charge—sent him home to go to Officer Candidate School. Captain Arthur seconded him to me for my little mission."

"Do you recommend him?"

"Without reserve, Admiral."

"Then maybe our Captain will assign him and his Fire Team to us. And what of ourselves?"

"Officially," said Dan, "his orders are to get us to the States, then return to the Australian theater as fast as he can. But *unofficially,* we're to see whether we can pick up that shadow. The problem being that Captain Arthur doesn't even think we *have* a shadow to worry about."

"And whose idea is it that we four introduce ourselves to the United States of America?"

"Well, Jake has told you what he intends to do in America. But you heard him say there was more. I am now prepared to tell you that. Matthew believes we might be able to recruit troops in strength, then somehow signal *Argo* to come pick us all up so that we can join the war effort in the Nine-o'clock Quadrant. He told me the greater nuisance we can make of ourselves away from this system, the more assets the United Systems Navy would need to redeploy away from Earth, long enough for him to overthrow the United Nations."

"And how might the United States government receive such a suggestion?"

"With great enthusiasm, if Matthew is right. They're committed to the war themselves. They want nothing less than the freedom to come out and walk and build on the surface again."

"But wouldn't they have need to retain as many forces here on Earth to fight their part of the war?"

"They might, except for one thing: they know as well as Matthew does that we must all distract the enemy wherever we can. And Jake and I have other reasons to get back into space."

"What might those be?"

"Not so much what, but who. Jake, maybe you can go first."

"Gladly. Once in space, I can renew some of my Syndicate contacts, find out what goes on, and get the Syndicate to help. I know enough now to convince the Syndicate to throw in with the Free Systems in the Nine-o'clock Quadrant. We can do a lot of damage, *and* we can gather some very valuable intelligence."

"I'm sure you could," said Jacques-Yves—and now it was his own turn to affect a sardonic smile. "And you, Doctor: whom would you be trying to contact?"

"The Morgens."

"Do you mean to say that *they* are interested?"

"That would be one Morgen in particular: Emperor Kress."

Jake Boddicker stared back at Dan in open-mouthed astonishment. Obviously, that name impressed him—and Dan had never mentioned his acquaintance with Kress before. "You are quite serious?" he asked.

"Oh, yes. If we can impress him, he'll throw in with the Free Systems and also give us any aid, direct or indirect, that he can. As a matter of fact, he has commissioned the largest warship you or I ever saw—a real battleship, is the word I have. But his honor won't let him deploy it unilaterally. I don't know all the details, but as I understand it, he wants to see whether it will have a worthy crew and strike force. If so—well, Admiral, that ship would become your flagship."

Now Jacques-Yves truly was without voice. A chance to walk the deck of a spaceship again, this time in command of a task force. The very thought took his breath away. Then he remembered something else. "I might have known that Kress would think in those terms," he said. "Surely he remembers when he, Matthew Morrow, and I all intervened in the Morgen Civil War. At one point, I commanded a task force of a motley collection of ships, whatever was available in that theater. Matthew commanded one of those ships—and distinguished himself, too. Kress had his own role to play on the surface of his people's homeworld. Yes, of course, he would want to reunite the old *Bonaventure* fellowship; it would be just like him. What do you suppose he'll say, Natalya, when he finds you alive?"

Natalya smiled a very broad smile. "I would definitely look forward to such a meeting," she said. "I can only imagine what he must have felt, when ... well."

"You know how I feel to see you alive again," said Jacques-Yves. "But of course, our American Acting Captain knows nothing of this. I suggest we not burden him with it. Particularly when this ship has a more immediate mission—to find out whether a threat under the sea exists. In that regard: do you both think Captain Arthur is qualified to handle such a threat?"

"There's not but one way to find out, Admiral," said Dan. "Besides that, he's the best-qualified officer who can command this ship. But the problem remains: he doesn't accept the threat and thinks of us as mere passengers and himself as a fully independent commander. He won't balk you directly, but it'll be there—a slight resentment if you assert yourself as OTC when he doesn't expect it."

"Then we shall have to be more subtle. We'll require access to information on the position of this ship and anything her sensors detect that could possibly pose a threat. And I'd rather not have to get it from a member of the bridge watch."

"There should be no need for that," said Dan. "All information, of whatever kind, goes into the ship's server network. Access is a matter of proper identification and clearance."

Jacques-Yves realized the problem at once. Now he stood up and took a more careful look around his quarters. "You are saying," he said aloud, "that I would need a console, plus an account on these servers, plus the means by which to identify myself. I had wondered earlier why he left me this beautiful-looking but decidedly antique drafting table."

"In other words," said Dan, "you don't have a workstation."

"I see none here. But I also see no legitimate military reason why I should not have one. Therefore, I shall ask. In the process, I shall discover just how much consideration a distinguished passenger on a warship deserves. Do either of you have any further questions or any other information you think I ought to have?"

Dan, Natalya, and Jake each said, "No, sir."

"In that case, that will be all. By the way: have any of you been taking your meals in the wardroom with the other officers on board?"

"Well, we did," said Dan, "but we rarely spoke to the ship's regular officers. And now that you're on board, I sense that the steward's mates will have orders to serve us all here in your cabin."

"Yes, I can certainly predict that. Very well, then I'll see you all at 1200, here in this cabin."

The three other officers left. Jacques-Yves then crossed to one installation he did have: a simple intercom. This had a speaker and a keypad, obviously for dialing a combination of some sort. It sported four rows of three buttons, the top three rows numbered 1 through 9 (with a group of three letters above each of the numerals 2 through 9), and the bottom row labeled "*", "0", and "#". But of course. A telephone dial, reproducing exactly the standard telephone dials of the twenty-first century. These people must be superstitious about changing ship's systems.

Well, if this dial followed the original convention, then if he dialed zero, he should reach the communications shack. So he pressed that button.

"Intercom operator," said a voice from the speaker. "What can I do for you, Admiral?"

Impressive. "I would like to speak to Captain Arthur," he said.

"He should be in his sea cabin. I can signal him and then transfer you. Can you hold?"

"Yes, I'll hold."

Silence. Then: "Good morning, Admiral de Grasse. This is the Captain speaking."

"May I see you for a moment? I have a sensitive matter to discuss."

"Sure. I was about to check things out on the bridge, but I'll be glad to see you. Come on over."

"Tout de suite."

The speaker fell silent. Jacques-Yves turned and left his suite, moving down the same passageway he had used before. He identified himself to the single Marine guard, who knocked, received some sort of assent, then admitted him.

"Good morning, Admiral," said the Captain, smiling and holding out a hand. "Are you squared away?"

"I am if I comprehend correctly," said Jacques-Yves, taking the offered hand. "But I'd like to ask a small favor."

"Sure thing—but first, won't you have a seat?"

Jacques-Yves took the offered place on a sofa. "I have no workstation in my quarters," he said.

Captain Arthur didn't answer straight away. He hesitated for only a moment, but long enough. Then he said, "My apologies, Admiral. I had thought *I* had your quarters squared away."

"Captain, let us be frank with one another. You did not anticipate that I would have need of a workstation in my quarters. And the cause—excuse me, the reason—for that is that you'd like to think this is simply a ferry run, and here am I, the inconvenient ranking passenger about to, how does one say it, 'pull rank.'"

Arthur laughed with a bare hint of nervousness. Then he said, "Touché, Admiral. All right, I'll lay it out. Captain Jones told me to pick someone up from the French wine country, then ferry a bunch of people to the States. The trouble is that one of them—you—outrank me. But this isn't exactly a task force. We're just one ship, on a routine cruise."

"Your pardon, Captain, but this cruise is *not* routine. You have reason to believe—or a least *I* have reason to believe, from certain briefings I have received—that you are about to cross an ocean having at least one, possibly more than one, submarine in it, whose Captain may be friendly—or hostile. Aside from helping to land a strike force and then conducting a shore bombardment with, as I understand it, a single shot, you have no other combat experience. I *have* combat experience—in a space-borne navy, to be sure, but still … combat. And, though you would not have gotten this brief, combat against a stealthy enemy. So perhaps my insights might prove valuable."

"You're talking about those sonar ghosts we saw on the way to Australia, aren't you? Those are nothing. Random echoes."

"But they're not, are they? Minor magnitude-one seaquakes, at regular intervals?"

"Oh, *now* I get it. You've been talking to Commander Thakur. But he's a doctor, not a line officer."

"That was merely his formal training. In fact, I consider him knowledgeable enough to evaluate a possible combat threat. You don't have to know all his history, but only that *I* know it, and I trust and value his judgment."

Jack Arthur sat in silence.

Jacques-Yves let him sit for a minute, then said, "You need not trouble yourself overmuch. I do not propose to be your Officer in Tactical Command. I merely would like access to certain information, of an admittedly combat-sensitive nature, for myself and for the three persons who now form my staff—Commander Thakur and Lieutenants Bronskaya and Boddicker. That information will go no further than to us four."

"This is all highly irregular, Admiral. Surely you know that. I am an officer of the United States Navy. You four are effectively officers without a navy—with the possible exception of Commander Thakur. But his case is worse because he claims to be an officer in a rebel navy."

"And furthermore," said Jacques-Yves, "my remaining officer is what you would call a 'crook.' Well, I don't like him, either, but I trust him. I also understood that the United States of America was formally at war with the United Nations and the United System. Wouldn't that give us the status of military allies?"

"Maybe it would," Arthur said. "But we don't even know what we're dealing with."

"That is the exact problem, is it not?"

"All right! But the United Nations took down their entire wet navy centuries ago!"

"Stood it down, yes. But did they necessarily scuttle every ship they had? Mightn't they have saved at least two or three submarines?"

"They wouldn't want anything like that! They were concerned about disturbing the whale migration routes!"

"That consideration might apply to a surface vessel. And to any ordinary submarine of the period. But I happen to know that the Japanese Naval Self-defense forces built and tested two prototype submarines having magneto-hydro-dynamic drives."

That rocked the Captain. "Where did you hear that?" he asked, drawing back.

"Where else but *Jane's Fighting Ships*? When I left France, I left behind a library containing that series, up to its last volume. And haven't you confirmed that just now? And if you have, haven't you *also* confirmed that those 'sonar ghosts' worry you more than you care to admit?"

Arthur fell silent once again. This time Jacques-Yves let him think on the matter. Eventually, the Captain said, "You win, Admiral. You'll get your access. But it's with the clear understanding that I remain in command of this ship. Any suggestions you have to make about how to fight this ship, to meet any threat whatsoever, you bring directly to me—not my officers or crew. Do you understand?"

"Perfectly. Indeed I would never act in any other manner."

Arthur got up from his place and crossed to his intercom. He keyed in a sequence of five button strokes. A man's voice answered. "Chief Sutton here."

"Chief, this is the Captain. I'd be pleased to see you in my cabin right away."

"Aye-aye, sir."

Three minutes later, the cabin door opened. The young Black man, uniformed the same as any other member of this ship's crew, but wearing the rate and rating devices of a senior chief petty officer in information services, walked in.

"Rear Admiral Jacques-Yves de Grasse, may I present Senior Chief Information Technician Barry Sutton, formerly of your Navy, now a member of ours. Chief, Rear Admiral de Grasse will require access to all command-level intelligence, for himself and for three other officers. This has my direct authorization."

"Aye-aye, sir," said the Chief, smiling.

"That will be all, Senior Chief. Will that be all, Admiral?"

"Yes, and thank you a million times."

"Don't mention it."

The Chief gestured to Jacques-Yves, who accompanied him out into the passageway.

As soon as they were out of earshot of the Captain's Marine guard, Jacques-Yves spoke: "Did I understand your Captain correctly? Did you once serve in the United Systems Navy?"

"Yes, sir. At Bethesda Naval Hospital. Matthew Morrow himself recruited me."

"Matthew Morrow," said Jacques-Yves slowly, watching the younger man carefully, "was once my second officer and chief project officer."

"Then you commanded *Bonaventure VI* and *VII!* Pardon me, Admiral, but I have always wanted to meet you. And say—don't mind the Captain. He doesn't know your reputation, as I do. Anyway, the Captain said you can see all command-level intelligence. That pretty much means whatever you'd like. What did you have in mind?"

"Live streams of the radar and sonar consoles, and of course, this ship's position, heading, and speed."

"Ah. Our 'sonar ghosts.' I take it you believe the submarine theory?"

"I *accept* it, yes. More to the point, my command instincts—which have definitely returned to me now that I am walking a ship's deck again—tell me that this ship is under threat and, in fact, is a hunted ship. Your Captain—and this goes no further than your ears—does not appear to comprehend."

"Got it. Well, he's got one thing right. He trusts you. Maybe not completely, but far enough. So: first, we'll get a workstation installed in your cabin and the cabins of our three other officer guests, Commander Thakur and Lieutenants Bronskaya and Boddicker. Then I'll create an account for you and design a role that will let you create other accounts. You'll have full access to anything this ship can see or hear, by any manner of sensor you can name—and full authority to share that with any account you create."

"Excellent. If I may say so, I could have used someone like you on *Bonaventure*. Either one."

"Well," said Sutton, grinning, "I suppose I've got the next best assignment now."

* * *

"Unto Almighty God, we commend the soul of our departed comrade-in-arms, Private First Class Lawrence Shannon, United States Marine Corps, and we commit his body to the deep, in sure and certain hope of the Resurrection unto eternal life, through our Lord and Savior Jesus Christ, at Whose coming in glorious majesty to judge the universe, the sea shall give up her dead, and the corruptible bodies of those who sleep in Him shall be changed, and made like unto His glorious body, according to the mighty working whereby He is able to subdue all things unto Himself."

Captain Arthur nodded to Hospital Corpsman First Class Andrea Riley USN, who stood next to the longboard upon which the body of Private First Class Sutton rested, with the forty-one-star American flag draped over it. Now she raised the board, and his body slid over the portside railing and onto the temporary ramp that rested on the ship's hull. Jacques-Yves de Grasse, with Natalya Bronskaya and Dan Thakur flanking him, watched as the body slid down the very long ramp and eventually fell with a soft splash into the waters of the Bay of Biscay.

Captain Arthur continued his service, "I heard a Voice from heaven, saying unto me, 'Write: from henceforth blessed are the dead who die in the Lord, even so saith the Spirit, for they rest from their labors.'"

After this, the entire ship's company turned out on the flight deck and fell silent for half a minute, hats in hand. At last, the first lieutenant—now acting as executive officer, or so Jacques-Yves understood—said, "Ship's company, cover!"

Everyone present put on his hat.

"Chief petty officers, dismiss your divisions!"

That took some time, with each chief giving a dismissal order to his respective contingent. The only voice Jacques-Yves recognized was that of Senior Chief Barry Sutton, saying, "Information technicians, dismissed!" When all the enlisted personnel had left the flight deck (except those who were assigned to it as their regular duty), Captain Arthur nodded to Jacques-Yves.

He took a deep breath, then said, "Commander Thakur, Lieutenant Bronskaya, Lieutenant Boddicker, come with me," as he left the flight deck with his "staff" in tow.

He didn't feel like returning to his cabin but instead led his three fellow officers through the deckhouse and onto the forward-weather deck. They gathered next to the missile launcher. For a while, no one said anything as the ship continued on her way through the Bay of Biscay. Behind them lay Cape Ferret, which they had rounded earlier that day, leaving Arcachon Bay behind.

Natalya spoke first, "Admiral, I … I must say I have never before felt the inadequacy of life in our former service. These people treat everything with a solemnity we never matched."

"They do seem to take their Christianity seriously," said Jacques-Yves. "Do you suppose there's any truth in it?"

"Had you asked me that while we were running through the Gascony Regional Forest, I would have doubted it. Now … now I'm not so sure. I actually start to wonder. There's a lot that doesn't make much sense. But these people take great comfort in it, and they have something we lack. It was all I could do to maintain my composure back there, and I'm not ashamed to say it."

"Dan?"

"It's way out of my league, Admiral. But I have to agree with Natalya. There's something there, all right, though I don't begin to understand what it might be."

"And you, Mr. Boddicker. You're awfully quiet. And your trademark smile is gone."

"Oh, you noticed that, did you, Admiral? OK, I admit it. The way this crew keeps to its religious traditions gets to me, too. Especially that rigmarole—no, that's not the right word for it. They know what they're doing. But I don't get it at all, and it gets on my nerves."

"Perhaps I might be able to find a clue."

"How?" asked Dan. "Where?"

"I'll let you know," said the Admiral. "That will be all for now."

The three other officers re-entered the deckhouse. Jacques-Yves de Grasse stood where he was, looking out over the Bay of Biscay—to starboard, away from the Spanish north shore he knew he would see to port. Then he turned forward, looking past the gun mount to where the bow sloped down abruptly to slice the water as it went.

Into the unknown, that voice in his head said again. How true that was.

Chapter 8

Matthew Morrow heard the soft chime of the wake-up alarm he had set. He sent a silent command to the charging alcove in which he had literally stood all night long. The alcove shut down and released him—fully charged, and ready in all respects to face another day.

His network interface told him it was five-thirty in the morning. But he always preferred to verify things like that externally. So he left the alcove, crossed the deck of the flag-quarters conference and chart room, and walked out the door. He exchanged salutes with the Marine guard and made his way down the passageway to a hoist to take him to the weather deck, then outside, forward of the multi-level deckhouse. Then he made his way past the missile launcher, past the big shore gun, to the end of the ship's bow. From here, he had a nearly unobstructed view of all the stars.

He made out the Chameleon, the Octant, and the Bird of Paradise, hanging over Cruria Australis. He could tell his exact latitude from those constellations even without a sextant. More to the point, their orientation, and the positions of several other constellations, let him tell the time directly.

He frowned as he remembered coming out to this deck at 2100 to see two constellations that held particular significance to him. One was Cetus— the whale. The most relevant star in that constellation was Tau Ceti. The Elves came from there.

The other was Orion—the Hunter. Now he frowned even more deeply, recalling an action at the star known as the Hunter's Leg. Rigel. On the sixth planet out from that star, his friend Natalya had ended her organic life. Never had he thought he would see her again after that—and under such circumstances. *Turned into a not-quite-machine, like me. And for what? To attack some of the finest people the powers-that-be will ever know. That's why we're making revolution.*

He could see neither constellation now. Nautical twilight had set in. In less than forty-five minutes, the sun would rise.

Finally, he decided he'd seen enough. So he went back into the deckhouse and took the hoist to the ship's bridge.

The two senior Navy officers were already on the bridge: Brevet Rear Admiral Jones, standing off to one side, and Captain Lance Aaronson, the ship's commanding officer.

"Field Marshal on the bridge!" the on-duty petty officer announced. Everyone started to stand up to salute.

"As you were," Matthew said with a wave of his hand. The bridge watch then returned to what they were doing. This was what "making all preparations for getting under way" looked like in this room.

"Good morning, Field Marshal," said Admiral Jones. "The Captains are all reporting in. We'll be ready to depart on schedule."

"Good," said Matthew. "Any radar or sonar contacts?"

"None, except our own ships," said the Admiral.

"How about the LCG—actually, I must apologize. During that entire operation I ran overland, I never thought to give her a name. If she's going to be under your command, she needs one."

"I already thought of that, Field Marshal," Jones said with a smile. "I worked it out with Captain Blakely. She now answers to the name *Magpie*. They have those birds in these lands—and in fact, those birds had to learn to be wild all over again. Back when Australia and New Guinea were civilized, the people used to feed them. In the American Reservation, they still do."

Matthew smiled. "As good a name as any, I suppose," he said. "Good job. If you have no other questions for me, I'll leave you to it."

"Thank you, sir. We'll definitely depart on schedule."

"Good. In that case—"

"Admiral," said the radio operator, "we just got a call from *Magpie*. Sounds urgent. Captain Blakely wants to speak to you."

"On speakers," said Jones.

"Aye-aye, sir. Switching to speakers now."

"Very well … *Magpie*, this is Admiral Jones. What have you got, Blakely?"

"Admiral, we're reading a high-level atmospheric disturbance—an organized low-pressure cell with clockwise winds and distinct rain bands. We evaluate this as a low-level tropical cyclone."

"Position, heading, and speed?"

"Fifteen degrees south, ninety degrees east, heading zero-eight-zero at two five knots."

Jones whistled. "Roger, *Magpie*. Message received. Stand by; you'll be getting a new course. Out." He made a slashing motion above his throat. The radio operator understood. "Contact broken, sir," he said a second later.

"Signal all ships," Jones said next. "Make all preparations for getting under way. Now. Have all ships report readiness. And then we will head about two two five, and thread the Kupang Strait. We'll turn to course three zero zero after that. Send that message and request acknowledgment."

"Aye-aye, sir."

While the radiomen and signalmen were passing the message on, Jones turned to Matthew. "That cyclone will be here in three days," he said. "I want to be long gone before it arrives."

"I see," said Matthew. "So you're going to make your way to Borneo at best speed."

"That's right. Through the Java Sea, then north-northwest between Borneo and Sumatra. Then, God willing, straight to Vietnam. But there's just one other problem we'll have."

"And that would be?"

"Typhoons. When we cross the equator, we'll be right in typhoon alley—and the northwest Pacific basin, which is typhoon country, is the most active tropical cyclone basin on Earth. The other thing to worry about is that typhoons, on average, are the worst tropical cyclones we know."

"Seasonality?"

"There is none—not for typhoons. Oh, it's rare to get a typhoon this late in the year. But all the old records say it was not unheard-of, by any means."

"All ships acknowledging signal, Admiral," said the radioman.

"Very well," said Jones. "Steer the course as ordered."

Chapter 9

A harsh sound, vaguely resembling a boatswain's whistle, sounded from the intercom.

Jacques-Yves placed a bookmark in his Louis Second Bible, marking a place in *Genèse seven*—the chapter describing the launch (or the carrying-away) of *l'arche de Noé*. Then, setting it down on the small table next to his sofa, he got up, crossed the deck, and walked to the intercom. "This is Admiral de Grasse," he said. "To whom am I speaking?"

A man's voice answered in French: "Here, Commander Thakur. Admiral, there is something on sonar I should like to show you."

"Come to my cabin *tout de suite*. We can discuss it here. De Grasse out."

In less than a minute, the Marine guard—actually one of Sergeant Jameson's Marines—opened the door to admit Dan Thakur. As soon as the doctor-cum-secret-agent entered, the Marine closed the door behind him.

Jacques-Yves already had his new workstation warmed up. Now he beckoned to Dan to join him. "Now, Commander," he said—in French, since Dan had opened in that language—"talk to me. Do I take it the sonar ghosts have returned?"

"Oh, yes, Admiral. Exactly as I remember hearing about them. If I may?"

Jacques-Yves nodded and shifted slightly to his left. Dan settled in and took over the console. Making rapid-fire touch motions on the screen, including using the virtual keyboard, Dan brought up the readings of which he had spoken. "They're very hard to discern, Admiral," he said, "and frankly, I expect the bridge watch either to miss them or dismiss them as 'error of system' or 'sea return artifact,' or…"

"'Echo of hazard,' could be?" By which he meant *random*, of course.

"Exactly. But I assure you, these readings are *not* of the hazard. Something is shadowing us again, staying just out of range."

"Where away? Ahead? To starboard?"

"No, Admiral. Deep. Very deep."

"How deep would that be?"

"Frankly, Admiral, that surprises me. I make it as deep as five hundred meters."

"*La vache!* That's deeper even than the three deepest-diving submarines in the original United States Navy could dive."

"And that goes to why the bridge watch wouldn't recognize it. I wrote an enhancement to the sonar resolution program to highlight it."

"Such an enhancement would be prodigiously nonspecific, would it not? Or at least, that's what Captain Arthur would say."

"Captain Arthur does not know just how good his equipment is. The microphones that make up the passive sonar systems are exquisitely sensitive, *if* one knows how to process correctly the sounds they pick up. Not even a submarine below the thermocline can escape my notice. I assure you, Admiral, I am quite certain of my interpretation of the data."

"So—where does that leave us? We *do* have a shadow—but a shadow deeper than we thought. How fast are we traveling at the moment?"

"We are making about thirty-seven kilometers per hour—actually, twenty 'knots' to be exact. That is…"

"I know what a 'knot' is. It's from their measurement system. I learned that much from *Jane's Fighting Ships*. Natalya keeps trying to encourage me to start using the *système patriotique américain d'unités*. Perhaps someday, when I have more time. And yes, I know that Matthew uses it, too."

"If I may say so, Admiral, you will find it more commodious to use the American system if you must speak to the Captain about these findings."

"A valuable point. Now tell me this: are you sure this shadow isn't the original USS *Seawolf* or either of the other two members of her class?"

"What would cause you to ask that, Admiral?"

"Simply this: *Seawolf, Connecticut,* and *Jimmy Carter,* the three ships of that class, were never accounted for after the Great Climate War. Vanished, like this ship and *Michael Monsoor.* The *Lyndon Baines Johnson,* of course, was lost."

"Lost in battle to this very ship, in fact."

"Just so. But we do *not* know what happened to those three submarines. Of course, our shadow *cannot* be a ballistic-missile submarine—for even though the USS *Alaska, Tennessee, West Virginia,* and *Wyoming,* all operating in the Atlantic Ocean, also were unaccounted for, none could dive as deep as our shadow. But if our shadow *is* a *Seawolf,* then it is a clear and present danger."

"But can we not assume that those unaccounted-for submarines would not have been friendly to the United Nations?"

"I fear not. Recall that *LBJ* was UN-friendly. And it would be in keeping with the Machiavellian calculations of the United Nations to hold one or two or all three *Seawolfs* in reserve. "

"All perfectly reasonable, Admiral, except that none of the *Seawolfs* could dive to five hundred meters. Four hundred ninety meters was their test depth. No ship would dive deeper than test depth to carry out surveillance, even of this ship."

"But if it isn't one of those three vessels, then it is still another vessel, of a class that can dive deeper. But who would build it?"

"That takes us back to your earlier point, Admiral. In truth, we cannot know whether the shadow is friendly or hostile."

"And that," said Jacques-Yves, "brings up another problem. If the shadow were hostile, then by rights, she should have wiped out the American fleet—which would effectively destroy the entire United States Navy as it now exists—before they got anywhere near Australia. Which Captain Arthur will cite as the more reason to dismiss these echoes as of the hazard."

"So—what would you wish done?"

"Stay on it, Dan," said Jacques-Yves. "Refine your detection algorithms so that they will leave no doubt. If the echoes remain through tomorrow, then on the next day, I ask to see the Captain."

"*D'accord, mon amiral.*"

"That will be all, then."

But as Dan was about to leave, Jacques-Yves thought of something else. "Wait a moment."

"Sir?"

"Find Natalya for me, if you please. My compliments, and I'd be pleased to see her in my cabin *tout de suite.*"

"Yes, Admiral."

Jacques-Yves went back to reading his Bible at the passage he had marked. Ten minutes later, the cabin door opened. Natalya came in, exchanged salutes with the Marine guard, and crossed to where Jacques-Yves was sitting after the door closed. "You asked to see me, Admiral?" she asked.

"Yes. Pray, seat yourself."

She did. As she did, she said, "I see you are reading your Bible. The story of *Juge Débora,* could be?"

"No—though that is a story for another day. I was reading about the Deluge and the cruise, if you can call it that, of the Ark of Noah. Fascinating reading, to be sure."

"Does it read true?"

"I'm not at all willing to concede that. A flood that literally covered all the land areas of the Earth, to a depth of at least fifteen arm's lengths? Scarcely likely. It would have to rise to more than eight point eight five kilometers."

"To cover Everest, you mean? Yes, that would be a problem … but Matthew told me about an engineer from the twentieth and twenty-first centuries who claimed to explain the Deluge."

"And how might we obtain a copy of his work?"

"Well, you won't find his work in any United Systems library. The United States Library of Congress might have it, though."

"The more reason to reach the United States as soon as possible. But that aside, this story still draws me. Genesis chapters seven and eight read exactly like a ship's log, apart from such fanciful elements as The Eternal 'remembering' Noah and his crew and somehow 'sending' a favorable wind. And yet the story names a mountain where the Ark ran aground—and no one ever found it on any mountain by that name."

"If you mean 'Ararat,'" said Natalya, "*I* might be able to help you there. I'm conversant in Hebrew, as is Matthew. That word isn't necessarily a proper name. It could mean an eddy in a flow."

"Meaning, then, that the Ark was lying-to in a pocket of relative calm with raging seas all round it, by cause of a favorable wind. Yes, that would make sense. But all that can wait for another time." He set the volume down and turned to face her. "I'm more interested in this 'American Patriotic System of Units' you keep urging me to adopt. You told me Matthew had somehow equipped you to use it. Is it that much better than the Interstellar System?"

"Oh, yes. When you think about it, Admiral, the Interstellar System, far from being 'cosmopolitan,' for lack of a better word, is very Earth-centric. It all stems from a unit of length that is, or was, a quarter-meridian on Earth. Now, what does that say about other planets, having different dimensions from Earth?"

The concept struck him without voice, as so many things did. Finally, he said, "I never once thought of that. But of course, you have right. When he designed the metric system that forms the basis for SI, Joseph Lagrange wanted to impose consistency. To that end, he avoided human dimensions. Instead, he chose a dimension from the Earth herself, never imagining that our species might walk on other worlds and make contact with those who originated on them."

"But maybe abandoning human dimensions was the actual objective."

"How so? You know that no human's foot is exactly as long as any other's."

"The Americans solved that problem. They declared an average foot and kept its length the same."

"Still," Jacques-Yves reminded her, "they defined it in terms of the meter."

"True—they did. Not anymore."

"Oh?"

"They have redefined it in terms of the speed of light in a vacuum. And redefined units of all the basic quantities directly in terms of realizable constants. They didn't have to redefine time; the second already had a defined constant, and they'd no cause to change it. But they redefined all the others."

"But wait. Wouldn't that violate coherence? Even if they kept the same unit of electrical current, they would still have to use a non-unity multiplier to relate their unit of energy to their unit of electromotive potential."

"Not if they were prepared to change the size of the latter."

"They didn't!"

"Oh, yes, they did."

"Do you want to say," said Jacques-Yves slowly, "that a 'volt' as they use it aboard this ship is not the same as the 'volt' that Engineer Shaka used aboard *Bonaventure?*"

"That's exact. In fact, the American 'volt' is stronger than the SI 'volt.'"

"But *why?* Why go to so much trouble?"

"For two reasons. One, they no longer had access to the International Institute of Weights and Measures. Remember that the United Nations, of which that Institute is a part, tried to destroy them. Two, they wanted nothing to do with anything that originated in any movement that smacked of collectivism."

Jacques-Yves sighed, "I must admit they have the right of it there," he said. "The French Revolution began well, when it was all about getting rid of hereditary kings and foreign-blooded aristocrats. If the Americans think the Revolution turned collectivistic, we can blame Robespierre. But that still doesn't answer why the American system is inherently better than the Interstellar."

"Dan could probably tell you that. You see, the average human foot is roughly the same as an average Neo-Inuit foot or an average foot on any other world. Except one."

Jacques-Yves thought about that. Then he said, "The Elves?"

Natalya nodded. "The Elves," she repeated.

"And according to you and Matthew," he said, "the Elves are not our friends."

"No, sir. They definitely are not."

Jacques-Yves sat for a long time. Then he came to … well, a temporizing solution. "The reason for wrestling with this measurement question now," he said, "is that Dan and I will soon have a presentation to make to the Captain." He briefly described the problem of the "sonar ghosts" and their suspected origin. "And when I present anything to him," he went on, "I must do it in units of measure he will comprehend."

"A submarine at five hundred meters … that would be deeper than sixteen hundred feet. But I have fear that it might be of a class of which you never heard, or maybe you thought all units of the class were scrapped."

"And what class of ship would that be?"

"A Russian *Akula*. Specifically, K-335 *Gepard*, the only member of a special deep-diving variant of that class. He had a test depth of 520 meters and was rumored to dive to 600."

"Did you say 'he'? Aren't all ships 'she'?"

Natalya smiled. "Not in the Russian Navy, Admiral," she said.

Jacques-Yves waved that off. "That signifies nothing," he said. "What *does* signify is what you said earlier about classes of ship—or submarine—of which certain units were unaccounted for."

"Then I have hope I will not shock you when I tell you that the *Gepard* was listed as 'still on patrol' after Russia also fell in the Great Climate War."

"But I thought all Russians signed on to the Novy Mir project?"

"Legends tell of a remnant of patriotic Russians who did not bend to the United Nations. We have no legend of an underground society, no. But according to one legend, the last President of Russia vanished, along with his family. Vanished along with a number of Russian submarines of the Northern Fleet. One of them…"

"Called itself *Gepard*," Jacques-Yves finished. "Any others?"

"K-295 *Samara,* which can dive almost as deep. But I can name three others that could dive much deeper."

"*La vache.* Which might these be?"

"TK-208 *Dmitri Donskoy,* last of the Typhoons, and K-550 *Aleksandr Nevsky* and K-549 *Prince Vladimir.* And Admiral," said Natalya, suddenly turning more sober, "those three carried ballistic missiles."

"Do you suppose the United Nations knows anything about these vessels?"

"Almost certainly. They would be very afraid of any Russian Naval assets for which they could not account. More to the point, we cannot be sure that any missing *American* Naval asset is friendly or hostile. Any one of those three 'Seawolves' could be another *Lyndon Baines Johnson.* Admiral, the Captain must know, and he must know fast. And we must make him comprehend."

"And more than that," said the Admiral, "the Captain needs all the resources he can muster to deal with the threat, if threat it is. That includes our maglev AFV. Could you adapt its sensory and weapons systems to use American Patriotic units?"

"Oh, yes, Admiral. All I need do is interface with the system and change values and notation for the Seven Constants."

"Range values will be ridiculously large, however."

"Actually, no. The American system defines other units as multiples of the base unit for different applications. They're not multiples of ten, but they don't have to be. Their unit for combat range, the yard, is very close to the meter, only slightly shorter."

"Good. I'm going to propose to present that vehicle to the Captain, and train two of his pilot officers to fly it."

"If they can fly an inherently unstable vehicle like a helicopter, they can fly an SSF maglev," said Natalya. "But we can't have them calling it 'SSF 616' any longer."

"Definitely not. I'll let the Captain handle that detail."

* * *

"I can definitely prove it now," said Dan Thakur.

The four were seated in Jacques-Yves' sea cabin, breakfasting on *gaufres Belgiques* and blueberries. It was MJDN 204198—or *Quartidi* in the Third Decad of *Frimaire*. Or, going back to a calendar he thought he'd never use, Thursday, December 14th, 2417.

"Please share," said the Admiral.

What he heard convinced him. *Yes, the time had come.*

"How much time will you need to get your presentation together?"

"I'm ready any time."

"Good." Jacques-Yves stood up, crossed to the intercom, and keyed a combination.

"Captain's office," said the voice of the yeoman at the other end.

"Here ... this is Admiral de Grasse. Please convey my respects to the Captain and tell him I must see him at his earliest convenience."

"He can see you at one-triple-zero hours, Admiral."

"Agreed."

* * *

"With all due respect to our friendship," said Captain Arthur, "this had better be good."

"It is, if I properly comprehend you," said Jacques-Yves. "My ... flag secretary, for lack of a better term, has a finding to share with you—a finding of a highly likely threat."

The Captain sighed, "All right, then, let's hear it."

Dan Thakur stood up. "Thank you, Captain," he said. "First, let me compliment you on the exquisite sensitivity and precision of your passive sonar systems. I was able to enhance the processing of their signals, perhaps to an extent that never occurred to your navy. And a good thing—for I can now show that this ship is under surveillance, at least, and under threat at worst."

"Since you mentioned sonar, I assume you mean a submarine. Is this about those sonar ghosts that the sonar watch keeps reporting?"

"It is. I've also noted the two times your senior sonar operator ran diagnostics on your systems. So I already know that your equipment is without error. Now, Captain, your original signal algorithmic processing routines were not written to evaluate any sound source sixteen hundred feet or deeper. But they *were* written to find a submarine below the thermocline—the depth below which most sounds simply bounce back to the deep. So your passive sonar could already find a submarine eight hundred feet deep. I simply enhanced it further. So I have a 'type' on our shadow.

"Captain, I evaluate the source as a deep-diving fast-attack submarine, similar to two classes of submarine, certain units of which remain unaccounted for. They could be members of the original *Seawolf* class, all of which vanished during the Great Climate War—except that none of those vessels could dive quite as deeply as the one following us. *Or* they could be members of the Russian *Akula* class, two of which vanished at about the same time, that could dive deeper. I am aware of other submarines that also vanished during this period, but the one following us is much smaller than they."

"Before I evaluate that interesting theory," Arthur said, "I need to hear your 'type.'"

"Right away, Captain," said Dan. "May I use this console?"

"Have at it," said the Captain.

Dan sat before the offered console and made several rapid-fire finger strokes. Not long afterward, the display filled with an obvious sound waveform. For several seconds they heard only random sounds from under the sea. But every ten seconds, they heard something else—something that sounded very like a seaquake.

"Captain," Dan went on, "there's more. I have ninety-five percent confidence that I have accurately generated a top outboard plan for our shadow."

"Let's see it."

The screen changed again, this time showing a simplified drawing of what a submarine might look like if one overflew it while it was in drydock.

"Yeoman," said the Captain to a waiting petty officer, "be so kind as to fetch me my copy of *Jane's Fighting Ships.*"

"Aye-aye, Captain."

"I see you possess that series as I do," said Jacques-Yves.

"Well, I see I didn't do you justice, Admiral," Arthur said. "You and I do think alike, after all, that it is better to have a hardcopy that you can hold in your hand."

The yeoman brought the volume, and Arthur took it, opened it, and started rapidly turning its pages, making his long practice apparent. Then he stopped at the pages he wanted, spread the book wide, and turned it around so that his guests could see it.

"That's it," said Dan. "That's the plan."

"And that," said the Captain, "is the Russian fast-attack submarine K-335 *Gepard*, or at least a vessel built to that specification, or close to it. Except, I'll bet she never sounded like that. You were right, Admiral; that's a magneto-hydro-dynamic drive, all right. Which begs the question: *what in God's Name is she doing here, and where has she been for all these centuries?*"

"Your pardon, Captain," said Natalya, smiling impishly, "but that should be, 'What in Bog's Name is *he* doing here.'"

The Captain grinned. "*Tushye, tovarishch,*" he said.

"Another question presents itself," said Jacques-Yves. "And you know what that is."

"Meaning, is she—or he—friendly, or hostile? But … wait a minute. If that vessel were hostile, it could have sunk us all when we left port on our way to Australia or certainly taken part in the Battle of Sydney Harbor—against us."

"But this isn't the only ship of her class that went missing."

"No. And this finding changes the whole ballgame."

"That's quite close to how *I* would have put it, Captain. So: what are you going to do about it?"

Captain Arthur did not move or speak for several seconds. Jacques-Yves waited.

At last, the Captain said, "We continue on our present course until we round Cape Ortegal. But after that, we make our course for Nova Scotia, not our original destination of the Straits of Florida. Until I know who's in command of that vessel and exactly where his loyalties lie, I'm not going to risk leading him straight into our harbor. Unless you think we should risk that?"

Jacques-Yves shook his head, "No, Captain. I'm inclined to agree with you."

Dan raised his hand.

"You have something to add, Commander Thakur?" the Admiral asked.

"Yes, Admiral—and Captain. I was just thinking that we *could* try to communicate with that vessel. If your *active* sonar is as good as your passive, I'm sure I can build a modulator good enough to transmit a voice."

"I would do that only as a last resort. But … yes, come to think of it, voice transmission by active sonar would be a nice capability. But while we're doing that: Admiral, I want that magnetically levitating vessel you came in on. It would make an excellent anti-submarine weapons platform."

"I thought you might see that possibility, Captain," said Jacques-Yves, and made his proposal to modify the maglev and train two American pilots on it.

"That's very kind of you," said the Captain when Jacques-Yves had finished. "Very well, I accept. But I also want that new processing program your man developed."

"That goes without saying, Captain. But I'm curious: what will you call her?"

"Does she have a name at the moment?"

"No."

"I see. Well, I'm not going to go on calling her the Six-One-Six, that's for sure. That number has an arguable, but dark, significance in our traditions. Since she's the first maglev vehicle in the Navy catalog, her registry number will be Mike Lima Victor Double-ought One. As for a name … I'll name her *Hummingbird,* after the only known bird that can hover. Yeoman, make a note."

"Aye-aye, sir."

"And another thing. Does she carry any armament for ground attack?"

"Now that you mention it," said Jacques-Yves, "she *can* carry high-explosive charges. The SSF sometimes use them for ground assaults. In fact, I imagine she's fully loaded with that sort of ordnance."

"It's worth checking. But more to the point: we should modify her to carry torpedoes."

"You mean the same armament your Seahawk carries. Yes, with that, I would agree. But as I recall, the British Royal Navy, less than two decades before the Great Climate War, was still deploying an anti-submarine weapon called a 'depth charge,' that they were dropping from helicopters."

"Ye gods, that's ancient!" said Arthur. "We got away from depth charges by the time they built this ship. They're useless in a deep-water sea battle anyway."

"Not necessarily, Captain," said Jake Boddicker. "A weapon like that is good to have, especially if your enemy doesn't expect you to have it."

"Still, I wouldn't expect an enemy sub to feel a thing from little firecrackers like that."

"But, what about if they carried a more powerful explosive?"

Arthur seemed to take a few moments to think about that. Then he said, "You mean improvised chemistry?"

"Improvisation is my middle name, Captain," said Boddicker—and that feral grin of his was back. "I'll bet I could make a depth charge that would shock any submariner, in more ways than one."

Arthur took a deep breath. Then he said. "All right. Get on it. I'll tell the gunnery officer to give you everything you need."

"Aye-aye, Captain."

* * *

"Admiral, what do you make of all this?" Natalya said (in French) as she, Dan, Jake, and Jacques-Yves made their way back to what even the Captain was calling "flag quarters."

The Admiral didn't have to hear twice what Natalya was talking about. The walls of the narrow passageway sported a curious sort of decoration. Bright colors prevailed, with red, green, silver, and gold dominating. Here and there, three spotted legends read "MERRY CHRISTMAS."

"Maybe I can help you there," said Dan. "I've been reading up on American religious customs. This happens to be their Advent Season. The Second Sunday in Advent had just passed when we came aboard. Advent has two more Sundays to run, and after that…"

"Noël," said Jacques-Yves. "Joyeux Noël. That's what my ancestors, going back to the original Admiral de Grasse, would have been saying this time of year. I suppose I ought to have mentioned it earlier. But these Americans are the only ones I know who observe the custom today."

"But what does it signify?" Natalya asked.

"Literally a celebration of the birth of that personage the Captain mentioned at Private Shannon's funeral. Jesus Christ."

"Christ … Christianity … The founder of Christianity."

"Yes, Natalya. And, according to my Louis Second, the son of the Eternal himself."

"I need to ask Sergeant Jameson about this. I think he keeps the custom, too. If…"

The harsh boatswain's whistle sound interrupted them. And after that came the Captain's voice: *"Now hear this!"*

The three stopped abruptly—because they noticed that everyone else within sight was also stopping to listen to the nearest public-address speaker. When the Captain spoke that way, it had to be important—and ominous.

"This is the Captain. I have a very serious announcement to make. Some of you might guess what it is, and maybe the rest of you are wondering whether it's even possible. This ship is now in Threat Condition Delta."

He paused.

"Repeat: this ship is now in Threat Condition Delta. The four most distinguished guests we have on board, to wit, Rear Admiral Jacques-Yves de Grasse and his flag secretary, flag lieutenant, and weapons consultant, have just been in to present to me their evaluation that we are not alone in this ocean. We have picked up a shadow—a very deep diving shadow."

An angry murmur began to sound.

"What does this signify?" asked Natalya.

"This is a destroyer, Natalya," the Admiral said. "Her usual mission is anti-submarine warfare. And a deep-diving shadow can only be a submarine. You can now imagine how her crew must feel."

"I must emphasize that at the present time, we have *no* reliable evaluation of the shadow as either friendly or hostile," the Captain's voice continued. "Admiral de Grasse has generously pledged his full support of our endeavor to evaluate the shadow properly. But until we know more, we are *not* going back home. Not yet. And I'm sure you all understand why.

"We will remain in this state of heightened alert until further notice. It's tough to have this break this close to Christmas, but threats never did take a pause for Christmas in the history of the United States Navy. And if the shadow belongs to an enemy, then it likely belongs to our most likely enemy—which is an atheistic enemy."

Another angry murmur, louder this time, broke out.

"I am, however, glad to announce that this ship has acquired another anti-submarine asset. The Admiral has *given* us that magnetically levitating vehicle he and his flag lieutenant flew in on. Assignments will be forthcoming to select pilot, copilot, and crew for this vehicle. Lieutenant Bronskaya has signaled her willingness to provide whatever training any selectee might need—subject, of course, to qualification. And Lieutenant Boddicker has begun a project to equip her with an ancient type of ordnance he believes he can enhance to very good effect. We're also getting enhancements to all our detection systems. We will meet any threat that presents itself.

"And last—in the short time that it has been my privilege to be your commanding officer, I have never had reason to expect less than the best from any of you. This is a proud ship, and a proud ship is a winning ship. Let's keep it that way. Are you with me?"

"AYE-AYE, SIR!" The ship rang and echoed with her entire crew speaking with one voice.

"I thank you, and the United States Navy thanks you," said the Captain's voice in reply. "So, for what it's worth, let us praise the Lord, pass the ammunition—and Merry Christmas."

Chapter 10

Jacques-Yves de Grasse could not sleep. Impatiently he reached for the wrist chronometer on the shelf above his bunk. Holding it in front of his face, he read the dial. 0205. And the date: SAM (for *Samedi*, or "Saturday" as they called it on this ship) and 16.

His first impulse was to signal the bridge. But as soon as he thought of that, he remembered. He had no authority to ask to speak to any member of the bridge watch, not even the officer of that watch—unless said officer happened to be the Captain. He was just about to try to go to sleep again when he heard that harsh boatswain's-whistle sound again.

Involuntarily he said in French, "Here, Admiral de Grasse."

And a voice answered him, also in French: "Here, Commander Thakur. Admiral, I think you should use your workstation to access the enhanced sonar display. There has been a change."

"Oh?" Jacques-Yves was now wide-awake. Quickly he got out of the bunk and stowed it. Then, after putting on his robe, he crossed to the small table and switched on the workstation. Quickly he navigated to the new sonar display and studied it.

Their shadow stood out in stark relief, no question. And it had risen more than one hundred meters. Out of curiosity, he asked for measurements in American Patriotic. And he just stared.

Twelve hundred feet deep—and coming rapidly to the surface.

"Notify Natalya and Jake!" he barked. "I want you all to report to my cabin *tout de suite!*"

"Yes, Admiral!"

No question of going back to sleep now. He swiftly shucked the nightclothes and put on his utility uniform. He was just applying the last accouterments when he heard a rapid-fire bugle call on repeat. A voice followed: "General quarters! General quarters! All hands to battle stations!" And finally, a very loud, repeating alarm, ringing like a gong, over and over.

At that moment, his cabin door opened, and Dan, Jake, and Natalya rushed in. "We just heard the general alarm, Admiral," said Dan. "Where to now?"

"To the bridge," said Jacques-Yves. "All of us. That includes you, Dan."

"Yes, sir!"

"Wait! Jake, how are those 'depth charges' coming?"

"I've got a batch ready to drop right now, Admiral," said Jake. "In fact, I've got a standing chit from the Captain to be on hand at their first deployment."

"In that case," said Jacques-Yves, "you will lay below to the hangar deck and report to the pilot of *Hummingbird. Toute de suite!*"

"Aye-aye, Admiral!" said Jake, who left immediately.

"You two," said Jacques-Yves to Natalya and Dan, "follow me." He led the way, relying on long practice. On the way, he had to dodge several sailors rushing past him, ahead and behind, each carrying helmet and life jacket to their particular battle station.

They reached the bridge just as the alarm stopped sounding. Jacques-Yves saw a room in deceptive calm. Any place would be calm after all that rushing about in the passageways. He heard when a young yeoman-third-class called out, "Admiral on the bridge!" The only lighting in the room came from the various flat-panel displays that filled it. Each one had a petty officer bending over it, and these non-comms were calling out to one another what they were seeing. All very efficient—but he could feel the tension emanating from everyone around him.

"Ah, Admiral," said Arthur's voice from a tabletop display that dominated the room. "You might want to see this."

Jacques-Yves came closer. He realized the display was actually an electronic "chart" showing the waters surrounding this vessel. And sure enough, it prominently featured the submarine, showing her depth, bearing, and lateral range—and the designation "UNK."

"That," said Captain Arthur, "is our 'ghost.' Coming up to talk to us, I have no doubt—or in any event, not even caring whether we can see them."

"In that case, if I may say so, I see no reason to maintain silence."

"I definitely concur," said the Captain. Then he raised his voice and turned to one side. "Sparks!" he called.

A first-class petty officer looked up from a console with three screens and an apparent push-to-talk microphone. "Comms, aye-aye," he said.

"Hail them."

The petty officer—obviously a radioman—poked his center screen several times to bring up a new display. Jacques-Yves guessed the Captain must have ordered that the bridge radioman would guard the sonar modulator as well as the radio set. Then the radioman picked up his push-to-talk microphone, thumbed the switch, and began to speak.

"Unidentified submarine, this is the USS *Elmo Zumwalt*," the young man said. "Please identify yourself and state your intentions."

The radioman let the button pop back up. Silence greeted him.

He pushed the button again, saying, "Unidentified submarine, this is the United States Ship *Elmo Zumwalt*. We ask you again, identify and state your intentions."

More silence.

"Bogey depth eight hundred feet and still climbing," said another petty officer, turning from a screen showing four concentric circles with cross-hairs. This must be the sonar operator.

Captain Arthur stepped to his own console, poked another display, then picked up his microphone. "*Hummingbird?* Bridge," he said. "Report."

"We've got him, Captain," came the voice of what must be the pilot of the maglev. "Torpedoes ready to drop, plus those new depth charges."

"Stand by." The Captain turned to the sonar operator, "How deep is he now?" he asked.

"Six hundred fifty feet. Hull-popping noises starting to quiet some. I think he's slowing down."

"Have you heard any other noises?"

"Well, I wouldn't expect him to be running with torpedo tubes flooded, and I haven't heard any flooding noises … Stand by one … He's moving away from us, and forward. Confirm: bearing zero-zero-zero relative, lateral distance one triple-oh yards. If he's after another target, I can't see it."

"Depth?"

"Five hundred fifty feet and still climbing."

And then another voice cried out from an unexpected quarter: "Conn, radar! New contact bearing two two five absolute, altitude one-double-oh thousand, and closing fast! It's a missile!"

"*Right full rudder!*" cried the Captain. "*All ahead full! Missile watch, intercept!*"

As Jacques-Yves watched through the forward window, a bright streak lit up the night sky, giving him after-images for a few seconds. At the same time, he felt the inertia pulling him to port. He grabbed a vertical handhold to hold himself steady. Out of the corner of his eye, he saw Dan and Natalya doing the same.

Then, as another flash turned the night into day, the radar operator said, "Target destroyed, Captain."

"Make your course zero-zero-zero," said the Captain. "Sonar, what's our shadow doing?"

"Still on his base course … Another sonar contact, Captain! A big one! Range one-five-double-oh, bearing zero-niner-zero, depth three double-oh feet, and climbing. Sorry, sir, but I did *not* see that one coming."

"What is this, some kind of big party? What's the first one doing?"

"He's already at periscope depth … Stand by one … He's coming about, turning to port."

Then "Sparks" spoke again, "Captain, he's answering our hails!"

"What took him so long? Scratch that. Let's hear him."

Another man's voice filled the room—speaking Standard, or something like it, with a thick Russian accent. "USS *Elmo Zumwalt*, here the Atlantic Federal Ship *Leopard*. You have come under attack from low Earth orbit. We advise you to maintain your present course and speed. We are attempting a counterattack."

"Who's 'we'?" asked Arthur. "And what's this 'Atlantic Federal Ship' malarkey?"

For answer, the radio operator pushed his transmit button again—he had never set the microphone down. "*Leopard,* this is *Zumwalt.* We request clarification of your identity. Do you copy?"

"Ask him about that other sonar contact," the Captain ordered.

"*Leopard,* this is *Zumwalt.* We show another sonar contact, in addition to yourselves. Will you identify?"

"That's the *Vladimir Putin,* and he is with us, *Zumwalt.* Stand by one … *Zumwalt!* The enemy has fired another missile! Advise you steer left, heading two seven zero, and make flank speed!"

"You heard him, Helm," said the Captain. "Do it!"

"Aye-aye, sir."

And now Jacques-Yves had to shift his hold, to keep from falling over to the right. As he did so, the Captain half-shouted to no one in particular, "How could a platform in orbit fire another missile so quickly?"

"It's in a forced orbit," said Jacques-Yves. It was the only thing that made sense. And it meant that this ship was a prime target.

"'Forced orbit?' What's that?"

The sonar operator interrupted them: "Bogey Two is now at one-double-oh feet … Holy Moses! Six missile hatches opening … Six missiles breaching surface … Six missiles away!"

"Confirm, Captain," said the radar operator. "Six sub-launched ballistic missiles. Speed one double oh knots, now two double oh … Three double oh … Four double oh … Five double oh … Six double oh…"

A gigantic thunderclap sounded—how odd in a starlit sky.

"They just broke the Barrier, Captain," said the radar operator. "One of them just broke formation, gunning it for all she's worth … Incoming missile destroyed. Five missiles continuing on … Out of range, Captain."

The Captain poked his screen some more, obviously changing the channel. "Lookouts, bridge!" he shouted next. "What do you see?"

"Captain, we have five bright points of light heading roughly one niner five relative to us … Now merging into one, they're just too high to resolve distinctively … Fading fast … We've lost them."

"And now, Admiral," said the Captain. "You were saying?"

"I was describing a forced orbit. When you go faster, or slower, than orbital speed for any given altitude. That platform—or vessel—has slowed drastically, perhaps even to station-keeping, and is maintaining altitude using retro engines, just to be able to fire more missiles at us. We have definitely caught the eye of the United Systems Admiralty, and no mistake."

Suddenly the lookout's voice came back: "Holy cats! Captain, we've got a fireball! Very bright, bearing one niner five … Now one niner zero, looks like a comet … One eight five … One eight zero and steady," the voice fell silent again, then came back one last time, sounding more sober, "Lost it over the horizon, Captain. Bearing one eight zero. It was headed straight down."

"*La vache*," Jacques-Yves whispered.

"Yes, Admiral de Grasse?" Arthur asked. "It sounds as though you have quite an evaluation."

"I have, Captain. What you have just witnessed is the danger of firing missiles at a ground or sea target from a forced orbit. Particularly if you're orbiting too slowly. A counterattacker can drop you right out of orbit. Which is what we saw."

"Then do you evaluate those submarines as friendly?"

"Oh, yes, Captain. They said they were counterattacking, and that's exactly what they did."

The Captain raised his voice again, "Helm! All stop, and steady as you go."

Jacques-Yves felt the ship slow to a stop.

"Sparks," said the Captain next, "hail *Leopard*. Give them my thanks, and ask their intentions."

The radio operator spoke again into his microphone: "AFS *Leopard,* this is USS *Zumwalt.* We thank you for that last intercept but would like to know your further intentions. Over."

The stranger spoke again: "USS *Zumwalt,* the Atlantic Federation extends its friendship to the United States of America. We request permission to send a delegation to board your vessel for the purpose of negotiating a treaty of alliance."

"Sparks, let me talk to them," said Arthur, picking up a handset of his own. A moment later, the radio operator nodded to him. So he said, "AFS *Leopard,* this is Captain Jack Arthur of the USS *Elmo Zumwalt.* I'd like to speak to your commanding officer ... Hello, who? ... Pleased to make your acquaintance, Rear Admiral. Many thanks for that operation ... Absolutely. Permission granted. We'll send out our own whaleboat ... And I'm looking forward to talking to you, too. Thank you again. Out." He replaced the handset, then barked another order: "Have the whaleboat prepare to launch. Sonar, where's our friend?"

"Coming alongside to port, sir. Still at periscope depth ... Correction: he's surfacing."

And so it was. Jacques-Yves looked out the port windows. As he watched, a conning sail broke the surface. It was somewhat elongated but looked almost like a truncated version of the deckhouse aboard the *Zumwalt.* The rest of the submersible followed. He couldn't see much, but he saw enough.

"Send out the whaleboat," the Captain ordered next. Then, turning to Jacques-Yves, he said, "Admiral, I'd like you and your staff to join me. Especially Lieutenant Bronskaya. I suspect we'll need her to translate."

* * *

In the boathouse below the flight deck, Jacques-Yves watched as powerful winches brought the inflatable craft back out of the water and into its cradle. Not long after that, the large hatch swung up to close with a loud, reverberating thud.

The two officers riding in the inflatable wore combination caps typical of Naval officers. They wore dark greenish-blue uniforms with gold accouterments: two Cyrillic letters "АФ" on each lapel and the usual shoulder boards of rank. For the senior officer, one outlined star above one narrow and one broad stripe. For the more junior, one bright solid star above two narrow stripes.

As the two officers stepped aboard, Jacques-Yves appreciated the full height of the senior man: 180 centimeters—no, *five foot ten*. This American Patriotic measurement system had something to recommend it, after all. Based as it was on human dimensions, it lent itself easily to estimation of a man's height, at least. His junior companion stood slightly shorter, at five foot eight.

The Command Master Chief, standing next to the Captain, blew the traditional three notes on his whistle.

The senior stranger waited, then said, "Permission to come aboard, Captain."

"Permission granted," said Captain Arthur. "I am Captain Arthur."

"And I," said the other, "am Counter-admiral—that is, Rear Admiral Kiril Vassilyevich Yevgenov of the Atlantic Fleet. With me is Senior Lieutenant of Fleet Infantry Andrei Dobrynin, my aide. I am doubly pleased to make your acquaintance at last."

"Oh? Can I really have such a reputation?"

"Well," said Yevgenov, smiling, "not so much you personally, as this ship, and what she represents. But … you, sir," he said, noticing Jacques-Yves for the first time. "Forgive my manners. Shouldn't I be talking to the OTC?"

Jacques-Yves smiled, "Have no fear, my good Rear Admiral," he said. "I'm not anyone's Officer in Tactical Command. Captain Arthur here is merely ferrying me to his home port. I am Rear-Admiral Jacques-Yves de Grasse, formerly of the United Systems Navy. These three other officers are my unofficial staff. I present Lieutenants Natalya Fyodorovna Bronskaya and Jacob Boddicker of the Revolutionary Forces for a Free Earth, and Commander Udayan Thakur of the Free Systems Navy."

Dan Thakur spoke first, "Pleased to meet you, Rear-Admiral," he said.

"I'll second that," said Jake Boddicker.

And then Natalya said, "*Vy by prednochli govorit' po-Russky?*"

The other officer, mouth agape, said, "*Vy govoritye po-Russky?*"

"*Da.*"

"*Vy na samom delye Russkaya?*"

"*Da,*" said Natalya, smiling broadly.

Yevgenov gasped. Then he smiled and said, "I think, perhaps, we should speak English for the benefit of our fellow officers." Then to Captain Arthur, he said, "Please to forgive that last. I was not expecting ever to meet a Russian again, outside of our society. As you will have guessed, we are mainly Russian, with a slight admixture of American. I see we all have much to learn from one another."

"I would certainly concur," said Jacques-Yves.

"And I," said Captain Arthur. "Let us continue this conversation in the wardroom. You'll find it much more comfortable. If you will all follow me, please?"

* * *

"This has been an extremely interesting development, to say the least, gentlemen and lady," Captain Arthur began. "For the benefit of our guests, we were already an effective alliance of three. Now, it would appear that a fourth party wants to join. So the time has come for some serious comparing of notes. Wouldn't everyone agree?"

Everyone nodded.

"Rear Admiral Yevgenov, you should definitely start. I had learned that the original Russian Federation died at about the time of the Re-Wilding … That is, the Great Climate War, and that something actually called 'Russian Soviet Federated Socialist Republic' replaced it, took its seat in the United Nations, and pledged its cooperation with the New World Order."

"And I can corroborate that last," said Jacques-Yves. "But perhaps you can tell us what happened from your perspective … And what exactly *is* the Atlantic Federation, and how comes it to be primarily Russian? Do we, in fact, see, in the Atlantic Federation, a continuation of the Russian Federation?"

"I regret that I must disclaim that honor," said Yevgenov. "For us, nothing can replace the *Russkaya Fyedyeratsiya* except a restoration of that polity on actual Russian soil. The *Atlantichyeskaya Fyedyeratsiya* began when a *very* small proportion of true Russians managed to escape in a small collection of submarines. They were the ballistic missile submarines *Dmitri Donskoy, Aleksandr Nevsky,* and *Prince Vladimir,* with the attack submarines *Gepard* and *Samara* for escorts."

Jacque-Yves nodded to Natalya and caught her knowing smile.

"Had we not had the *Dmitri Donskoy* with us, plus the *Aleksandr Nevsky* and *Prince Vladimir,* our civilization would have died. We decided to take all our wives with us—and most of them had to travel aboard the missile carriers. You cannot imagine the crowding, even aboard so large a vessel as the *Dmitri Donskoy* was."

"The *Dmitri Donskoy* was then the largest submarine still active, was it not?" asked Natalya.

"*Da* ... That is, yes. A member of our Typhoon class."

"Please go on, Rear Admiral," said Captain Arthur. "This is already an amazing tale."

"Well, our last President was aboard *Aleksandr Nevsky,* and gave the order to proceed to the American coast. Intelligence had reached us that the celebrated inventor Leon Vincent, in addition to his ventures in automobiles and aerospace, had founded a marine-science company. The last report said this company, Vincent Marine, had been building a city on the North American Continental Slope, just off the Charleston Bump. According to the report, its depth was to be more than two hundred meters—and before you ask, Captain, we were still using the metric system then."

"Wait, wait, wait," said Jacques-Yves. "Captain Arthur, did you know anything about such a venture?"

"Actually, Leon Vincent did mention it after General Crawford's men broke him out of Sing Sing," Arthur said. "He had hoped to find another source of rare-earth minerals to support his space exploration efforts. But come to think, by the time we managed to reconnect all the elements of what became the new United States, not one employee or dependent of a

Vincent Marine Company remained. It was as if that company never existed."

"That's because," said Yevgenov, "they joined us. That, of course, would come later."

"I can't wait to hear that part of the story. But please, take up where you left off."

"Well, to this day, we observe the anniversary of the day when—thank Bog—we found the undersea construction camp that was indeed building a city under water. At the time, the vessels serving that camp consisted of one surface freighter, one highly efficient surface worker transport, and six American Naval submarines—the fast-attack submarines *Seawolf* and *Connecticut* and the *Ohio*-class submarines *Alaska, Tennessee, West Virginia,* and *Wyoming*. Actually, at that moment, *Connecticut* was not with the project but was on reconnaissance. When she returned, she told the story of this very ship, its battle with its sister ship *Lyndon Baines Johnson,* and its joining with its other sister ship, *Michael Monsoor.* And then the tale grew more incredible. It seems those two ships made rendezvous with a ship of the Carnival Cruise Line—and from what *Connecticut* could see, nearly all its passengers were women."

"In fact, Rear Admiral," said Arthur, "they were the wives of the original crew of this ship and her sister ship."

"As everyone thought when *Connecticut* returned to make her report. So our President, ever the romantic that he was, made a proposition. A shore party would seek out, and make contact with, the spouses of those who had been working on the city project and the crews of the American submarines. We would use the surface worker transport, plus the *Dmitri Donskoy* and two of the Ohios, to rescue them. If we could do all that, the Americans would accept Russian leadership—which, our President pointed out, would actually be logical because we Russians were the best undersea shipwrights in the world and had built submarines that could dive deeper than any others."

"The original crew of USS *Trieste* might dispute that," said Arthur, smiling. "That is, if *Trieste* were still afloat."

"Well," said Yevgenov, smiling more broadly, "as you probably have guessed, a certain young infantry officer, Captain Grigoriy Aleksandrovich

Yevgenov, my direct ancestor, proved himself equal to the challenge. Hundreds of women joined us, and the Atlantic Federation was born."

"Starting with that one city?"

"Yes, the city we call *Atlantida*—Atlantis—to this day. If the project hadn't been ten years along when we first joined it, we might never have survived. But as it was, Atlantis was almost sustainable. With our crews joining in, we made it sustainable—and then immediately began scouting for more locations. We had to—Atlantis was bursting at its seams when the women joined it. But the Americans had proved the concept, and the Russian contingent supplied the know-how for building structures even deeper. We built our next city, which we named Chernava, at a depth of fifteen hundred feet. And before you ask, we took one suggestion from the Americans: abandon the metric system and adopt their customary system. Some of us, familiar with the measurement system we used in Tsarist days, tried to argue the matter—but, because few of us even remembered how to define the old units, they gave up. So I think you'll find that we use length, mass, and temperature units similar, or perhaps identical, to yours."

"Did you also, by any chance, redefine the units of electric current, amount-of-substance, and luminous intensity?" Jacques-Yves asked.

"After much discussion, yes, we did," said Yevgenov. "We soon realized that we would never again have access to the General Convention on Weights and Measures. And that, in any event, coherence demanded such a redefinition."

"We thought the same," said Arthur. "We'll have to compare notes to see whether our units are the same as yours."

"*I* have a question," said Jacques-Yves. It was definitely time to broach this. "Rear Admiral, you named six vessels of the United States Navy that took part in the Atlantis Project. I am something of a naval historian in my former society—and I was able to account for all but seven submarines that disappeared, besides this vessel, the *Michael Monsoor*, and five wooden vessels."

"We know about those," said Yevgenov. "We followed your little fleet to Australia."

"Ah, so it *was* you, or one of your fellow officers, who shadowed us," said Captain Arthur.

"That's for later," said Jacques-Yves. "For now, do you know anything about a submarine named *Jimmy Carter?*"

"A moment, Admiral," said Yevgenov. He turned to his aide. "Andrei," he began, then asked a question in rapid-fire Russian. The younger officer answered in the same language, accompanying it with gestures indicating vessels of two different lengths.

Finally, in Standard, Yevgenov said, "My aide informs me that the vessel you named was the third member of the *Seawolf* class—and considerably longer. No, Rear-Admiral, we have never seen him. You are saying you list him as 'still on patrol'?"

"That's exact."

Silence greeted those words and lasted for half a minute. Then Arthur said, "Jacques-Yves, are you sure about that? I mean, absolutely sure?"

"Jack," said Jacques-Yves, using the other's first name for the first time, "I have made it my affair—no, how do you say it—my *business* to research the entire naval history of Earth. For fifteen years, have I engaged in this research. One does need something to do with one's time, even if one runs a vineyard and winery. Naval history was, in fact, my passion before I even entered the Naval Academy. I am quite certain of my facts in this regard."

"And that means," said Yevgenov, "that we have a hazard on which we did not reckon."

"Kiril, I have great hope that your Fleet takes great care to watch out in case the United Nations decides again to field a Navy in the oceans of Earth."

"Of this much, I can assure you, Jacques-Yves. *Nothing* passes in these oceans without the knowledge of our Admiralty. But I shall certainly mention this in my next dispatch."

"Let us talk about something more pleasant for now. How deep can your Fleet dive today?"

"To the very bottom of the Atlantic—though we rarely venture into the Pacific, Indian, Arctic, or Southern Oceans. In fact, our society has, by now, expanded to twenty-two other cities on the continental slope of the southern United States, and the floor of the Sargasso and Caribbean Seas and the Gulf of Mexico, in addition to Atlantis and Chernava."

"Why the Gulf?"

"Petroleum, Jacques-Yves. As we learned how to build cities ever deeper, we built one next to the old Deepwater Horizon well, which we have reopened."

"Then you're already close to the Matagorda Inlet!" said Jack Arthur.

"Exactly. Our city of Novy Kh'yuston services the Deepwater Horizon well and exports petroleum to all our other cities. That is how we spotted your flotilla on its way to Australia. We have, in fact, had a watch on this ship since it left that port. Two of our submarines are in the Southern Ocean even now, watching the operations in that theater. One carries the name *Marlin*. The other is a ballistic missile submarine, like *Vladimir Putin*, which we have named *Yekaterina Velikaya*."

"So why haven't you contacted us earlier?"

"Perhaps," said Jacques-Yves, "the Atlantic Federation had to watch you in action, to learn whether to trust you. Is that not so, Kiril?"

"It is. But every now and again, a Mayor of Atlantis will propose to bore *into* the continental slope to try to reconnect with the American society that, according to my celebrated ancestor, simply retreated underground."

"Whoa," said Arthur, holding both palms up. "I wouldn't advise that, not without proper co-ordination. If you bore in any further north than the former Myrtle Beach, North Carolina, you're likely to run into the society that calls itself New Aztlán. But if you bore in from where I think you are, you could wind up connecting into someone's private dwelling cavern, and that wouldn't be pleasant for either side."

"All of which," said Jacques-Yves, "must wait. For now, we must all realize something important: we are all under threat. A definite, though delayed, threat from space, and a very likely threat from under the sea. If *Jimmy Carter* was never accounted for—and I repeat that this is the exact case—then she represents a threat. We must, in fact, assume that the United Nations will re-activate her."

"Would they preserve her that long, do you think?" asked Jack Arthur.

"Without a doubt, especially a ship that could dive to sixteen hundred feet. Simply bringing her out of drydock and placing her back into service would be ridiculously easy.

"But more to the point, gentlemen, and lady, this is definitely a long-term combat situation, now involving more than one vessel. Kiril, how many vessels accompanied you?"

"I came here with the two you know of: *Leopard* and *Vladimir Putin*."

"Will you place yourself and those two vessels under my command?"

"You talk like one having combat experience, so yes, of course."

"Jack?"

Captain Arthur took a deep breath, then said, "Yes."

"Very well," said Jacques-Yves, who suddenly felt like someone was draping a mantle on his shoulders. "For everyone's benefit," he went on, "I do indeed have combat experience. My experience is in outer-space combat, to be sure, but it is no less extensive for all that. I will now give you my history, and that of the two officers accompanying me so that you can better appreciate my experience—and the overall strategic situation.

"The United Systems began in earnest after the United Nations declared victory in the Great Climate War. It consisted at first of two systems: the United Nations of Earth—also known as Sol d, by the way—and the Planetary Federation of Tau Ceti, where lies Elfhaven—the home of the Elves. They are a bipedal race, like us, except that they stand an average of eight feet tall and are known for their pointed ears and other 'elfin' features—hence their name. The Elves had, in fact, been surveilling this Earth for over one hundred fifty years at least, and possibly longer, before making contact.

"They made this contact after Juan de Cuellar took off in a modified rocket ship belonging to Vincent Aerospace—and used one of their modified drilling rigs as a launch platform—and demonstrated faster-than-light travel. The Elves came to Earth and made common cause with the United Nations—and intervened in the Great Climate War. I'll let Captain Arthur describe that further, as I assume he's had a full briefing on that history."

Arthur nodded pointedly to acknowledge that.

Jacques-Yves went on to describe his service record and a history of the Metamorphic War. "And then," he said, "my service came to an abrupt end. My second officer—Lieutenant Commander Matthew Morrow USN—reported a strange finding in what is still known as Protected Wild Space on the continent you still call North America but which the United Nations has called Aztlán for centuries. Shortly thereafter, the Special Security Forces boarded my ship and took him into custody. That happened fifteen years ago. At the same time, I received orders to surrender my ship for decommissioning, and my officers and crew were scattered. I received a raise in rank and my retirement papers. For fifteen years, I have lived on my family's vineyard near Cadillac on the Garonne River. That is, until Natalya here came ashore to find me and recruit me.

"At this point, I'll let Captain Arthur tell you the history of his society, and all about what 'Protected Wild Space' means. In fact, every continent on Earth has its Protected Wild Regions—though the one in North America is more extensive than most, except perhaps for the Amazon Basin in South America or the jungles of Africa. But in the North American case, this was a punishment. Since Captain Arthur is most familiar with that, I shall let him continue from here."

Arthur gladly took the floor and held forth for five minutes, giving the history of the United States from the Great Climate War to the present day. "We have been sending hunting and foraging parties aboveground for centuries to acquire wild game, fruits, and grain and vegetable seeds to improve our diet," he said in conclusion. "But not until recently did we solve a particularly nagging mystery—namely where some of our children had been disappearing to, never to return. That's when Matthew Morrow came. He made contact with the Seventh Marine Armored Cavalry Squadron and personally led a raid on a pedophile game preserve, where he rescued quite a few children. In …"

Kiril Yevgenov, mouth agape, interrupted him. "How is that, you say?" he asked. "A *pedophile game preserve?* What exactly does that signify?"

"A facility where some very cruel adults released kidnapped children into a forest and allowed guests to hunt them down," said Captain Arthur with a look as if he had a bad taste in his mouth. "I will let you guess what happens to such a child upon capture."

"I have great hope," said the Russian admiral, grimly, "that your friend Captain Third Rank Morrow executed the men running that preserve. That installation sounds like the most disgusting thing of which I have ever heard."

"Well, he did, in fact, kill a lot of men, including almost the entire guard force and some high-profile guests, in that action. Actually, some of the children he rescued contributed to that, as I understand it. He also took several high-profile prisoners and *then* had to fight another action to bring them to justice in our courts and, where appropriate, in the United States Congress. Not that we routinely pass bills of attainder, you understand, but simply that some of those high-profile criminals were Members of Congress, to say nothing of the involvement of the President himself. So you don't have to say it: we have undergone a profound social upheaval.

"But that's nothing compared to the story Matthew Morrow told us about himself. I think I'll let Lieutenant Bronskaya brief you about that."

"Thank you, Captain," said Natalya. "Before I touch on that subject, I should share my own origins and service record." She then described her life on Novy Mir—a story that shocked both the Russian officers present, but especially Senior Lieutenant Dobrynin. When she described her apparent death-in-action on Rigel g, and waking up "wearing" a total-body prosthesis, the briefing stopped. Young Dobrynin blurted out a heartfelt diatribe in Russian. Natalya smiled at him, saying, "*Angliski, Angliski!*"

The young man took a deep breath, then said, "I apologize, sirs. But I … I can't believe it. I had wondered where you got that slight golden sheen to your skin. But I never imagined it was artificial! Do you mean to say that you are made of metal and plastic?"

"Yes," she said, smiling. "But my central nervous system is as organic as yours."

"How … how could anyone do this to you without your consent? How could you stand it?"

"That, young man, I owe to my friend, Lieutenant Commander—make that *Captain Third Rank* Morrow. You see, he is a 'cyborg,' like me."

"*Solkyn syn!* And did the same people do this to him?"

"Different people, but the same project," said Natalya. "That would be a long brief."

"I … I cannot believe it. This is the sort of cruel trick that Baba Yaga might play on someone!"

"Well, it *was* a trick, I'll give you that. We each are products of a project intended to build an army of cyborgs like us, to attack the *Amerikantskii*. Of course, they did not know of your Federation. In fact, no one knows that any Russians exist, beyond those who tried and failed to re-create the old *Sovyetskiy Soyuz* on Novy Mir."

"I must apologize for my young friend," said Kiril Yevgenov.

"Oh, please don't be embarrassed on my account," said Natalya. "The young man serves to remind me that I am still human, and for that, I thank him."

Dobrynin blushed crimson and held his peace.

"In any event," Natalya went on, "Matthew and I have a mission of revolution. Quite apart from any personal resentment either of us has, we simply do not care to see an army of half-human, half-machine entities like ourselves loosed on inoffensive targets. Matthew has taken overall command of what we call the Revolutionary Forces for a Free Earth but sent me on this special mission, which was first to contact Rear-Admiral de Grasse here and escort him to America. But which now has extended itself, now that we have discovered you. But you have two more persons from whom you should hear. Dan, you're next."

Dan Thakur described his service record, especially during the Metamorphic War—and then the history of the settlement of the Nine-o'clock Quadrant and the rebellion that had lately broken out there over a tax dispute. After he finished, Jake Boddicker described his Syndicate connections and how he hoped to renew them.

"So as you can see," said Jacques-Yves when all had spoken, "you three—Kiril, Andrei, and Jack—are servants of free societies on Earth, Commander Thakur is a not-so-covert agent of another, Natalya here is a direct revolutionary, Jake Boddicker is a one-time mercenary turned freedom fighter, and I am a recent defector. So we can all agree that we serve a common cause, which is—how do you say it, Captain Arthur—'liberty and justice for all.'"

"Agreed," said Arthur, smiling for the first time.

"But we also are in a dire strategic situation and an even more dire tactical one. We face a threat at sea—most likely under it—and a threat from space. Furthermore, we have a duty to protect at least two of our societies from detection."

"Which will be doubly difficult now," said Yevgenov. "The enemy, no doubt, know of each of our societies, but they do not know where we are based—or where *you* are based, Captain Arthur. Or at least we can hope they do not know this. And we ought to keep that secret from them as long as we can, even though it means we can expect no reinforcement."

"An excellent point," said Jacques-Yves. "Which brings me to my first order of business. Kiril, I want you as my Operations Officer."

"Thank you very much, Admiral. I will be glad to serve in that capacity."

"And I appreciate your service. Commander Thakur will serve as my Flag Secretary and Intelligence Officer. All reports, of any nature, concerning the detection of any enemy or any unknown vessel must go to him."

Yevgenov and Arthur both nodded in agreement.

"And Lieutenant Bronskaya will be my Flag Lieutenant."

Natalya inclined her head to the group.

"Lieutenant Boddicker's special expertise is in weapons development. He has already enhanced our anti-submarine capability. I will make him available to you, Kiril, to enhance the weapons of *Leopard* and *Vladimir Putin*. Please do not hesitate to ask."

Boddicker grinned his usual wolfish grin.

"I will not have a formal Chief of Staff. Instead, Rear Admiral Yevgenov will be second to me in line-of-command."

Yevgenov smiled and nodded.

"Now, I certainly remember that the Russian Naval deck rank structure is significantly different from the American—and even different from the rank structure to which I am accustomed. For everyone's benefit, Natalya, Dan, and I come from a naval tradition that derives from the British Royal Navy. Mr. Boddicker has agreed to work in that tradition. Let me assure you, Captain Arthur, and you, Kiril, that I have no desire to impose a uniform rank structure on any ship that has always operated on another. As to orders coming down from me, let's remember that the line of command flows from myself to Rear Admiral Yevgenov and then to individual ship's Captains. As long as we remember that, we should have no difficulty with naval etiquette. Does everyone concur?"

"Hear, hear," said Captain Arthur and Admiral Yevgenov.

"Now then, unless anyone has any further questions, I will adjourn this meeting—after which I would like Admiral Yevgenov, Senior Lieutenant Dobrynin, Commander Thakur, and Lieutenant Bronskaya to join me in my quarters."

Chapter 11

"**H**ere we are, gentlemen," said Jacques-Yves as he led the way into what was now definitely flag quarters. "Commander Thakur and Lieutenants Bronskaya and Boddicker are already familiar with these quarters, of course. Do either of you have any questions?"

"I see that this ship's crew celebrates *Christovym*, just as we do," said Kiril Yevgenov.

"If I comprehend that word correctly, yes, they do."

"You do not observe it?"

"In my society, that tradition is long since forgotten."

Kiril smiled. "But not entirely, no? You at least remember what it is."

"Well, to be more accurate," said Jacques-Yves, "we've begun to educate ourselves. Which reminds me: your calendar must be sixteen days behind that which this crew uses, no?"

"We adopted the Gregorian calendar when we formed the Federation. That is yet another idea we took from our American friends. In that year, we simply began our Fast of the Nativity thirteen days earlier than planned and thus, could synchronize exactly with the American Christmas and New Year. Actually, that was my ancestor's idea. He learned much from the women who took part in the Great Run to the Sea. Especially," he added, smiling slightly more broadly, "from one woman in particular who became my ancestress."

Jacques-Yves had to smile in his turn. "Yes," he said, "I can well imagine. But now, duty calls. If you'll all gather around this drafting table, we can begin."

Young Dobrynin's eyes bulged. "Is that a real drafting table that I see?" he asked.

"Yes, it is. This ship's Captain rather thoughtfully provided it. If I didn't know any better, I'd have guessed he knew he would have a guest on board with a fondness for antique maps and the like. He finally told me I share that fondness with his own commanding officer—or rather, his predecessor in command."

"Then Captain Second Rank Arthur is not the duly assigned commanding officer?"

"Ah, you caught that, did you? We must all adapt to circumstances that include lack of a channel of instant communication with our command authority, must we not?"

Both the Russian men nodded knowingly.

"Now then," said Jacques-Yves. "You see before you the chart of our current 'area of patrol,' for lack of a better term, in the Atlantic Ocean. Somewhere within—or more likely outside—this area is at least one enemy submarine. We do not know how capable she is, other than assuming that she has the same capabilities of the former USS *Jimmy Carter* SSN-23."

"Which would be formidable enough," said Kiril. "She was one of the original *Seawolves,* so she could dive to sixteen hundred feet. That might still be her limit—for if the United Nations really did preserve that vessel, they would not have had time to improve her. Of course, if they hadn't scrapped all their member Navies, they could have made improvements to the type, same as we made improvements to the original *Akula* class. But we can make no assumptions as to the industrial capacity of the United Nations, can we?"

"Actually, we can. I don't know how much your original intelligence service told you shortly before your people had to take flight. But the United Nations and Systems abandoned all farming, animal husbandry, and industry, apart from a device they call a 'printer' that can duplicate any object upon command. The United Systems does have a shipyard in orbit around the planet Sol e—that is, Mars—for space vessels only. In point of fact, the United Nations has not kept a wet-naval shipyard for three centuries."

"*Solkyn syn,*" said Kiril, softly. "How could anyone be so complacent?"

"In the supreme confidence that all your original vessels are indeed 'still on patrol,' that something called Russia was back in the fold of the New World Order, and that the United States of America no longer existed."

"One would think they learned differently from the Great Run," said Kiril.

"Maybe they assumed that the vessels your ancestor used, to take all those women off, are *also* 'still on patrol.' In any event, you are the first person to tell me any part of that tale."

"Truly?"

"Truly," said Jacques-Yves. "I look forward to hearing the rest sometime."

"It will be my pleasure to tell it to you—after we make our plans. For now: we must also assume that the enemy can see this ship as well—or at least see the wake she makes. In fact, that is all we could see, in addition to the forms of the wooden vessels that this ship and her sister ship escorted to *Avstraliya*. We do not completely understand how this ship could hide her physical form. But a ship can hide her form but not her wake."

"Still, the Americans can make detection slightly more difficult. But I take it you do *not* recommend continuing to port—yours or any American port."

"Definitely, *negativno*. We must assume this vessel makes a wake visible from space. The only reason that original flotilla made it to *Avstraliya* as they did was that they had the cleverness—and the steel—to steer on the fringes of a hurricane along the way. And one wonders why no one detected them in the Southern Atlantic Ocean, which does not have tropical cyclones or any storms remotely as violent."

"That's because no one was watching," said Natalya. "The United Nations Oceanographic and Atmospheric Administration does not even keep satellites to watch that part of the ocean, for the very reason you just cited, Admiral."

"And, unfortunately, we cannot use a similar ruse ourselves. For one thing, the tropical cyclone season is past. For another, we are much too far north for tropical cyclones."

"But perhaps, if we head further north," said Jacques-Yves, "we can make detection from orbit slightly more difficult."

"But surely the enemy have satellites in polar orbit?"

"They have, but not so many. And orbital insertion is inherently more difficult."

"Admiral," said Kiril, an ear-to-ear grin spreading across his face, "I think I have a solution."

"Please share."

"If we steer now toward Iceland, we can enter the Arctic Ocean, and specifically the Barents Sea, while the ice has not yet gathered to its full extent. This ship's cloaking device will render her invisible from any shore lookout. And the ice, while still navigable, will smother most of her wake. I am sure we can safely escort her through the Arctic Ocean toward *Alyeska*. But before we come near, our 'bogey' will come out on the hunt. And I am sure we can surprise her."

"Rather a drastic detour, don't you think?" asked Jacques-Yves. "Do I take it you have an idea where *Jimmy Carter* came to harbor?"

"No, Yakov-Ivo, that I have not. But the idea is to lure her in, no? And what better place to bring her to battle?"

"Perhaps. But afterward, we'll be seriously out of our way."

"Perhaps, Admiral," said Natalya, "but perhaps not."

"I beg your pardon?"

"The Americans, or so Matthew told me, were planning to breach the Great Circle Tube system when Matthew went on his last operation in America. And more than that, our highest-ranking prisoner confirmed that the Americans had indeed taken over the Rio-to-Ho-Chi-Minh Tube Line."

"*La vache!* Another thing that Ramón did not see fit to tell me."

"And who is this Ramón?"

"Vice-Admiral Ramón Ordoñez-Pizarro, Director of Naval Intelligence," said Jacques-Yves. "He came to see me shortly before Natalya showed up at my door. He told me of Matthew Morrow's revolution, but I see now that he told me not half of what he surely knew. But to your point, Natalya: do you want to say that we can contact the Americans from a point in the Arctic Ocean?"

"Yes, Admiral," said Natalya firmly. "It's a risky bet, but it might be the best we can manage."

Jacques-Yves stared at the chart for a few seconds—thinking about many battles in which such "risky bets" had made the difference between victory and defeat. Then he looked up. "Risk is the essential hazard of war, can we not all agree?" he asked.

Everyone answered in the affirmative.

"Natalya," he said, "call Captain Arthur. Let's get his input."

* * *

"You've got something there, Admiral," said the Captain. "Of course, Lieutenant Bronskaya could tell you as much about the breach of the Great Circle Tubes as I could. After all, she attended the same briefings. But what you really want to know is whether I'm willing to navigate in the Arctic."

"And are you?"

"Definitely. I'll show you—just a moment." He turned to the waiting yeoman, saying, "Please bring every hardcopy chart we have of the Arctic Ocean and, specifically, the northern coasts of Europe and Russia."

"Aye-aye, sir," said the petty officer, who saluted and left.

"Those charts will take time for him to pull," said the Captain. "But to your point, Admiral Yevgenov, those waters should still be navigable at this time of year. It'll be a near thing, of course. But that's all to the good—the ice will be just enough to muffle our wake but not enough to block us. And with the cloaking system, no one can see us onshore unless we want them to."

"It would certainly help, however, if the Americans could expect us."

"I've been thinking about that," Arthur said. "In the old days, this ship was equipped for satellite communications. And technically still is. I wonder whether your Flag Secretary could help adapt our systems for satellite surveillance."

"You mean, to 'hack' the satellite network?" Dan asked, his face lighting up with enthusiasm.

"That's exactly what I mean."

"I'd love that challenge. That could tell us directly what the enemy knows."

"And more than that," said the Captain, "if we can sniff out what those satellites can see, I'm sure the American Admiralty can. It would make sense for them to get right onto a thing like this. Anyway, we can try."

The yeoman returned then, bringing the charts. Captain Arthur selected the chart of the Barents Sea and spread it on the drafting table. After spending a minute looking it over, he said, "As I thought, Admirals. We round the coast of Norway; then, we take our chances with the icebergs. They'll never find us there. And very likely we'll see *Jimmy Carter* long before we get there."

"How so?"

"They won't *want* us to get into the Barents Sea. They'll do everything they can to stop us. And the only thing that will be able to, is that submarine."

"And what about another ship in orbit?" asked Kiril.

"As to that," asked Jacques-Yves, "your task force just showed the enemy that we can strike him, even from the sea, if he dares get close enough to strike us."

"There's one thing I still haven't figured out," said Arthur. "Why don't their ships simply have at us with DEW cannons?"

"Ozone, Captain," said Jake Boddicker. "You must have forgotten just how well your ozone layer protects you. That layer will reflect any coherent-light beam. You can't shoot through that layer with DEW weapons—only with missiles."

"Or meteors," said Arthur grimly. "That's how the Elves smacked us back in 2035. But none of us ever wondered why they hit us that way, and not with big ray cannons. We can hope they can't pull the meteor stunt twice."

"They can't," said Jacques-Yves. "By now, they've used them all up for mineral resources."

"You're kidding!"

"No, Captain, I assure you I do not joke about this. The major reason for sending a colony expedition to Proxima Centauri b—Berks' World, the world Matthew Morrow came from—is that they had already exhausted the iron and nickel from the Mavericks of the Solar System. Absolutely none are left.

"You do have a point: they could summon another ship to try to fire missiles at us. But if we move smartly, we'll be so close to shore that they won't dare. Apart from the radiation hazard, they don't want to risk further exposure."

"You do realize, I trust," said Kiril Yevgenov, "that you have just named another reason the United Nations would attack the Atlantic Federation. They don't have the mineral resources they once had. We do. And we are even now testing technologies to help us expand into the Pacific Ocean, to build colonies near enough to undersea volcanoes. Admiral, if they knew even half of this, we would be prime targets."

"Kiril," asked Jacques-Yves, "did these considerations occur to you when you joined battle against that orbiting warship just now?"

"A calculated risk, Yakov-Ivo. But one I would gladly take again. A chance perhaps to reclaim what we lost? To prove ourselves worthy of the heritage of Aleksandr Nyevskii and Tsar Pyotr? That's what impelled me to begin with. Now, after meeting a fellow Russian—and after meeting *you*—I am more confident than ever that I made the right choice."

Jacques-Yves blinked and turned to Natalya. Managing a smile, he said, "Well, Natalya, my new second-in-command has paid you a high compliment."

Natalya smiled broadly. *"Bolshoye vas spasibo,"* she said.

"Vy eto zasluzhili," said Kiril.

Out of the corner of his eye, Jacques-Yves spotted Andrei Dobrynin bracing his shoulders—and blushing again. What could that signify? Time to draw the subject back to the affairs at hand.

"Then we have decided," he said. "We set a course for the Barents Sea, by way of Iceland. The next question becomes, how does each of us get there?"

"If I may suggest, Admirals," said Arthur, "I think the submarines should travel separately from this ship. They're going to be looking for us and will assume the submarines are following below us. In fact, there's no reason for us to stay together, so as long as we agree on a meeting place, the enemy need never know where our undersea assets are."

"You would risk navigating alone?" asked Kiril. "After what almost happened to you?"

"Risk is my business, Admiral," said Arthur. "As you pointed out, your risk is greater. Furthermore, I would never expect you to communicate. Communication always risks detection."

"And I take your point," said Jacques-Yves. "Nevertheless, we follow prearranged courses so that each of us can seek out the other if we catch one echo of that enemy submarine."

"I don't entirely like that last, Admiral," said Arthur. "But it does have one thing going for it: we'll be able to search a wider area for that sub as we go."

"Just so. Kiril, what course will you follow?"

"We follow the Mid-Atlantic Ridge to within sight of Iceland. After we pass two seamounts southwest of the Reykjanes Peninsula, we turn toward Norway."

"In that case," said Captain Arthur, "I recommend this ship head toward Norway—with just enough zig-zagging to bring us near the Norwegian coast in as much time as our friends will take."

"*D'accord*," said Jacques-Yves. "Kiril, how many days will you require for your passage?"

"Six days," said Kiril. "We could make it faster in an emergency, but we would prefer not to. We … That is, I am about to reveal something that must not leave these quarters."

"You have that assurance," said Jacques-Yves.

Kiril smiled a little more, then said, "Our civilization has perfected the ultimate in silent propulsion: the magneto-hydro-dynamic drive."

"We deduced as much," Arthur said. "Though you can thank Admiral de Grasse and his staff for recognizing it first."

"The more important consideration," said Jacques-Yves, smiling in turn. "is that the *Jimmy Carter* will *not* have this kind of drive."

"Let's hope not," said Arthur. "As careless as the UN obviously was to stand down all the navies of their member States, I still don't like to make a war plan that depends on a stupid enemy."

"Fools are neither sown nor reaped; they appear by themselves," said Natalya.

Kiril burst out laughing. "How true!" he said. "I take it you don't find this lapse so incredible?"

"I do not. Sir."

"Besides, this is the best plan we have," said Jacques-Yves. "Kiril, what is your best speed with this drive?"

"Twenty knots, Yakov-Ivo. With propellers, we could move twice as fast in an emergency."

"So—we will agree upon an interim destination." Jacques-Yves looked closely at the Barents Sea chart, and at the northern fjords of Norway near its boundary with the Atlantic Ocean. He pointed decisively at the longer inlet. "There," he said. "Just at the mouth, in case we must abruptly take refuge inland. Does anyone have any further questions?"

Everyone present shook their head, "No."

"*D'accord.* Commander Thakur, start working on breaking into the satellite network. Admiral Yevgenov, Lieutenant Dobrynin, you should return to your ship and depart. Lieutenant Boddicker, you've seen some of the weapons our new friends carry. If you can advise them, now's the time. Captain Arthur, I'll ask you to work with Commander Thakur on the satellite-intercept project."

"Will do."

"In that case, you are dismissed. Natalya, please remain."

Arthur and Thakur left first and were already talking about where to begin. The last words Jacques-Yves heard from either man was the name of Senior Chief Information Technician Barry Sutton. The two Russians—Atlantians—whatever they chose to call themselves—left next. Jacques-Yves caught something in the older man's attitude toward the younger. *Discipline,* he told himself. *That young man will hear a stern lecture about professionalism; I shouldn't wonder.* Jake Boddicker left with them.

"You're worried about Andrei, are you not?" asked Natalya as soon as the door closed.

"Yes, as a matter of fact," said Jacques-Yves. "And not only him, but you, too. After all, you'll likely be working together again the next time we can all meet. Will that present a problem?"

Natalya laughed, "Not for me, I assure you, Admiral," she said. "But I worry about him, too. I know when a man has a crush on me."

"Pardon me for asking, but are all young Russian men as impetuous as this young man seems to be?"

"No more nor less than other young men," said Natalya. "But they take concepts like love and chivalry very seriously. Happily, they also take their duty equally seriously. Admiral Yevgenov will take him in hand, I'm sure."

"And how can I help?"

"You already are helping," she said. "Andrei obviously respects you as well as his own superior. He will not challenge your authority in any way. He will treat you as he might have treated my own father, had he lived."

"How *do* you feel about coming back into contact with Russian culture?" he suddenly asked.

And now Natalya smiled more broadly. "Despite this little problem," she said, "I feel happier than I thought possible. Andrei and his admiral remind me of a Russia that once was, and that I had thought dead. Hearing the tale of the finding of Atlantis, and the Great Run to the Sea—it's like something out of a Sergei Eisenstein movie. Even to the name of one of the original submarines—did you catch it? Aleksandr Nevsky. The man who drove German and Swedish invaders out of Russia in the twelfth century of the Common Era."

"And Prince Vladimir?"

"Ah, yes. Vladimir the Great. He, it was, who chose Christianity over all other faiths."

"Really? I did not know that the original Soviets would celebrate a man like him."

"Oh, but the submarine that bore his name was a product of post-Soviet Russia," Natalya explained. "That other Vladimir, whose name you heard today, commissioned that vessel."

"Vladimir Putin," said Jacques-Yves. "Easily the most controversial head-of-state Russia ever had. The United Nations mentions him only to condemn him."

"Yes, and that is supremely ironic because he was once a ranking officer in the Committee for State Security in the old Soviet regime. How soon people forget. An interesting man, for an interesting and pivotal time." Then she turned more serious as she said, "Truly, Admiral, I have high hope the Atlantic Federation has a man like Putin in command of it today."

"Let us hope their situation does not become as dire as *that*," said Jacques-Yves. "I'm more interested in whether our new acquaintances have what it will take. Though truly, I think they have. Admiral Yevgenov spoke of the steel of that tiny remnant of the United States Navy—including five wooden vessels—using a hurricane for concealment."

"If they respect 'steel,' as they put it," said Natalya, "I think we can have reasonable hope that they have it themselves."

The boatswain's whistle sounded again. Jacques-Yves got up, crossed to the intercom panel, and touched the button. "Yes?"

"Admiral, this is Captain Arthur," said the voice from the speaker. "Our two Russian friends have disembarked. We'll recover the gig after they have boarded their vessel, and then we can be on our way."

"*Bon.* As soon as your boat is secured, follow the agreed-upon course."

"Aye-aye, Admiral."

Chapter 12

"**W**e left Timor just in time, I'd say," said Admiral Jones. "The winds were just what we needed to cross into the Java Sea. Had we waited, the winds would have been worse than contrary, and we'd be contending with that cyclone by now."

Matthew Morrow looked again at the chart on the drafting table. He was looking at a small weight his friend had placed on the chart to show where the little fleet was moving through the Java Sea toward Borneo. "And how long to Vietnam, would you estimate?" Matthew actually had his own estimate, but whatever else he was, he was not a seaman. Ronald Jones was.

"Six days, Matthew," said Jones after a few seconds. "Assuming our luck holds with the winds. We need to pass west of Borneo, and it's going to be hit or miss with the winds. In fact, without these islands, we'd be in a dead flat calm right now. But after we cross the equator, we take the opposite risk."

"I assume you are using our LCG as a storm scout?"

"Absolutely. Any pair of eyes makes a difference."

Just then, both men heard a knock on the flag-quarters door.

"Come in," said Jones.

The door opened, and a yeoman, wearing undress whites, came in. "The Captain's respects, Admiral, Field Marshal," he said. "He thought you ought to see this. Report from Captain Blakely aboard *Magpie*." He handed Jones a clipboard with a small sheaf of papers on it.

Jones signed the sheet on top, then detached it and handed it back to the yeoman, keeping the other sheets. "Carry on, sailor," he said.

"Aye-aye, sir," said the yeoman, who saluted and left.

Matthew started to read the report, then remembered he had company. "The usual salutations," he said. "Andrew notes that we're passing out of satellite range for cybernetic networking, at least through the usual channels. He's working on a way to restore connectivity without arousing suspicion."

"Does that have anything to do with all these islands being deserted?"

"That it does. I would also expect the powers-that-be to harden the force-field generators in these parts. My virus didn't get much beyond Timor and New Guinea."

"Which virus was that?"

"The one I used to take down all the force fields on Australia. Andrew knows that eventually, we'll have to take down all the force fields that guarded Java, Sumatra, Borneo, and all the other islands of Indonesia. I'm going to let that ride. Best not to let the authorities know too much … Ah. Here's the part that concerns us most."

"Storm warnings?"

"Yes. Three of them."

Jones whistled, "That's pretty active, even for this basin," he said. "Where are they?"

"Here," said Matthew, handing over a single sheet of paper.

Jones looked the sheet over. "Well," he said, "the bottom two will stay well out of our way. One's headed for the Russian Far East, the other toward the Bering Straits. She'll dissipate long before she gets there." Jones stepped closer and pointed to the top listing. "This," he said, "is the problem."

Matthew took the paper back and read more closely. "Maximum sustained winds, one five zero knots."

"And very wide, too. But that's not the half of it. She's a straight runner. Headed straight for Vietnam."

"And when will that affect us?"

"On our present course and speed, when we round Borneo, we'll be directly in its path."

Matthew glanced at the page again. "Moving roughly westward at thirty knots, I see," he said.

Jones nodded grimly. "This ship could outrun her, maybe," he said. "But *not* our wooden vessels. They just need to stay out of her way. I wouldn't even want to try to outrun a typhoon in this vessel. You may or may not have heard, but one of the deep concerns about vessels of this class was that their extreme tumblehome configuration is very unstable. It's an open question whether this ship or *Constitution* would do better in that kind of rough weather."

"But we might not have a choice," said Matthew. "I've just finished the rest of the report. Andrew has intercepted a general intelligence watch officer's alert. It would appear that the space missile cruiser USS *Courteous* spotted your old ship, the *Zumwalt*, in the North Atlantic. She fired a missile, then used retros to go into a forced geosynchronous orbit—at low-orbit altitude—and fired another missile."

Jones winced, "Did *Zumwalt* get hit?"

"No," said Matthew. "This is the strange part. A ballistic missile submarine that strongly resembled a submarine of the last two ballistic-missile classes in the Russian Maritime Fleet fired a brace of missiles that second time. One of them destroyed the incoming missile. The other five continued into orbit and destroyed *Courteous*. Disabled her engines, and then she dropped like a meteor. Straight into the Atlantic, near the equator."

Jones whistled again. "And what does that mean for us?" he asked.

"It means we can expect to deal with a threat from orbit ourselves," said Matthew. "The Admiralty will desperately try to find us and destroy us."

"And why do you say we might not have a choice with that typhoon?"

"We might need to take cover under her clouds."

"Are you sure you want to risk that?"

"You did it before, Ronald."

"Yes, I did. With a hurricane that packed max sustained winds no stronger than eighty knots. That monster northeast of Borneo is almost twice as strong and could get even stronger if she doesn't pass over some land."

"Well," said Matthew, crossing to the chart table and looking at the chart, "there are the Philippines."

"They might slow her forward speed, but not her winds. But wait. You said a minute ago that a ballistic-missile submarine surfaced near *Zumwalt* and fired missiles into space. Did I hear you right?"

"You did. That is a complete mystery to the Admiralty. In point of fact, no one is supposed to have submarines of any kind, especially not capable of firing hypersonic sea-launched ballistic missiles." Matthew looked up at his friend. "This *could* work in our favor. The Admiralty will want to focus on the Atlantic."

"You don't really believe that, do you, Matthew?" asked Jones. "After that operation you ran to liberate Australia? And with our Marines investing the Great Circle Tubes? No, they won't overlook us. Much as I hate to contemplate it, we'll need a plan to use that typhoon for cover."

"Have you one?"

"I'll get on it right away. And I'll also need more intelligence." He crossed to the intercom and keyed a combination. Both men heard the voice of a radioman answer, "Yes?"

"This is the Admiral. Send that yeoman back to me. I'll have several orders for him."

"Aye-aye, sir."

Jones clicked off, then turned to face Matthew. "I was just thinking," he said. "All the way down to Australia, our sonar listeners kept hearing 'ghosts' of some kind. None of us could make any sense out of them, and no one made contact with us. But that report you just read makes me think we were missing something."

"Very likely you were," said Matthew. "And I'd like to believe that something was friendly, though, at the moment, I can't imagine who it might be if it's not your Navy."

"I assure you, it isn't."

"Were your sonar operators still hearing 'ghosts' right before or after the Battle of Sydney?"

"I seem to recall something along that line."

"Then, if I may suggest, Ronald, have your sonar operators stay fully alert in case those 'ghosts' come back. Friendly or hostile, we have to know where they are."

"Good point."

The yeoman came back to the flag quarters. "The Admiral sent for me?" he asked.

"Yes. Take this down. First, my compliments to Captain Aaronson and have him tell the sonar watch to keep a sharp ear out for any out-of-the-ordinary sounds, 'sonar ghosts,' whatever they call them. Second, my compliments to Captain Blakely aboard *Magpie* and tell him to watch that monster typhoon very closely—the one that's headed for Vietnam. Let's see—we'll assign the name *Yolanda* to her. This brings me to my third order: pass this storm warning to all captains. Violent typhoon, designated Yolanda, max one-minute winds one five zero knots, last reported position one zero north, one three five east, heading two seven zero at speed three zero knots. Updates will go out as available. All ships mind her location, steer clear, and make all preparations for rough weather. Is that clear?"

"Yes, sir," said the yeoman, who repeated the orders.

"You got it," said the Admiral. "Carry on."

The yeoman saluted and left.

"Well, now that we've settled those questions—at least for now—that still leaves the question of who those 'ghosts' might be."

"Well, according to this report, even the Admiralty doesn't know that," said Matthew. "But they're clearly afraid of them. Andrew has intercepted enough chatter to know that."

"I should think so, if they actually shot one of your former Navy's ships out of orbit. The question still is, why?"

"That," said Matthew, "we'll have to wait to find out until we get back into cyber-network range. Until then, we concentrate on our own operation."

* * *

Diary entry, 18 December 2417, or MJDN 204201, 0700 hours local time. Field Marshal Matthew Morrow recording.

Our fleet has rounded the western shore of Borneo and is on direct course toward Saigon and the Mekong River Delta. My friend Andrew Blakely appears to be enjoying his role of "storm chaser." He reports that

Typhoon Yolanda has actually picked up speed, however illogical that might sound, considering how fast she was traveling when we first detected her. He also confirms that Yolanda is also on a direct course for Saigon and will likely cause a nine-foot "storm surge."

As I look at the now re-wilded, hence totally deserted, shores of Borneo, I can only imagine the devastation a typhoon like Yolanda would wreak four hundred years ago when thriving nation-states shared Borneo and the twenty thousand islands in this part of the Northwest Pacific Basin ...

Matthew abruptly paused his silent dictation as he heard the intercom chime. He sent a silent command, both to his own secondary memory and to the ship's mainframe, to save his work and close the file. Then he looked up at the door and said, "Enter."

A Marine opened the door and took one step in. "Admiral Jones' respects, sir," he said. "He requests you join him on the bridge."

Matthew reached for his combination cap and put it on. "Right with you," he said. "Let's go."

The Marine led him to a hoist, which took them up to the top deck— the bridge. On the way, Matthew noticed that the ship was pitching and rolling more than usual. *Typhoon Yolanda? Or another storm?*

When the hoist door opened, a master-at-arms snapped to attention, saying, "Field Marshal on the bridge!" Several men started to rise from their stations.

"As you were," said Matthew. He crossed to where he saw Ronald bending over an electronic chart display. When Ronald saw him, he saluted. Matthew returned the salute. "Report," he said.

"You noticed the ship is laboring a little worse than before?"

"Yes, I did."

"Typhoon Yolanda," said the Admiral grimly. "We rounded Borneo at exactly the wrong time. She's in our area and on course to intercept."

"Then I assume you are already plotting a course to evade the storm."

"We were," said Jones. "But now we've got another problem. Our sonar ghosts seem to have solidified."

"If I take your meaning," said Matthew, "we definitely have a submarine pursuing us."

"You got it. I recommend we try to contact her."

"Go ahead," said Matthew. "She obviously knows where we are, and I want to know who she is."

"Thank you," said the Admiral, who then nodded to the middle-height officer wearing four stripes on his shoulder boards. This officer was Captain Aaronson, who commanded this ship.

Aaronson turned to the sonar operator. "Range, bearing, and depth of target?" he asked.

"Bearing two seven zero relative, range three double-oh yards," said the operator. "Periscope depth."

Aaronson picked up a push-to-talk microphone and pushed the talk button. "Lookouts, conn," he said. "What do you see?"

"Conn, port beam," came a voice over a loudspeaker. "One periscope, off our beam, about three double-oh yards away."

"Pass the word to the signal watch. Flash 'Unidentified vessel, this is USS *Michael Monsoor*. Identify yourself and state your intentions.'"

"Aye-aye, sir."

The Captain turned to the Admiral, "Shall I launch the helicopter?" he asked.

"Negative. The ship is laboring too badly for that."

Then they all heard another voice over the loudspeaker—a man's voice, in the baritone range, speaking seemingly broken English with an accent Matthew recognized at once: Russian. *A Russian? Here in the Northwest Pacific?*

"USS *Mikhail Monsoor*, here Atlantic Federal Ship *Marlin*. We have detected an apparent warship in low Earth orbit. He may be preparing to attack. Suggest you steer due north and make best possible speed."

"What the … Captain Aaronson, I want to talk to those guys myself," said Jones.

The Captain turned to the radio operator, who nodded. Now the Captain picked up a telephone handset and handed it to the Admiral.

Jones put the handset to his ear and said into the mouthpiece, *"Marlin,* this is Rear Admiral Ronald Jones, United States Navy, commanding Task Force One. Why should we trust you, and why should we steer into the path of a violent typhoon?"

Matthew, with his extra-sensitive hearing, heard the spirited reply in the earpiece. He could barely make out the words: "Rear Admiral, this is your only chance! If you can get under the cloud cover, the orbiting ship can't see you. But you must hurry!"

Jones turned to Matthew—and Matthew read the question in his eyes.

Matthew was about to nod when another voice sounded over the loudspeakers—Andrew Blakely's voice. "Admiral Jones!" he fairly shouted. "There's a warship in orbit—a heavy cruiser. He's slowing for a forced stationary low orbit and is aligning to fire missiles at the surface!"

"Radio," said Jones, "acknowledge that last." Then he realized he was still holding the handset. He put it back to his head and said, "Very well, *Marlin,* we show the same. Out." He put the handset back into its cradle, then seized the push-to-talk mike again. He started shouting orders into it: "Signal all ships! New course zero zero zero, best possible speed!" He put the microphone back into its bracket and nodded to Captain Aaronson.

That officer turned to another officer wearing lieutenant's bars. "Sound general quarters," he ordered. "Hands to battle stations, and secure for rough weather."

"Aye-aye, sir." Soon after that, a loud, repeating gong sounded throughout the ship. Matthew saw the bridge watch putting on helmets and life jackets. A Marine handed him a set, which he put on—a purely perfunctory exercise for him, but he must set the example.

"All stations manned and ready, sir," said the Lieutenant, now wearing a helmet with two bars on it, and the legend "ASST. GUNS" below this.

"Very well, Mr. Kelvin," said the Captain. "Pass the word to radar and lookouts to keep a sharp eye for incoming missiles. Helm, make your course zero zero zero. Ahead twenty knots."

"Aye-aye, sir," came two acknowledgments. Other than that, no one said a word for the next five minutes. Matthew could feel the tension, even if he *was* a cyborg. He had always sensed the tension of battle in his days aboard *Bonaventure VI*. Then after Dr. Girard had removed his emotion-blocking chip, he could feel it, too. *Fighting on land with air support was never like this. At sea, as in space, your weapons platform is also your world. And in space, you rarely had to contend with anything like rough weather.*

"Conn, weather," said another petty officer at a station forward and to starboard. "Barometer's down, sir. Twenty-nine seventy and falling. Winds out of north-northwest, one five knots."

"Very well," said the Captain, who reached for the push-to-talk mike again. "Lookouts, conn. What's the sky look like?"

"Conn, port bow. We're moving into some dense clouds, with a lot of rain."

"Very well," the Captain lowered the mike and turned to the assistant gunnery officer, "Mr. Kelvin," he said, "reduce speed to one zero knots. Maintain course."

"Aye-aye, sir."

Then Ronald Jones said, "Signal all sailing vessels to reef sail at discretion."

"Aye-aye, sir."

"Weather, conn," said the Captain, "Report."

"Barometer twenty-nine fifty and falling. Winds now out of the northwest at two zero knots."

The Admiral said, "Signal all ships. New course zero niner zero. Best possible speed."

"Aye-aye, sir," said the assistant gunner—and now Matthew understood. This officer was functioning as the officer of the deck.

"Helm, right full rudder," said the Captain. "Steady on zero niner zero. All ahead two-thirds."

"Aye-aye, sir."

Then a voice from a station forward and to port shouted, "Conn, radar! Missile contact one eight zero absolute, altitude two five triple-oh! Incoming!"

"Sound collision!" cried the Captain. "Hard left! All ahead flank!"

"Signal a ninety-degree turn to port!" cried Admiral Jones.

Matthew grabbed the nearest stanchion to keep from falling over to starboard as the ship took the tight turn.

Then the sky around them lit up almost blindingly.

"Incoming missile destroyed," said the radar operator.

The Captain picked up his microphone again. "Lookouts, conn," he said. "Report anything at all."

"Conn, stern. Nothing but clouds and wind-driven rain. The wind is coming from our port beam, I'd say. The afterglow from that missile detonation has already faded … Wait! Correction! Fireball taking a dive straight into Borneo … Holy …! It just slammed right into that island! There's a nine-foot mini-tsunami headed straight for us!"

"Signal all ships! Course zero zero zero! Maximum speed!"

"Helm, you heard him! Course zero zero zero! All ahead flank! All hands, brace yourselves!"

Matthew held on to the stanchion. Without thinking, he looked dead astern and saw the big wave bearing down on the ship.

Then he felt the ship lifting him up. *Why, it's just like that amusement-park ride I took back in south-central Virginia—the Intimidator!*

Then the wave had passed, but now the ship was laboring harder than ever.

"Weather, conn," said the Captain, "Report."

"Barometer twenty-nine twenty-five. Winds two seven zero at three zero knots."

"Signal all ships," said Jones. "New course zero niner zero. Best safe speed. Captain Aaronson."

"Yes, sir?"

"Take your damage report as soon as you can. We'll hold this course until the winds start to calm down. When the wind speed slackens to ten knots, let me know."

"Aye-aye, sir."

"In the meantime, signal all ships to report damage and casualties."

"Aye-aye, sir."

Matthew looked out to starboard. In the distance, he made out the north shore of Borneo—and one very large jungle fire.

"I could almost wish that typhoon was running on a path a little bit more to the south," said Ronald Jones, coming to stand beside Matthew. "Except that we would then be right in her path. But I so hate to see a good forest—or jungle—burn out of control."

"I'm more concerned about how that could have happened," said Matthew. "Do you really believe that one submarine destroyed a ship in low Earth orbit? And with a name like *Marlin*, she's a fast-attack submarine."

"I take your point, sir," said Jones. "But there's one way to find out. Captain Aaronson, I'd take it kindly if your radio man could signal *Magpie*. I want to talk to Captain Blakely right away."

"Aye-aye, sir. Sparks, you heard. Raise *Magpie* and tell them the Admiral wants to talk."

"Aye-aye, sir," said the radioman. As Matthew watched, he pressed several buttons, then said into his microphone, "*Magpie,* this is *Monsoor.* Admiral Jones calling for Captain Blakely. Over."

A few seconds later, Andrew's voice carried on the loudspeakers. "Blakely here," he said. "The Admiral is calling?"

Jones looked toward the radioman, who nodded. Then Jones raised his voice slightly and answered, "That's right, son. This is the Admiral speaking. Full report."

"Well, you're actually in a good spot to get away from the center of the typhoon and still stay under cover. As to what just happened: six hypersonic ballistic missiles launched out of the sea. One of them took out the missile aimed at you. The other five slammed into that warship and dropped her right out of orbit. She had slowed to station-keeping in low planetary orbit, which is always a dangerous thing to do. Either her captain didn't get the memo about the disaster that befell that other cruiser over the Atlantic, or it never occurred to him that whichever navy deployed one ballistic-missile submarine might be deploying another, in these waters. In any event, that ship crashed straight into Borneo, and I think we just confirmed that alert we intercepted."

"Your evaluation?"

"Well, maybe it's not my place to make one, but…"

"Belay that, son. It certainly is. The Field Marshal has briefed me fully on your record. Now out with it."

"Yes, sir. Well, sir, I evaluate that the Admiralty has yet another enemy—an undersea enemy. And one capable of operating in at least two theaters at once. If—that is, I advise you to respect them, and to befriend them if you can."

"Well, that sounds sensible enough. The Field Marshal and I will be considering it right now. In the meantime: you will signal us *at once* if you detect *anything* that might indicate another space-born threat. Is that clear?"

"As crystal, sir."

"Carry on." He made a throat-cutting gesture to the radioman, who threw another switch. "We're off, sir," he said.

"Well, Matthew," said Jones, "you overheard. There are two subs out there, without a doubt—one fast-attack and one that carries ballistic missiles that can strike in low-Earth-orbital space. Matthew, I certainly don't want to make enemies of that other naval force. And did you catch how else they identified themselves?"

"Yes. 'Atlantic Federal Ship.' But I never received any briefing on any 'Atlantic Federation.'"

"Me neither. But there's a legend in my family about an incident that happened toward the end of the Re-Wilding War. Of course, 'legend' means 'rumor' in a historical context. Well, according to that legend, the great inventor, Leon Vincent, had another project going, one that *hasn't* continued in United States society. I've never been able to find out what it was. But the legend says that this project would have a large number of men separated from their wives and children for months at a time. And then, after the Re-Wilding War broke out, an armed force came ashore in southeast Florida—and gathered all those women and children together and took them away. Somewhere. No one ever found out where. But you want to know what the strangest part of that legend was?"

"What?"

"That armed force was Russian. Russian Naval Infantry."

"Russian … yes, and maybe we have our answer."

"How so?"

"Didn't you catch the accent of the voice from that submarine?"

"Well, it's an accent I never heard before, but…"

"A Russian accent."

"No…?"

"No question," said Matthew. "That could have been Natalya Bronskaya's cousin speaking to you."

"But how on Earth…!" Jones paused.

"We need to reconnect with the network as fast as we can," said Matthew. "And it's going to be difficult. That typhoon is very powerful. We're fortunate that we didn't have to travel any closer to the center than we did. When she makes landfall in Vietnam, she's going to wreak havoc."

"Yes, I know," said Jones. "We'll make our own landfall, all right. And then have to fight a pitched battle with a humanitarian disaster all around us. I'm not looking forward to that."

Just then, Captain Aaronson walked up to them. "Pardon me for interrupting, sirs," he said, "but the winds have slackened as you predicted, Admiral."

"Good. Signal all ships to run before the wind wherever it leads. A wide and gradual left turn. When our heading matches our bearing for Saigon, we steady up on that course and sail straight in."

"Aye-aye, sir."

Chapter 13

Jacques-Yves was writing in a paper ledger that he used for a log. Senior Chief Barry Sutton had wondered why he hadn't cared to type or speak his log into the ship's computer. But after an hour of diligent search, he had found this ledger left over from the days, centuries ago, when Officers of the Deck would keep handwritten logs. In fact, Sutton had been amazed to learn that he was serving under an OTC who actually practiced the lost art of cursive handwriting!

"*Mardi 19 décembre 2417,*" he wrote in French. "Ireland lies well to our east, and we hope to pass Scotland tomorrow as we continue toward Norway. Morale on this ship is as high as ever, but I also detect a small degree of tension among officers and enlisted as we approach our intended *rendez-vous* off the northernmost coast of Norway, where we shall enter the Barents Sea. Certain members of the crew derived no small satisfaction on knowing that their ship had actually detected at least one submarine that is one of the quietest ever built.

"We also are receiving intercepts from the United Nations satellite network, now that Commander Thakur and Chief Sutton have succeeded in breaching it. Of course, we never expected to intercept reports of popular uprisings. But we *have* intercepted reports of certain areas of Sol d going dark and other areas becoming physically inaccessible. Lieutenant Bronskaya concludes that the Great Circle Tube Lines are thoroughly invested with American troops. This seems to have affected civilian morale, especially in the polity known as *le Nouvel Aztlán*, although why the Americans don't seem to have bothered invading that polity yet, is difficult to imagine…"

A knock sounded on his door. "*Entrez,*" he said. Then he realized he had spoken that order in French—and yet the order was obeyed. Obviously, this crew had grown used to him.

It was Natalya—and she seemed more eager than usual to see him.

"Good morning, Lieutenant," he said. He checked his wrist chronometer. Six hours and seven of the morning! "You're up early, and I notice you rather scrupulously guard your sleep cycle. What brings you to me at this hour?"

"Something you're going to find difficult to believe," she said. "But, Admiral, this is something you urgently need to know."

"Then, by all means, please share."

"Admiral, do you remember my telling you about the nanobots that Matthew carried?"

"And gave to you. Yes, I do remember. Is there a fault with them now?"

"To the contrary. Admiral, I did not tell you more than a fraction of what these nanobots can do. Let it suffice that they can facilitate telepathic communication between any two intelligent beings who possess them in sufficient numbers."

"Are you telling me that you are in contact with Matthew?"

Natalya briefly wore a long face. "Oh, how I wish I could stay in touch with him," she answered. "I miss him terribly. But I just made contact with someone else."

"What! But that's impossible. Surely no one else aboard this ship is so equipped."

"Close range does not require itself, Admiral. What *does* self-require is closeness to network adapters and uplink hardware, including the cybernetic communication facilities of this ship. That goes double now that we have breached the satellite network. Yesterday I thought I heard a new voice in my head—and when I realized where it might come from, I asked Chief Sutton to enhance my quarters so that I could use the ship's digital antenna."

"I do have hope," he said sternly, "that you or he cleared this with Captain Arthur. I esteem him far too highly to presume upon his hospitality by failing to consult him on such a matter."

"Chief Sutton gave me the impression that Captain Arthur has cleared you—and by extension, Dan and me—for anything."

"Generous of him," said Jacques-Yves. "*Very* generous indeed. Do I take it you confirmed your impression?"

"Yes! And you'll never guess whom I was able to contact."

"Pray don't keep your Admiral in suspense, Lieutenant."

"Ayelet Cohen!"

"I have fear that I do not know such a person."

"She's no other than the Lady of the Lamps!"

Involuntarily, Jacques-Yves shot to his feet, barely keeping his hold on his ledger and stylus. Then he said, slowly, "Are you absolutely positive?"

"Absolutely. I'd know her anywhere. We've met if you remember my telling you."

"I remember your making a vague suggestion that you knew who she was. You have met her? Before she made her suicide run … Wait, wait, wait. She didn't commit suicide, after all, did she?"

"Matthew and I discussed that very possibility. But I never expected to hear from her again—and certainly not this way!"

"But what opportunity could Matthew have had to invest her with a nanobot army?"

Natalya lowered her voice. "That goes to what I was reluctant to tell you, Admiral," she said. "About how Matthew gave such an army to me. I did not want to shock you with the story if it wasn't relevant. But—the fact of the matter is that the best way a person with nanobots can give them to another is through intimate contact."

Jacques-Yves couldn't help smiling. "In other words," he said, "you and Matthew renewed your love affair—no, that expression does *no* justice to what you and Matthew have. If you would prefer, I can assure you this will go no further than these quarters. But what you're also telling me is that Matthew and Ayelet must have shared at least one night before he turned up on Botany Bay."

"Yes, they did," said Natalya. Then she smiled and said, "Have no fear, Admiral. Matthew and I discussed that. We have no secrets from one another. In fact, her death—or what he thought was her death—hit him hard. But in all our discussions about her, he completely forgot that he had taken the nanobot treatment *before* that last night with Ayelet. A few stray nanobots must have gotten into her system. As many as five would have sufficed. For them to replicate would have taken a long time, given the limits of a human diet—after all, one *cannot* expect a human to eat dirt, sand, or especially metal."

"Was that your diet after you acquired your nanobots?"

"Briefly, yes. The cravings eventually decline to a manageable level, just enough for the nanobots to maintain their numbers. But Ayelet's nanobots only recently attained the numbers sufficient to support telepathy. Several days ago, she started reaching out to anyone who could hear. I think she's trying to contact Matthew again—and again, have no fear; I am not jealous of that."

"Does your telepathy help you avoid that?" asked Jacques-Yves.

"Absolutely. In any event, I finally was able to contact her—and she is *very* glad to have that contact. More than that, she has already pledged to support you however she can."

"Now, *that* is the most important thing you've said all morning," the Admiral said. "Do we need to continue in your quarters?"

"Happily, no," said Natalya. "If you will permit me, I can modify your intercom for that."

"Are you *certain* you have the Captain's permission?"

"Well, Chief Sutton seemed to think I had."

"I'll apprise the Captain anyway. But I will permit it now, on my own authority."

She crossed to the intercom panel and covered it with her right hand.

And then Jacques-Yves saw something he never expected. A swarm of tiny gunmetal-gray creatures literally flowed out of her mouth, along her shoulder, then down her arm, to where her hand rested against the panel. Then the swarm covered the panel and began to move over it. Jacques-Yves fancied he heard barely perceptible noises, like microscopic hammers, chisels, and other tools. This racket went on for five minutes, after which the entire swarm retreated up her arm and into her mouth.

"Done," she said with a note of satisfaction. "And I have contact again. Ayelet sends you greetings, Admiral, for I've told her all about you."

"Give her my greetings in return," he said, "and explain to her our problem with the enemy submarine."

"Aye-aye, sir," she said. And after that, she fell silent. Jacques-Yves waited.

Finally, Natalya said, "She says she knows, or has a good theory, where that submarine might be found. It would be at the original Soviet Russian naval base in Murmansk, upriver from the Polyarnyy Inlet into the Barents Sea."

"And where does she find herself now?"

"Near Le Havre. She was hoping to make contact with elements of the United States Marine Corps. That makes sense because we know the Marines seized control of the central spine of the Great Circle Tube Lines— the ones that run from Rio de Janeiro to Ho Chi Minh City in Vietnam. A branch of that line runs from Beijing to Le Havre. And from that branch runs a sub-branch that serves Murmansk."

"Has she sufficient forces to commandeer the Tubes and then attack Murmansk?"

"The Tubes are already falling into American hands," said Natalya. "She says she will gladly attack Murmansk, at your word, and stop that submarine from sailing."

Could it be as easy as this? Never mind—there was not but one way to find out.

"Tell her to make it so," he said.

"As good as done," said Natalya with a feral grin.

"Your nanobots impress me greatly," said Jacques-Yves. "Have they any practical limits?"

"I do not know," she said. "I haven't had time to test them properly."

"I suspect we'll soon find out what their limits might be," he said. "Er ... Natalya, are you certain there's no sure way to transfer nanobots, except through intimate contact?"

"That's certainly the best way," said Natalya, smiling again. "We could try another way, but…"

"Let us postpone that discussion for another time, shall we?"

"Yes, if you prefer. But if I may point out, Admiral, perhaps I should double my nanobot numbers. If I had to invest another person with nanobots, they would need a full load at once."

"What would require itself for that?"

"You probably would prefer not to have the details, Admiral," she said. "Have no fear; I'll ask the metalsmith and the shipfitter. They'll probably think it strange, but they can supply me with what I need."

"Make it so—so long as you do not risk your health in the process."

"Have no fear of *that*," she said.

* * *

Jacques-Yves stood on the weather deck, next to the missile launcher behind him, and looked out to starboard. He raised the pair of antique *jumelles* he had brought with him and strained to focus on the land that was barely visible.

Norway. One of three lands that were once home to the Vikings, one of the greatest seafaring peoples that had taken to the seas so many centuries ago. How many modern Norwegians even remembered their storied past? Not many.

"A sou for your thoughts, Admiral," said a soft, feminine voice— speaking in French but now affecting a thick Russian accent.

"Good morning, Natalya," he said, lowering the *jumelles* and letting them dangle on his neck by their strap. "I was thinking of where you and I are and how far we've come. Not merely in distance or even in time, but in the choices we have made."

"Begging the Admiral's pardon, but to have doubts is only natural."

"Doubts? No, not that. The evidence is too strong. Matthew would never lie to me, and neither would you. Then we have the evidence of this very ship, a ship everyone thought was long at the bottom of the sea. Still…"

"I know," she said. "It's hard to realize that your entire life has been a lie. That's what Matthew realized. And as you can imagine, I didn't need much convincing."

"Yes, I can well imagine," said Jacques-Yves. "Your young Russian swain was right. What happened to you and Matthew both was nothing short of criminal. And for more than twenty years, I was too blind even to consider the possibility. As I was too blind to consider much else."

"Such as?"

"Such as the printers adulterating everyone's food and drink with a psychoactive drug. And to think I didn't grasp the implication when Matthew had to correct an 'error of code' not once but *twice,* first on *Bonaventure VI* and then on *Bonaventure VII.* An enemy is never well-placed, except *inside* the authority one serves."

"Dan once told me that an organic body has defenses that usually fight against external invasion," said Natalya. "But sometimes those defenses turn against the body itself."

"As long as we're talking about medical metaphors," asked the Admiral, "is there one for a part of the body that is not part of its defenses, but against which those defenses ought to turn, to save the body from death?"

"Oh, yes," said Natalya, with more spirit. "Dan told me all about the mRNA preparations intended—or so everyone heard—to prevent or defend against infection by the 2019 Coronavirus. I asked him about that to make sense of something Matthew told me—and also something I have from Ayelet, now that I'm used to having her in my head."

"Speaking of whom, how are you holding up? Does sharing thoughts with her present a problem?"

"It did at first; I won't deny that. But Ayelet and I are very good friends. We trust one another. Trust is essential between two people with any kind of telepathic rapport."

"I'm glad to hear that. But you said you had something from her?"

"Yes. She rediscovered the State of Israel, you see, and they confessed to her and Matthew that they had … The expression she used translates as 'to burn incense on the high places.' It means to place too much confidence in something that pretends to save you but is, in fact, dangerous."

"And how does that apply?"

"Residents of the original State of Israel nearly all took those preparations," she answered. "And nearly half of them died before their time."

"*Degueulasse!* One wonders just how long this sort of thing has been passing—official measures that bring more harm than good."

"Centuries, Admiral. In nearly every human society, a cadre of elite actors arises that believes that only they are fit to live. The rest of us live on sufferance. Perhaps the safest societies today are the ones who had to go underground, like America and Israel, or under the sea, like the real Russia."

"The Atlantic Federation?"

"Yes. Named for Atlas, like this ocean we're on. But this is the real Russia, all the same."

"And how goes our Lady of the Lamps and her campaign?"

"Actually, Admiral, that's what I came here to share with you. Ayelet has reached Murmansk and made valuable contacts at the graving dock. It positively buzzes with activity, all of it new. *Jimmy Carter* is there, all right, and they truly are making her ready for sea. They're not taking time to enhance her deep-dive capabilities, but they *are* equipping her with torpedoes that can dive to two thousand feet. But they are also turning her into a minelayer."

"Definitely something for Kiril to know. Has Ayelet a plan to stop that submarine from putting out to sea?"

"Oh, yes," said Natalya. "She understands how important that is."

"We can hope she will succeed. But we have to consider what to do if she fails."

"Ayelet has been thinking about that," said Natalya, now looking almost grim. "She suggests it would go better if even one of the submarines could communicate with this ship."

"Communicate they can, but they don't dare," said Jacques-Yves. "You know that. A submarine functions best by keeping silent."

"I do know that, and so does Ayelet. But, as you have now had an opportunity to observe, there are other forms of communication."

What other forms could there be? The minute he asked that of himself, he saw the answer—and it chilled him to the bone. "The nanobots?" he asked.

"By now, I've doubled my supply," she said. "As I said I would."

"*La vache*. Natalya, I … I could never give you such an order."

"That is not important, Admiral," she said, managing a smile. "I volunteer."

"And for that, I thank you. Nevertheless, let us say no more about it until you hear again from Ayelet. Let her carry out her operation, and we will proceed as her results require."

"Aye-aye, Admiral."

* * *

"Hail the *Leopard*," Captain Arthur ordered.

The radio operator turned to. "AFS *Leopard* ahoy. This is USS *Elmo Zumwalt*. Come in, please."

They didn't have long to wait. A voice—doubtless from the same radio/sonar operator aboard *Leopard* who had first answered them six days before, answered back: "USS *Elmo Zumwalt*, here AFS *Leopard*. We hope you had as pleasant a voyage as we had. Over."

"*Leopard*, that's affirmative. Stand by one." He turned in his seat and said, "You're on, sirs."

Jacques-Yves looked at Jack Arthur, who nodded back. Now Jacques-Yves picked up the handset and spoke into it. "*Leopard*, this is Admiral de Grasse. I would like to speak to Admiral Yevgenov."

That same voice said in his ear, "Please to wait."

A minute later, Kiril's voice sounded: "Here, Admiral Yevgenov."

"Kiril, it requires itself that you and I talk. Aboard this ship."

"Agreed. Shall I have my aide accompany me?"

"Of course. This will be a full conference."

"Agreed."

* * *

"We saw no sign of our quarry," said Kiril. "Did you?"

"That's what we need to talk about," said Jacques-Yves. "We've definitely located *Jimmy Carter.*"

"How?"

"That can wait. For now, know this. The good news is that *Jimmy Carter* is not yet at sea. She's in Murmansk, where she has been all these centuries."

"And the bad news is that she could put to sea at any time."

"Essentially, yes. Our intelligence is inexact on that point. But when, as, and if she *does* put to sea, she will have improved torpedoes, capable of striking targets as deep as two thousand feet."

"Admiral, you *must* tell us how you know all this!"

"I agree; it's time. Natalya, would you like to take it from here?"

She did, describing her nanobots and their ability to facilitate telepathic communication either at close proximity or over a network. Then she spoke of the Lady of the Lamps. As she spoke, Jacques-Yves watched young Andrei Dobrynin closely. The look in his eyes had spoken of shame when he first stepped aboard. Now it spoke of wonderment. The boy leaned forward, seeming to hang on Natalya's every word. But he kept silent.

Kiril did not. "*Udivityel'no!*" he cried. Then, continuing in Standard, he said, "*Leytenant* Bronskaya, that is the most astounding tale I have ever heard. You really can communicate with your friend over so many hundreds of leagues?"

"Yes," said Natalya. "And at need, we can each see what the other sees."

"I had heard of identical twins who could do that. But it never occurred to me that a mechanical device could enhance such communication. But the important thing is: your friend is in Murmansk and is preparing to strike, yes?"

"Yes. We'll know soon whether she succeeds ... or fails," Natalya lowered her head.

"*Ya ponimayu*," said Kiril, before remembering to speak Standard. "That is, I understand. Failure could mean death, and you would feel her die, yes?"

Natalya nodded. "Yes," she whispered.

"Natalya Fyodorovna, I salute you," said Kiril. "I wish there was something I could do."

"I doubt anyone could help me in that event," said Natalya. "But I thank you anyway."

Seeing Natalya confess weakness of any kind unsettled Jacques-Yves. Eager to change the subject, he said, "We all need to plan what we shall do if Ayelet's operation fails. May I assume you have been conducting combat drills?"

"Oh, yes. As I would assume you would have."

"That is also correct ... Wait. Natalya?"

Natalya was holding a hand up as if to say, "Stay." She said nothing.

"I do not understand..." said Kiril.

Jacques-Yves laid a finger on his lips. Kiril, taking the hint, nodded.

Then Natalya spoke, "The operation has begun," she said.

All eyes turned to her at that.

"Ayelet is attacking—but with such a tiny force! Only fifty!"

"What?" cried Dobrynin. "A single platoon?"

"Yes ... so far, they are making great progress. Night has fallen where they are, and they have surprised them ...Wait ... Oh, no! She's led them straight into a trap! ... Oh ... Oh, *Bog!* So many casualties! ... Run, Ayelet, run! Get out of there!"

"Why won't she run?" asked the young man again.

"She's lost half her force and is making a last stand. Someone is raising a weapon ... That's it. She's lost consciousness," Natalya bowed her head.

Jacques-Yves caught Kiril's eye. He was sure his own visage mirrored the grim expression on the other's face. Aloud, he said, "I think we must assume mission failure."

Kiril Yevgenov nodded.

"This meeting is in recess," Jacques-Yves said next. "Kiril, the chief outside can conduct you and Andrei to visitors' quarters. I will summon you later, as appropriate."

The two Russians left. Natalya remained.

"Tell me, Natalya," he said, as gently as he knew how, "Is it death?"

"It is not death, Admiral. I have the impression that she is still breathing, and her heart still beats. But she perceives nothing. We must assume she is a prisoner of war."

"I thought as much. But there's more; I know it."

"Yes, Admiral. *Jimmy Carter* was ready to launch. Once she heads down the inlet, she will pass Polyarnyy within hours and then be out into the Barents Sea."

"If you require time to recover…"

"There isn't time! Admiral, I must initiate a transfer. At once."

"But surely … stay. Do you want to say that you want to give your spare nanobots to someone already aboard this vessel?"

"Yes. Admiral, every second we sit here, *Jimmy Carter* is that much closer to joining battle with us. She will head west, toward the Norwegian coast. Ayelet is sure of it, and I have no reason to doubt that."

Jacques-Yves took a deep breath and considered the problem. The only sort of person who could make a difference with a nanobot army would be one of the Russians. And that could only mean one Russian in particular.

"You have selected that blushing young swain, have you not?"

Natalya actually smiled. "Yes," she said.

"He's only a boy, and I don't think he has the slightest concept of what such a change would signify."

"He's also a Marine. Did you catch that qualifier Admiral Yevgenov gave at our first meeting? He called him a senior lieutenant *of infantry*. In Russian Naval parlance, that makes him a Marine."

"And you being a Marine yourself, you respect that. Do you consider him qualified?"

"Yes, I do. I also find him honest, fiercely loyal, and honorable. Indeed he reminds me of Matthew at his age."

"Speaking of whom, how do you expect Matthew to feel about what you propose?"

"He will comprehend; have no fear. I regret that I cannot consult him about it, or at least not yet. I don't know why he doesn't try to communicate this way. Perhaps he does not know—yet—all the things nanobots can do. But he knows me, and I know him. It's very difficult to explain, but telepathic rapport places all participants at a level of understanding that completely eliminates jealousy."

"A state of which, I have fear, I shall have to remain ignorant, I suppose. Very well, then. I shall speak to Kiril. That's the sort of thing fathers do in Russian culture, yes?"

"That's exact," she said, smiling. "And thank you for comprehending so well."

"I don't comprehend a word that has just passed between us," he said. "But I shall arrange it any way."

* * *

"You want my aide to do *what!?*" Yevgenov didn't quite shout but came close.

"I admit it's outlandish in the extreme," said Jacques-Yves. "But let's think it through. The worst hindrance our task force faces is lack of communication between the surface contingent—meaning this vessel—and the undersea contingent—meaning your submarines. Now imagine how much more effective we could be if even *one* of your submarines, specifically the fast-attack submarine, could coordinate an attack—or a defense—with this ship."

"You want to say that *Leytenant* Bronskaya could communicate with *Leytenant* Dobrynin, even through water."

"During the Cold War between the United States of America and the Soviet Union, the two respective submarine commands could give orders at all times to their ballistic-missile submarines. So one must admit that it is theoretically possible."

"All right, I'll admit that. But why must it require such an intimate exchange?"

"Kiril," said Jacques-Yves, "you and I both know, even without asking Commander Thakur—who, as he told you, is medically trained—that we do not have time to harvest billions of nanobots and simply ask a man to open his mouth and let them pour in. As unprofessional as it sounds, the method Lieutenant Bronskaya proposes really is the fastest method. And speed is of the essence."

Kiril fell silent for half a minute. Then he said, "If we were negotiating a marriage contract—and we are indeed negotiating something very like it— I would expect you to test the spirit of my 'son' with vodka. But I gather there is not sufficient time for that."

"No, Kiril. Besides," said Jacques-Yves, smiling, "my 'daughter' finds your 'son' having more than sufficient 'spirit,' as you put it. You see, like him, she is an officer of naval infantry."

Kiril burst out laughing. "You sly fox!" he bellowed. "Why did not you tell me that at first?"

"But, Kiril, you did not ask!" said Jacques-Yves, putting on his best innocent smile.

"Very well, Yakov-Ivo—you know, you never told me your father's name."

"How does that relate … Oh, I comprehend now. My father's name was Jean Dominique de Grasse."

"Very well, Yakov Ivanovich, I will explain matters to my young aide. He may wonder whether I have suddenly shoved it under the collar—that is…"

"Gotten thoroughly soused. You'd be surprised how many Russian sayings Natalya has shared with me on this voyage."

"In any event, in the end, he will comply. Have your aide wait for him in her quarters; that would seem the safest option. I will make my explanation, and then … Oh, pancake! There is likely no liquor permitted on this vessel, yes?"

"Regrettably, no, Kiril Vassilyevich. The United States Navy always was a 'dry' Navy."

"Ah, well. From adversity springs wisdom. We will endure the wait. But someday, before you and I part, you must come and share vodka with me in my flag quarters aboard *Leopard*."

"I look forward to that."

The two men shook hands, and then Kiril left. As soon as the door closed, Jacques-Yves used the intercom. From long practice, he dialed Natalya's number.

"Yes, Admiral?" she asked—in French.

"The plan is approved."

He did not have to wait but two seconds before she said, "I comprehend. Specific orders?"

"Wait where you are."

"Thank you, sir," she said—and Jacques-Yves could actually hear her smile.

At a time like this, there was nothing further to say. He broke contact without another word. Then, from a small compartment in his quarters, he drew out another item Captain Arthur had thoughtfully provided him: a chess set consisting of a metal board and magnetized wooden pieces. He had just finished placing the last black pawn when he heard another knock. "*Entrez*," he said.

Kiril Yevgenov walked in—and smiled when he saw the chessboard.

"White, or black, Kiril Vassilyevich? Your choice."

"Black will do."

Jacques-Yves swiveled the board around so that the black pieces stood away from him. Kiril drew a chair and sat down across from him.

Jacques-Yves opened with his queen's pawn, moving it two spaces forward. "In my service," he said, "we play chess on a board with three levels, with smaller movable boards added."

Kiril moved his own queen's pawn directly opposite the white one. "Would it surprise you," he said, "that we play chess the same way?"

As Jacques-Yves moved his queen's bishop's pawn next to his queen's pawn, he said, "You do surprise me, Kiril."

"Because we confine ourselves to a planet? You forget that the ocean has depth as well as latitude and longitude." And with that, he moved his own queen's bishop's pawn forward—one square.

Jacques-Yves moved his king's knight over the row of pawns to land on the third bishop's square. "Another thing to look forward to," he said.

Kiril moved his own king's knight to mirror the move Jacques-Yves had just made.

Jacques-Yves then moved his king's pawn forward—one square.

That moment, Jacques-Yves would reflect later, was when all conversation stopped. After that, nothing took place except move and countermove, move and countermove…

Many moves later, a knock came on the Admiral's door.

"Check," said Jacques-Yves. Of course, Kiril moved his king out of check—but he smiled a rueful smile, knowing what was to come.

The knock sounded again.

"Check," said Jacques-Yves again after making another move. Again a countermove.

And a third knock.

"Checkmate," Jacques-Yves said next. Then, "*Entrez.*"

Natalya came in—and Andrei Dobrynin followed close behind. Of course, Natalya's face had not changed its golden tone, but Jacques-Yves still detected a bright light in her eyes. Andrei's face was flushed.

"Success?" Jacques-Yves asked.

"Success, Admiral," said Natalya. "Oh, and … Admiral Yevgenov, your aide has proved an excellent student. I think you'll find him more than qualified."

"As a telepathic communicator?" asked Kiril.

"Absolutely—and more than that."

"Oh?"

The young Lieutenant answered, "The Lady of the Lamps is alive, Admirals. They do not treat her well in the brig, but that's to be expected. But she wants us—wants me—to remember something Natalya said earlier—that fools are neither sown nor reaped but appear by themselves."

"Do not speak to your superiors in riddles, young man," said Kiril. "The milk on your ears is still too wet for that."

"But it's no less true, Admiral. And in this case, I want to say that, as far as the Lady of the Lamps has determined, the former USS *Jimmy Carter* might seem a formidable adversary—but as we all suspected, he does not have the benefit of our silent drive. He will come after us as if he were smashing his way through the forest. I can show our Captain how to put that boat under his belt."

"You're going to have to show *me* first, young man," said Kiril.

"Is it not obvious, Admiral? The enemy might possibly hear this vessel, but not the *Leopard*. Because they do not have the silent drive, they will not be silent—and will not know what to listen for. And that would be true even for a crew trained as well as ours. This crew will not be. The Lady of the Lamps informs me that they took ratings trained on spacecraft to serve as the crew of a submarine. The same holds true for their officers. But the rules of combat under the sea are entirely different from those in the sky. Indeed that boat will not be at full complement because their underground transportation network is thoroughly compromised. The Lady of the Lamps said to tell you that she knows it would have been better to stop that boat from sailing. But our boat is still more capable; this crew is better trained, and—thanks to Natalya here—our boat can coordinate with this vessel.

"In fact—and I understand this would be highly unorthodox—I believe we can capture that vessel."

"You have right—that is highly unorthodox," said Kiril. "Submariners do not surrender unless they have positive word their cause is already lost. You will not have that advantage."

"But if we can overwhelm them with our coordination—Admiral, I repeat: this crew will be utterly inexperienced. Such coordination as we can achieve, particularly with the tactical advantage the silent drive gives us, will overwhelm them."

"Suppose we do capture that enemy vessel," Jacques-Yves asked. "What then?"

"Then we use it on a rescue mission."

"Have you taken leave of your senses, young man?" asked Kiril.

"No, he hasn't," said Jacques-Yves. "Indeed, I have deep shame for not thinking of it before he did. But he is absolutely correct. The usefulness of that vessel as a prize is obvious to me now. I'm sure Captain Arthur would leap at the chance to lend his ship to such a challenge with all her armament. Kiril, you surprise me. Weren't we just talking about playing chess in three dimensions?"

Kiril stared as if thunderstruck. Then he began to laugh—softly at first, then much louder. "And so we were!" he said. "Very well. Andrei Aleksandrovich, let us return to our vessel. We have much to discuss with Captain Antonov, and we ought to begin at once."

"And how will you signal us when you are ready to depart?"

Natalya answered that question. "Can't you guess, Admiral?" she asked with a smile.

Jacques-Yves clapped a palm to his right temple. "Of course!" he said. "They will signal *you*. You have right, Kiril—you should go back to your vessel at once. Natalya and I must brief Captain Arthur. Until then: success!"

"Success!" said the Russian Admiral. And again, he and Jacques-Yves shook hands on it.

Chapter 14

Matthew Morrow heard the intercom chime again. He left his charging alcove, walked to the intercom panel, and pressed the call button. "Morrow here," he said.

"This is Admiral Jones. I think you might like to join us all on the bridge. We're being hailed."

"Another United Systems vessel?" *I certainly hope not.*

"Negative. It's our Russian friends, or 'Atlantic Federal' friends, whatever they call themselves."

"On my way." He clicked off, picked up his combination cap, and left the cabin. He took less than five minutes to reach the bridge, where he did indeed find all the ranking officers in attendance.

"Field Marshal on the bridge!" said the duty yeoman. As ever, everyone started to rise from his seat.

"As you were," Matthew said with a palm-down gesture. He exchanged salutes with Jones, then said, "Report."

"As I said, that Russian-sounding officer who gave us that initial warning is hailing us. He'd like to talk to the most senior officer on board, and that's you."

"Very well. Have your radioman put us on voice."

Captain Aaronson nodded to the radio operator, who keyed in a few commands, then turned and nodded.

"To the task force commander now contacting us, this is Field Marshal Matthew Morrow, commanding the Revolutionary Forces for a Free Earth. To whom have I the honor of speaking?"

"Marshal Matthew Morrow, here—this is Rear Admiral Yuri Stepanovich Andreyev of the Atlantic Federal Fleet, commanding Pacific Special Task Force One. Greetings to you."

"Then do I have you to thank for the warning given us two days ago about the attack from space?"

"Yes, I did have that honor, Marshal. Did all your ships survive?"

"We did, as a matter of fact—and we thank you also for your effective counterattack. But I now seek to learn more about your fleet and the civilization it guards."

"I would rather discuss that with you in person. Would that be possible?"

"I'm afraid we're a bit rushed at the moment…" then Matthew stopped, because he saw Ronald Jones gesturing to him with an upraised finger and then with his right hand cupped around his mouth. "Stand by one," he said, then made a throat-cutting gesture to the radioman. That petty officer touched his screen once, then nodded again.

"Matthew, if you're thinking we don't want to be delayed getting to Vietnam, I think we can manage," Jones said. "Why don't we send the sailing ships on toward Saigon while we rendezvous with these Russians?"

"They'll be out of our protection, Ronald," said Matthew. "Are you sure you want to do that?"

"Better than conducting a treaty negotiation and a strategic planning session over open airwaves, Matthew. Besides, those Russians could have us for lunch any time, and haven't done it. I think we should trust them."

Matthew had to admit: Ronald's logic was sound. He nodded again to the radioman, who touched his screen again, and nodded back.

"Admiral Andreyev, your proposal is agreeable," Matthew said. "We'll lie to here, long enough to take you and your staff aboard. We can send our sail craft on, but we don't want them to get *too* far ahead of us."

"I understand perfectly. We can come aboard, and then we can be under way again while we talk. Your sail craft can make not much more than twenty knots, true?"

"True."

"I think both our vessels can make higher speeds than that. We will surface when we observe you heaving to."

"Acceptable. Morrow out." Again he made the throat-cutting gesture, and this time the radioman said, "Contact broken, sirs, but we can re-establish it any time."

"Very well," said Jones. "Signal *Constitution* to take charge of the wooden fleet and continue on toward Saigon at their best possible speed. Then signal *Magpie* and tell them I'd like them to drop Captain Blakely onto the landing deck. When we've done that, let's heave to and send out the gig."

* * *

"I represent and act on behalf of the Atlantic Federation," said Andreyev when he and his flag lieutenant had come aboard. Those two officers were with Matthew, Ronald, and Andrew Blakely in the flag quarters. *Monsoor* and *Marlin* were chasing after *Constitution* and the other wooden vessels at twenty-five knots.

"We are a group of twenty-four interconnected cities on the floor of the Atlantic Ocean, most of them in the Sargasso and Caribbean Seas and the Gulf of Mexico, and on the eastern continental slope of North America."

"And you are the first officer, other than an officer of the United States Navy or Marine Corps, to call that continent by that name," said Matthew.

"Really?" asked Andreyev. "What do others call it?"

"Aztlán."

"An Aztec name? But why?"

"The name *America*," said Matthew, "is never spoken in polite company in the society I once served."

"*Solkyn syn!* Yet this is a combat vessel of the United States Navy, no?"

"Yes. The United States of America, and the State of Israel, are allied with me. The United States of America consists of a network of deep-underground caverns with pneumatic and other tubes to connect them. The State of Israel is a much smaller network of caverns slightly north and west of the largest city in New Aztlán. But you have been observing our operations in the South Atlantic, Indian, Southern, Southwest, and Northwest Pacific Oceans for some time, have you not?"

"Again, you score. Our Admiralty dispatched my task group—which consists of this ship, the *Marlin,* and the ballistic missile submarine *Yekaterina*

Velikaya—to follow your task group and evaluate you as potential friends or enemies."

"So you did note the departure of our ship, the *Zumwalt*, back to the North Atlantic."

"Yes. We dispatched an unmanned drone to follow your ship back into the Atlantic and to report as soon as it came within sonar range of the Sargasso Sea."

"We intercepted a United Systems Navy watch officer's network alert describing the destruction of one of their ships over the Atlantic," said Andrew.

"Then my Admiralty has entered the war, and on your side, as it were," said Andreyev. "You can be certain the Atlantic Federation stands with you. Centuries ago, the United Nations, with what we all speculated was extraterrestrial help, chased our ancestors out of Russia. We fled in a small number of fast-attack and ballistic missile submarines to the one place in the oceans where we might find safe harbor—the Atlantis Project of the Vincent Marine Company."

"So *that* was it!" said Jones. "Then the legend is confirmed—that is, your society is a legend in ours. A very spotty legend, it's true—no one dares believe that seemingly fanciful tale of a Russian ground force rescuing a bunch of women and children from one of Leon Vincent's facilities in Florida before the Re-Wilding finally erased all trace of civilization above-ground."

"Ah. The Great Run to the Sea. I assure you, my friend, that it actually happened."

"I've heard enough," said Matthew, "to tell me that I should trust you. So here is my plan. The United Nations built the Great Circle Tube Lines centuries ago and have maintained them ever since. They serve the major continents, except for Australia, which they turned into a vast prison complex, and Cruria Australis—that is, Antarctica—which never had any permanent settlement, but only expeditionary bases, now abandoned. These islands we are leaving behind were once civilized and are now completely wild. In all the Pacific Ocean, only New Zealand and Hawaii, among all island political entities, remain—and Ronald, you know more about Hawaii than I do. Would you call Hawaii a civilized country?"

"I wouldn't know *what* to call it," Jones said. "The United Nations evacuated all Caucasian people from those islands and erased all signs of civilizational development that weren't there before the first Christian missionaries arrived. That's the legend, anyway. We've never visited it."

"Nor have we," said Admiral Andreyev. "The larger point is that these Great Circle Tubes serve only the two Americas, Asia, Europe, and Africa, true?"

"True," said Matthew. "But now the Americans have breached them. United States Marine expeditionary forces actually occupy the Tube station in Saigon—or Ho Chi Minh City. I am trying to get there, with as large a Marine contingent as my ships can carry, with elements of United States Cavalry from the American Reservation—which once occupied the western third of Australia—to supplement them, and lift the siege."

"And you are using that great storm to soften up your enemy before you land," said Andreyev, smiling and showing all his teeth like a wolf. "Exactly as I would have done. My task force carries Naval Infantry that might be able to assist you. But how is it that you are using sailing vessels?"

"That, *I* can explain," said Jones, smiling in turn. "Those vessels were all museum ships. One of them was still an active combat vessel of the United States Navy at the time. The rest—all replicas of some of the original ships that carried the first settlers to North America. When the Re-Wilding happened, all those ships fled. This vessel that we're on went to assist our sister ship, the *Zumwalt,* when she had to fight a battle with the third member of our class, the *Lyndon Baines Johnson.* This entire task force, including *Zumwalt,* subsisted for centuries after the Re-Wilding War until finally, we made port at Matagorda Inlet in the Gulf of Mexico. And you might as well know—this task force is all that's left of the United States Navy, which is more than we can say for all the UN Member States. All of them scuttled their navies after the Re-Wilding War."

Andreyev whistled, "In my society," he said, "we have a saying: fools are neither sown nor reaped, but appear by themselves. What this means is that you can expect no ships to oppose you but only a rudimentary shore fortification."

"That's what we hope."

"You would do well, then—as I'm sure you've already decided—to overtake your wooden vessels, take the lead, and bombard any enemy shore positions first. We can escort you and make sure you have no Naval opposition. *Yekaterina Velikaya* can even do shore bombardment of her own; not all her missiles are ballistic. One thing, though—we were barely able to track you. We could see your wake but not your hull above water. How do you manage that?"

"This vessel is cloaked," said Jones. "Matthew here showed us how to do it. It was the next step after designing a vessel with a complete tumblehome."

"Ah—the inward slope of her hull and superstructures, no?"

"Exactly."

"We have our own stealthy refinement. Our submarines carry magneto-hydro-dynamic drives. But these can only run at twenty knots' speed, so if I may suggest, we race ahead of your wooden sail craft, then slow to twenty knots so that our vessels can run with total silence."

"One thing, Yuri," said Jones. "You use the word *knot*. Is that the same as one minute of arc at the equator?"

"It is. We ended in adopting American units of measurement when we created a civilization with American help."

"Does that include such units of length as *feet* and *yards* and so on?"

"Oh, yes. I am sure that will not present a problem as we coordinate our movements."

"Excellent. Matthew, I think we've got the makings of a revised plan. Let Yuri here get back to his vessel, first of all. Then we make max cruising speed, go past *Constitution* and her group, and we might even be able to catch up with Typhoon Yolanda."

"It will be a near thing," said Andrew. "Yolanda is picking up speed as she gets closer to Vietnam. Thirty-five knots forward speed already."

"Then I suggest we move with dispatch," said Andreyev. "Obviously, we can't run silent; we must simply run."

"Right you are." Jones held out his hand. "It's been a pleasure to meet you, and it will be an even greater pleasure working with you."

Andreyev shook the offered hand. "And the feeling is mutual," he said.

* * *

"Field Marshal on the bridge!" said the duty yeoman.

"As you were," said Matthew, almost as quickly. This time he had come onto the bridge wearing his helmet and life jacket; he calculated that this ship would soon be in battle. He could tell that someone—maybe Captain Aaronson—had made the same calculation. Every member of the bridge watch was wearing a helmet and life jacket.

He strode directly to the weather station and read the display. It told him all he needed to know, as if the pronounced rolling of the ship, and the cloud cover dead ahead, didn't offer their own clues—barometer 29.50 inches of mercury; winds out of the south at twenty knots.

"We're in the fringes of the typhoon again," said Jones behind him. "We're already heading slightly head-into-wind, just to maintain course."

"How fast are we traveling?"

"Four-oh knots. I'm trying to get within shooting range just as the storm makes landfall."

"A good plan as far as it goes," said Matthew. "It's your task force."

"Thank you, sir."

"Where are *Constitution* and the others?"

"Lagging behind, of course, because they could never keep up with us. I estimate they'll take twelve hours to catch us."

"Which gives us those twelve hours for shore bombardment. How are you communicating with our friends?"

"Blinkers. *Marlin*'s periscope is well equipped for that kind of communication."

"And *Magpie?*"

"Keeping up with us. I had her escorting *Constitution* for awhile, but the weather back there is as good as it gets, so Captain Blakely suggested he could do better as a scout. I took him up on it."

"Good, so long as he doesn't reveal himself to the enemy shore watch before we're ready to strike. Which should be how soon?"

The answer came over the loudspeaker: "Conn, starboard bow. Land ho."

Captain Aaronson picked up his microphone. "Starboard bow, conn," he said. "This is it. I want continuous reports on all activity on shore. Acknowledge."

"Aye-aye, Captain."

"There's your answer," Jones said to Matthew. Then to the Captain, he said, "Signal *Magpie*. We're going in."

"Aye-aye, Admiral," said the Captain. Then, slightly louder, he said, "General quarters! Battle stations! Sparks, pass that signal on!"

"Aye-aye, sir," came several responses.

The gong-like alert sounded; Matthew could almost hear it through the decks and bulkheads, echoing throughout the ship. He could definitely feel the footfalls as the crew rushed to the gunnery, missile, and other stations.

"Conn, starboard bow," came the lookout's voice. "The storm's definitely moving in. But we can definitely see some shore batteries. They must have rushed in some heavy guns recently, sir."

"Give an exact report, lookout," said Captain Aaronson. "The gun watch will need range, bearing, and elevation. Give them."

"Aye-aye, sir. Got one we can make out very clearly. Range, five triple-oh, bearing zero three zero relative, elevation one-double-oh."

"Mister Kelvin! Pass that on to the gun watch. Fire when ready."

"Aye-aye, sir," said a young man wearing lieutenant's bars, and also wearing the sidearm that the Officer of the Deck always wore. Then he raised his voice: "Gun watch: shore battery, range five triple-oh, bearing zero three zero relative, elevation one-double-oh. Advise when ready to fire."

Matthew watched as the ship's single gun, farthest forward, swung up and about, then settled at a slight up angle thirty degrees to starboard.

"Target set, sir," came the voice of a petty officer wearing the rating symbols of a first-class gunner's mate.

"Fire at will," said Lieutenant Kelvin. "Destroy it."

"Aye-aye, sir."

The ship shook as the gun fired its round. Almost at once, Matthew saw a bright flash on shore.

"Direct hit," said the gunner's mate. "Target destroyed."

"Got another one! Range four five double-oh, bearing three four five relative, elevation zero five zero."

The gunner's mate didn't wait this time. The gun swung slightly to port and angled itself further down. "Target set, sir," said the gunner.

"Fire," Kelvin said again.

Same process, same result.

Then another voice, calling out in alarm: "Conn, radar! Incoming! Bearing zero zero zero relative, range one five double-oh and closing fast!"

Another gunner's mate made several rapid-fire finger strokes on his screen. Then the missile launcher, behind the big gun, sent a missile of its own.

"Incoming missile destroyed … Watch it! Another one…!"

The missile detonated. Everyone ducked as the forward windows shattered. One man cried out in pain as several pieces of shrapnel buried themselves in his chest. He fell over, dead. Then Matthew saw Lieutenant Kelvin holding his left arm—and bleeding between his fingers.

"Gangway!" Matthew shouted. About five men in his path scattered as he raced to Kelvin's side. Deftly Matthew took hold of the pressure point he knew where to find, and pressed. It was enough; the bleeding stopped.

Behind him, Captain Aaronson shouted, "Corpsman! To the bridge, on the double!"

Three minutes passed, during which Matthew paid the battle only scant attention. The Captain seemed to have the battle well in hand. Matthew concentrated on binding the fallen officer's wound.

At last, the corpsman arrived with two hospitalmen in tow. "Thank you, Field Marshal, sir," he said. "What's the problem?"

"He's bleeding from an artery."

"Yes, I can see that. Here," he said, handing Matthew a large white bandage. "Press that on the wound, if you would, sir."

Matthew did and held it in place while the corpsman tied the bandage down with a cravat. "That's done it," he said. "We'll take him below."

Matthew released his hold as the two hospitalmen stood on Kelvin's two sides. The corpsman looked the officer in the eye with a small penlight, then said, "Can you hold on?"

"I think so, Corpsman," said Kelvin—a little weakly but still determined.

"We'll try it, sir." He nodded to the two hospitalmen, who then interlocked their arms, hands forward of the elbows, to form a seat. Matthew and the corpsman helped Kelvin stand long enough to sit on this seat and draped his arms around the shoulders of the two hospitalmen. In that way, the three carried the officer into the hoist. Matthew watched as the hoist doors closed.

Only then did Matthew notice the whistling wind blowing loudly throughout the bridge. Jones and Aaronson had to shout to get the bridge personnel to hear them. Somehow they succeeded.

"Signal *Marlin,*" said Jones. "Send 'Plan B.'"

The Captain passed that order on. A very large submarine, which could only be the *Yekaterina Velikaya,* surfaced and fired several missiles of her own.

"Helm, reduce speed to minimum headway," Aaronson ordered next. "Gun and missile watch stand by. Have someone take Gunner's Mate Quigley below—we'll eventually bury him at sea."

"Sir, incoming message from *Marlin*," said the radioman.

"On voice."

"Aye-aye, sir."

Then Yuri Andreyev's voice sounded: "Admiral Jones, this is Andreyev. The Captain of *Yekaterina Velikaya* reports no more shore activity. He will shortly land his infantry. Do you require assistance?"

"Negative, but thank you just the same," said Jones. "We've taken battle damage, but nothing we can't handle."

"Very good. We will remain with you until the rest of your fleet arrives."

"Thank you, Admiral. We'll lie to here. Jones out." Jones made the usual throat-cutting gesture, then turned to Captain Aaronson. "You heard," he said. "You might as well concentrate on repairs. What damage do you have?"

Aaronson took a quick look around the various bridge stations. He was just about to answer the Admiral's question when a machinist's mate stepped off the hoist. As soon as he stepped onto the bridge, he snapped to attention and saluted.

The Captain returned the salute. "At ease, Machinist's Mate," he said, "and give me your report."

"The cloaking system will be out for six hours, sir," he said. "That last warhead severed several key connections. The missile launcher is out, too, but we expect to get that back in two hours. The big gun is still serviceable but limited to about thirty degrees each side of dead ahead."

"Casualties?"

The Machinist's Mate's face grew more somber. "Five killed and six wounded on the weather deck, sir," he said.

"Very well," said the Captain. "Return to your station and pass the word to expedite repairs to the gun and the missile launcher, then the cloaking system."

"Aye-aye, sir." The petty officer saluted, turned about-face, walked back into the hoist, and pressed a button that closed its doors.

"Well," said Jones, "we could have suffered worse, I suppose. What about you, Matthew? What's your plan, if I may ask?"

"Call me when *Constitution* comes alongside," said Matthew. "That was a good operation, by the way. I'm going to lay below and see to your Lieutenant Kelvin and those other wounded sailors. Oh—one more thing. On my old service, I would have seven decorations printed, but you don't do that kind of thing. Does your quartermaster carry medals in his stores?"

"He does," said Captain Aaronson. "And he should have plenty of the kind of medal I'm sure you're thinking of."

"Very well. I'll pass along your best wishes."

"And I'm sure they'll appreciate that as well as I do," said Aaronson. He and Jones saluted. Matthew returned the salute, then entered the hoist and punched a button to go below.

His first errand was to the quartermaster. After the obligatory exchange of salutes, he said, "This ship has seven wounded men aboard her. I'll want to award the Purple Heart to each of them."

"Seven Purple Hearts, coming right up, sir," said the quartermaster, who didn't take long to fetch the medals. Matthew stopped to look at one of them: purple and silver ribbon, supporting a heart-shaped emblem with the left profile of General George Washington, Commander of the Continental Army. He remembered a newly-installed President of the United States awarding him an identical medal in the chamber of the United States Senate. But of course, that medal now rested in a storage facility somewhere in Cumberland Caverns. It was one of many things he'd left behind—even his memories, until the Navy had caught up with him. And that was after he'd run a lengthy operation covering all of Australia.

He put the medal back into its case, exchanged salutes once more, and took it and the six others to Sick Bay. At the Sick Bay door he took off his helmet, put the seven medals in their cases inside it, and cradled it under his left arm. Then he knocked. A hospitalman opened it, then snapped to attention and saluted. Matthew returned the salute, saying, "As you were."

The lead doctor, wearing a blood-stained dull green pookie suit and cap, with a face mask slung around his neck, looked up and managed a salute. Again Matthew returned it.

"Come to see the wounded, sir?" the doctor asked.

"Yes, Doctor Collins. First, were you able to keep them all alive?"

"It was a near thing with some of them," said Lieutenant Commander Luke Collins. "But one of them insisted on giving them all a pep talk. I thought doctors made the worst patients, but I think bridge officers run a close second to that. Somehow, it helped; I'll say that for him."

"Field Marshal, sir!" said the patient on the far end of the ward, who could only be Lieutenant Kelvin. He actually raised his bandaged arm in a half salute—a little difficult, seeing that it was in a sling.

Hastily Matthew returned the salute. "As you were, Lieutenant," he said, "and save your strength. None of you should have to salute me anyway; can't you see that I came into this space uncovered?" That drew a few chuckles.

"Now that I have your attention," Matthew went on, "I brought presents for you. I'll be disembarking within several hours, and I thought you all ought to have a small token of my regard for you and your country's regard. You—hospitalman—come here."

The hospitalman who had admitted him to Sick Bay approached.

Matthew handed him the helmet, saying, "Be so kind as to pass these out to these wounded sailors, and to the Lieutenant here."

The hospitalman—remembering what Matthew had said about not saluting an officer not wearing helmet, cap, or other cover—made a slight bow and took the helmet. Then he went from bed to bed, handing out the seven medal cases. In one case, he had to set it on a small table; the patient had not yet regained consciousness.

Matthew took back his helmet, again cradled it in his left arm, and stood in the middle of the ward, where all could see him. "Physicians, nurses, corpsmen, and hospitalmen, bear ye witness," he said. "For having been wounded in battle against an enemy of the United States, and an enemy of the Free Earth, I, Matthew Morrow, as Field Marshal of the Revolutionary

Forces for a Free Earth, do hereby award each of these men the Order of the Purple Heart."

Dr. Collins—whose eyes were positively glistening, Matthew saw—raised his hands and brought them together in a clap. Again. And again. And again. And then in rapid-fire applause. Within a quarter minute, everyone in Sick Bay, except the seven patients, were joining in the ovation.

Matthew then walked the length of the ward, offering a hand and saying, "Congratulations." When he got to the unconscious patient, he settled for laying a hand on the man's forehead—after first satisfying himself that the man had a pulse.

When he offered his congratulations to Lieutenant Kelvin, the officer smiled. "Thank you, sir," he said, "for this, and for making sure I'd live to get it."

"That was nothing, Lieutenant," said Matthew. "Elementary battlefield first aid."

"Still, if you hadn't done it, we wouldn't be talking, sir. I'm never going to forget this. Ever."

"And now, remember what I said," said Matthew. "Save your strength. This ship's career is far from over." He looked up again and addressed the entire ward: "Hear this, all of you. We won the battle. Soon I will go ashore to carry the war inland. Each of you made that possible, in his own way. And for that, I thank you more than I can say."

Now it was their turn to applaud, mostly by knocking on their bed rails, except for the unconscious man.

Matthew waved at them all, then stepped up to Dr. Collins. "You'll no doubt have to tell that one man that the medal belongs to him," he said.

"I certainly shall," said the doctor. "And may I offer my thanks as well? I think you just made my job an order of magnitude easier."

"I'm glad to hear that," said Matthew and meant it. "In any case, it was the right thing to do. Carry on, Doctor."

"Aye-aye, sir."

Matthew could stand no more. As quickly as dignity allowed, he left Sick Bay. He had to take a moment to dab at his eyes before putting his helmet back on and continuing down the passageway. On the way, he passed a chronometer built into a bulkhead. The time read 0830. Remarkable how little time had passed. Less than an hour—and it had seemed an eternity.

* * *

"Unto Almighty God, we commend the souls of our departed comrades-in-arms, and we commit their bodies to the deep, in sure and certain hope of the Resurrection unto eternal life, through our Lord and Savior Jesus Christ, at Whose coming in glorious majesty to judge the universe, the sea shall give up her dead, and the corruptible bodies of those who sleep in Him shall be changed, and made like unto His glorious body, according to the mighty working whereby He is able to subdue all things unto Himself."

Admiral Jones intoned the prayer before a solemn assembly of the crew on the landing deck. Then he nodded, and six hospital corpsmen raised six stiff boards and tipped six bodies into the waters of the South China Sea.

Admiral Jones went on: "I heard a Voice from heaven, saying unto me, 'Write: from henceforth blessed are the dead who die in the Lord, even so, saith the Spirit, for they rest from their labors.'"

Matthew watched as that assembly, hats in hand, kept silence for half a minute. He carried his combination cap in his hand, waiting like all the rest.

The executive officer then said, "Ship's company, cover!"

Matthew put on his cap and noticed everyone else doing the same.

"Chief petty officers, dismiss your divisions!"

Matthew waited for the various enlisted personnel to leave the landing deck, unless that was their regular duty station. Finally, Admiral Jones strode up to Matthew. "The *Constitution* should be along soon," he said. "I assume this is goodbye?"

"Not at all, Admiral," said Matthew. "It's when I disclose the next part of the mission plan. Now that we have reassembled our fleet, we are going to take it straight up the Soai Rap River."

"You mean to Saigon?"

"That's right. We just had to fight a battle here, so the enemy is trying desperately to defend that city."

"Are you sure that river can accommodate our draft?"

"I'm sure even this ship can get within missile striking distance, even allowing for the re-accumulation of silt after they suspended dredging. *Constitution* can sail further up-river, and the other ships can sail further still."

"This … this might sound a little banal, Matthew, but did our burial ceremony make any sense to you?"

"We bury our dead with almost as much ceremony as I saw here," said Matthew. "But we have no 'God' to invoke. I've been hearing a lot about that concept lately. I'm sure you wouldn't invoke it if it wasn't very important."

"Well," said Jones, "I could say it's what keeps us sane, and what kept us sane for all those centuries until you came into our lives. Some of us regard you as God's instrument on Earth; I think you should know. But it goes deeper—way deeper—than that. If I may make so bold as to suggest, you really ought to speak to our Chief of Chaplains. If your travels take you back to Cumberland Caverns, I would highly recommend it."

"I will certainly consider it," said Matthew, "if only on account of the importance you just placed on the concept."

"I don't know how you do it, sir," said Jones. "I read the brief before our task force set out for Australia. How *do* you stay sane?"

"Your brief cannot have been complete," said Matthew, "and that's mainly because I did not share half my childhood experiences with anyone at Cumberland Caverns. But to answer your question, two things availed me. One was my music—especially the ability I eventually gained to interpret music properly, and then to compose it. The other was and is my sense of justice—in the full realization that, in order to get justice, I must give it."

"Now that much of a brief I did get—about your work with the Navy JAG, and all those treason trials. I still have trouble wrapping my mind around the practices you exposed—and stopped."

A voice came over the public-address system: "Sail ho. Dead astern and approaching."

"That will be the *Constitution*," said Jones. "So to confirm: what are your orders?"

"To signal all ships to steer into the mouth of the Soai Rap River. Have them proceed up-river in this order: *Discovery II* first, then *Godspeed II*, then *Susan Constant II*, then *Mayflower II*, then *Constitution*. This ship will go in last."

"Let me guess: in the order of increasing draft."

"Precisely. I wouldn't advise risking any ship grounding and blocking the passage of any other ship."

"Sensible enough. Shall we lay up to the bridge?"

"Yes. After you, Admiral."

Chapter 15

He had never stood this kind of bridge watch, nor imagined standing one like it, Jacques-Yves reflected.

He glanced again at his wrist chronometer. SAM 23, and three hours and a quarter. In such darkness, that should be of the morning, not of afternoon. If it were the latter time, this vessel would be in nautical twilight. Even the moon did not appear, which deepened the darkness.

Zumwalt was at full battle readiness. Natalya stood next to the Captain, but her eyes had a faraway look about them. The nanobots, Jacques-Yves had no doubt. A rating sat at every console in this room.

Jacques-Yves glanced out the window to port. A hundred meters—no, a hundred *yards*—off the beam, almost like a second, low-lying moon, hung the *Hummingbird*. Jake Boddicker, as Jacques-Yves knew without asking, was aboard the maglev.

"Entering the Barents Sea now, Captain," said the navigator.

"Is *Leopard* keeping up with us?" asked Arthur.

"Affirmative," said the sonar operator. "Hugging the bottom—which is the best they can do, since the bottom, here in the Bear Island Channel, is about 400 feet."

Jacques-Yves grimaced. Arthur caught it. "Are you thinking what I'm thinking?" he asked.

"Oh, yes," said Jacques-Yves. "In such shallow waters, *Leopard's* deep-dive advantage is wasted. And we dared not risk *Vladimir Putin* in these waters."

Arthur turned to Natalya. "How about you?" he asked. "Are you in touch with your friend?"

"He's alert and at his post, Captain," she said. "Still no sign of *Jimmy Carter.*"

"That won't last. The instant that other submarine makes an appearance, I want to know it."

"Aye-aye, Captain."

"Where *is* the *Vladimir Putin*, anyway?"

"Keeping station in the Norwegian Sea, at or close to her test depth," said Jacques-Yves.

"Well, she has plenty of room for that, certainly."

"Yes, and the idea is that she should *not* be a target. That's our job."

"Don't remind me."

Neither man spoke for about three hours. During that time, Jacques-Yves alternated between looking out the port and starboard windows. To starboard lay the Kola Peninsula, which also held what was once (and maybe still was) the Murmansk Oblast. To port lay the Svalbard islands. The channel through which Zumwalt had sailed lay between them, with *Leopard* trying to thread her way over an uneven and shockingly shallow bottom. Jacques-Yves didn't envy *Leopard*'s captain in the least.

At six-hours, two steward's mates asked permission to enter the bridge. They each bore a tray, one of sandwiches, the other had cups of coffee. Everyone was grateful for the food but not all that grateful for the interruption. The steward's mates took the hint: they dropped off their wares and got out. Jacques-Yves accepted a simple lettuce-and-tomato sandwich—the steward's mates knew of and respected his vegetarian choice—and a cup of coffee with cream and sugar. For the millionth time, he reflected on how much better even such a simple drink as coffee tasted aboard this ship. No printers here, except those that produced documents and the occasional spare part in the machine shop. This coffee came from freshly ground beans and had real cream in it. He could taste the difference.

Another half-hour passed. Then another, and another. He could recognize the nautical twilight beginning to show forward…

"Conn, sonar! New contact bearing one three-five, depth one double-oh, range two five double-oh, speed one five knots! Designate contact Bogey One!"

"Lieutenant Bronskaya…" the Captain began.

"Andrei has it. He's reporting it to his captain now."

"Sonar, how loud is that contact?"

Without looking up, the sonar operator said, "Compared to our friend? Loud enough almost to drown out the whale sounds."

"That's *Jimmy Carter*, all right," Arthur said. Then he picked up his communications handset. "*Hummingbird*, conn," he said. "Make your course one three-five, move out two triple-oh from our position, and drop some buoys."

"Aye-aye, sir," came a voice from a speaker somewhere.

Jacques-Yves watched as the maglev moved off roughly past the starboard bow, to the prescribed distance. Several small objects dropped from her underside and splashed into the water.

"Getting dimensions on Bogey One now, sir," said the sonar operator. Then he said, "Length about four five-oh, and beam four-oh."

Arthur nodded knowingly. Jacques-Yves needed no further confirmation.

"Range now one triple-oh," the sonar operator went on. Then, "Nine double-oh … Eight double-oh. He's bearing down on us, sir. Stand by one … Hull-popping noises. Coming shallow."

"Helm, make your course one three five."

Jacques-Yves understood at once. The narrowest possible target a ship like this could present was a bow elevation. By steering bow-on, Arthur was making it difficult for the enemy to score a hit with torpedoes.

"Bogey One, coming to periscope depth."

The captain picked up his handset again, "*Hummingbird*, conn. You are authorized to attack at will."

"Aye-aye, Captain."

And then two torpedoes dropped from the maglev and hit the water.

"That's done it!" cried the sonar operator. "He's crash-diving."

Jacques-Yves glanced at Natalya. She was staring forward as if in a trance. Only Jacques-Yves knew better. She was making sure young Andrei Dobrynin was getting all of this.

"*Hummingbird*, conn," Arthur said next. "Rattle his cage."

"Aye-aye, sir."

As Jacques-Yves watched, the little maglev started dropping small canisters into the water in a circular pattern.

"Hold-down, Captain?" he asked.

"You bet, Admiral," said Arthur, grinning like a wolf. "I've been reading up on ancient depth-charge doctrine; goes back to the Second World War. And from the look of things, your 'weapons consultant' came up with a winner. I'll admit I thought he was a snake, and still do. But he's grown on me today."

Jacques-Yves looked out and saw the point at once. He could see the shockwaves from the undersea explosions the depth charges were making.

After another minute, Arthur picked up his handset again. "*Hummingbird*, conn. Ceasefire."

The little canisters stopped falling.

"Sonar, what's Bogey One doing?"

"Just sitting on the bottom … Correction: he's picking himself up and hugging the formations. He must think he can come to our broadside."

"Helm, you heard him," said the Captain. "Don't let him. Keep our bow pointed at him at all times. Sonar, call off your bearing on the target."

"Aye-aye, sir … Now bearing one double-oh … Now zero-niner-five … zero-niner-zero … Whoa! Two torpedoes just passed right over his sail! … Torpedoes detonated. They hit the wall on the far side of him."

"Now, where did they come from?"

"Where do you think, Captain?" said Jacques-Yves with a smile. "Again, you see the benefit of instant communications between a surface ship and a submersible when an enemy cannot suspect it."

Arthur made a visible effort to keep from laughing out loud. Finally, he managed to gasp out, "Sonar, conn. Keep calling depth, range, and bearing."

"Range five double-oh, bearing zero eight five, depth … Stand by one … he's coming shallow again. In fact, he's just blown his ballast."

"*Hummingbird,* conn. Can you see him? If not, drop some more buoys."

"Aye-aye, sir. Stand by one … Yep, we've got him. Coming right up. Should be breaking surface … now."

The incredibly-long submarine broke the surface, sail first, then the rest of her. Jacques-Yves read the number 23 on her starboard bow.

Captain Arthur glanced at Jacques-Yves with a question in his eye. The Admiral nodded.

"Sparks," said the Captain, "hail them and order them to surrender."

"Aye-aye, sir … USS *Jimmy Carter,* this is USS *Elmo Zumwalt* DDG one triple-oh. You are ordered to surrender your vessel. Over."

Fifteen seconds passed.

"USS *Jimmy Carter,* this is USS *Elmo Zumwalt.* Repeat: you are ordered to surrender. Please respond. Over."

Five seconds.

"Conn, port bow," came another voice. "Our Russki friends are surfacing now."

The Captain turned to the sonar operator, who raised a thumbs-up signal.

"Sparks, hail them again."

"USS *Jimmy Carter,* this is USS *Elmo Zumwalt.* Will you surrender?"

And finally, a voice came back: "USS *Elmo Zumwalt,* this is USS *Jimmy Carter.* We surrender. What are your terms and conditions?"

Jack Arthur looked back at Jacques-Yves and smiled.

Jacques-Yves reached for the handset, and the Captain gave it to him.

"Attention USS *Jimmy Carter,*" he said. "This is Rear-Admiral Jacques-Yves de Grasse, commanding…" Just *what* was he commanding? What should he call this task force? Then he looked at Natalya, who smiled back at him.

"Commanding Free Earth Allied Expeditionary Force Number One," he finished. "You will set course for Bear Island and make for it at thirty knots—on the surface if you please. Be advised that you will travel under close escort. When you reach that island, your entire crew will disembark. Is that clear?”

“Yes, Admiral de Grasse.”

Jacques-Yves nodded to Captain Arthur, who made a throat-cutting gesture to the radio operator. When the operator nodded back, the Captain asked, “Why Bear Island?”

“Because it had not but a handful of permanent residents even before the Great Climate War. Today it has undergone the retro-savage rendition— that is to say, ‘re-wilding.’”

“Yes, but wouldn’t it have a force field surrounding it?”

“Not likely, since it is inaccessible except by boat. But I would advise you to send the *Hummingbird* to reconnoiter it, just to make sure. And remember: no force field can extend all the way through the atmosphere.”

“Got it. So if we find a force-field generator, we shut it down. Sparks, put me through to *Hummingbird*. I have some orders for them.”

* * *

“They’re all formed up, Admiral,” said Sergeant Jameson. “All one hundred forty-one of them. Fifteen officers, seventy-five Navy ratings, and fifty-one Marines—or ‘Naval Infantry’ as they call them. Ye gods, I’d forgotten how top-heavy the original United States armed services were with officers. But one of the extra officers is … I can hardly believe it…”

“If it pleases the Admiral,” said young Andrei Dobrynin, “the word your *starshiná* is looking for is *zampolit*. Short for *zamyestitel komandira po politrabote*. That is, deputy to the commander for political work.”

“*Degueulasse, en effet*,” said Jacques-Yves. “How hard has my old service fallen that they have to employ officers to remind the crew whose side they are on. Very well. Pray, separate the officers from the enlisted, and send that—what did you call him—that *zampolit* to the rear, under close guard.”

“If I may, Admiral, you might wish to let *Leytenant* Bronskaya guard him.”

"No. Lieutenant Boddicker is perfectly capable of that duty. I need you and Lieutenant Bronskaya by my side when I address the prisoners. Where did they come from, by the way?"

"That is the most ironical thing we have observed, Admiral," said Dobrynin, smiling more broadly. "This is a predominantly Russian crew, selected because they know this land and are familiar with its weather. The *zampolit* comes from England, and I believe I have identified two, maybe three of the officers from *Novy Aztlán*. They include the ship's surgeon, his assistant, and a psychiatrist—all as fanatically political as the *zampolit*. I shudder to think of the sort of medicine they practice.

"But the other officers, and all the enlisted crew—all Russian. Of that, I am certain."

"Sergeant Jameson!"

"Yes, sir?"

"Pass the word to Lieutenant Boddicker. I want those three medical officers, and the *zampolit*, escorted aboard *Zumwalt*. Close guard, and a thorough physical examination."

"Aye-aye, sir," said Jameson, who signaled two U.S. Marines to follow him.

Natalya walked up to join them. "*Zdravstvuyte*, Andrei Aleksandrovich," she said with a smile. Then she held out her hand to him. He took it. For a few seconds, the two stood, facing one another, saying nothing—but Jacques-Yves now knew better than to suppose they were not communicating. At first, Andrei blushed all over again, but gradually he relaxed.

Finally, Natalya said, "We are ready, Admiral. We assume you would like us to translate for you."

"Yes. You understand the problem?"

"Oh, yes, Admiral. I understand—and between us, we can make it not a problem."

"Good. Then let us address these officers and this crew. Walk with me."

"Do you mind if I walk with you, Yakov Ivanovich?"

"Ah, Kiril! Yes, of course. You can translate to me if you feel we have need."

"That will be a pleasure."

The four walked toward the prisoners—one rank of officers in front, their captain in the center, and five ranks of enlisted behind them. Jacques-Yves and Kiril walked in the center, with Natalya and Andrei to their left and right.

"Greetings, officers and crew of United Systems Ship *Jimmy Carter*," he began—and waited briefly as Natalya and Andrei translated that. "I am Rear-Admiral Jacques-Yves de Grasse, formerly of the United Systems Navy. You will guess why I bring these two officers with me to address you. I now ask each of them to introduce themselves," he said, turning to Natalya and Andrei, "to you all."

"*Ya Leytenant Natalya Fyodorovna Bronskaya, raneye slushil v Kosmicheskoy Morskoy Pekhotye Soyuza Sistem.*"

Kiril whispered in his ear, "Do not worry. *Leytenant* Bronskaya is introducing herself as a former member of your United Systems Naval Infantry—forgive me—Marines. Except that she used the Russian word for an outer-space Naval infantry."

"I comprehend."

Andrei spoke next: "*I Ya Leytenant Andreii Aleksandrovich Dobrynin, iz Morskoy Pekhotye Atlanticheskoy Federatsii.*"

Jacques-Yves nodded and smiled. "I don't really need you to translate *that*," he said. As he did, he looked closely at his audience. They had been skeptical at first, if not openly hostile. For the most part, they still were—but they regarded Andrei with a curiosity none of them could conceal. Who was this obvious Russian, and what was this Atlantic Federation of which he spoke? Hopefully, they would hold on to that curiosity as he spoke further.

"As you can see—or rather, hear—I show you two officers in my command who are as Russian as you. I, of course, am not Russian; I am French—though this gentleman to my side *is* Russian. Kiril, perhaps you can introduce yourself?"

"Ya Contre-admiral Kiril Vassilyevich Yevgenov, iz Flot Atlanticheskoy Federatsii."

Jacques-Yves resumed: "The larger point is that we are all human. And more to the point, we are all people of honor. What I am about to tell you, I know you will find difficult to accept. I ask you to hear me out, and then hear directly from my two translators.

"Officers and enlisted, your government has deceived you. It deceived Lieutenant Bronskaya and me as well, so naturally, we have much to tell you that your government would rather you did not know. Lieutenant Dobrynin, however, has a somewhat different story to tell. And because you are all Russians, I think his story will inspire you.

"I will now ask Lieutenant Bronskaya to tell you her story."

He nodded to Natalya, who then launched into a speech in such rapid-fire Russian that he could not follow—though he did hear a name that sounded like *"Metyu Morrou"* and could readily translate *that* name. Kiril filled in for him at that point: "She is mentioning how she knows Matthew Morrow. That's a name I gather they have been taught to fear. But they will still listen to your officer of Naval infantry because they will listen to a fellow Russian."

"Somehow, I knew that would be important."

"It is. And now she has just mentioned the pedophiles. They will listen to her now. You should know, Yakov Ivanovich: pedophilia is as thoroughly un-Russian as it gets."

Finally, she raised her voice and shouted, *"Vy posleduyete za nami?"*

And the crowd answered as if with one voice, *"Da! Da! Da! Da! Da! Da! Da!"* Even the officers joined in that chant.

"She just asked whether they would follow us," said Kiril.

"Do I take it they are enthusiastic about that?"

"Oh, yes, Yakov Ivanovich. Your officer can orate with the best of them. I am impressed."

Natalya smiled across at Andrei, then spoke some more Russian to the crowd. After that, Andrei began to speak. He began, *"Ya tozhe Russkii, kak i vse vy!"*

"Prevoskhodno!" said Kiril. "He just reiterated that he, too, is Russian, like all of them. And now … yes, he is telling them about the Great Race to find *Atlantida*—what we call Atlantis. Truly I never knew my young aide had it in him! And … Oh," Kiril dabbed at his eyes, "He just mentioned the one word that will capture the heart of any Russian."

"What word is that?"

"*Rodina.* Which means 'Motherland.' Remember I told you the Atlantic Federation could not call itself Russian because it is not on Russian soil? We hold our land—our *Rodina*—sacred. It has been the one constant in our history, perhaps the one thing that held our society together in the days of the *Sovietskiy Soyuz.* As thorough a mess as that was, the *Rodina* never changes. Never."

Finally, Andrei raised his voice and delivered a very impassioned peroration: *"Vremya prishlo! Verni to, chto prinadlezhit tebe po prabu! Prisoyedinyaityes k nam, kogda my sovyershim revolyutsyu, chtobi vosstanovit' slavy, svobody, kotorye my poteryali!"*

Kiril, barely able to contain himself, translated along with Andrei's speech: "'The time has come! Take back what is rightfully yours! Join us as we make revolution to restore the glory, the *freedom,* that we have lost!'"

And again, the listeners chanted *"Da! Da! Da!"* over and over, this time raising their right fists in a repeated thrusting motion.

And then something happened that maybe none of them quite expected. Someone braced his shoulders back in rigid attention and broke out in song:

"Rossiya — svyashchennaya nasha derzhava,

"Rossiya — lyubimaya nasha strana!"

And several other men started to chime in:

"Moguchaya volya, velikaya slava—

"Tvoyo dostoyan'ye na vse vremena!"

Natalya and Andrei then raised their hands, almost like conductors, as they started to lead the song:

"Slav'sya, Otechestvo nashe svobodnoye,

"Bratskih narodov soyuz vekovoy,

"Predkami dannaya mudrost' narodnaya!

"Slav'sya, strana! My gordimsya toboy!"

Kiril translated the refrain: "Our glorious Fatherland, age-old union of fraternal peoples, fount of ancestral and popular wisdom, glory to our country, we are proud of you."

The song carried through two more stanzas and a repetition of the refrain. And on the last repetition, Jacques-Yves couldn't help himself. He made his best effort to join in. Now that he understood what the words were supposed to mean, he could sing them with the proper cadence and emphasis. Kiril joined in, too—and from the look of him, he could not have been more pleased.

Jacques-Yves was heartily glad he had let Natalya and Andrei speak for him. They had given these people something else to fight for, as he could never have done alone.

Sure enough, when Natalya spoke apparent words of dismissal, the two officers approached him. "We were just as surprised as you, Admiral," said Natalya. "We ought to have predicted that at least one member of that crew would have a collection of *samizdata* that would include the National Anthem of Russia!"

"Pardon, Natalya—*samizdata?*"

"Underground literature," said Andrei, also smiling. "I have to assume that one particular *starshiná* was brave enough to start singing that song, and eventually, all who also knew those words joined him. By the way, Admiral, your pronunciation of the chorus in Russian was nearly perfect."

"I will second that, Yakov Ivanovich," said Kiril.

"Thank you a thousand times. But give credit where it's due, Kiril. You taught me what those words mean. Someday I will sing for you the national anthem of France."

"I look forward to that."

Jacques-Yves turned to Natalya. "Do I take it this crew will join us?" he asked.

"Oh, yes, Admiral. For the chance to break this regime and to have the Russia we all love. For that, they will gladly fight and die."

"I must commend you, young man," said Kiril. "That was the finest recruitment speech I've heard in a very long time. I only regret that it means my losing an aide."

"What can you want to say by that, Kiril?" Jacques-Yves asked.

Kiril smiled, "Surely even you, Yakov-Ivo, recognize that this young officer's talents are wasted in the office of flag lieutenant," he said. And to Andrei, he said, "Would you like to command a Naval infantry unit in our next operation?"

"I would like that very much, Admiral," said Andrei. "And I truly believe I can be of great help to our ally onshore, the Lady of the Lamps. She calls to me, and has already made known to me how to approach and enter the installation at Murmansk. In fact, that elongated boat out there came with a platoon of naval infantry."

"Yakov Ivanovich, we must begin at once to plan that operation. Shall we reconvene aboard *Zumwalt*?"

"Yes, of course. Ah, I see the next vital shore party arriving now." He indicated the rigid boat from *Zumwalt* now beaching on the island. Out stepped the ship's chief cook and a squad of cooks, bringing what looked like a hearty meal for *Jimmy Carter's* crew. Jacques-Yves led the small party to the boat, which they used to return to *Zumwalt*.

* * *

"You were wise to separate out those four officers from *Jimmy Carter*," said Dan Thakur when the council-of-war reconvened in Jacques-Yves' "flag quarters" aboard *Zumwalt*. "I have never seen such fanatical devotion to a cause I never really thought could inspire such an emotion. The *zampolit* I can readily accept. But those three Aztlánians are supposed to be physicians. They practically blurted out to me what they were doing. Would you believe they were explicitly doling out neochlorpromazine to that entire crew, plus the Marine contingent onboard?"

"*Nauseabond,*" said Jacques-Yves.

"I agree. Thoroughly bad medicine. Violative of every precept of the Oath of Hippocrates. That oath requires one to 'keep pure and holy one's life and one's art.' Those three have violated a sacred trust, and they literally don't care."

Jacques-Yves glanced at Andrei and could see him turn green. He, himself, took fifteen seconds to process what Dan had just told him. Then he said, "Once again I am without voice. What kind of customs prevail in this *Nouvel Aztlán?*"

"Don't forget, Admiral," said Natalya, "that the Five Ladies came from there—four of them, anyway."

"Forgive me," said Kiril. "But … Five Ladies?"

"Those Five laid the philosophical and moral basis for what the United Nations became," said Jacques-Yves. "Together with the Elves, they laid the philosophical and moral basis for the United Systems. And Natalya has right: four of them did come from *Nouvel Aztlán*. They sought to bury every principle of nationalism—and, frankly, of honor. Today the United Systems Navy Director of Naval Intelligence descends directly from one of the Five."

"Now I know of whom you are speaking," said Kiril. "We remember them, too. Only we don't call them 'Ladies.' We call them *'Pyat' vedm.'* The Five Witches."

"I have learned enough about what it signifies to be a Russian," said Jacques-Yves, "that I cannot blame you in the slightest. But that is of no import now. Now we must do what we returned aboard to do—plan the next operation. First: Captain Arthur, I must commend you again on your part in the recent action. Nicely done. You'll be happy to know that we have turned an enemy into an ally."

"Thank you, Admiral."

"That's of nothing. What I'm sure you'll appreciate the more, is that I will want you to take an even more active role in the operation to come. Which is: to attack Murmansk, and offer rescue to the Lady of the Lamps and what remains of the force she led in the abortive attempt to prevent

Jimmy Carter from sailing. Now, if you'll all gather round the drafting table, I can explain our position."

The group got up from where they were seated, then stood around the drafting table, where Jacques-Yves had already spread a chart of a narrow part of the northern, or Arctic, coast of Russia.

"This," he began, "is Murmansk. And this," he said, pointing to a narrow inlet leading into that city, "is Polyarnyy Inlet. I'll want to converse with the Captain of *Jimmy Carter*—what is his name…?"

"Captain Third Rank Ivo Rostov, Admiral," said Dobrynin.

"I will want to confirm this with Captain Rostov. But we have to assume that the Inlet is well-guarded. Except for one thing."

"I've got it," said Captain Arthur. "With our cloaking system, the sentries wouldn't see anything but our wake, and that would be in the daytime. This time of year, the sun is down all day."

"Just so," said Jacques-Yves. "And they'll be expecting *Jimmy Carter,* so she can sail all the way up the Inlet and arouse no suspicion. And *Leopard,* of course, has that magneto-hydro-dynamic drive, which they will *not* expect."

"I think I see what you are thinking, Yakov-Ivo," said Kiril. "You want to sail up the Inlet in this ship, with our prize coming in, in apparent triumph."

"Something like that."

"But there's no need for such stealth as that. *Jimmy Carter* had a mission to seek out and either capture or destroy this particular ship, no?"

"That's exact."

"Then why not pretend that *Jimmy Carter* succeeded? Let this vessel sail in openly, with *Jimmy Carter* on the surface. *Leopard* can accompany us submerged, of course; they will *not* expect him. And one other vessel besides."

"*Vladimir Putin?*"

"Have him come in surfaced, also as if he were a prize."

"But they won't expect *Putin*, will they?" Jacques-Yves asked.

"Oh, but they will," said Kiril. "You forget that *Putin* destroyed a ship of their Cosmic Fleet."

"Yes, that I can understand—up to a point. And that is: *Putin* is our most powerful vessel. I agree we should have *Putin* as part of the operation—but submerged, with *Leopard* as escort. Let's not let the enemy know that she— or as you say, he—is even anywhere near the Barents Sea, much less coming straight up Polyarnyy Inlet. Add this to it: the enemy would never believe they could capture such a vessel. An operational submarine that could dive to three thousand feet?"

"Ah, of course. I take your point. Of course, *Putin* can dive deeper than that, but their own histories will speak of ballistic-missile submarines that could dive to the depth you named. You have right, Yakov-Ivo; *Putin* should come in with his accustomed stealth."

"*Excellent,*" said Jacques-Yves, giving that word the French pronunciation. "So: two vessels coming in openly, and two by stealth. Therefore, I will command the open task force, and you the stealthy one. But you, Lieutenant Dobrynin, will play a different role. Now, as I understand it, *Jimmy Carter* carries a platoon of Naval infantry with its own leader. Correct?"

"Correct, Admiral. However, I do not understand. Am I to play the role of an adviser in that landing?"

"Actually, no, my young friend," said Kiril, smiling warmly. "Let me anticipate what my friend Yakov-Ivo will want to know next. Between *Leopard* and *Putin*, we can make up a platoon-sized landing force from the security forces of both vessels, plus some of the *Amerikantski* Marines. It will fall to you to coordinate a landing from two vessels, *Jimmy Carter* and *Leopard*. I am assigning you to command that joint landing force—with the temporary rank of Captain of Naval infantry."

Andrei blushed all over again. "I … I do not think—"

Jacques-Yves eyed the young man to see why he had stopped short and could see—he had caught Natalya's eye. Natalya was looking at him with absolute confidence. No, not confidence—at least, that was not all. That look held a message: *I will be with you.* And with the telepathic rapport they had, she probably communicated that to him directly.

"That is, I will endeavor to prove myself worthy of your trust," Andrei finally said.

"And I'm sure Sergeant Jameson and his fellow Marines will be honored to serve under you," said Jack Arthur. "It will give them a chance to do what Marines do: storm a beach."

"I should meet them all immediately to start building a platoon," said Andrei.

"In fact," said Kiril, "you can introduce the *Amerikantski* to the Naval infantry contingent aboard *Leopard*. I ought to send him back to the Norwegian Sea straight away, to signal *Putin* to join us. In fact, I shall join that vessel. We should meet again on Bear Island, to accomplish an exchange of personnel and make our final plans."

"Very well," said Jacques-Yves. "I'll want to brief—and debrief—Captain Rostov. You should start on your voyage as soon as you can. Let us meet on Bear Island, where we'll settle on our final plans. Oh, there's just one more thing. I am aware that your crew, Jack, and your crews, Kiril, are looking forward to celebrating Noël. But as I'm sure you understand…"

"Perfectly," said Jack Arthur. "Somewhere in an enemy maritime city, a woman sits captive who tried to do us a big favor. We owe her rescue just as soon as we can bring it about. I'm sure God will understand if we delay our celebration until after the operation."

"Agreed," said Kiril with a solemnity unusual even for him.

Jacques-Yves nodded. "Then we all agree," he said. "In that case, you are all dismissed."

As they all filed out of his cabin, Jacques-Yves caught Natalya's eye. He could tell that she was very much pleased. For herself or someone else?

Chapter 16

Matthew looked out yet again from his place on the bridge of USS *Michael Monsoor*. Ahead and to the north, the waters of the winding Soai Rap River stretched toward Saigon. They had passed the first bend and now were entering the second one. A gentle breeze blew from slightly east of south, so all the sailing vessels were running under full sail.

"We're making good time, I'd say," said Ronald Jones. "But your precautions were correct. In about an hour, this ship will be able to go no further. *Constitution* might get a little further upriver. But the replicas—they just might make it all the way into Saigon. Even *Mayflower II* draws only fourteen feet, and this river should still be deeper than that."

"Will you be able to lend fire support to our forces landing in Saigon?"

"Oh, sure. With missiles, certainly. And even with our big gun, though, we'd need precise coordinates of any target."

"We should be able to provide that," said Matthew.

"'We'? Well, that says it. You'll be going ashore?"

"Yes. In fact…"

He stopped talking.

"Sir?" said the Admiral.

Matthew waved him off, saying, "Sh-h-h. I think I hear something."

He *did* hear something—but it wasn't a sound anyone else on this bridge could hear. In fact, it was not a sound at all, but a thought. A thought from outside of himself, trying to intrude into his thoughts. But it was just out of reach. Now maybe …

"Ron," he said, "be so kind as to pass the word to the Captain that I need this ship's antenna aligned at precisely three five two degrees."

"Charlie?"

"Got it, Admiral," said Captain Aaronson. "Sparks?"

"On it, sir," said the radioman. He brought up a virtual dial on his display, highlighted a specific field, and made three keystrokes.

"That's done it," said Matthew. "Now, let me concentrate."

The thought came in much stronger. No, not a thought. A voice! *Now, what was that voice saying?*

Matthew! Is that you? Oh, Matthew, I need help!

Matthew nearly collapsed where he stood. *That was Ayelet's voice!*

Ayelet! I thought you were dead! What's happening to you?

And then he knew. Indeed, he literally saw. Metal bulkheads and a cold, hard deck. A rectilinear room. No windows. One face of this room apparently open—except that it wasn't. He could recognize something Ayelet could not, even if he had to "use" her eyes to see it. An electromagnetic containment field. And most vitally of all: a location. Murmansk, in the northernmost reaches of Russia. In fact, it was near the innermost part of Polyarnyy Inlet.

What are you doing in Murmansk?

A new vision—of an ancient U.S. Navy deep-diving fast-attack submarine. A submarine that, Ayelet had to assume, had put out to sea.

Ayelet, listen to me. Are you listening?

Yes.

He quickly queried her nanobots—for they were the means by which he could communicate with her. All he needed to ask was one simple question: a total count.

He got it—but it was not quite enough. Not for what she needed to do. *But maybe …*

Ayelet, listen carefully. You don't yet have enough nanobots to take down that force field. But if you let them feed on one of the side bulkheads, they can grow in strength. Then they need to penetrate the bulkhead and strike at a circuit at these coordinates. He passed them on.

Got it. Will you be coming for me?

I am on the Soai Rap River, making my way to Saigon.

Yes, I can hear you more clearly. You must be getting closer.

Then he heard other voices—real voices.

"Thirty feet, Captain," from the sonar operator.

Then Captain Aaronson's voice, very reluctant: "All stop."

"All stop, aye," from the engine-telegraph operator.

I'll have to break this contact, Ayelet. I have to transfer to another ship, and eventually, I'll come ashore. Hang in there.

I will, Matthew. And try not to worry. I've made a couple of new friends.

Oh? What kind of friends are these?

It took Ayelet a comparatively few clock cycles to tell him about Natalya. And—a senior lieutenant of Atlantic Federal Naval Infantry!

Ayelet, follow through with Natalya and Andrei. I will make my way to Murmansk as fast as I can get there. In the meantime, execute that maneuver I just gave you.

Will do.

Breaking that contact was the hardest thing he'd ever done. But he had to do it.

"Admiral," he said aloud, "send someone to pack my kit. I need to transfer right now."

"To which vessel?"

"*Discovery II*. I need to get as far upriver as I can get, and then go ashore. In the meantime, I'll have some comprehensive signals for you to send, intended for the vessels carrying our Marines. Listen carefully, and take notes."

He rapidly dictated a long series of orders. The Admiral looked quizzically at him at first, but gradually a realization started to dawn on him. When Matthew finished, the Admiral smiled.

"Now, this is one operation I very much look forward to carrying out," he said. Then he turned to a waiting yeoman. "Yeoman!" he barked. "You heard the Field Marshal. Lay below to his cabin and pack his gear, as he said. Have it brought to the boathouse."

"Aye-aye, sir."

"Wait, Yeoman," said Matthew. "I'll ride with you." He then turned back to the Admiral, "Goodbye, Admiral," he said. "It has been a pleasure sailing with you."

"And likewise," Jones said. The two exchanged salutes, and then Matthew entered the hoist with the yeoman.

The hoist descended to the quarters deck, and the two men got off. Matthew and the yeoman had Matthew's "gear" packed within five minutes. All of it fit into a metal-and-canvas backpack that only someone like Matthew could carry. All but one piece: his Mark Eight heavy DEW rifle. He let the yeoman assist him into his backpack and picked up the DEW rifle. Then they carried it back aboard the hoist and rode it several more decks below—to the boathouse.

A rigid inflatable boat was already waiting for Matthew. He boarded, set down his gun, and slipped out of the backpack, which he set down beside him. Then to the young boatswain's mate who obviously served as the coxswain, he said, "Shove off."

"Aye-aye, sir."

Behind them, the aft bulkhead lowered itself into the water like a ramp. Then the boat slid down a set of tracks and into the river. The coxswain started the small inboard motor and reversed it, pulling the boat out of the boathouse and away from the ship. Then the petty officer put the motor into a forward gear and steered to *Monsoor*'s port side, passing her with increasing speed.

As Matthew watched, the boat left *Monsoor* behind. Catching up to *Constitution* took a little longer because she was still sailing upstream. But she would soon stop—as Matthew had ordered. He could already see signal flags flying from *Monsoor* for all the other ships to see—or at least for *Constitution* to pass along up the line.

One by one, the boat passed the sailing vessels: *Constitution, Mayflower II, Susan Constant II,* then *Godspeed II*. At last, the boat drew alongside *Discovery II*, where a crew was already lowering a cargo net for Matthew to use to climb aboard.

He climbed quickly, with his gun slung over his right shoulder, while the ship's crew threw over several lines to haul Matthew's backpack aboard. It took him two minutes to reach the gunwale and then haul himself over it, to stand on the main deck. As he did so, he noticed the inflatable boat pulling away and heading back downstream.

It was almost like stepping back in time. The crew, though they were dressed in modern uniforms, were all at the stations appropriate for a ship under sail. A young officer, wearing the double silver bars of a lieutenant, met him as he finished saluting the ship's colors.

"Permission to come aboard, Captain?" Matthew said.

"Permission granted," said the other officer, saluting. "Lieutenant Jack Farmer, in command of this vessel, at your service. It's a pleasure to have the Field Marshal aboard."

Matthew returned the salute, saying, "Belay the third-person talk, Captain. We're about to go into action. Did you get the signals?"

"Yes, sir."

"Good. Follow them exactly. I expect split-second timing from you and your strike force."

"Aye-aye, sir."

"Questions?"

"Only one, sir. Why the flags instead of radio?"

"Come now, Captain Farmer. You know why."

The Captain furrowed his brow for a few seconds, then said, "Of course! Radio silence!"

"That's part of it. The other part is that we face an enemy that has forgotten that visual signals even existed, and certainly has forgotten how to read them."

Slowly Farmer's lips took the shape of a smile—then a broad, ear-to-ear grin. "*Now* I get it! Sir," he said.

"Carry on, Captain."

The young officer saluted, waited for Matthew to return it, then raced off to his station on the quarterdeck.

Matthew looked forward. Ahead, the Soai Rap was going into the second bend. Almost casually, he strolled toward the ladders that would take him up to the quarterdeck.

His backpack waited for him, leaning against the port rail. Now he unslung his Mark Eight and carried it at alert carry while he looked over the port rail toward the shore.

For another half-hour, the small ship kept moving until, at last, Matthew could see the city and the docks. Those docks were now deserted. Centuries ago, they must have been bustling with activity. Today the entire installation looked like a museum.

He barely caught the movement. Hastily he re-slung his weapon and raised his binoculars, focusing on an object on shore. Now he could see more clearly.

Troops were moving south and downstream—out of the city and away from these docks.

Then he realized he had company. He turned to see Captain Farmer standing to his right, also looking through a pair of binoculars. "Do I see the enemy moving downriver?" he asked.

"You do," said Matthew. "A Company has landed and has attracted the enemy's attention."

"Shall I send the hands to battle stations?"

"When I tell you, Captain. I don't want this ship to attract attention. Let them thin their ranks a little more."

That didn't take much longer. Matthew watched the troops move out for five minutes more. During that time, *Discovery II* drew even with the docks. Then he caught the waiting Captain's eye and nodded.

The Captain gave a hand signal. Across the main deck, the boatswain returned it and gave several signals of his own.

Quickly the sail watch reefed all the sails. The helmsman steered directly toward the docks. And from below, a section of Marines came on deck, all ready for action.

Matthew drew on his backpack and descended to the main deck, holding his Mark Eight at tactical carry. As the docks drew nearer, he looked out for any sign of any enemy.

He spotted several sentries in several buildings. Now he raised his gun and fired several shots.

The leading Marine sergeant took that as a signal. As soon as *Discovery II* came near the docks, even before the line handlers could jump to the docks to moor the ship, the Marines were over the bulwarks and swarming onto the docks.

Matthew saw the first enemy try to return fire. Instantly he locked on and burned the SSF soldier where he stood. The other Marines followed his lead, some taking aim at targets inside the buildings, the rest laying down suppressive fire.

Matthew felt pure pleasure—he had achieved complete surprise. Better yet, these Marines knew their business.

He took the point, toward a building bristling with antennae. He could not only see those antennae; he could feel them—or at least their emanations. And now he found he could read their signals. What had been merely an objective was now also a source of intelligence.

"Sergeant!" he shouted. "There's a 'pillbox' bearing three one five, distance one double-oh. You should send a squad up that narrow driveway, bearing zero-zero-zero. Have them continue for two blocks, then turn to head two-seven-zero. They'll be right on top of it."

"Yes, *sir!*" said the sergeant, giving a quick salute. Then he changed a setting on the radio set he had built into his helmet. "Squad six!" he shouted. "Head down that alley, bearing zero-zero-zero, two blocks, then turn left. Your objective is a pillbox bearing three one five!"

"Roger that, Sergeant. Squad six on our way."

"Go! Out!" Then the sergeant turned back to Matthew. "Any other pillboxes?"

"No, just a few enemy in those buildings. Let's keep them occupied until the squad confirms hitting the pillbox. Then we have another objective. Their vehicles are all parked in an open-air building bearing two six-five, distance about one five-oh."

"Got it, sir!"

For another two minutes, the rest of the platoon kept up their pretense. Then Matthew saw a bright burst of flame from the northwest and heard the concussion that would have ruined everyone's hearing, except for Matthew's special built-in protection and the earplugs the Marines wore. Then a voice: "Sarge, Squad Six here. That was the pillbox."

"Roger that! Stand by one!" He turned to Matthew. "Further orders, sir?"

"Send them heading two seven zero," said Matthew. "They'll be just the distraction we need."

"Right!"

And just as Matthew had predicted, the SSF drew off to the northwest, trying to deal with Squad Six. Matthew had the sergeant lead the rest of the section toward the vehicular parking deck. The guard force there tried to put up a fight—and Squads Four and Five annihilated them. All but a handful who tried to flee to the north—and ran into Squad Six. They at least had the good sense to surrender.

Matthew, looking over the armored fighting vehicles they had just captured, was still tapped into the local wireless networks. Now he could intercept the frantic enemy reports of the disaster that had just overtaken them.

The bulk of the Special Security Forces still stood between the docks and the Great Circle Tube Terminal. But all their reinforcement was gone—because A Company and First and Second Platoons of B Company had by now neutralized them. Matthew, of course, was with the second section of Third Platoon—and now the first section, which had disembarked from *Godspeed II*, was on its way to join them.

"I'll take one of those AFVs, Sergeant," he said.

"Yes, sir."

Matthew climbed into the AFV and quickly brought it from "cold" to ready to run. After that, he waited for the first section to arrive—in more maglev AFVs. The platoon sergeant was with them.

Matthew conferred quickly with the leading sergeants and gave them simple orders: re-form the platoon, then follow him straight toward "downtown" Saigon—and the Tube Terminal. Which, of course, was under siege. U.S. Marines from Third Regiment held it, but the SSF were pressing them.

Matthew used his interfaces to search the AFV's systems. Yes! This AFV could drive autonomously. Now he unlatched the door, swung it open, and jumped. No organic could have done what he did next: kept up with the AFV without falling and possibly getting crushed. The AFV kept going as its door slammed shut in the slipstream.

Now he raised his heavy Mark Eight and fired the heaviest burst this gun could produce at the nearest tank. Abruptly the enemy vehicle settled to the pavement and gouged it. That produced just the result he needed: the besiegers turned around to deal with the threat that had just hit them from behind.

His advance ground to an abrupt halt—he expected that. But the enemy couldn't afford to press him, either—because now, between him and the contingent from Third Regiment, he had the enemy surrounded. But this enemy was a dogged one. They were *not* going to give up this easily.

Matthew knew he needed to experiment. He would have liked to get into the communications building to take over its equipment, but he couldn't do that and hold this position at the same time. But there might be a way …

He tried to extend his tap and force the enemy system to send a message. It worked. Now he used it to send a message to the captain of B Company: *Get yourselves up here ON THE DOUBLE!*

Now he took stock of his situation—and saw at once where the enemy were about to break through! He rushed to the spot and fired several shots with his Mark Eight. Several Marines quickly stopped the breach—but another one was about to open up. Without even thinking about it, he took a flying leap, gun in hand, at an angle he calculated precisely: fifteen degrees up-angle, that put him where he needed to be without exposing himself too much. A few more shots and the hard-pressed Marines reinforced that hole, too.

He was just wondering how much longer he could keep this up—when he saw the Third Regiment taking the initiative. Instead of sitting where they were in a clump waiting for the enemy to pick them off or drive them back into the Terminal, now they were out, fanning out and forming two long arms, trying to squeeze the enemy between them. The problem was that the enemy were too many. The Third Regiment couldn't contain them. But at least that was better than sitting and waiting to die!

Now he "reached" for another remote circuit. Yes, this was the one! "Sergeant!" he shouted.

"Yes, sir?"

"Listen carefully," said Matthew and gave some rapid-fire orders.

"That'll stretch us out pretty thin, sir."

'Can't be helped. We either do it or watch the enemy gain the advantage."

"Yes, sir." Was that reluctance Matthew heard? No—it was grim determination. It was do-or-die time, and this sergeant knew it.

So the Third Platoon did spread itself out thinly—but gained confidence as they realized that Matthew had taught them a new tactic, and it seemed to work. And it did—for about fifteen minutes. Surely there had to be away to close the circle!

That's when the rest of B Company arrived. This was all the reinforcement Matthew needed. Five minutes later, they had closed the circle.

Third Regiment obviously had taken the hint. They, too, started tightening the circle.

Fifteen minutes later—an hour after this firefight at the Terminal had started—Matthew saw a white flag from the enemy position.

Matthew went forward, cradling his heavy gun, toward that white flag. As he did, he noticed that all the firing had now stopped.

Three men stood ahead of him—two SSF sergeants, each with his hands in the air, and an obvious SSF officer—a colonel—with his hands behind his back.

"Bring those hands out where I can see them," Matthew ordered.

The other officer ignored him. "Oh, so it's 'Field Marshal,' is it?" he asked.

"You at least know how to read rank insignia," said Matthew. "But is your hearing at fault? I said bring your hands out where I can see them."

The officer whipped out a handgun and fired.

Matthew raised his electromagnetic shield—barely in time. Then he hardened it to reflect the beam.

The colonel dropped his weapon, then fell supine, with a smoldering hole in his heart. After that, Matthew heard the clattering of many weapons and saw many SSF stand up and put their hands in the air. A few seconds later, he watched as several Marines appeared—Third Regiment, and B Company—to take them all into custody.

Then Matthew saw a familiar face he was glad to see. "Ho, Colonel Campbell!" he called out.

A Marine colonel looked up—and smiled broadly. "Field Marshal on deck! Ten-HUT!" he shouted. Around him, nearly a hundred Marines snapped to attention.

"As you were," said Matthew as he strode up to Colonel Joe Campbell. The two clasped hands warmly. "It's good to see you again, Colonel," Matthew said.

"And likewise, Field Marshal," said Colonel Campbell. "By God, you cut it thin, if you don't mind the impertinence."

"From you, never," said Matthew. "I expect that of you—as I also expect results. And I like the results I see."

"Thank you, sir," said Campbell. "From what I can tell, I'd say Saigon— or whatever they call this place—definitely belongs to us. No question. The civilian population is with us—ironic, but true. Those SSF think they know how to fight, but they're used to subservient prisoners, not real soldiers."

"One of your former officers will be here shortly," said Matthew. "He should be with A Company, further downstream. You'll find that I brought well-trained forces with me. But I'll be taking a small force—maybe a platoon—with me to Murmansk."

"What's in Murmansk, if I may ask?"

"A Naval task force, consisting of *Zumwalt* and, if the intelligence I have is correct, a small task force of submarines."

"Submarines, sir? Who would have submarines?"

"Another set of allies, who call themselves the Atlantic Federation. I'll make sure you get a full brief later, but for now, these are Russians, descendants of a small Russian submarine force that fled the Second Russian Revolution. I had help from another of their task forces in the South China Sea."

"Where have they been hiding all this time?"

"Under the sea."

"Say again?"

"Their name *Atlantic Federation* doesn't refer only to the ocean. It refers to the first underwater city that Leon Vincent had started to build."

"I'm sure that *will* be a long brief," said Joe Campbell. "To answer the question I think you have, I'm confident I can hold things here. The SSF are now wiped out. As I read it, you and I just took care of their last effectives. If your mission is urgent, I'm sure I can rustle up a tube train for you that can carry you and one platoon."

"In that case," said Matthew, " Third Platoon of B Company will accompany me to Murmansk. I'll need a train and a crew."

"Coming right up. If you'll all follow me, I can take care of that right now."

Chapter 17

Once again, Jacques-Yves de Grasse was on *Zumwalt*'s bridge, looking out at a starlit night. These stars, he knew, would all be stars of the northern sky. Polaris, of course, would be keeping station at a very high angle—more than eighty degrees. But the largest benefit, as ever, was the twenty-four hours of night.

He checked his wrist chronometer. The day-and-date display read LUN 25, and the hands told the time as two hours.

Slightly aft and to port, the former USS *Jimmy Carter* (now renamed AFS *Zhimiy Karter*) kept up with *Zumwalt*, making twenty knots. Kiril would no doubt say that the submarine was "out of his own plate." Submarines, certainly since the twenty-first century, were built to move better submerged than surfaced. That had not always held, as Jacques-Yves well knew from his naval history studies.

Below the waters of Polyarnyy Inlet, *Leopard* and *Putin* followed—submerged. Not even their periscopes showed. Kiril was, of course, aboard *Leopard*, his old flagship. But this time, Andrei was not with him. Instead, Andrei was aboard *Zhimiy Karter*, with the First Platoon of what was now called the Allied Expeditionary Naval Infantry Strike Force. The Second Platoon, with the good Sergeant Jameson serving as its leading sergeant, was aboard *Leopard*.

Jacques-Yves looked around him. As before, Captain Arthur sat in his command chair, where he could see everyone in the room. Natalya stood next to him. "Conn, starboard bow," said a voice on the squawk box. "We have the town of Polyarnyy and the old Number Ten Shipyard in sight. Zero activity."

"Conn aye," said Arthur.

Polyarnyy. Namesake of the very inlet they were in. During that period of international strife known as *la guerre froide,* Polyarnyy had been the real downstream base for the Red Banner Northern Fleet. Murmansk had been the research center of the Soviet Navy and later the Russian Navy, but Polyarnyy had held the drydocks that actually serviced the operational ships and submarines of the Northern Fleet. It had always been a closed town; now, it was a ghost town.

"Natalya," Jacques-Yves asked, "are you still in contact with Ayelet?"

"Oh, yes," said Natalya, looking grim. "She's wide-awake."

"Sleep deprivation?"

"More than that. She just took a bucket of cold water in the face."

"*Degueulasse.* It's a wonder she hasn't broken by now."

"She won't break," said Natalya, her jaw set. "Not if I can help it."

Of course. That telepathic rapport again.

"And … Admiral, I remind you," Natalya went on. "She has more than just me."

"Young Lieutenant—excuse me, *Captain* Dobrynin?"

"That's exact," Natalya said with a smile.

Jacques-Yves looked out the starboard windows. From here, he could barely make out the outlines of Polyarnyy as they slipped by. "I wonder," he said idly, "why they didn't tear it down, as they tore down so much else."

"Just lazy, I guess," said Captain Arthur. "Maybe old Soviet-era naval installations didn't excite the kick-in-the-gut resentment that American cities did. Or maybe they still maintain it as a lookout station. Well, anyway, we're maintaining the illusion, and the more reason to keep radio silence."

"How much longer to Murmansk?"

"About three-quarters of an hour."

Fifteen more minutes of monotony ensued, with only the occasional course-correction order to break the remarkable near-silence of this ship's bridge. Then Natalya burst out laughing.

"What amuses you so?" asked Jacques-Yves.

"When you're going to torture someone," she said, "at least try to make sure her tastes haven't adapted to suit the moment."

"What can you possibly signify by that?"

"Someone just shoved a handful of dirt into her mouth and commanded her to eat it."

"And how can that be pleasant?"

"Admiral," said Natalya, smiling even more broadly, "think. Dirt is actually mineral. What better substrate for a nanobot 'culture.'"

"Of course. How could I forget—but you wouldn't have known since you weren't aboard. One fine day some nanobots got loose aboard *Bonaventure*—that would be Number Six, of course. They were literally eating their way through bulkheads, overheads, and decks. If it hadn't been for Matthew, plus my genius of a stepson, the ship would have been lost with all hands."

"How did you manage to gain control?"

"Not I," said Jacques-Yves, actually smiling at the memory. "Credit Matthew and Paul. They simply gave them proper organization so that they would behave like a real organ and not a cancer. By the time Matthew and Paul were through, they turned their energies to repair. Just in time, too, for almost immediately, we were in action. Near-certain defeat turned into total victory. The ship gained yet another unit citation, and Paul was detached from the ship and admitted to the Academy."

"Odd," said Natalya. "Matthew made light of it when he told me."

"And that," said Jacques-Yves, "is Matthew for you. But more to the point, you are telling me that Ayelet will actually be stronger for the experience."

"And she knows it. She's gotten good at putting on an act. She just managed to 'persuade' her torturers to give her more dirt to eat."

"She can't keep that act up forever, you know."

"Admiral, remember: fools are neither reaped nor sown but appear by themselves. Though anyway, they've gotten tired of that game. And I think the base just went on alert. Someone must be keeping watch at Polyarnyy, and must have seen us pass."

"Well, Captain, it seems you had right a moment ago," said Jacques-Yves.

"Then, with that confirmation, I should do something else. Chief Watson?"

The Command Master Chief snapped to attention. "Sir?" he asked.

"Battle stations, silent."

"Battle stations, silent, aye, sir!" He saluted and used a portable digital device to pass the word—but softly. For the next fifteen minutes or so, Jacques-Yves felt slight vibrations in the deck as the ship, which had been half asleep until now, started to wake up fully.

Five minutes later …

"Conn, radio," said "Sparks," the radio operator. "Intercepting ship-to-shore chatter."

"Put it on speaker."

"Aye-aye, sir." And the speaker clicked on with a voice speaking Standard: "… this is United Nations Naval Station Murmansk. Identify yourselves at once."

"Murmansk, this is USS *Jimmy Carter*, returning from Operation Radish. Bringing in a prize. That ship you see is the former USS *Zumwalt*."

"You are properly identified, *Jimmy Carter*. You may pass."

Everyone on the bridge grinned ear-to-ear.

Now Captain Arthur picked up his handset. "Hangar, conn," he said.

"Hangar, aye."

"Prepare *Hummingbird* to launch on my command. Get the Seahawk ready, too; we may need it. And throw over a sonar buoy."

"Aye-aye, sir."

The sonar buoy was for alerting *Leopard* and *Putin* to be ready for action.

"Radar, conn," said Arthur. "Stand by to cloak."

"Standing by to cloak, aye-aye."

"Gunnery, conn. Target zero-four-five relative, distance three triple-zero. Track and prepare to fire."

"Aye-aye, sir."

For three minutes more, no one spoke. And then …"

"Cloak!"

At once, the scene outside seemed to get even darker. Several displays changed at once, no doubt reflecting enhancement.

"Commence firing!"

The big forward gun rapidly swung round nearly to the beam, then fired. The recoil shook the ship. A moment later, Jacques-Yves saw the explosion onshore.

"Launch *Hummingbird!*"

"*Hummingbird* away," came the voice from the air boss.

Jacques-Yves glanced outside the port windows, barely in time to watch *Zhimiy Karter* submerge. Then from shore, came an answering shell. Except that it splashed into the water a hundred yards behind and to starboard of *Zumwalt*—because, of course, Captain Arthur knew the first rule for a cloaked vessel: always keep moving.

Suddenly several ground-attack missiles broke the surface, lit their engines, and streaked toward the source of the incoming gunfire. *Putin.* Good for Kiril! Now the shore defenders would have *two* sources of bombardment to contend with.

"Conn, starboard bow. Our two subs have surfaced near shore. Discharging landing forces."

"Conn, aye."

Natalya spoke next. Smiling, she said, "Andrei has just stepped ashore. He knows exactly where to go … Wait! They're taking machine-gun fire. Pinned down."

"Where from? Belay that! Gunnery, conn! Take your targeting instructions from Lieutenant Bronskaya, and fire at will!"

"Aye-aye, sir!"

Natalya shouted a relative bearing and distance to the gunnery officer, who passed these on. *Zumwalt's* gun lit up the night sky with its next shot, then one more. Then Natalya said, "It's all right, Captain. Andrei is on the move again."

Another shell detonated off the port bow—where *Zumwalt* had been. And another ground-attack missile broke the surface, ignited, streaked toward the source, and detonated.

"How far does Andrei need to travel?" the Captain asked.

"About three hundred yards," said Natalya.

"Hangar, conn. Launch helicopter."

"Launch helicopter, aye-aye."

A minute later, the Seahawk, making the usual thumping sounds, lifted off from the landing deck and raced toward shore.

Jacques-Yves turned from the window to watch Natalya. Now that a helicopter and a maglev were in the air to provide close air support, Natalya left the gunnery station alone and started relaying targeting instructions to the two craft. Her face showed the same determined concentration as before.

"Ayelet is free!" she cried, her face suddenly showing elation. "She's using her nanobots to defeat the force field holding her in her cell. She'll be out in no time!"

"I don't comprehend," said Jacques-Yves. "Didn't they restrain her with metal shackles?"

"As I, myself, know, Admiral, metal restraints can be quite tasty to nanobots."

"Then why didn't she free herself earlier?"

"Well, we *have* been providing quite a distraction, wouldn't you say?"

"I would indeed. But I hope I'm not distracting *you*."

"Have no fear, Admiral. Andrei and his forces are inside. He can coordinate directly with Ayelet now. The pilots of our two small craft know what to do, outside. It won't be long."

Indeed, within five minutes, "Sparks" spoke again: "Conn, radio. Message from shore."

"On speakers."

"Aye-aye, sir."

Then a lilting female voice filled the air: "USS *Elmo Zumwalt*, you can cease firing now. This installation belongs to us."

"Sparks," asked Captain Arthur, "can she hear me?"

"She can now, sir."

"Very well … This is Captain Jack Arthur of the USS *Elmo Zumwalt*. To whom have I the pleasure of speaking?"

"This is *Shofet* Ayelet Cohen, also known as the Lady of the Lamps. Your excellent Captain Dobrynin is with me. I understand you have some officers on board who will require rapid transport to America. Is this true?"

Captain Arthur smiled at Jacques-Yves and gestured to him to speak. Jacques-Yves took the hint, "I am Rear-Admiral Jacques-Yves de Grasse, formerly of the United Systems Navy—and now serving the Revolutionary Forces for a Free Earth. You and I should talk. Would you like me to come ashore?"

"Yes, Admiral. I look forward to meeting you."

"I will be ashore within the hour." He nodded to Captain Arthur, then said, "Natalya, with me—and ask Dan Thakur to join us also. And Jake Boddicker."

"Shall I contact Admiral Yevgenov?" the Captain asked.

"Oh, yes. Give him my compliments, if you please, and say I would be pleased to see him ashore with his current aide."

* * *

The inflatable whaleboat chugged in to the pier, or what was now left of it after the recent action. Jacques-Yves had little trouble identifying the greeting party. There was Andrei Dobrynin, of course, his shoulder boards sporting the accouterments of a Captain of Naval Infantry. Next to him stood the young lady who was the reason for this last excursion. Five-foot five inches tall, a little on the stocky side (but muscle, not fat), and with hair the color of this dark Arctic night.

As he stepped onto the pier, he first accepted the smart salute of young Captain Dobrynin. Then he turned to greet the young lady. "Ayelet Cohen, I presume?"

"You presume, correctly, Admiral de Grasse," she answered. "And Natalya Fyodorovna—how wonderful to see you again. I must apologize for letting you think me dead."

"Oh, Ayelet, just seeing you alive again more than makes up for that." And as if to make the point, the two embraced.

As she broke the embrace, Ayelet Cohen asked, "Admiral, won't you please introduce me to these other officers?"

"Yes—and forgive my lapse of manners. May I present Rear Admiral Kiril Vassilyevich Yevgenov of the Maritime Fleet of the Atlantic Federation?"

"Greetings, Judge Ayelet," said Kiril with a slight bow. "Your reputation precedes you."

"Thank you, Admiral. Your Captain Dobrynin has told me about your Federation. I had known of rebel cities underground, but not underwater."

"And this," said Jacques-Yves, "is Lieutenant Commander Udayan Thakur, my Flag Secretary—and of course, you know Lieutenant Bronskaya."

Dan Thakur said, "May I congratulate you on your rapid recovery."

"Oh, *that,*" said Ayelet. "Nanobots confer several significant advantages."

"Yes, like instant nano-surgery—even intravascular, I shouldn't wonder."

"You are a physician?"

"Yes."

"Perhaps I ought to submit myself to you for a physical examination— after we discuss certain vital matters."

"And finally," said Jacques-Yves, "I present Lieutenant Jacob Boddicker, formerly of … that is…"

Jake Boddicker smiled. "He means I am a former gangster," he said with an ironic smile. "I specialized in weapons, before the authorities sent me to The Rock. Matthew Morrow broke me out, you might say."

"If I may suggest," said Jacques-Yves, "I have flag quarters aboard *Zumwalt*. They would be far better for our purpose than an open pier."

"Point well-taken, Admiral. Shall we embark?"

* * *

"It's actually wonderful to meet you at last," said Ayelet Cohen when they were all seated in Jacques-Yves' flag quarters. "Your reputation as the Captain of a space warship precedes you, of course. But I had no idea you were such an excellent Naval historian. And let me assure you that those exquisite historical artifacts you had to leave behind, and your library, are all in safekeeping. If something were to happen to the cybernetic network, those would be the best references we would have—and it was very generous of you to lend them to us."

"And by *we* and *us* you mean…?"

"The Zealots, of course. We're well-organized by now. Having to return to Earth in the heart of Europe was the best thing that could have happened to me. The greatest concentration of the Zealots is in the heart of France.

"But enough of me—Natalya has already told you how I survived. Let's talk about you. Of course, I shall always be grateful to you for rescuing me. But more than that, I tried to help you out once and didn't do very well at it. I'd like to try again."

Jacques-Yves laughed, a little nervously. "You haven't the least thing to apologize for, Mademoiselle Cohen—or should I simply say *Shofet* Ayelet?"

Ayelet smiled. "It's taken me a long time to get used to that title, but yes, I'd like that."

"Very well. Actually, I suspect you can help me, and my staff," he went on. "We urgently need to reach America as quickly as possible. Captain Arthur here was ferrying us to the shores of his country when we met Kiril and his little task force. Now I believe we have a more urgent errand. Natalya, Dan, Mr. Boddicker, and I need to get off this planet and make contact with other freedom fighters elsewhere in the Galaxy."

"Not to mention the Syndicate," said Boddicker. "I have my own contacts to renew."

"And the Americans would do well to establish physical contact and a full alliance with the Atlantic Federation."

"And yet you broke off from that errand to rescue me," said Ayelet. "I am more grateful to you for that than you can know."

"Well, we did, after all, have to deal with what was then a threat. And as I recall, Murmansk was always the best-connected city in the northern parts of Russia. And still is, or you would not have conceived of a plan to try to stop that submarine from sailing."

"In that case," said Ayelet, smiling more broadly, "we *can* help you. First, Natalya, I need to tell you what I told Andrei. Maybe you still can't contact Matthew Morrow, but I did."

Natalya gasped. "You've heard from Matthew?" she asked. "How is he? *Where* is he?"

"He contacted me while he was in Vietnam, and as I understand it, he's making his way toward Murmansk. This brings me to how my Zealots and I can help you. As you may or may not know, the United States Marines are in complete control of those parts of the Great Circle Tube system that serve the west coast of North America, and also the continent of Europe, and the lands of Russia. Now, thanks to you, we control much of Murmansk. All we need do is get you to the Tube station we used to launch our first assault on this sub pen."

"And that," said Andrei, "is where I come in. I now know that enough people still remain in Russia to make an effort to redeem our *Rodina* from the present regime. Murmansk will be as good a place as any to establish a base from which to launch such a War of Redemption."

"You won't have but so many forces to begin with, young man," said Kiril. "Two platoons, from one of which you will lose many of your *starshini* and other non-commissioned officers."

"That is only temporary, Kiril Vassilyevich. I am confident I can recruit and train others to take their places—as difficult as that might prove. Which reminds me: the *Amerikantski* Sergeant Jameson served me well in this last operation. I understand that he is trying to reach America in order to train to be an officer. It will give me the greatest of pleasure to write for him a letter of recommendation."

"And I can think of none better qualified to write one," said Kiril. "You make me proud, young man. If anyone among us could do what you have set out to do, you can.

"But that makes your errand, Yakov Ivanovich, the more pressing. I am certain that, once the *Amerikantski* can connect to *Atlantida,* many will wish to come here, willing to fight to reclaim Russia at last.

"But it does leave one more—how do you say it—loose end. *Kapitan* Arthur, where will you go?"

"Well," said Arthur, "seeing that I won't have any ferry mission to perform, I just need hydrogen—I'm sure we can improvise an electrolysis plant for that—and some victuals. And then it's back to Australia, or Vietnam, or perhaps China. That's where the real action is, I'm sure."

"I will consider it an honor to escort you part-way there. Sadly, we cannot cross the Arctic Ocean—well, our submarines can, but you cannot. It's ice-locked now. Trying to pass through the Arctic seemed a good idea at the time, but—well, that's quite impossible this time of year. So for you, it's back the way we came, then to follow a great-circle course to Cape Horn, round it, then chart another great-circle course to Australia. But: you will pass directly over the undersea territories of the Atlantic Federation, and as such, you will enjoy the complete protection of the Atlantic Fleet. I see no reason why you could not travel at maximum speed until you have crossed the Sargasso Sea. By then, the Admiralty will assign you another escort— but you will have to run at twenty knots only."

"I understand," said Jack Arthur. "That way, your ships can run silent and still keep up with us. Nevertheless, I like the idea. It means we'll have circumnavigated the globe."

"And we can also resupply you at sea. We can even make sure you have a full load of hydrogen, so you need not take on much more than you will need to return to the Atlantic. And at this time of year, you need not worry about Atlantic hurricanes."

"And I will have quite a story to tell. Especially to Matthew."

"Then it is agreed," said Kiril. "And now I think we should celebrate. In fact, we already have an occasion to celebrate, do we not?"

"We certainly have," said Captain Arthur, grinning. "Merry Christmas!"

"*Joyeux Noël*," said Jacques-Yves.

"*Schastlivogo Rozhdestva!*" said Kiri and Andrei, in chorus.

And then everyone turned to Ayelet to see what she would say.

And she smiled and said, "*Chag molad sameach.*"

Natalya smiled broadly. "Does that mean you will join our celebration?"

"With the greatest of pleasure," said Ayelet.

"In that case," said Jacques-Yves, "since we now control this installation, we should use it to celebrate properly. Can we?"

"We can," said Andrei. "We can use the large graving dock that once housed the Typhoons in the old Soviet days."

"Then let us make it so," said Jacques-Yves. "We'll rotate the crews ashore for, say, sixteen hours. And then—then we part ways."

"Perhaps we can delay thinking of that for later," said Kiril. "For now, let us celebrate our victory—and a much older victory."

"In that case," said the Admiral, "this meeting is concluded. Natalya, please remain a moment. The rest of you may leave."

As they filed out, Jacques-Yves noticed Ayelet making a point of keeping up with Andrei. At last, the door was closed. At once, he asked, "Do I detect the beginnings of a friendship between our Andrei and *Shofet* Ayelet?"

"That's very possible, Admiral," Natalya said. "Andrei is such a romantic, and Ayelet very much appreciates what he did. In fact," she said with a light laugh, "I've just had to break my connection with those two, to allow them at least *some* privacy."

"I take your point. By the way, what was that Hebrew phrase she used?"

"She wished us a happy Nativity. She knows what that signifies, even though she hasn't yet brought herself to believe in it. Of course, it would have been nice to celebrate her Festival of Lights, but that was over with two weeks ago.”

“Which is how long we two have been traveling together. Remarkable!”

“Yes, we have definitely come a long way, in experience as well as distance. And I assume we’ll travel even farther.”

“Indeed, yes. I definitely will join the Free Systems Navy. And I’ll want you in its Marine Corps—in command of as large a contingent of Marines as the Americans can launch into space. But until then: shall we join the celebration?”

* * *

The celebration couldn’t have gone better, Jacques-Yves decided. The cooks from the *Leopard* and the *Putin* were eager to show their American counterparts how to cook a proper Christmas feast in the Russian Orthodox tradition. And the crew of *Zhimiy Karter* were still marveling at the taste of real food that came from a true galley, not a device that tried to pretend to be one, but … did not succeed.

For his part, Jacques-Yves strolled around the cavernous sub pen, staring at the impossibly high overhead. Kiril caught up to him.

“And how do you like your experience with Russian architecture?” he asked.

“If you want to say, how do I like standing in a building that could swallow the first ship I ever commanded, then, of course, I find it overwhelming,” said Jacques-Yves. “Do you Russians always build such large structures?”

“Oh, yes. You should tour some of our cities someday. Even this structure, as large as it is, could not hold *Putin*.”

“I am almost without voice,” said Jacques-Yves. “But then, so many things have struck me without voice in the long voyage I have just taken.”

“If I understand what you want to say,” said Kiril, “I could say the same. I congratulate you on a truly glorious campaign—and thank you for setting in motion the redemption of our sacred *Rodina*.”

"And I thank you, for your part in that campaign, Kiril Vassilyevich. We have indeed made a good team. I am desolated that our team must soon dissolve."

"That is of no import, as you Frenchmen like to say. You have other campaigns ahead of you in the *Kosmos,* and I, perhaps, will have campaigns to run at sea. You have taught me much that I will not soon forget. Including even some new chess moves."

"Ah, yes. You did promise me a game of chess in three dimensions."

"As a matter of fact," said Kiril, for the first time indicating the *porte-documents* he was carrying, "I brought my three-dimensional chessboard and pieces with me. Compact, you see, as is the case with any submariner's personal effects. Shall we find a space and play a short game?"

"Lead on, Kiril."

As the two admirals made their way to a corner of the hangar, they caught sight of two young people sharing a nearly intimate moment. Kiril reached out and caught Jacques-Yves' arm just as he recognized them: Andrei and Ayelet.

"I think," said Kiril with a wink, "we ought to search elsewhere for a place to play."

"*D'accord.*"

They walked on, to one of many tables set up for eating. It happened to be vacant, so Kiril opened his case and drew out a very complex assembly, which with a few pushes and pulls, turned into a true three-dimensional chessboard array almost identical to the one Jacques-Yves was used to playing on. It featured three eight-by-eight boards, mounted one above the other with telescoping pillars. And as Jacques-Yves remembered, the black pieces started on the top level, and the white at the bottom level on the opposite side.

"White for you, Yakov-Ivo?" asked Kiril.

"*D'accord.*"

After twenty moves, the two men realized that they had a large audience consisting of half the other attendees. But this game did not end as the other had. After twenty more moves, the game reached an impasse.

But that did not stop the crowd from breaking out in sustained applause.

* * *

Once again, Jacques-Yves and Natalya were wearing haversacks, holding all that belonged to them. But this time, Dan Thakur and Jake Boddicker were with them, also wearing haversacks. Sergeant Jameson was also part of this party, at the head of a mixed Russian-American platoon. Naval Infantry Captain Andrei Dobrynin and *Shofet* Ayelet Cohen rounded out the party, together with a section of Zealots.

Facing them were Rear Admiral Kiril Yevgenov and Captain Jack Arthur.

"Well, this is goodbye," said Arthur. "I must say that it's been a pleasure having you aboard my ship—and even serving under you. I learned a lot on our cruise together."

"I'm glad to hear that," said Jacques-Yves. "And, Kiril, I promise you I will see to a connection between your Federation and the Americans."

"I eagerly await that, Yakov Ivanovich. But now you must go. In fact, we all must."

After a few handshakes all around, Jacques-Yves and his party watched as Captain Arthur and Rear Admiral Yevgenov each boarded a boat to take him to his respective vessel.

Jacques-Yves allowed himself only a quarter of a minute to watch the small boats move across Polyarnyy Inlet before turning in-shore—and toward a network of deserted streets.

Ayelet took the point with her Zealots. Jacques-Yves, Natalya, Dan, and Jake followed, with Andrei's mixed Russian-American forces surrounding them.

Murmansk seemed to Jacques-Yves to be a mere shadow of her former self. And yet … something about this city troubled him almost at once— nothing he could readily define, but still there.

And then he recognized that feeling.

"Natalya," he said firmly, "we are not alone in this city."

"No, we definitely are not," said Natalya. "But let's not make it obvious that we know."

"Do Andrei and Ayelet know?"

"They do. They just asked me to join in their 'conversation.'"

And they wouldn't do that if the situation did not require it. "Your advice?" he asked.

"Walk as you are, but be ready to get down when I tell you."

He nodded.

Five minutes later, they were just about to round the corner leading to the hoist—or the lift—to the underground tube station, when …

"*Down!*" Natalya cried.

He flattened himself to the still-paved road—not very comfortable even in the best of circumstances. He could almost feel the DEW beams crisscrossing the space where his body had been, and could definitely hear the guns sending those beams.

He struggled to see the battle raging all around him, then gave it up. Sadly he saw the body of a Zealot lying where a DEW beam had pierced it. Now and again, he heard the rattle of Sergeant Jameson's pellet gun.

Then the battle changed. He had not the slightest proof, but he knew: Andrei, taking advantage of another pair of eyes (those being Ayelet's), had taken his mixed platoon to hit the enemy from behind, even as the all-Russian platoon kept up their defense. Jacques-Yves could tell that the Russians had suffered two more casualties—but now they were on the move, toward the station.

Bad. How did anyone propose to dislodge the enemy from the station? They would need to take it intact, so they could use the lifts to get down to tube level.

And suddenly, the enemy came boiling out of their position! What could have driven them out? Then he saw the American Marines, in hot pursuit.

Then, in less than a minute, the enemy had thrown down their weapons and surrendered.

Finally, one of the lifts slotted into place at the ground-level stop. The doors opened. Out stepped a man—at least it looked like a man—carrying a heavy-duty DEW long gun at tactical carry (muzzle up, braced with the left hand, the right hand holding the grip with the finger near, but not on, the trigger), and wearing that same odd uniform Natalya wore, but with five stars arranged in a pentagonal array on each shoulder. A "man" with golden skin.

"Matthew!" cried Natalya, who leaped up from her position and rushed to the gold-skin man. Hastily he laid his weapon aside and spread his arms wide. The two met in a heartfelt embrace.

As they broke the embrace, Ayelet Cohen stepped forward. "Hello, Matthew," she said softly.

"Hello, Ayelet," said Matthew Morrow—for it could be no one else. He reached for her hand, and she placed her hand in his—but only for a moment.

"Captain Andrei Dobrynin, front and center," said Matthew.

Andrei Dobrynin stepped forward and saluted. Matthew Morrow returned it, then offered his hand to shake. "Congratulations on your recent operations," he said.

"Thank you—Marshal."

"No, Andrei Alexandrovich. *I* thank *you*. Would you like to command in this theater?"

"I would like that very much."

"And so you shall. If you can read my mind as well as I can read yours, you can be sure that I consider you highly qualified for this command." He shook Andrei's hand briefly, then stepped forward to meet Jacques-Yves. "Hello, Captain—or Admiral. It is well that we meet again."

"I feel that I ought to apologize ... *Maréchal.*"

"That would not be important, Admiral," said Matthew. "What *is* important is that you are with us—and, though you've heard it before, I congratulate you on your recent campaigns, and especially on finding an ally on the sea that can strike at a target in orbit. Though you might as well know: the Atlantic Federation sent another task force to remain in the Southwest Pacific theater, and they had to do the same favor for the task force that carried me to Vietnam. But now, I need you to get out into space and lend your skills to the Free Systems of the Nine-o'clock Quadrant. And to find Kress, and see if he'll join us."

"I understood that our old fellow officer wants us to prove ourselves."

"You understand correctly. And I can think of no better officer to send than you."

"Even as old as I am?"

Matthew smiled, "You're not going to tell me you're 'getting old for this sort of thing,' are you? After you just fought two campaigns in the Barents Sea, and likely saved our revolution?"

Jacques-Yves managed a light laugh. "Point taken, Matthew," he said.

"All right, then," said Matthew. "Now, let's see you off to America. I'll accompany you as far as the Beijing station, where you'll go your way, and I'll go mine. I need to return to the Southeast Asian theater as quickly as I can get there. By the way—where's *Zumwalt?*"

"I understand she'll be sailing the Atlantic and rounding Cape Horn on her way back to the Southeast Asian theater," said Jacques-Yves. "But Sergeant Jameson is with me."

"Excellent. Now one more thing." He turned to Natalya and Ayelet and said, "I apologize for not communicating with you sooner, Natalya—and to you, Ayelet, for having to break off as I did. By the time I realized that I could and that you, Ayelet, were in trouble, I had problems of my own, which I had to concentrate on. We have solidified our hold on Vietnam and need to expand into Laos, Cambodia, and China. Happily, Joe Campbell is in command in that theater. As soon as I could hand the theater over to him, I came as quickly as I could to offer rescue. But I must congratulate you, Ayelet, on effecting your own escape."

Ayelet smiled, "It wasn't quite as simple as that, Matthew," she said. "This wonderful young man," she went on, indicating Andrei, "provided enough of a distraction so that I could deploy my nanobots." She lowered her voice slightly and said, "Thank you again for those."

Matthew could not blush, but Jacques-Yves would swear that he would have if he could. "You're welcome," he finally said. "You surprised me by reaching out to me as you did. Then again, I never thought of all the things nanobots can do."

Matthew turned to Natalya, "As difficult as it will be to part again," he said, "your mission orders still stand."

"I understand, Matthew. Do *you* understand all that I have done?"

"Yes. Giving nanobots to Captain Dobrynin was a stroke of genius. Of course, you both will have to counsel him on what a wonderful gift he has and how to use it."

"We will," said Natalya.

"Don't worry about that," Ayelet smiled almost impishly and nodded.

"In that case," said Matthew, "I leave this theater in your capable hands, Ayelet. Take care of it—and your people."

Ayelet smiled and then rushed to embrace Matthew. Jacques-Yves comprehended. This was about remembering old times and much else.

"And now, Admiral," said Matthew, "please gather your staff together, and let's be off."

Jacques-Yves simply nodded, and Natalya, Dan, Jake, and Sergeant Peter Jameson fell in with him.

Matthew Morrow led the way into a large lift car. When all were inside, Matthew turned and waved through the still-open doors. Jacques-Yves caught a glimpse of *Shofet* Ayelet and Captain Andrei Dobrynin waving back at them.

Then the doors closed, and the lift car plunged in near free-fall down its shaft.

THE END

We, Too, Shall Enlist

The Terra Prime Series

Book Four

Terry A. Hurlbut

Chapter 1

Jacques-Yves de Grasse felt a gentle but firm hand rouse him. He opened his eyes and, at first, wondered where he was. A bunk, certainly—but in a room, if one could call it that, having a curved wall that extended continuously into the overhead. And no windows, either. *What was this?*

Wait, wait, wait. This was no room; it was a tube car, part of the Great Circle Tube system on Sol d. If the configuration of the walls and overhead were not convincing, the throbbing certainly was. *How fast are we traveling, anyway?* He would have to ask.

Lieutenant Commander Udayan "Dan" Thakur—of the Free Systems Navy, no less—smiled. "Good morning, Rear Admiral," he said—in French, too, out of respect for this old man he accepted as his commander.

"And good morning to you, too, Dan," he said. "And thank you." He rubbed his eyes and levered himself out of the bunk. "Do I gather we're getting close to the Beijing Junction?"

"Yes. The Marshal sends his greetings and would be pleased to see you before we arrive."

Field Marshal Matthew Morrow had formed, and now commanded, the Revolutionary Forces for a Free Earth. Strange to think of his old second officer as his superior in rank—though not expecting subordination, but alliance.

"Pray, greet Matthew for me," said Jacques-Yves, "and tell him I'll join him shortly."

"Aye-aye, sir." Dan saluted and left the tiny cabin.

Jacques-Yves got out of the bunk, then half-walked, half-stumbled to the tiny wash station. He drew enough water to splash into his face. The cold water was bracing—just what he needed to come fully awake. After that, he took five minutes to see to himself, including a shave. Then he put on a uniform—with two stars on each shoulder, as befitting his rank. As he pulled on the tunic, he glanced down at the ribbons on display above the left breast pocket: battle stars—too many—plus various gallantry decorations and an occasional decoration for wounding in battle. And all of it, he suddenly realized, was part of an old era. And he had barely begun to adjust to the new. With that bittersweet thought, he put on one more accessory—his wrist chronometer with the analog hands and the mechanical date and day-of-the-week display, now showing MER 27. Now he was ready to leave the private cabin.

The other five occupants of the tube car were waiting. Dan, of course—of Hindu extraction, with the medium-brown skin and dark hair that went with that. Next to him sat Sergeant Peter Jameson of the United States Marine Corps—United States of *America*, if you please. African, with the short, curly hair and enhanced lips of members of his race. On the other side of this room sat Natalya Fyodorovna Bronskaya, uniformed as a first lieutenant. In every particular but one, she looked like a classic Russian and sported bright red hair—except that the hair was artificial and her skin golden. She was not exactly human anymore but a cyborg—a disembodied central nervous system "wearing" a total-body prosthesis.

Seated next to *her* and across from Sergeant Jameson sat Jake Boddicker, easily the most thoroughly un-military person present. He wore a Naval uniform and sported the two silver bars of a lieutenant. But the uniform did *not* fit his personality or his sardonic attitude toward life. But then again, he had a direct commission in the Free Systems Navy—assuming that service would actually accept him. What he *really* was, was a member of the Syndicate. His specialty: weapons of all kinds, generally illicit. He had proved his value in the last two operations Jacques-Yves had run, but Jacques-Yves still made no effort to conceal his distaste. Boddicker smiled back at him—a crooked smile. He knew. So at least he and Jacques-Yves understood each other.

And standing in the middle of the room, uniformed with *five* stars on each shoulder, arranged at the points of a pentagon, stood Matthew Morrow. Six feet tall, looking as if he should weigh about 185 pounds—except that, like Natalya, he too was a cyborg. Piercing blue eyes (real eyes, but with enhancements Jacques-Yves didn't care to think about) regarded Jacques-Yves from inside a golden face topped with brown "hair."

"Good morning, Admiral," said the cyborg in a voice that still managed to sound human—but in Standard, in deference to the others present. "I trust you slept well?"

"I did indeed, *Maréchal*. Thank you."

"At your service," Matthew Morrow said. "And first names will serve between us. We are now approaching Beijing. There, we part ways—you to continue to America, and I to return to Indochina, which is still the most hotly contested theater of the revolution."

"In that case," said Jacques-Yves, "have you any message to convey to your American friends?"

"Yes," said Matthew. "Tell the Speaker of the House that I, in fact, met her distant cousin—a sergeant in the United States Cavalry from the American Reservation. She will understand."

"If *I* understand correctly, then that message should please her, should it not?"

"It will."

"I'll be sure to pass that on," said Jacques-Yves, smiling.

"Thank you. And thank you again for everything you did in the Atlantic and Arctic Oceans."

"That was only natural," said Jacques-Yves. "I had great help in those operations. Besides, we must all act to ensure our survival—long-term rather than short."

"True." Matthew paused for a few seconds, then said, "The sensors tell us we have nearly arrived."

"And everything is in readiness," said Sergeant Jameson.

"Thank you, Sergeant." Jacques-Yves then turned to Matthew and said, "Well, Matthew, this is where we say farewell."

"Actually, in your native language, it's where you say 'to see you again' or even 'to God.' I've been looking into that concept. You must acknowledge that many of our allies take it seriously."

"And how likely would you say that it is real?"

"Had you asked me that before my arrest, I wouldn't have given it the slightest thought," said Matthew. "But much of what I've seen and heard gives me reason and leads for further investigation."

"Really?" said Jacques-Yves. "Well, if I find anything of import along that line, I'll at least try to signal you with it."

"I would certainly welcome that."

The car now slotted into an obvious enclosure with a slight bump. Then two doors—so well hidden that Jacques-Yves had forgotten they were there—slid open. Outside lay a prominent platform. Jacques-Yves read the legend BEIJING, in Roman and Cyrillic letters, together with what he assumed was a Chinese ideogram, on the far wall.

All six left the car, Matthew leading the way. *One could almost believe we were in a regular city underground. But one does not reach such an underground in a hoist—or elevator—that falls nearly free for several minutes. Just looking up makes me wonder whether a large weight is going to crush me at any moment.*

But they did not use an *ascenseur* this time but instead used an *escalateur. La vache, didn't l'Académie Française have a problem with* that *concept!* But, by whatever name, it worked. They found themselves one stage down and on another platform within a minute. But Jacques-Yves saw none of the crowds he would expect to see. Instead, he saw American Marines, some clustered in squad-sized groups, some standing guard. Nevertheless, the direction signs remained, with one of two legends: RIO DE JANEIRO and HO CHI MINH CITY, repeated in Cyrillic and Chinese ideography as before.

"This is definitely where we part," said Matthew. "You will take a car toward Rio and disembark beneath San Francisco. I will return to Saigon, which, incidentally, is the original name for the Eastern Hemispheric terminus of this line. And one more thing," Matthew took a rather curious object from his pocket: a thumb drive. "Use this on the communications portal on your car," he said. "It holds several messages from me and clearance for you."

"I comprehend—well, I don't quite, but I have implicit confidence in you. So now I say goodbye and good luck."

Jacques-Yves and Matthew shook hands. Then Matthew shook hands with the Marine Sergeant who accompanied them, and with Dan, then with Jake. He actually embraced Natalya—well, of course, since those two shared more in common than many husbands and wives did, Jacques-Yves dared say. Finally, Matthew left them, obviously to make his way down yet another level to the platform of the Indochina Line that, like the Le Havre Line on which he had just traveled, terminated in Beijing.

As he left, another tube car passed through the force field separating the main tube from the short siding that tube cars had to use to enter any station. Jacques-Yves knew why that had to be: the Great Circle Tube system used evacuated pneumatic tubes.

The car had two Marine drivers; a single Marine, with the chevrons and bows of a sergeant major, greeted the four as its side doors opened.

"Rear Admiral de Grasse and party?" he asked.

"I am Rear Admiral de Grasse," said Jacques-Yves.

"I am Sergeant Major Lloyd Anderson, United States Marine Corps. Please step aboard, sir. Next stop: San Francisco," he finished without a hint of irony.

Jacques-Yves let his party aboard the tube car. They all found seats, which included seat belts. Jacques-Yves looked questioningly at their guide, who said, "They are necessary, sir. Yes, we've figured out how to turn on the gravity compensators, but they're not exactly up to spec. In fact, those seat belts are a recent addition. We found them just that way when we took this system over."

Jacques-Yves had many questions but decided they could wait. He found a seat and strapped himself in. The other three members of his party did the same. Then the Marine sergeant walked to a wall panel that sported a touch screen and a display above that: 0 KT. He tapped some kind of code into it using the touch screen and waited.

The tube car's doors closed, and Jacques-Yves did indeed feel it start to move. A slight sensation, but definite. The wall panel speed display changed almost too rapidly for him to follow. Within seconds it was showing a three-digit speed, that passed 150 … knots, he assumed. And it kept climbing. The left digit advanced to 2, 3, 4, 5 … and then the speed readout started to slow. Eventually, it settled down at 650 knots.

"I see you've changed that speed display away from SI, Sergeant Major Anderson."

"Yes, we did. We use American Patriotic measurements here now. Are you familiar with them?"

"Yes, as a matter of fact. Lieutenant Bronskaya here briefed me on my voyage. Now at this speed, how long to San Francisco?"

"A little over eight hours and forty minutes, sir," said Sergeant Major Anderson. "Then comes the slow part: Cumberland Caverns in about seven and a quarter hours."

"Why so slow?"

"We have a lot to learn about how this system works, I can tell you. Even with three hundred eighty years, we never developed gravity compensation or electromagnetic force fields. So the fastest we can make a train travel is three hundred miles per hour—and this baby makes six-fifty *knots*. Takes my breath away just thinking about it; I don't mind saying, sir."

"How did you penetrate this tube system?"

"Underground, sir. Punched a hole right into San Francisco station and took it over."

"That was brave of you, considering how this system functions."

"We did what we had to do, sir."

"And do you plan to invade the western coast of *le Nouvel Aztlán?*

"Actually, yes—and the eastern coast as well. We would have been content to let them stew for a long time while we devoted our resources to other theaters. In fact, your establishment of a Russian theater on land will definitely help. But we're going to need to acquire some of those gravity landing craft, in order to assist you."

"Assist me?"

"In getting off the planet. I don't know much more than that—except that I have orders to assist you in any way with transportation to, and communication with, the Admiralty."

"Speaking of communications, have you established a channel of secure communications from this car?"

"That's one of my orders, sir. This particular car is cleared for full-duplex communication even at the top-secret level. In fact, Admiral Scott would very much like to talk to you ASAP."

"If I comprehend that correctly, you must mean *tout de suite*. I'll require privacy, of course."

"Yes, sir. This is a VIP car—in fact, the First Secretary used to use this car on occasion. Through that door, you'll have a cabin all to yourself. All other sleeping cabins are forward."

"Thank you. If you'll excuse me?"

"Aye-aye, sir," the Sergeant Major saluted. Jacques-Yves returned the salute and walked aft. As he entered the cabin—which he found even more luxurious than the one he'd used on his way to the Beijing Terminal—he closed the door. Then he looked for the workstation he expected such a car to carry and found it easily. When he switched it on, the screen took a minute to cycle through several starting-up routines, then projected a blue screen with a simple message in Standard: AWAITING AUTHENTICATION.

He took the thumb drive from his pocket and looked on the workstation for a slot that could receive it. Once he found it, he inserted the drive. And *now* he got results. A seal bearing the legend UNITED STATES NAVY greeted him. The emblem was in blue, gold, silver, red, and brown and bore an eagle holding a gold anchor in its talons, with a silver chain surrounding it and several apparent sun rays emanating from its head. A dark blue background surrounded this.

Beneath this seal, Jacques-Yves read another legend in white: STATE YOUR NAME, RANK, AND NATIONALITY.

"Jacques-Yves de Grasse, Rear Admiral, formerly of the United Systems Navy. I am a Frenchman."

WHAT IS YOUR DESTINATION?

"Cumberland Caverns." As good a place name as any, though he knew no more than that.

VOICE AND SPEECH PATTERN AUTHENTICATED. STAND BY TO JOIN CALL.

What? How could this system authenticate him … but of course. Matthew. He could record merely by listening, and his recordings would suffice to establish a voice profile. For that matter, his recorded "memories" were admissible as evidence, as Natalya had explained.

The screen now showed only the seal of the United States Navy. Jacques-Yves waited. He could guess whoever wished to talk to him was on a radically different diurnal cycle. Jacques-Yves glanced at the digital wall chronometer on the forward bulkhead of this cabin: 8:00 a.m. Eight hours of the morning. Depending on where Cumberland Caverns were, their time might be eleven hours out of synchrony with his. Hopefully, that would not present a problem at this hour.

He drew out his chronometer and set its hands to tell the time listed on the display. Then the screen changed again, presenting a button labeled JOIN CALL. He reached with his right pointing finger and touched it.

At once, the screen changed radically to reveal an office with a broad desk. At that desk sat a man in what must be a Naval uniform. Five stars showed on each shoulder board. Above his head was a repeat of the Navy emblem.

"Rear Admiral Jacques-Yves de Grasse, I presume?"

"You presume correctly."

"I am Fleet Admiral Jack Scott, Supreme Commander of the United States Navy. On behalf of the United States of America, I greet you—very warmly. And thank you for your service."

"Can you have gotten a report so quickly?"

"Not from our ship, the *Elmo Zumwalt,* if that's what you mean," said Admiral Scott. "But I've seen a preliminary report from the Commandant of Marines. And that thumb drive, I assume you used, contained full particulars from a *very* good friend of ours."

"Would that be Matthew Morrow?"

"It would. Now, if you don't mind waiting a moment, I'm going to see what we've got here."

"*D'accord.*"

"Say again?"

"Ah. That is, I agree."

"Thank you." The screen didn't darken or change. Instead, Admiral Scott simply turned away from the camera and started to stare intently at a flat screen beside him, occasionally reaching to touch it. "After-action reports, mostly," he said, so softly Jacques-Yves almost didn't catch it. "Won't *that* be a happy legend? Not even 'Ike' or 'Mac' ever stormed a riverbank as General Morrow did."

General? Jacques-Yves said to himself. *Doesn't he mean Marshal?* Then he remembered these Americans never used the title "Field Marshal." Instead, they used the title "General of the Army." And he remembered who "Ike" and "Mac" were: the two highest-ranking field commanders of the United States Army during the Second World War, one in the European theater, the other in the Pacific.

Then Scott looked back at Jacques-Yves—or rather, at the camera. He uttered a long, drawn-out whistle. "I don't know how our friend does it," he said. "How could anyone invent something so fast—and in such detail?"

"If we're talking about Matthew Morrow, then I suppose anything is possible with him," said Jacques-Yves. "If you recall, I had him as my second officer—which, among other things, entailed directing special projects. Some of these were quite urgent. I will say right now that he saved my ship and the lives of my crew on too many missions to count. As to *how* he makes things so, my dear friend and former ship's surgeon tried to tell me once, and I confess her explanation went—how do you say it—completely over my head. Something to do with the total integration of his mind with one central processing and arithmetic logic unit, and several ancillary processors."

"That's already too much Greek and Latin for me," Scott said. "And I don't know how it is in your educational system, but I had the benefit of studying Greek *and* Latin. But enough of that. I haven't told you what I just came across."

"And that would be?"

"Complete specifications for a new kind of military body armor. No, not armor. An exoskeleton—and amazingly simple in concept. Powered, too—and that'll be the hard part. Admiral, do you suppose they use anything like that—but wait a minute. It'll save time if we can get onto a first-name basis. Is that agreeable?"

"*Certainement*—that is, certainly. My name is Jacques-Yves."

"And my friends and advisers call me Jack. Pleased to make your acquaintance."

"As am I. But to answer your question—Jack—the United Systems Marines never used anything of that sort. I don't think they use it yet. Did Matthew tell you that the authorities of my former society tried to build cyborgs like him and Natalya to be the ultimate soldier? Invulnerable, all-powerful, ready to crush all the enemies of the United Systems, external and internal?"

"He did indeed," Jack said grimly. "I was present when he briefed the President on that very point. He said he was the first prototype—and I gather your Natalya is another prototype. After reading his description of her case, I'd like you to tell her, from me, that she has my deepest sympathies."

"I'll be sure to convey that, Jack."

"But that means your former society likely never used its imagination to invent something like this. It would have saved them a lot of headaches, and we'd never have had a chance against them. With this, *we* can get the jump on *them*. That is, if we can implement the power pack. The energy density involved is something you have to see to believe. In fact, our ancestors messed—that is, *tried* to get something like this to work about four hundred years ago. We have a legend that someone invented a literally limitless power source that could fit in less space than a haversack and provide power for a structure we once called a 'single family residence.'"

"Or perhaps my old house on my vineyard," said Jacques-Yves.

"Yes, I can imagine that. Anyway, our ancestors would have needed that kind of power source to make this 'powered armor' work. As I suspect we'll need it now."

"I know someone who might be able to help," said Jacques-Yves. "That is if you can get me close enough to persuade him to defect and offer him rescue."

"Another former member of your crew?"

"Exact—that is, correct. Ian O'Reilly, Warrant Officer First Class—I believe that reads 'Master Chief' in your rank structure. There was next to nothing he couldn't do when I knew him."

"Do you have any idea where he is now?"

"I have—that is, I fear not—that is…"

"Got it. You don't know—so we'll just have to find out. See here, Jacques-Yves: *you* have my deepest sympathies if I understand correctly where you're coming from. You had your command taken from you, your ship scrapped, and your officers scattered hither and yon. That's got to hurt. Under any other circumstances, my sympathies are all I can offer you. But you're telling me that some or all of these former officers and 'warrant officers' can help you. Correct?"

"Correct."

"In addition to which, you have Lieutenant Bronskaya—and in fact, Matthew writes that he gave her specific mission orders to at least *try* to reassemble your old wardroom—or as many members thereof as we can find. According to this, Matthew already found three of your former officers—that would be Commander Kendrick, Doctor Diane Conway—and Lieutenant Bronskaya, whom *nobody* thought to see alive again. So I gather that the first two officers I named already have their roles to play in the Southeast Asian Theater. But if you'd like to have back anyone else in your former crew, we'll find them for you. That's a promise."

Again, as he had so many times, Jacques-Yves was overwhelmed. "I … forgive me, but I am without voice. I never imagined earning such a favor."

"Think nothing of it, Jacques-Yves," said Jack. "That's actually a favor we owe Matthew. Besides, we need all the experts we can get on our side. Next—well, this is something interesting and something we can whistle up right away. A personal re-entry capsule."

"Now *that* is something with which my old service *was* experimenting. I believe you'll find that one of my staff officers—my present Flag Secretary—used such a capsule to parachute into Sydney, Australia."

"Yes, Matthew mentions that. I confess I never thought of deploying troops the way you would fire ship-to-ground missiles. This must be something to aid you in your mission into space. Here on Earth, we'll just use ordinary parachutes.

"But now we come to another problem, an order of magnitude more difficult. What's this I read about an undersea civilization in the North Atlantic? And would that have anything to do with a big fireball some of our foraging parties observed, together with what looked very much like a brace of ballistic missiles launching from the sea?"

"It would indeed, Jack," said Jacques-Yves, who went on to talk about the Atlantic Federation, and the best account he could give of his adventures while in command of an impromptu task force consisting of USS *Elmo Zumwalt* DDG-1000 and the Atlantic Fleet Ships *Leopard,* a fast-attack submarine, and *Vladimir Putin,* a ballistic-missile submarine. Scott winced when he heard about the destruction of a space warship in low Earth orbit but kept silent while Jacques-Yves continued his account. The story of the Battle of Murmansk interested Scott the most, especially the involvement of the former USS *Jimmy Carter* SSN-23.

"And where is that former Seawolf now?" Scott asked.

"Admiral Yevgenov did not share that with me. When I left that task force and accepted escort to the Murmansk Tube Station, I left Yevgenov in command of that task force. How he deployed his submarine assets, he did not share with me. Though I would assume that he seconded *Zhimiy Karter,* as they call her now, to assist Naval Infantry Captain Andrei Dobrynin in his drive to make revolution throughout Russia. That's what I would do in his place, seeing that *Zhimiy Karter* lacks the magneto-hydro-dynamic drive that all submarines of the Atlantic Federation Fleet carry."

"I suppose that makes sense, seeing that Yevgenov has to cross an ocean or at least get within safe hailing distance of his home bases," said Scott. "Matthew Morrow's message advises me that *Zumwalt* will get another escort from the southern border of the Atlantic Federation, all the way to and around Cape Horn, then out to the Australia and Indo-China theater. And he *also* advises us to start drilling a tunnel out to sea, to a target within the Charleston Bump, beyond the Frying Pan Shoals, at six hundred fifty feet below sea level."

"Where," said Jacques-Yves, "you should be able to establish contact with the city of Atlantis, or *Atlantida* as they say it in their language."

Scott whistled again. "Jacques-Yves, if anyone had told certain of my predecessors that someday, Americans would make contact with a *Russian* undersea civilization camped literally on our country's doorstep, he would have thought that man was a fool or a communist. Never mind—times change, and enemy identification changes with them.

"Now, according to this message, this undersea city of yours is fifty-five nautical miles out—well beyond the old Contiguous Zone, by the way. We'll start boring at once, of course, but it will take a little time to reach them."

"How 'little,' would you say?"

"Oh, maybe nine days—assuming they make no effort to bore toward us."

"*La vache!* You can tunnel that fast?"

"Our best tunnel borers can make six nautical miles a day with the usual support. Can we at least count on those people to assume we're friendly?"

"Yes," said Jacques-Yves without hesitation. "They've been trying to work out a plan to connect to your civilization almost since their founding but, of course, did not wish to risk breaking into an inhabited cavern or tunnel. They have their own tunnel borers ready to move, and furthermore, they would build a transparent plastic tunnel toward the slope and bore from there. If they hear you, they'll start construction immediately and home in on your noise."

"You wouldn't have any idea how fast they could bore, would you?"

"Not a precise idea, no. But don't forget that they've had three hundred eighty years to develop their own technology, not only for undersea cities but also for the infrastructure to connect them. I'm sure they can bore through any kind of ground, at least as fast as you can, or faster."

"Good. Because connecting with them could be critical."

"How so?"

"Think about it. These newfound allies, bless their hearts, just drew first blood against an asset our enemies had in space. Make that two—because according to another of Matthew's after-action reports, the Atlantic Federation has a task force operating in the Pacific Ocean, off the coast of Vietnam—and *they* managed to knock *another* space warship out of orbit. Now, do you want to bet against an enemy coming in force to subdue Earth?"

Now it was Jacques-Yves' turn to wince. Finally, after several seconds, he said, "I take your point, Jack. They haven't done it yet, primarily because they are hard-pressed on the other side of the quadrant. But once they realize they are in serious danger of losing the homeworld—yes, they will come. You can be sure that the Atlantic Federation is fully committed, or will be, once Admiral Yevgenov makes his report. Still, one does not withstand siege forever."

"Precisely my point, which brings me to our next subject. Jacques-Yves, was it your intention to go up into outer space and make contact with any possible friends out there?"

"Yes, it was—and is. In fact, that staff officer I mentioned earlier, who used a re-entry capsule to come to Earth, comes from the Free Systems. They have a ship in the outer reaches of this system. He came to connect with me and as many of my former officers as he could reach."

"Oh-ho," said Scott. "Does your reputation extend to the Free Systems, then?"

"I suppose it must, though I never imagined that reputation would still hold after so many years."

Scott grinned like a wolf. "Jacques-Yves," he said, "don't forget the reputation you have right here on Earth. Matthew told me personally all about you and all the other members of the wardroom of *Bonaventure* Sixth and Seventh. And that campaign you ran in the North Atlantic and then in northern Russia clearly shows you haven't lost your touch. Have no fear, Jacques-Yves. The United States Navy—including what will become its space branch—will assist you in every way so that you can get out there and bring us enough forces to lift the siege we *both* know will come."

"May I ask what form that assistance will take?"

"We are planning an operation against New Aztlán and hope to capture some of those 'LCG' craft Matthew Morrow told us about, Like the kind he captured in the Lucketts raid. We're hoping to use them to place you, as much staff as you have and can recruit, plus a full troop of Marine armored cavalry—no, belay that. Powered exoskeletons would be too heavy for Marines to carry vehicles of any sort—but Matthew also shared specifications for mortars, grenade launchers, and rocket launchers that a soldier in a powered exoskeleton could carry easily. Add to it the specs on this exoskeleton—why, if we could solve the power problem, we could enable infantry to move as fast as cavalry, or faster. So I should say: we hope to place a company of infantry, all equipped with and trained on this new body armor, into space, in addition to some launches to place Marines into several key theaters on Earth."

"If I may suggest," said Jacques-Yves, "the Atlantic Federation Fleet would be most interested in detaching some of their Naval Infantry units for such missions, particularly into the heart of Russia."

"Naval infantry … is that what they call 'Marines'?"

"It is. And in my experience, they fight as well as your Marines."

"I'm liking this even better. Well, that's enough chatter for now. I've got to get things moving on that project to connect to Atlantis *and* that new equipment Matthew invented. Those are gilt-edged priorities. I'll call you if I think of any further questions to ask. Have you anything else to share?"

"Yes. I'll be bringing with me one of your Marines—a Sergeant Peter Jameson. He comes well-recommended for your Officer Candidate School—and I take great pleasure in adding my own name to those recommendations."

"Jameson … Jameson—didn't he take part in the landing on Australia?"

"He did indeed and then boarded the *Zumwalt* for passage home. Of course, our discovery of the Atlantic Federation, and our operations in the

Barents Sea, required that he use a different mode of transport to return home."

"Yes, I see his name here, in another after-action report. He comes highly recommended indeed. Technically he needs to take exams for OCS, but I see no reason why he can't take those exams en route. I'll speak to the OCS Commandant, so we can get that in train. Anything else?"

"No, Admiral."

"Very well. The hour is late here, but not where you are. Tell Sergeant Jameson to expect to sit for those exams within the hour. Scott out."

And the screen went dark.

* * *

"Sergeant Jameson," said Jacques-Yves as he re-entered the common area.

"Yes, sir?"

"Congratulations are in order—or so I infer. You will prepare to take an examination."

"You mean I'm accepted into OCS?"

"Tentatively, contingent on your passing that examination."

"You mean, when arriving at Cumberland?"

"Oh, no, Sergeant. You will take it within the hour."

"Wow!" said Jameson. "I never knew Marine High Command to move so fast."

"War has a way of expediting certain matters," said Jacques-Yves, drily. "Speaking of which: Natalya, you, Dan, Jake, and I must prepare to return to space. Admiral Scott has promised me the use of enough space vehicles to place ourselves, and a full company of Marines, into orbit and, we hope, Dan, to make contact with the ship that brought you here."

"Wow. I can't wait for Captain Park to see us all," said Dan with a grin.

"What kind of space vehicles are we talking about?" Natalya asked. "Matthew didn't seem to know about anything beyond the LCG that Ayelet used."

"Well, Sergeant Major Anderson told us about that already, did he not?"

Anderson, recognizing his name, asked, "Oh, did Admiral Scott brief you on that operation?"

"Yes, he did. Come to think of it; I might be of some assistance in planning that operation."

At that point, he heard an interruption coming from his private cabin. "My excuses," he said. "It seems I have another call." Again he entered the private cabin, closed the door, and sat down at the workstation. Sure enough, the JOIN CALL button showed again. He pressed it.

Jack Scott smiled at him from his office. "Is your Marine sergeant ready to take a test?"

"I've just informed him."

"I've just spoken to the OCS Commandant. The examination will be ready for Sergeant Jameson to take in—let's see—that will be oh-nine-hundred where you are. Will you so advise him?"

"*Tout de suite*, at least after you and I finish."

"And there's something else you should know. Our Seismology Office has picked up some noises they at first couldn't identify. When I passed the word about possible tunnel boring operations, it clicked. It seems your Atlantic Federation has already decided to come calling. So now—we're moving."

Jacques-Yves gasped. "Now even *I* don't know how they could get a report that fast ... Wait, wait, wait. Of course. Admiral Yevgenov surely dispatched an ultra-long-range torpedo carrying a sonar transceiver instead of a warhead. It's how their Officers in Tactical Command communicate with their bases."

"But surely they couldn't afford to send a thing like that on a whim!"

"Surely, Jack, you know that such a message would easily be urgent enough to justify the expense and the risk."

"Do you speak from experience, Jacques-Yves?"

"I do, as a matter of fact. It's a variation on the log-recorder buoys my service uses—a last resort when a ship faces imminent destruction."

"I'll take your word for that, Jacques-Yves. Now how would you advise in response to these drilling noises we're hearing?"

"Assume the obvious—as you said, the Atlantic Federation has implemented some kind of contingency plan. So start to bore toward them. You'll have to move *tout de suite*. Otherwise, they'll continue to bore all straight—that is, straight ahead—no matter what they're about to hit."

"I take your point. Well, you'll be happy to know that we don't permit expansion of habitation space on the coastal side of our East Coast tube. Also, we have spare borers stored in dead-end 'sidings,' again on the coastal side. That includes one pointed at the Charleston Bump—and as you and I were talking, I just cut the orders. We'll be able to contact Atlantis within a week."

"*Excellent*. I'll be sure to pass the word. And I'll have Sergeant Jameson in here at the appointed hour."

Chapter 2

Vice-Admiral Ramón Ordoñez-Pizarro sat, alone and feeling half resentful, half miserable, on a hard, backless bench of imitation wood in the passageway of the Admiralty Administration Building.

He asked himself for the hundredth time, *What am I doing here?* The events of the last months should have *vindicated* him! Vindicated not only him but his family, going all the way back to his ancestor Bernardo, the last *Comandante* of the celebrated *Fuerza Climática de las Naciones Unidas*, called UNCliFor in Standard. And before him, to Francisca Ordoñez-Pizarro, the first Director-General of *Nuevo Aztlán*.

Hadn't he told the Admiralty that *los Estados Unidos Americanos* still existed? Hadn't he dinned in their ears, over and over again, that they must strike again, even if the area *was* Protected Wild Space? *So why hadn't anyone listened?* But even that wasn't what stunned him now.

He looked up and locked eyes with the officer, wearing lieutenant-commander's shoulder boards and the multi-colored lanyard on the right shoulder that marked flag lieutenants and similar attendants on senior officers throughout the United Systems, and, no doubt, in naval services of all historical ages. The other officer met his gaze with … What was that?

Contempt! Oh, he knew, that insolent dog, who ought to cast his eyes down when addressing an officer of Ramón's rank! Three stars, that's what he had on his boards! Three stars … yet they were utterly meaningless now, and he knew it. And *that* explained his misery. Because the defeats the Admiralty had lately suffered had been so humiliating that they needed a scapegoat. Ramón had been so sure, *so sure,* that they would never light upon *him!* He, the direct descendant of one of the Five Ladies themselves! But, he now saw, who else could adequately atone for the loss of two battle destroyers? Each of them crippled and sent to a fiery re-entry and crash by a brace of hypersonic missiles. From vessels of a type no one on Earth was supposed to have. *Ballistic missile submarines!*

The United States of America had not been the only dangerous civilization with whom UNCliFor had dealt. There had also been *La Federación de Rusia.* The records still existed, damningly easy for him to find:

of several Russian fast-attack and ballistic-missile submarines, which had fled the final subsumption of the Russian Federation and the reconstitution of *La Unión de Repúblicas Socialistas Soviéticas.* No one had ever again seen those submarines that had fled out of Polyarnyy Inlet from Murmansk. So naturally, no one ever expected them, or anything like them, to remain in existence.

But everyone had forgotten that the Russians had been the best deep-diving shipwrights in the world they once knew. They must have built cities on the ocean floor—but *where?* No matter. For the Russians had literally returned to their old home, returned the way they had gone, and recaptured their ancient shipyard.

And what made it worse was that the Americans and the Russians were clearly allied. Not only that, but they obviously had help from United Systems Naval and Marine officers. Their names were the most damning of all. Lieutenant Natalya Fyodorovna Bronskaya, United Systems Marine Corps. Rear Admiral Jacques-Yves de Grasse, United Systems Navy. And Lieutenant Commander Matthew Morrow, United Systems Navy. Except that *Comandante* Morrow now called himself *Mariscal* Morrow—*Mariscal de Campo*, no less! And he, Ramón Ordoñez-Pizarro, had been instrumental in bringing those three together. That part would be the most difficult of all to explain.

He nearly jolted off his perch when he heard latch tumblers engage nearly in his ear. A door swung open—one of those oversized doors that graced every Naval installation for as long as he could remember. He looked up at the person with his hand on the knob—tall, the way the Admiralty liked all their human Ground Patrol personnel. Uniformed as a Chief, with the ratings of a master-at-arms, wearing a light gray helmet and having an armband on his left arm bearing the letters GP.

"The court will hear you now, Vice-Admiral," the Chief said tonelessly.

Ramón stood with all the dignity he could still muster and followed the Chief through the doorway.

Again, like all rooms in this building, this one was cavernous, with an overhead of at least three meters. Ahead of him sat the single armchair where all witnesses sat. Imitation wood, like all the furniture in this room—

because no one would commit the sacrilege of actually killing a live tree, especially not Central American mahogany!

The dais was of the color of that fabled Central American wood—artificial, of course. And now Ramón got a greater shock. He'd expected a less-than-sympathetic hearing. After all, this was a court of inquiry—and a court of inquiry that could judge the case of a Vice-Admiral was a formidable body indeed. But the president of this court was the tallest being Ramón had ever seen. In fact, he belonged to the race that was the reason official buildings, even on Sol d, were so cavernous. He stood two and two-thirds meters tall—slightly unusual for Naval officers but average for a member of his race. And in case Ramón had any doubt about the identity of that race, the court president sported the pale complexion and pointed ears that marked his race throughout the Six-O'clock Quadrant. In short, the chief of his inquisitors was an Elf.

"Raise your right hand," said the Elf in a silky-smooth voice that chilled Ramón to the bone upon hearing it. Ramón obeyed without a word.

"Do you solemnly swear that the testimony you are about to give in this inquiry shall be the truth, the whole truth, and nothing but the truth?"

"I do," said Ramón in what he knew was not much more than a squeak.

"State your name, rank, and position."

"Ramón Ordoñez-Pizarro. Vice-Admiral, United Systems Navy. I currently serve as Director of Naval Intelligence."

"Be seated, Vice-Admiral Ordoñez-Pizarro," said the Elf. If anything, his voice sounded worse—as if he were discussing a monumentally distasteful subject.

Ramón sat.

"Now then, this court has heard several reports of a most alarming nature." The Elf paused, swallowed hard, then said coldly, "Actually, 'alarming' doesn't half say it. As nearly as this court can determine, your involvement in our current troubles began when you visited retired Rear-Admiral Jacques-Yves de Grasse at his vineyard and winery. That would be…" the Elf paused to consult a laptop display, "MJDN 204195," he finished

"Yes, sir," said Ramón. "But as soon as I realized that Matthew Morrow had sent a covert operative to penetrate the French wine country…"

"So I note," said the president. "So you sent an operative to kill Admiral De Grasse and capture that cyborg operative." Then, in a chillingly severe tone, the president continued, "But you failed. Not only did you lose your operative, but your next attempt, involving a maglev shuttle, also failed. All of which was the perfect set-up for Admiral De Grasse to escape from France and join a ship of the *United States Navy*."

"Mr. President, if I may, I have told the Admiralty of the continued existence of *los Estados Unidenses* for many years…"

"Silence!"

Ramón's blood ran cold.

"I don't think you understand the precarious situation in which you find yourself," the Elf said. "Did you think you were here to give this court a litany of excuses? *You're here to show just cause why this court should not break you in rank and perhaps oust you from the Navy all together.*"

Now his mouth went dry.

"We face a situation we ought never to have had to face due entirely to your bungling," said the president. "It was bad enough before you got involved. Out of three prototype cyborgs, one is now destroyed, and the other two have turned renegade. We have lost the Botany Bay prison complex. We also face, apparently, *two* blue-water navies, one on the surface, the other beneath the sea. The latter is actually powerful enough to defend low-orbital space with ridiculous effectiveness. Not only that, but we face an air force that was *supposed* to belong to us and now belongs to our enemies.

"And who can know what else we face? Add to it that we have lost the use of the pneumatic tube system—or at least the part of it that matters. And the *reason* we've lost that is that our strongest enemy in this accursed world is underground, *and* at the level of the pneumatic tube system, and who knows how far below it!

"But the worst part of our situation is that we have utterly lost the cyborg project. I repeat what I observed earlier: out of three prototypes, one is destroyed, and the other two are renegade. And those are the two most dangerous renegades our society has had to deal with. And on *your watch*, that situation has gotten an order of magnitude worse. *What have you to say for yourself?*"

What could he say? This Elf had found his scapegoat, and Ramón was it. Or was there a way out?

Wait a minute…!

"My lord!" he blurted out. "There is yet hope. Those cyborgs you mentioned—they are running out of power!"

"Do not jest, Vice-Admiral Ordoñez-Pizarro. They can each recharge."

"Not for much longer!"

Silence descended upon the courtroom. Then the president spoke again. "Continue," he said.

"There is no reason to suppose that Matthew Morrow or Natalya Bronskaya understand the limits of the batteries they carry," said Ramón. Even as he said it, he desperately hoped it was true, and those two cyborgs hadn't had time to correct the fault. He plunged ahead anyway: "You cannot charge the batteries they carry more than a fixed number of charges. Matthew Morrow is surely nearing the limit. Natalya Bronskaya will reach *her* limit shortly thereafter."

"And then?"

"And then," said Ramón, managing a smile, "they will die."

The president leaned to his right to whisper to another court member. Soon all nine members of the court were whispering together. Finally, the president said, "Very well, the court will let you return to duty, on the assumption that those two cyborgs will shortly be incapacitated and we can bring this insurrection to a close." Then the Elf affected his most stern look yet as he said, "But be correct, Vice-Admiral Ordoñez-Pizarro. This court is being very generous in tolerating your mission failures thus far. *But this court will not tolerate deceit.* Do I make myself clear?"

"Yes, my lord."

"Very well. You may go."

Ramón picked up his officer's cap, stood up, and left the hearing room. He barely made it out of the Administration Building. Outside, he nearly stumbled, and half fell, into his staff car. He somehow managed to snap out an order to his driver to take him to the Military Intelligence Directorate. Once there, he went straight to his office, leaving orders he was not to be disturbed. Then—finally alone—he collapsed in his desk chair, trembling all over, and remained in that state for a good quarter of an hour.

Chapter 3

Sergeant Jameson emerged from the cabin at 1000 hours, wearing a broad smile.

"Do I take it," said Jacques-Yves, "that you have passed your examinations?"

"I certainly have."

"Congratulations—although I'm not sure I understand how you could pass such an examination so quickly."

"These are adaptive tests, sir. With each answer you give, the program selects the next question—more or less difficult, depending on whether you answer right or wrong."

"Well! As quickly as you completed these tests, you must have done very well on them."

Jameson shrugged, "I suppose so," he said. "Hey—I'm in. In fact, I have some preliminary reading assignments already."

"Now that *is* fast!"

"Well, sir, I have a theory about that," said the sergeant. "It occurs to me that the Marine Corps very much wants to assign me to your space-launch mission. I don't like to presume, but…"

"You are absolutely correct, Sergeant," said Jacques-Yves. "I won't claim any direct knowledge of any such orders, but your analysis makes perfect sense. I commend you—it means you're already thinking like an officer."

"Why … thank you, sir."

"Of nothing. What's more important is that you should start your studies. Ask Sergeant Major Anderson to help you. Tell him I said you're to have everything of which you have need."

"Thank you, sir." Jameson saluted, and Jacques-Yves returned it.

As the sergeant left, Jacques-Yves turned to Natalya. "Keep your eye on him, Lieutenant," he said.

"I've been watching him, Admiral," she said, smiling. "I look forward to having him in my strike force—and I'm sure *he* looks forward to taking a combat leadership role again."

Three alarm tones sounded. Jacques-Yves turned to where they seemed to be coming from and found himself looking at another bulkhead clock, which was now flashing 11:00.

"Time zone change, Admiral," said Natalya. "We're not on Beijing time any longer. We're on Vladivostok time."

"I see." Again he raised his arm to check his wrist chronometer. But before he could advance the hands, Natalya stopped him.

"I wouldn't do that just now if I were you, Admiral," Natalya said.

"Why not?"

"Because we're going to make many more time-zone changes, and even a date change, before our journey ends."

"*La vache.* How do regular United Nations subjects handle such changes?"

"The wristwatches they wear do more than tell time," she answered. "They synchronize automatically with a network time server. No one in United Nations or United Systems society ever sets a timepiece."

"*Dégueulasse.* Total passivity. I was a fool to think I could last forever in such a society. Then again, I'm accustomed to command, and command requires a measure of autonomy that civilians in this world never had. What other functions does a typical wristwatch perform? Or dare I ask?"

"Same as some of the wearables you and I used in the Navy, Admiral— aboard *Bonaventure VI.* Vital signs, for one thing—and even dietary monitoring."

"And to think they're *enforcing* that disgusting drug regimen Matthew discovered! I'd rather keep this wrist chronometer, thank you very much. However often I must adjust it, I control it, and it does not control me."

Natalya smiled. "I can't argue with that, Admiral," she said.

"But I'll take your other point. I might as well wait until the time adjustments become a bit less frequent than they are likely to be."

"I've been wondering about that," she said. "Your mechanical chronometer seems designed for far less frequent time changes than one every half hour. Couldn't someone have improved such a timepiece to enable a semi-automatic adjustment?"

"What do you want to say by that?"

"It seems to me that if you could advance the hands exactly one hour forward or backward with a single button press or lever pull, such a device would be far more convenient."

"Yes, I can see that it would," said Jacques-Yves. "Then again, the electronic chronometers took over after the Jet Age was only a few *décennies* old. No one would look at a mechanical chronometer again, much less think about how to improve it as you suggested."

"Ah," said Natalya, smiling more broadly, "but I'll wager that our old friend Eric Shaka could improve the design that way."

Jacques-Yves shook his head, "I doubt my old engineering officer would ever take an interest in anything mechanical," he said. "But, now that I think about it, Warrant Officer O'Reilly might have. He was the one person aboard who could repair this when I asked him to. Except he would never have seen much point in such a quick-adjustment mechanism."

"Why not, do you think?"

"Because in space, there's never a need for it. As I'm sure you remember, all United Systems Naval vessels keep Coordinated Universal Time in synchrony with Sol d—or rather, Earth. Which is the City of London, capital of the United Kingdom."

"I never thought of that! Why solar days and not sidereal days?"

"Sidereal time," said the Admiral, "might be appropriate for travel within a particular star-and-planet system. Or it might have *been* appropriate in the days of lightspeed communications, when one needed to define a day by the orientation of a particular point on the surface of this planet, regardless of whether it was daytime or nighttime. But planetary orientation makes no difference in the modern era of interstellar travel and hyperluminary communications. And the United Systems still regards this world as the 'homeworld.'"

"Even after everything that's happened?"

"Those *happenings* have been fairly recent if I understand correctly."

Natalya nodded. "True, Admiral," she said.

* * *

The tube car went through three more time changes, then a date change—strange, to *gain* a day after *losing* three hours. But after Natalya explained it to him, it made sense. After that, it went through four more hour advances before its compass heading changed to south-southeast. But in addition to losing eight hours and gaining a day, eight *more* hours had passed. So he was not surprised when the wall chronometer told him it was 2330 hours on the day *before* he had awakened. And soon, it would be midnight on the day *of* his awakening. So by forbearing to adjust his chronometer, he wouldn't have to adjust the day.

He set about packing his kit bag, for he knew to expect a transfer. Within fifteen minutes, he was finished. After another fifteen minutes, he felt the tube car slow again. He took his kit bag in hand as the car slotted into the siding at the tube station.

"San Francisco, sir," said Sergeant Major Anderson. Not long afterward, the car came to a stop, and the doors slid open.

The San Francisco station looked no different from the Beijing station, except for the signs telling him where he was—until he went down one level. Then the difference between San Francisco and Beijing became obvious. The line leading eastward through the interior of the United States of America—beneath the vast area called Protected Wild Space—was clearly improvised. Instead of a neat hole, this one showed every sign of a recent, and hurried, connection. Loose rocks lay everywhere, and the sign indicating a direction toward the New York Caverns was actually *hand-painted*. Jacques-Yves was just about to comment on that when he sensed another tube car approaching.

This car showed every sign of moving much more slowly. It also looked like an older model. In fact, it came out into the open air as it entered one of two open tracks that merged into one. It came to rest next to a ram-like stop at the end of the single track. That's when Jacques-Yves realized that this was not a single car at all, but a train. An apparent locomotive with a sloping windscreen capped each end of the train, which had four cars between the two locomotives.

"I see that your philosophy of tube transport differs greatly from that of the United Nations," he said to Sergeant Major Anderson.

"If you mean we like modules that we can string together to serve different transportation purposes, yes," said the sergeant. "Our system is slightly more adaptable. We can piece together any kind of VIP transport we need or transport large numbers of people in the same direction. Shall we board, sir?"

"Yes, by all means," said Jacques-Yves, who had noticed the open doors.

A train, he soon realized, required slightly stricter safety rules than a single long but jointed car. Where one car joined another, gaps could open up. Perhaps for that reason, all the cars had doors at each end.

"This will be your car, sir," said the sergeant, indicating the car they had entered by passing to the left of the galley car where they had boarded. "The rest of us will sleep in the car nearest the loco on the other end."

"Won't the noise annoy you?"

"We're used to it, sir. So much so that we hardly notice it. Besides, those engines are fairly quiet as engines go. They're electric."

Jacques-Yves took the point at once. Electric motors were the quietest of all. And nothing else would serve in an underground society.

And so, with his wrist chronometer still reading MER 27 but now displaying the time as 12:30, Jacques-Yves felt the train move out of the San Francisco terminal and onto a two-rail track. Gently it picked up speed—but *not* the very high speed of the pneumatic tube car. He guessed he was moving at not more than half that speed.

He didn't bother trying to sleep; that would be useless, given that, for all intents and purposes, it was four and a half hours in the afternoon and *not* midnight and a half. *La vache,* how could these people endure such disruption to their daily rhythms? He couldn't wait to get back into space, which didn't require such frequent adjustments.

Seven and a quarter hours, Sergeant Major Anderson had said, and they would arrive at the Cumberland Caverns complex. In that time, he would cross three time-zone planes. So he would arrive in the late morning—eleven hours minus the quarter, to be exact. And he would better serve himself if he could be fully refreshed upon his arrival.

So he did the one thing that might bring the best results. He logged into the single console in his car and tried to program a meal. Then he remembered. *In this society, they don't "print" their food.* He would need help. So he stepped out of the car and entered the galley car.

"Can I get something for you, Admiral?" asked a young man, uniformed, Jacques-Yves guessed, as a Navy steward's mate.

"Yes," he said. "Bring me the heartiest vegetable-based soup this galley can produce."

"One bowl of split-pea soup, coming up, Admiral. And what will you have to drink?"

"Tea. Something relaxing."

"I recommend chamomile, sir."

"Chamomile it shall be," said Jacques-Yves with a smile. "I'll take it in my car."

"Aye-aye, sir."

He retired to his car, where, twenty minutes later, the young steward's mate brought him his soup and tea. The meal had exactly the effect he had hoped for. Within an hour of eating it, he found that he *could* sleep, and he did.

* * *

He sat in his conning chair aboard *Bonaventure VI*. Before him was the main viewer on the command bridge. Just now, instead of a star field, it showed a tactical display—a grim one. It showed his ship's strike force, all three platoons of it, laying siege to a fortress on the planet below. With a sick feeling of *déjà vu*, he recognized the landmarks. Rigel g.

Knowing he was reliving a mission he could not alter, he watched as Natalya's forces seemed on the point of breaching the fortress—when a troop of cavalry that must have ridden out the fortress' cleverly hidden postern gate ambushed them from each side. Somehow the Marines prevailed—but a call from an anguished S-6 carried the dire news. The strike force commander had been mortally wounded.

Jacques-Yves dispatched an LCG to pick up the commander. Then, with that same leaden feeling in his gut, he lay below and aft to the hangar deck to witness the off-loading of the commander's body. On that level, he met Débora, the ship's surgeon, who had a very grim look on her face. She must feel the same as him.

They waited until the LCG had re-entered the hangar. The hangar master must have activated the containment field, for he could read the hangar deck re-pressurizing, though the doors remained open. Then a green light in the passageway door told the two officers that the door was safe to open.

They opened the door and entered the cavernous space, walking swiftly toward the LCG. Jacques-Yves remembered to circle around the saucer-shaped vehicle to its stern—because the stern landing leg held the boarding ladder. As he and Débora approached the foot of the stern leg, a grim party was walking down the boarding latter, gently guiding a gravity litter.

Eventually, the captain and ship's surgeon met the litter, glanced down at the face of the patient on it … and here Jacques-Yves got a profound shock.

He had expected to find Natalya on that litter. But the patient looking up at him wasn't Natalya at all. *It was Matthew!*

* * *

Jacques-Yves sat bolt upright in his bed. He was in his private sleeping car on the train bound for Cumberland Caverns, in the underground society that was *Les États-Unis d'Amérique.* But he was not alone. Natalya stood next to the bed. He looked into her eyes—real eyes, capable of a sensitivity no camera could match—and of reflecting the full range of emotion.

She had been crying.

He said the first thing that occurred to him. "Matthew?"

She nodded, trembling. "How … how did you know? Sir?" she asked—in French.

"I had a very odd but pointed dream," Jacques-Yves answered in the same language. "And I know that only one person in the Galaxy could worry you so. What does Matthew have?"

"His batteries, sir. He hasn't been able to recharge for several days."

"What! Why did he not tell us?"

"Duty, Admiral. And perhaps not knowing how or whether you could help him."

"Lay that aside for the moment. Where is he now?"

Natalya's eyes suddenly glazed over. He was about to ask what *she* had when she relaxed visibly. "He's aboard the tube car in Saigon," she said. "A young man named Zachary Radner is with him. I should have thought of this: Zachary has his own nanobot army. He knew Matthew was in trouble. So he rather desperately signaled our friend Andrew Blakely—that is, the captain of an LCG that's part of that expedition. Andrew flew back to Western Australia, picked him up, and together they went directly to where Matthew had lost his energy and fallen. They're trying to keep Matthew going with continuous charging, but…" then she stopped, clearly unable to continue. Tears flowed freely from her eyes.

"Natalya," said Jacques-Yves, now leaving his bed so he could reach for her and try to offer her some comfort.

She turned her face from him.

"Look at me, Lieutenant," he said, using his stern command voice. "I order you."

She did.

Then in a gentler tone, Jacques-Yves said, "Never have fear to ask a fellow officer for emotional support. Especially not me, your commander. I performed that duty for Matthew, and I will perform it for you now. Have you or Sergeant Major Anderson made arrangements to transport Matthew to our destination?"

"Yes," she said, now beginning to recover some of her composure. "I couldn't think of any better place for him to come."

"You did well," said Jacques-Yves. "If anyone can help him, these Americans can. Surely we both know enough of them to respect their technology. But tell me this: are you subject to the same limitation?"

"I'm—that is, I have fear that I am. I perhaps have a few more days, or weeks, or months. I've not 'lived' so long as he has, and haven't had to go through as many cycles."

"Natalya, listen to me. Are you listening?"

"Yes, sir."

"We have hope of solving both your problems."

"How so?"

Now, for the first time, Jacques-Yves told her about Matthew's idea about powered exoskeletons. "So you see," he said in conclusion, "the Americans have already committed themselves to developing a radical new power source. Such a source should be eminently adaptable to you and Matthew."

"Oh, but have we *time?*"

"We shall have time," said Jacques-Yves, in a determined voice. "I shall see to that."

Natalya smiled. "Like old times … Excuse me. I almost called you 'Captain' just now."

Jacques-Yves smiled back, "I excuse you," he said. "After all, I *was* your Captain once. I have hope that this time, I'll serve you better than I did then."

"Rigel g?"

"That's exact."

"Now it's my turn to tell *you* to have no fear," she said. "The Admiralty conspired against me, making sure I would 'die' in that action. I told you that before, did I not?"

"You did. Lieutenant Kress, your successor in command of the strike force, was also sure of it. I don't know why he stayed in the United Systems Navy as long as he did. After they turned me out to pasture, as it were, and decommissioned my ship and scattered my crew, he returned to his own civilization. And I cannot fault him."

"Do you think you'll ever go back to being a vine dresser and winemaker?"

Jacques-Yves shook his head, "No," he said. "You had right to tell me that I was living—or existing—in a mausoleum. Furthermore, I have no heirs, unless you count young Paul Girard, Débora's son. And *he* is not likely to take an interest in agricultural pursuits. So I think I shall let our friend, the Lady of the Lamps, have the land."

"In the last century before the Elves came," said Natalya, "various preservation societies would look after the properties of famous persons who died and left no family."

Jacques-Yves had to laugh. "Do you really think I'll earn that sort of distinction?" he asked.

"One never knows."

"Still," he said, "I must visit the Caverns known as 'Mara Israel.' There I shall make my will and leave the land to Ayelet Cohen, or her heirs or assigns. I can think of no better steward."

"I should let you sleep, Admiral," Natalya said. "We've already passed into the next time zone and will pass through two more."

"You have right, of course. Have you any other questions for me?"

"No, sir. But thank you. Thank you for being the commander I needed. And for distracting me when I needed that, too."

"In such things," said Jacques-Yves, "I am always at your service. Never forget that."

She held out her hand for a handshake. He shook it—almost tentatively, remembering how powerful that hand could be. But Natalya knew her strength well; nothing untoward happened. Then she turned and left the car.

Jacques-Yves returned to his bed, wondering how he would compose himself for sleep a second time. It turned out not to be very difficult at all.

* * *

His dreams were much confused, though also much more pleasant, at least at first. One moment he was back on his old vineyard—the one his faithful retainer, Marcel, had burned after he and Natalya had left it. In the next, he was on the command deck of *Bonaventure VI*—which, in the middle of a battle, abruptly changed to the more streamlined command deck of *Bonaventure VII*.

And then, *a propos* of nothing, the scene changed again—to the bridge of USS *Elmo Zumwalt* DDG-1000. Except, this time, he was commanding that vessel directly and facing off against another vessel of the same model. Sure enough, that other vessel came at *Zumwalt* on a ramming course—and Jacques-Yves read the catalog number on her bow: 1002. USS—no, *NAS Lyndon Baines Johnson*.

And somehow, though he should scarcely be able to tell on short notice from the instruments on this bridge—he knew where he was fighting this battle—the Gulf of Mexico, and in a very narrow strait at that. The Florida Straits, with Florida off his starboard beam and Cuba off his port beam. As quickly as he realized this, the two ships were exchanging missile fire—but why was the big gun out of action? Of course—it had none of the special ammunition it required. The other ship had the same disadvantage, but—

A missile came straight at the deckhouse. He barely had time to shout an order to intercept …

And then he woke up.

The wall chronometer told him the time: 1130, with an R next to it. R for Romeo—but also R for a time zone five hours behind UTC, which the United States Navy called Z for Zulu. This, he knew, was the Eastern Time Zone, the same as the one for Cumberland Caverns. So he had fifteen minutes to see to himself, reset his wrist chronometer, and dress.

He accomplished all these things in five minutes and so was ready, with the rest of his party, when the train slotted into the Cumberland station.

When the doors opened, Sergeant Major Anderson led everyone out onto the platform. This was a very busy platform compared to those at Murmansk, Beijing, and San Francisco. Anderson led them all to an *escalateur* that took them up one level, then to a bank of *ascenseurs*. When the doors of one of them opened, Anderson led them all through into a very spacious car, then punched a button high on the triple column of buttons on a wall panel to one side of the doors. The doors closed, and the *ascenseur* started up—rapidly. That was good—at least these people knew not to force travelers to waste time in one of these things!

The car slowed, then stopped. The doors opened again, giving out into a space that actually *looked* like a natural cavern—with actual cavern walls. There another vehicle was waiting for them—an autobus with a twenty-passenger capacity.

But before they had an opportunity to board, a very light vehicle came toward them—with a driver and room for one passenger only. The vehicle pulled up to the party, then stopped. The driver—a civilian—wearing an identity tag labeled STAFF got out.

"Sergeant Peter Jameson?" he asked.

"That's me," said the Sergeant.

"The Commandant of the Officer Candidate School sends his compliments, Sergeant. He sent me to pick you up."

"Wow! How do I rate that?"

"Part of the service, Sergeant—or I should say, *Mister* Jameson. You're a cadet now. But if I may suggest, we should hurry. The Commandant doesn't like to be kept waiting."

"Whoa-ho! Well, in that case, let's go!" With that, Jameson loaded his kit bag into the vehicle. Then he turned to face the rest of the party one last time. "Admiral," he said, "it's been a pleasure serving with you."

"And it was my pleasure to have you on my staff," said Jacques-Yves. "But duty calls—and that likely goes for both of us. Good luck, Ser—ah, *Mister* Jameson."

"Thank you, sir!" He raised his hand in salute. Jacques-Yves returned it—and noticed every member of his party, except for Sergeant Major

Anderson, doing the same. Well, why not, after such a memorable association?

Jameson climbed into the vehicle, and the civilian employee drove him away. Then Sergeant Major Anderson led Jacques-Yves and the rest of his party aboard the waiting autobus.

This conveyance had plenty of room for everyone. Jacques-Yves took his seat directly behind the driver. Sergeant Major Anderson sat across the aisle from him, where he could talk to the driver more readily. After everyone was on board, the autobus rolled off—almost silently. He was accustomed to that—all the vehicles he knew had electric motors. But he was *not* accustomed to seeing so many vehicles. This society did not restrict vehicular operator's licenses or registrations nearly as tightly as the United Nations did. But somehow, traffic moved swiftly and safely, as far as he could observe.

Eventually, the vehicle slowed to a halt, and the driver opened the doors. Anderson led them all off, then down the motorway for about thirty steps, and then through a narrow passageway that gave onto a corridor for pedestrians only. Of course, he would have entered a building in Paris, Cadillac, or Bordeaux. So this was the equivalent of an underground society! After several more steps, the party emerged into a room filled with desks, computer consoles—and several clerks, most of them female, and most wearing aural headsets, staring intently at their screens and occasionally putting in a small piece of information, or a command, usually by touching the screen, but sometimes by touching other screens that rested on their desks.

Anderson led Jacques-Yves and the others across this room and through two doors into a spacious conference room. It was very long—Jacques-Yves guessed it was twenty feet long and ten feet wide. The overhead was no higher than seven feet—the same as aboard the *Elmo Zumwalt*. Or on that train that had brought him here, for that matter.

Along the centerline of the room rested a table of a wood that was a deep reddish-brown in color. He touched it, and it felt solid—and he could see the grains just beneath the mirror-polished surface.

"If you'll all find seats," Anderson said, "I'll make my report to the Admiral. He'll very likely want to see you."

"Make that *does*, Sergeant Major," said a voice at the door. Jacques-Yves turned to the owner of the voice. Tall (about six feet), of medium build, wearing a dress blue uniform and cap—with five stars, in pentagonal arrays, on each shoulder. Anderson raised his hand in salute. Jacques-Yves did likewise and noticed the rest of his party doing the same.

Fleet Admiral Jack Scott (for it could be none other) raised his own hand to return the salute. "Be seated, everyone," he said and took his own seat at the head of the conference table.

"Rear-Admiral Jacques-Yves de Grasse, I presume?" said Scott, extending a hand to him.

Jacques-Yves took the hand, saying, "Indeed, yes. And have I the honor of addressing Fleet Admiral Scott?"

"You have," said Scott, with a smile. "It's good to meet you in person. And you," he went on, looking at Natalya, "must be Lieutenant Natalya Bronskaya, late of the United Systems Marines. Or are you now a Senior Lieutenant in the Atlantic Federal Naval Infantry?"

Natalya smiled. "I haven't gone that far, Admiral Scott," she said. "But I *have* taken part in two operations with units of that service."

"So I gathered, from those after-action reports Matthew Morrow sent me … Wait a minute, Lieutenant. Did I just say something wrong?"

Jacques-Yves glanced at Natalya and saw at once that she was stricken with emotion. "I don't know whether you've heard," he said hastily, "but our old friend Matthew Morrow is in no small distress at the moment."

"I'm sorry to hear that," said Scott. "No doubt that was the subject of the latest message that reached my console just as I was leaving my office to greet you. What, briefly, is the problem, if I may ask?"

Jacques-Yves explained.

"Is he on his way here?" Scott asked after Jacques-Yves was finished.

"He is," said Natalya. "But he'll need a—how do you say it—connection at San Francisco."

"One moment," said Scott. He then drew out a small under-table drawer, which Jacques-Yves had not noticed when he entered. The drawer held a flat panel, about two feet long and slightly more than a foot wide. Scott touched it, and it lit up at once.

He then started to "play" the screen as swiftly and expertly as Matthew had once played the piano in the music room aboard *Bonaventure VII* when he gave those concerts to the crew. Concerts that would have been a forced courtesy—until Engineer Shaka had removed Matthew's emotion-blocking chip. That one act had enabled Matthew not only to interpret music in his own way, but to compose his own. Jacques-Yves found himself remembering some of those compositions—all sounding themes centering on truth, justice, *casus belli*, and righteous warfare.

Then the moment was gone, for Admiral Scott looked up at his guests. He wore a grim expression.

"I have given the requisite orders," he announced. "A special train is on its way to San Francisco—two power cars, a fifty-five-seater, a galley, and a mobile infirmary. That last will be slightly modified; that young man, Zachary Radner, has given an excellent report on Matthew's condition. But I won't minimize the situation, Lieutenant Bronskaya. "Distress" doesn't half describe his condition, as I understand it.

"Which makes our research project the more urgent, actually. Jacques-Yves, did you explain the particulars of Matthew's latest invention to your party?"

"To Natalya here," said Jacques-Yves. "Not to anyone else."

"I don't see Sergeant Jameson here," said Scott. "You didn't lose him, did you?" he asked with a smile.

"The OCS Commandant sent a civilian employee to collect him and take him to the school."

"Ah. I'm sure he'll settle in easily if his exam scores are any indicator—and yes, the Commandant shared them with me. You didn't brief *him* about that project, did you?"

"I didn't feel the need."

"Just as well," said Scott. "I'm going to make a command decision. Jacques-Yves and I are going to brief all the rest of you—with the clear understanding that the particulars of this project are not to leave this room. This is top secret, and I've already filed an order 'clearing' you all to handle material having that classification. Does everyone understand?"

Jacques-Yves looked at everyone present. Natalya already knew, of course. But in every other face—Jake Boddicker, Udayan Thakur, and Sergeant Major Anderson—he read a silent agreement to keep the secret.

"Very well," said the Admiral. "To put it most simply, Matthew Morrow has invented something that will revolutionize ground warfare—*if* we can develop a suitable power source. It's a powered exoskeleton—one that takes human or humanoid form but serves as body armor and can also amplify a soldier's movements and give him the effective strength of ten—at least. It is not only an exoskeleton but a completely self-contained suit—airtight, even watertight. I'm not sure Matthew intended it as a 'hard-hat SCUBA hybrid,' for lack of a better turn of phrase—but I'd love to talk to our new-found friends in the Atlantic Federation about that as soon as we make contact. Which, by the way, we're working on already."

"Excuse me, Jack," said Jacques-Yves. 'Hard-hat SCUBA hybrid'?"

Scott smiled. "You have me there," he said. "SCUBA stands for Self-contained Underwater Breathing Apparatus. 'Hard hat' refers to the kind of diving suit we used before SCUBA—a suit relying on air pumped in from the surface, and including a rigid helmet, hence 'hard hat.' The original SCUBA did not include helmets or, indeed, anything to counteract external pressure. But this new exoskeleton, in addition to containing pressure in a vacuum or near-vacuum environment, might also be able to *resist* pressure in a high-pressure environment—like an ultra-deep dive. That's why this should interest the Atlantic Federation. I can't imagine they have anything remotely like this—they probably used one-man submarines with mechanical armatures to build their cities. Now imagine how much easier they could expand, repair—or defend—their cities if they could use this exoskeleton for real dives.

"But that's for later. Even with the capabilities I've mentioned, a soldier on the ground, wearing such a suit, could outlast and outfight a battalion, perhaps even a regiment, of ordinary infantry. Matthew even gave it an electromagnetic shield, like his own. Between that and the outer skin, it would be proof against any ordinary hand weapon any enemy infantry would carry.

"But there's more—much more. If you have the strength of ten, you can carry ten times the load. Even allowing for the weight of its built-in life-support system and high-pressure air, or low-pressure oxygen, to supply it, you could carry weapons at least five times as heavy as any ordinary infantry weapon. Suddenly one soldier can carry, service, and fire what would normally be a crew-served weapon. So—artillery becomes obsolete.

"And this baby can move—faster than any of the tanks and armored fighting vehicles we use today. That's even allowing for carrying mortars redesigned for a man in a suit to service alone and rocket and grenade launchers that let him pack more punch than the biggest tank. Conventional armor—obsolete. Armored cavalry—obsolete. I'm not even sure spacecraft or aircraft would be effective against infantry equipped like this. A single infantryman could evade the most nimble bomber or attack plane—and carry anti-aircraft missiles that would have beat anything regular infantry used to carry.

"I want to make sure you understand what I'm getting at. Centuries ago, during the War Between the States, General Thomas Jonathan Jackson—known as "Stonewall" to his officers and enlisted—drove his men so hard in his campaign in the Shenandoah River Valley that members of other units called his brigade 'foot cavalry.' With this powered exoskeleton, *all* infantry units become 'foot cavalry,' and 'foot artillery,' all rolled into one mean fighting force."

"I say," said Dan Thakur, "shouldn't we have your Commandant of Marines in here?"

"I don't want to get his hopes up," said Scott. "Because the one thing that is going to hold this project back is power. The power source that can run this exoskeleton effectively, without requiring a recharge every hour, does not yet exist. Even Matthew wasn't sure we could develop it. And now, as I'm sure Lieutenant Bronskaya will be the first to tell us, that power source has become more urgent than ever. Without it, we're going to lose two very good friends—Matthew first, then the Lieutenant."

"Admiral, I'm not at all sure, but maybe this is where I come in," said Jake.

"I don't believe I got a full briefing on you, Lieutenant…?"

"Jake Boddicker's the name, and weapons are my game," he said, grinning that same wolfish grin that Jacques-Yves still couldn't decide whether he liked or hated. "And this powered exoskeleton of yours sounds great. Are you sure you've never tried to make it work before?"

"As a matter of fact, our society *does* have records of earlier experiments in powered armor," said Scott. "That's where I drew the insights I just shared with you on what it could do. But those experimenters ran into the same problem: power."

"Admiral!" said Natalya. "Don't you see it now? We need Eric! And Chief O'Reilly!"

"I was just about to mention them," said Jacques-Yves. "Jack, you've heard me mention them before. The two men she just named were, respectively, my engineering officer and my senior machinist in my last two commands. He was also the senior warrant officer on board."

"Yes, you told me," said Scott. "Now: do any of you have any idea where to find them?"

Everyone present pulled a long face.

"Then that's our priority," said Scott. "Find out where those two are and extract them." Scott keyed a few more touches into his flat-panel console, then looked up. "Your friend will arrive tomorrow morning roughly at oh-four hundred. We'll talk then. In the meantime: I've arranged accommodations in the VIP quarters. The reason you all rate that is that you have just shared top-secret material, and I don't want it to go any further. So for now, Admiral de Grasse, I'm going to make you my special consultant— and these other officers will continue as your staff. Now I'd like to know what services you're all commissioned in."

"Technically," said Jacques-Yves, "I am commissioned nowhere, except *perhaps* in the United Systems Navy—though, of course, I repudiate that commission."

"In that case, I'll commission you in the United *States* Navy, subject to your accepting another commission from an allied power when you contact them. Lieutenant Bronskaya?"

"My commission is in the Revolutionary Forces for a Free Earth," said Natalya.

"Ah. Matthew did that for you, right?"

"Yes, Admiral."

"And you two?"

"I hold the rank of Lieutenant Commander in the Free Systems Navy," said Dan Thakur. "Jake here holds the rank of Lieutenant in that service— though that's a commission I gave him."

"Do I detect a tentative note in that statement, Commander Thakur?"

Jake laughed. "He means, Admiral," he said, "that I'm a member of the Syndicate, which the United Systems considers a gang of criminals. Which maybe we are."

Scott chuckled. "From what I've heard already about the United Systems," he said, "I'd say you have no reason to feel embarrassed on that account. I'll respect your commission. If Admiral de Grasse accepts you as one of his officers, I'll respect that, too, so long as you respect *my* position."

"Of course, Admiral," said Jake. "That worked for Matthew and me, after all."

"Do I gather you respect Matthew Morrow?"

"He was the first officer of any military to respect *me*," said Jake. "In fact, he was the first person in any kind of authority, other than in the Syndicate, to treat me with any kind of respect. I'm still trying to get used to the idea of being what you call 'an officer and a gentleman.'"

Jacques-Yves stared at Jake Boddicker in shocked silence. Now he truly was "without voice." He had never heard anyone describe so brilliantly what was wrong with United Systems society.

He turned to look at Jack Scott, who looked to Jacques-Yves as if he were thinking much the same or close to it. Finally, the Fleet Admiral smiled.

"I'd say you're more than halfway there," he said, "if you could deliver an insight like that. I hope I can show you that respect is one of the things that binds our society together—and not just in the Navy and Marine Corps. You'll have a decision to make; I see that now. And only you can make that decision. I would definitely encourage you to reach out to your superior officer for guidance along that line. I have a hunch he can help you. Am I right?"

Jacques-Yves recognized that Scott had directed that last to him. "Absolutely," he said, turning to Jake. "Please feel free to ask me about what it means to be an officer any time we're not in immediate crisis. And I think we know one another well enough to tell that."

Jake Boddicker smiled—a different kind of smile. A man's smile. "Thank you, Admiral," he said. "I just might take you up on that."

Jacques-Yves, purely on instinct, turned and offered Jake his hand. Jake took it—and confirmed Jacques-Yves' earlier impression.

"Does anyone have any more questions?" Scott asked.

Jacques-Yves shook his head and noticed his companions doing the same.

"In that case," said the Fleet Admiral, "I adjourn this meeting. Sergeant-Major, my secretary will have all the billet assignments, including yours."

"Aye-aye, sir," said Anderson.

The Fleet Admiral left first. Then Anderson said, "Sirs and Lieutenant Bronskaya, if you'll follow me, please?" They did, first to one particular desk in the vast clerks' country, and then out into the passageway, about fifteen yards to another bank of *ascenseurs,* then up one level, then along two more passageways, to a short passageway with several doors opening on each side. The sergeant led Jacques-Yves to the first room on the left, then moved on.

Jacques-Yves spent about five minutes taking stock of his new quarters. They were at least as luxurious as the command quarters aboard *Bonaventure VI* or *VII,* and perhaps more. He actually had a suite, the outer room of which had a conference table easily big enough for him to hold a staff meeting—though, of course, Sergeant Major Anderson effectively replaced Sergeant Jameson, who was now in Officer Candidate School. The inner room contained a bed and end table (with an intercom set built into the wall near the headboard), a desk (fully equipped with a computer console), a closet, and a bathroom.

He sat at the desk and put out a hand to activate the console. The console was already programmed to recognize his voice, so he could get into the network easily. The first thing he looked for was routines for ordering a meal. Since this was Naval Headquarters, meals were on a ration system, just as he was accustomed to. This being mid-day, he ordered a meal of vegetable stew and coffee. He looked for an option to order wine and found it was not available. Well, alcoholic drinks were not available on the American Navy's ships, so he had to expect that they were not available at Headquarters, either.

The meal arrived within twenty minutes, and he found it tastier than anything he'd had at his home near Cadillac. But of course. Even at his home, he'd been using printers to prepare his meals. These people did not use printers for anything so basic to life as foodstuffs. Jacques-Yves had no proof, but he had no doubt either, that he was eating real vegetables, that someone had taken the trouble to grow in real soil. He must see an example of the gardens these people must keep.

After he finished eating, he buzzed for the steward's mate to take the crockery and utensils away. Odd, that. Aboard *Bonaventure VI*, he would have placed everything into a recycling chamber. Here they washed, dried, and re-used such things. He suddenly realized that such customs gave these people a sense of permanence that United Systems people could never know. Even the most common objects had to last more than a single use! So, of course, these Americans made everything to last.

And that, Jacques-Yves decided, is how they would win this war. If they respected even the simplest of objects they used every day, they respected themselves and one another, again as those in his former society did not.

After the steward's mate had departed for the last time, Jacques-Yves called up a routine to check the progress of Matthew Morrow's transit to these caverns. At first, he wondered whether his clearance would suffice—but then he discovered that he had Top Secret clearance. That allowed him to see anything he would ask for—with double scrambling on client-side and server-side.

Matthew was well past Beijing in the Great Circle Tubes, and the special train was on its way to San Francisco, where it would wait for him. Good.

Wait, wait, wait! Who else was traveling with him? Jacques-Yves had to look again. Zachary Radner, of course—Jacques-Yves couldn't wait to meet him. And … Diana Conroy! Actually, her full name was Diana Conroy Kendrick. So she had married his old executive officer—who now was serving as Air Chief Marshal in the Revolutionary Forces for a Free Earth. But who had detailed her to escort Matthew Morrow to the United States? Even this report did not say.

Never mind. It would be good to see her again, in any case. The old *Bonaventure* wardroom was coming together. Surely that must signify something—something very important.

* * *

Natalya had no appetite. She couldn't even muster the desire to taste organic food. Now that she was alone in her assigned quarters, she just wanted to collapse and cry all over again.

Oh, Matthew! She didn't try the computer console. Instead, she tried to reach out with her nanobots. But they couldn't connect. Even when she did activate the computer console and try to use it as a secondary antenna—and she could only guess whether that would work—she still could not connect. Matthew must be very deeply unconscious. That upset her all the more.

Natalya? Is that you? Calm down. Maybe I can help you.

Whose voice was that in her head?

Oh, come, Natalya. Don't tell me you've forgotten my telepathic "voice" already.

Ayelet? Is that you?

Of course, it is.

I didn't wake you, did I?

Oh, no. There is eight hours' difference between us. I'm in Murmansk.

Then have you heard about Matthew?

Did he run out of charge? I had wondered about that.

Yes! I can't reach him. He must be unconscious.

Well, he's with that fine boy he rescued from the Lucketts Game Preserve. I guess you don't yet have a strong-enough rapport with Zachary. I do because we've fought an action together. They're on their way to you.

Ayelet, please listen. We need to get in touch with two other former members of the Bonaventure *crew. Their names are Eric Shaka and Ian O'Reilly. Can you or your Zealots tell me where to find them?*

I'm afraid not. But someone else is traveling with Matthew. Do you remember Diana Conroy?

Diana? Yes! She's another former shipmate. But unless she knows something …

She might, at that. Zachary is a bit confused on this point, but he seems to be able to reach Matthew on some level. I can't begin to understand it, and I was once a psychiatric nurse. But chances are even that she knows where to find those two shipmates you named. Zachary had an instinct that Dr. Conroy should accompany them. That could be why. Sorry, I can't tell you more.

Oh, Ayelet, you've told me more than I thought possible. Thank you, thank you, thank you!

Baruch havat, *Natalya. Anything for a friend of Matthew, especially you.*

Even more tears flowed from Natalya's eyes now. Tears of joy.

After five minutes, she decided she should at least "charge up." The Navy had thoughtfully provided a charging alcove for her. She stepped into it and composed herself as best she could for recharging and rest.

What Did You Think?

Enjoying *We, Too, Shall Enlist?* Head on over to Amazon to follow me so you can pick up your copy. And, please leave me an honest review on Amazon, letting me know what you thought of *The Admiral's Choice*.

Thank You For Reading My Book!

I really appreciate your feedback about my books; your reviews make my books better!

Visit my online store at https://www.cnav.store/ to purchase patriotic gear and see my latest books and merchandise.

Thanks so much!
–Terry A. Hurlbut
www.conservativenewsandviews.com
https://www.cnav.store/

Acknowledgments

First and foremost, the character of Matthew Morrow has its basis, not in "case histories" of "persons on the Autism Spectrum," but on my personal experience. In that light, I couldn't possibly acknowledge everyone in my life who taught me a valuable lesson on what neurotypicals really think of persons on The Spectrum. Some of those lessons have been positive, some negative—but all have been valuable. In addition to which I acknowledge God, Who never fails in love or honor.

Next, I must acknowledge the "giants" on whose shoulders I have the privilege of standing. They start with men like C. S. Lewis, H. G. Wells, and Jules Verne. But they also include some less obvious names—like William Shakespeare and C. S. Forester. And perhaps even less obvious names, like Julius Caesar.

I must also acknowledge many, who would ask me not to identify them, who have apprised me of certain evils in the world in which we are now living. This applies equally to the ugly side of modern allopathic medical research, education, and services, as it does to certain criminal activities.

Next, I must acknowledge Jeannie Culbertson, who served as an invaluable guide through the weeds which every writer must travel.

And last, I must acknowledge my dear friend Andrea, without whose guidance and inspiration this work would not have been possible.

Terry A. Hurlbut
March 7, 2022
(MJDN 59645)

About the Author

Terry A. Hurlbut has been a student of politics, philosophy, and science for more than 45 years.

He is a graduate of Yale College and has served as a physician-level laboratory administrator in a 250-bed community hospital. He also is a serious student of the Bible, is conversant in its two primary original languages, and has followed the creation-science movement closely since 1993.

For more information and to read more of his writing, please visit Conservative News and Views at this link:

https://www.conservativenewsandviews.com/author/temlakos/.

www.ingramcontent.com/pod-product-compliance
Lightning Source LLC
Chambersburg PA
CBHW060859190726
48286CB00002B/305